bodyslick

bodyslick

Written and illustrated by

john h. sibley

VIBE STREET LIT
is a division of VIBE Media Group, LLC.
215 Lexington Avenue
New York, NY 10016
Rob Kenner, Editorial Director

KENSINGTON BOOKS are published by
Kensington Publishing Corp.
850 Third Avenue
New York, NY 10022

All Kensington titles, imprints, and distributed lines are available at special quantity discounts for bulk purchases for sales promotion, premiums, fund-raising, educational, or institutional use.

Special book excerpts or customized printings can also be created to fit specific needs. For details, write or phone the office of the Kensington Special Sales Manager: Attn.: Special Sales Department. Kensington Publishing Corp., 850 Third Avenue, New York, NY 10022. Phone: 1-800-221-2647.

Kensington Books Reg. U.S. Pat. & TM Off.

ISBN-13: 978-1-60183-004-3
ISBN-10: 1-60183-004-1

First Printing: July 2008

10 9 8 7 6 5 4 3 2 1

Printed in the United States of America

To
John H. Sibley, Sr.
(1927–2005)

"We expend enormous energy and vast sums of money to preserve and prolong life, but in the process our embodied life is stripped of its gravity and much of its dignity. This is, in a word, a progress as tragedy."

—Aldous Huxley's *Brave New World*

Acknowledgments

The following acknowledgments are for the people who have helped me forge a new vision and have helped steer my madness in a positive direction:

This novel is dedicated to my father John H. Sibley, Sr. (1927–2005), my mother Mattie Ramsey Sibley, Grandma Malone, Uncle Miles, my daughters Jacqueline and Brittany Sibley, their mother Deanna, my brother Kenneth, my sister Bernita Braswell, brother-in-law "Rhetoric Rodge," nephew Malcolm, cousin Cynthia, niece Kenya, Levi Wright, my cousin who inspired me in my youth to become an artist, and to all members of the Sibley tribe, and to many mentors and friends: Cleosophus Young, the late publishers of the *Robbin Eagle*, Larry Smith at *Parade* magazine, Richard Wright, Chester Himes, James Baldwin, Robert "Iceberg Slim" Beck, Steinbeck, Sartre, Fanon, Cornell West, Stanley Crouch, Poe, Harlan Ellison, Robert Silverberg, Phillip K. Dick, Samuel R. Delaney, Elmore Leonard, James Lee Burke, Tom Robbins, Justin Scott, John A. Williams, Leonard Shalain, Tom Clancy, Mario Puzo, Eugene Izzi, Baraka, Haki Muhadbulti, William Styron, Upton Sinclair, James Brown, Angela Davis, John Coltrane, Miles Davis, Yusef Lateef, Dave Brubeck, Earth, Wind & Fire, and Barack Obama for a new creative social paradigm. Friends: Jolyce Genus who invested in my talent years ago, Bart at Allegra, Carol Hagarty, *Beacon News*, artist Melvin King, William Tremaine, Editor Bike at the *Gazette*, artist Milton (git on da good foot) Roberts, 'Nam vet and boyhood friend Eddie Bolden, film director Anthony Colomate for his brilliant editing and suggestions, Diane Jamelah, Mark Sokolis, Mike Gentry, Jesse Ferguson, Dr. Emiel

Hambolin, a retired biology teacher at Dusable High School, Judith Hochberg in Hyde Park for her insightful critiques and political vision, Percy Richardson (Daddy Rich) who had a powerful influence on the youth in Robbins, Illinois, James "Dickey" Seafes for pimpnosis, my classy godmother Mrs. Bradley, Retha Murphy-Acox, a wise friend and mentor, Lionel and Derrick Spires management at the Westside Artist Switching Station lofts in Chicago, Rose, Bonnie, Phyllis, Carmalita, Jowon, Charlotte, Omega, Suki, Tina, *NLCN* publisher Isaac Lewis, who helped me open doors that I didn't see, professor/author John W. Fountain for his suggestions, former Chicago Bear Revey Sorey, First Jersey Shareholders, author Tony Lindsay for his insight, *Chicago Sun Times* sportscaster Dan Roan for the 2004 televised interview on Superstation WGN Channel 9 here in Chicago, a huge toast to *VIBE* magazine fiction book editor Rob Kenner, who had enough faith and vision in *Bodyslick* to get it published, Tashant my chess buddy, *The Voice* newspaper editor; Brad Cummings, Stanley Kincaid, founder of The African American Alumni Association at the School of The Art Institute at Chicago (SAIC). Also the entire *VIBE* staff and especially the incisive editing of Rakia A. Clark, who helped connect all the "dots" at Kensington Publishing Corporation, as well as production editor Ross Plotkin, who did a great job with the illustrations.

Preface

As you flip through the pages of *Bodyslick*, keep in mind that this novel is a product of ten years of my life (two Iraqi wars and three presidents). Ten years of squeezing in time to write, while simultaneously dealing with real world issues like marriage, fatherhood, bills, taxes, and raking up dog shit in the backyard.

In this urban sci-fi novel, I am more concerned with exposing the barbarity of human existence and shedding light on a possible "new genetic-reshaped underclass of servants, slaves, live sex toys, chimp/humans (humanzees) and yet-to-be-created xenografted Frankenstein monsters that in the near future will be lurking outside our windows, than I am with winning the Nobel Prize.

Will they be created because of the profit motive in commerce and science? Does love trump ethics when it comes to the selling of human organs? Is it unethical that a healthy white woman between the ages of twenty and twenty-nine can get $7,000 as an anonymous egg donor? Is it unethical that at this very moment you can sell your plasma and sperm but not your organs? Hopefully, after reading *Bodyslick* your views about the ethics of allowable and prohibitive biomedical research will be challenged.

As Jack Johnson once said, "Remember me as a man." I have always had immense pride in the fact that above all else I am a man first and the proud father of two lovely daughters. I have had all kinds of jobs: advertising salesman, CNN courtroom artist, commodity representative trainee, temporary laborer, janitor, USAF Security Policeman, caricaturist, Chicago double-decker tour guide, Windy City Carnival artist, and many years at Industrial Noise Control Inc. as a supervisor of the spot welding department.

Also, I briefly taught in the Chicago public school system and discovered how difficult it is to teach both middle and lower class black students within an anti-intellectual value system. (To apply oneself in school is "actin' white.")

I agree with John McWhorter, author of *Losing the Race* when he writes: "Black students from solid backgrounds mysteriously tend to hover at the bottom of the class, and baffled educators say this is a late-twentieth-century problem. Black students who reject school as 'white' do so while ones who lived when lynching was ordinary pursued education obsessively. Black parents who do not instill in their children a sense that failing in school is unacceptable, and are more inclined to complain about 'subtle racism' at the schools than to make sure their children do their best despite it, are a new phenomenon."

While writing *Bodyslick*, I have lost my home, filed bankruptcy, and been divorced. I have experienced loneliness, dread, despair, and at times an overwhelming sense of loss, pessimism, and even suicidal feelings.

Oftentimes, late at night, while the alley rats scamper outside my window (I now live in an artist's loft on the West Side of Chicago) and dogs howl piteously, perhaps at the restless ghost of unknown artists, and crackheads and prostitutes argue over drugs, I shudder with existential fear that maybe I am merely a mad artist raving in isolation. Thinking the unthinkable. Wondering if when I pray a personal God is listening. Or a God that is timeless? Because if God is timeless, He cannot be said to be thinking about me, or even planet earth, because thinking is a temporal activity. And if God is thinking about a wretch like me, He is subject to be destroyed when time no longer exists. Which translates into this: If there is no governance, no morality, in our Milky Way galaxy, we are all doomed.

As I write this, the death toll from the December 26, 2005

tsunami has reached 175,000—mostly women and children. But that pales in comparison to the million Hutus and Tutsis slaughtered in 1994 during the tribal war in Rwanda.

The fossilized, decadent cultural barons of American art have always kept me at bay. My entire career has been as an outsider. Outcast. The invisible man. Interloper. Picasso had a blue period. I had a blues period. All my life I have used painting and writing as a means of exorcising demons from my being in the world. Art has saved me from a life of dementia. If I didn't have art to channel my creative impulses, I'm absolutely certain those impulses would have compelled me to strike violently at the xenophobic barriers that have been imposed on me my entire life. The great heavyweight champion Floyd Patterson once said in a 1988 interview, "If it wasn't for boxing, I would probably be behind bars or dead!"

Like the Baroque artist Caravaggio, I have lived an unconventional and often violent life. I have had my battles with the police and have alienated potential friends because of my heretical beliefs and violent temper.

That cultural barricade I mentioned earlier has affected my survival as an artist. Early on in my life I embraced a "do or die" motto. I was full of idealism and hell-bent on surviving as an artist at any cost. Ultimately, my naiveté made me homeless. From September 1987 until January 1988, I lived on Chicago's mean streets.

I sang the Christian hymn, "There is Power in the Blood," along with hundreds of other lost souls at the Pacific Garden Mission on State Street before I ate my stale bologna sandwich. Then I had to strip off my clothing to take an Arctic-cold shower before I slept on the lice-infested cots of the mission. I preferred the concrete floor at the Metro train station on Michigan and Roosevelt.

Many a night I gazed up at the starry heavens asking, "God, why hast Thou forsaken me?"

I learned a vital lesson from that wretched period: family,

children, loved ones, and good health (both mental and physical) are far more important than the search for that elusive "bitch goddess called success."

Unlike an international city like New York where the legendary Apollo Theater is considered a national treasure, Chicago is a cold (hog butcher of the world), antiseptic and brutal town. It will bulldoze its most sacred cultural icons like the world famous Regal Theater on the South Side and the Maxwell Street open-air market, the home of the "electrified blues," where creators like Muddy Waters, Howlin' Wolf, Baby Face Leroy, Little Walter, Honeyboy Edwards, Jimmie Lee Robinson, Buddy Guy, Willie Kent and Junior Wells influenced English rock groups like the Rolling Stones, Cream, and Led Zeppelin, who all tried to pluck notes created by Maxwell Street bluesmen. I am deeply honored that in 2001 I was part of a landmark photo "A Great Day on Maxwell," in which blues legends gathered for an historic photo. Professor Steve Balkin, past president of the Historic Preservation Coalition of Maxwell Street, argues for the importance of establishing a "Blues Museum" to preserve the legacy of the Maxwell Street bluesmen. Now only a ghostly fog of death seems to hover over Maxwell Street, and there have been reports of unexplainable ghostly disturbances in the new University of Illinois at Chicago student dorms, built on that sacred ground.

I am now in the middle years of my creative production. If I am to leave a lasting legacy for future generations, it must be based on the creative and procreative flames I now have. But these flames are dwindling because of the constant struggle to survive in this ruthless, capitalist system.

When our average G-type star's (the sun) energy output gets too low, its stellar atoms extinguish. The death of an artist is like a star, and if black holes are the graves of *dead* stars we can use it as a metaphor for the darkness of existence for unknown artists; where no creative *light* or *genius* can escape; because of societal greed, entropy, alienation, racism, and wretched poverty.

A galaxy of unseen, sinister, societal forces that determine who is *in* and who is *out* of the art world have strangled the life out of untold geniuses, filling this nation's graveyard with thousands of unknown artists.

Prologue

Sergeant Malcolm Henry Steel
Charlie Company 1st Battalion
24th Infantry Division U.S. Army
December 24, 2003

Son,
    About an hour after I mailed my last letter to you
my Company Commander ordered us to move out.
Iraq's not as comfortable as Saudi Arabia, but with
all the reporters from CNN and NBC swarming in
and out of our area, I actually feel like a celebrity. I
don't know what they're putting on TV (maybe
you've even seen your dad once or twice), but don't
believe much of what they say. They keep telling us
to juice up our stories about the Iraqis, but there
isn't much to tell. Baghdad has broken down. Kids
younger than you are starving. No clean water or
medicine. Dead Shia and Sunni gangsters are lying
together in piles. But the animals here are what you
need to be careful of. We saw a seven-banded scor-
pion crawl up against my First Sergeant's ear when
he was asleep. A few hours later a snake with horns
(they tell me it's properly called a viper) snatched a
piece from the leg of an MP.

It's strange what will survive in this place. Some days it gets so hot that you can cook bacon on the hood of your tank, and the batteries behind your favorite CD will burst like little grenades. But the ugliest and nastiest things go right along crawling across the earth.

I just looked at what I wrote, and I can't make out some of my own handwriting. Give it your best guess. My hand isn't what it used to be.

We're lined up to go against the Iraqi heavy division soon. Company Commander says this division gassed more Kurdish towns than intelligence could keep track of. The boys around the post call them the "Jihad Corps." They're supposed to be holed up in a cove just over a berm of hills in a town called Samara to our north. Air Force has been pounding it for three days, so it should be clean by the time we get there. But like I said, things have a way of surviving here.

They're passing out gas masks now. Joey's dancing with it on backwards.

We've got to move out in a few hours, and my hands are getting worse. But you take care, and if you get some time between all your homework, think about picking up that pen I gave you and dropping your dad a note.

One last thing. Do me a favor and stay clear of your Uncle Will while I'm gone. I'll sleep better, and trust me, I do need my sleep.

Be good. Merry Christmas.

Love,
Dad

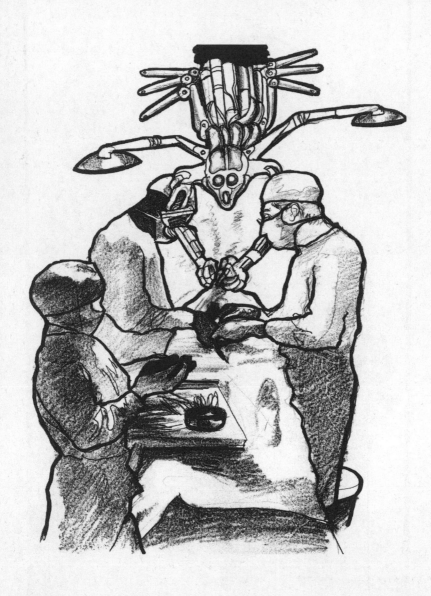

Chapter 1

Dr. William Jacob, world-renowned transplant surgeon, watched a blue ribbon of smoke curl upwards from the laser incisions his Robotic Operation Surgical Assistant was making with three-thousandths of an inch precision. The robot's kinesthetic sensing arm, equipped with eight-axis force sensors, slowly tracked above the flesh of a young boy's upper abdomen.

"ROSA, increase laser burst by twenty degrees," Jacob ordered.

Each ROSA unit had a specific voice recognition module, calibrated to the voice of its assigned control surgeon. The imprinting technology had come a long way to make each unit highly efficient in the operating room. When Jacob was an intern he would have made the incisions himself with a small electric saw; now the robots even wiped the patients down. He wondered if the hospital could still function without them.

ROSA's thin beam disappeared, and two assistants hustled up to the boy's rib cage with a chest spreader. Jacob was never easy with the noises it made. It was the same strained crackle wine crates made when they were pried open.

The assistants stepped away with the bloody spreader, and Jacob peered inside the boy's torso. The pericardial sac looked like a small basketball. The boy's heart had to be three times the normal size. Dilated cardiomyopathy: he had never seen it in someone so young.

"EKG tracing, nurse?"

"Normal, doctor. No change." Ruth Vaughan was one of the most meticulous nurses in the hospital. Jacob made a habit of working with her.

"His potassium levels?"

"Normal."

"Blood pressure?"

"The pulmonary artery pressure is rising slowly, doctor."

"Something's wrong," Jacob said. "Increase the dopamine. If pressure continues to fall, increase crystalloid fluid."

Ruth nodded. ROSA's sea green eyes—four color cameras, two for foveal vision and two for peripheral, all enclosed in a flesh-colored humanoid head—blinked as they sent topical and magnetic images through a neural data network to a display in front of Jacob. Digital meters pulsed across the screen as the drugs took effect.

"Blood pressure back to normal, doctor."

As ROSA made the final cut, Jacob glanced at the donor heart lying in a sterile basin near his tools. He checked to see if the old and new organs looked alike, even though he knew their appearance made little difference in the surgery's outcome. He was hoping for reassurance. The boy on the table was David K. Vanderbilt III, heir to a billion-dollar publishing empire and grandson of Louis K. Vanderbilt, the grand benefactor behind Jacob's transplant research at Baltimore Memorial Hospital.

Jacob carefully lifted the enlarged heart out of David's chest cavity and marveled that the boy could have lived with coronary arteries so hard and blocked; even the magnetic imaging scans had not caught the extent of the damage. ROSA took the old heart from his hands and lifted the new one from its icy container. It glimmered in comparison.

Jacob turned to his young surgeon who had been silently watching a few paces away from the operating table.

"This is when you start paying attention." Jones closed in on the table.

"First," Jacob continued, "we match up the donor heart's chambers with those of the patient. We do the same with the aorta and pulmonary arteries, reattaching the old arterial linkage with the new. You should have noticed that these consist of four anastomoses. Anastomoses is a big word for—"

"I'm familiar with the term," Jones said.

Fine, Jacob thought. He preferred to work in silence. He finished the rest of the stitching, his hands moving deftly around ROSA's arms. He knew the boy's immune system was already starting to attack the new heart. Jacob only hoped the arsenal of immunosuppressive drugs—cyclosporine, prednisone, and especially the recently approved trilexis—would neutralize the onslaught.

Rekindled blood flowed into the chambers of the new heart. Everyone stared into the boy's chest cavity, waiting, when suddenly the heart thumped. Jumped. Slowly it started pumping. Rhythmically. Its contractions were strong and vigorous.

Then it stopped.

"ROSA, defibrillator pads!" Jacob yelled. The serpentine robot lowered itself closer to the patient and extended two of its eight arms that carried defibrillator pads. Its green eyes blinked in anticipation of more orders.

"ROSA, follow the instructions of the patient's diagnostic database."

The robot sent a pulse of electrical current through the heart of the patient.

"Increase voltage!"

Defibrillator pads jolted the body up off the operating table.

"Increased by 15 percent, Dr. Jacob."

"Reading, nurse?"

"No movement."

ROSA blasted the heart with a higher voltage. Still nothing.

"The heart's dead, doctor," said Jones, quietly, after two more attempts had failed.

"Give ROSA instructions for closing the incision," Jacob replied, watching the unbeating heart. "ROSA, Dr. Jones has the floor."

"Thank you, Dr. Jacob. Have a good afternoon."

Jacob snatched off his surgical mask and strode out of the OR. A group of elegantly dressed people in the waiting room would not be expecting bad news.

The boy's family stood when he entered the room, everyone, that is, except the boy's grandfather. Louis K. Vanderbilt inched his wheelchair past his relatives up to Jacob's feet. He glared at him from inside a rigid navy blue suit. A navy blue silk blanket was ruffled in his lap. His shirt was baby blue. His tie was a cerulean blue, his eyes a royal blue. Jacob could not help thinking the old man was color-coordinated enough to be a pimp.

"The new heart failed," Jacob said. "For a brief moment we thought a miracle was on our hands, but as I mentioned earlier, your grandson's rare AB blood type tripled the chance of rejection."

"So what now?" Vanderbilt replied, seemingly unmoved by the news.

"I'm afraid little is left in our power."

"What do you mean little is left?" The old man's eyes stayed fixed on Jacob.

"Sir, David is now on a ventilator. His brain, lungs, kidneys, virtually all his major organs are healthy. So he is alive. Without a heart . . . but alive."

"Then you can do something."

"But—" Jacob began.

"But what?" Vanderbilt asked, his voice rising. "I have been generous, Jacob, very generous. Don't tell me that I did not buy my grandson's life."

"Sir, David will remain on the ventilator while we search for another donor. David's heart is of the utmost importance to this hospital, but I have to warn you, the possibility of finding another heart in the little time we have is slim."

"That will not do."

"Rest assured, sir, we will exhaust every possibility." It was the standard script for patients' families.

"When can we see him?" the old man asked.

"Once the nurse takes him out of the recovery room, which . . ."—Jacob glanced at his watch—". . . will be in a couple of hours. But I would prefer if you came back tomorrow."

"We will, but just remember: our support is unlimited. Absolutely unlimited. I want David back, do you understand?"

"Of course, Mr. Vanderbilt."

Jacob answered a few more questions before managing to excuse himself with the pretense of having another appointment. His intern was waiting for him in the hallway.

"How's the family?"

"In denial."

Jacob did not stop to talk. Jones popped off the wall to trail him down the hallway.

"ROSA finished up smoothly."

"Good to hear."

"That machine is light years ahead of the university's Genesis system. Genesis is less—"

"Not to be rude," Jacob interrupted, "but there's not much you can tell me about the Genesis system. I was using it when you were in preschool. Although if you want my opinion; yes, I agree that the system is less invasive, but the cable instruments are too cumbersome."

Jones knew where this was going. Another white doctor who assumed the black surgeon could not keep up.

"Listen, I did graduate at the top of my class at the University of Chicago. I certainly understand the anatomical structure of the heart, so there is no need for condescension," Jones said, his voice sharpening into an edge. "What I don't understand is why you didn't implant the Jarvik 12 artificial heart, which would serve as a bridge until you get a transplant?"

"Dr. Jones, with a patient as important as Vanderbilt there is no room for instant death because of mediastinal infections, bleeding, fit complications, or a defective pneumatic pump!"

Jacob stopped at a coffee machine and punched in an elaborate mixture of espresso, vanilla, milk, and hazelnut. There was an awkward silence as the cup filled. Jones began to wonder if he had gone too far.

"How are you going to find another heart?"

Jacob did not answer right away. Instead he blew on his drink and slurped up its foam.

"I don't know. It took a year to get the last one. There's nothing on the list." He brushed the foam from his lips and stared at it on his finger. "Donor demand still outpaces supply, not to mention the added ethical problems with taking vital organs from the freshly dead."

Jacob had hoped the government with its donor tax incentives, anatomical gift acts, and free funeral grants would have corrected the trend. But people refused to be persuaded, and the chances of receiving transplant surgery were skyrocketing into odds resembling the lottery. Soon, he feared the dead would be more valuable than the living.

"What about bodimorphs?" Jones asked. "You know, like the ones they're using at Philadelphia General?"

Jacob had read about the facility there. They kept cadavers on life support systems until they needed their organs for surgery.

"That's why the medical personnel there recently went on strike. It's too stressful. One day a finger jerks on a body and the family thinks their loved one is back from the dead. Try convincing them it's just a spinal reflex. You try telling Vanderbilt that. He'll take both our jobs before he believes you. He has donated enough to this hospital to own it."

Jones leaned in closer. "Can I say something off the record?"

"Sure," Jacob said, still more interested in his beverage.

"If you consider what I'm about to say unethical, will you forget you ever heard it?"

"Yes, get on with it."

"If that family has the money you say they do, I have a source in Chicago that can supply a heart in twenty-four hours."

"You mean illegally?"

Jones shrugged.

"What's his name, your, um . . ."

"Finder? He goes by Bodyslick."

"Bodyslick?"

"That's what they call him in the business."

"He wouldn't be reliable," Jacob said to himself more than to Jones.

"I think that would depend on how much you're willing to pay him."

Jacob stared deeply into his beverage before throwing the rest down his throat and gesturing in the direction of the elevators.

"Contact him. Get all the data you need from Mr. . . ."

"Bodyslick."

"Sure. Sort out the equipment you'll need to transport the heart from Chicago. Cardioplegic solutions, cryonic organ cooler, saltwater solution—the basics. Take the Learjet to Chicago and if necessary, arrange for a helicopter to take you to a location to meet this Bodyquick."

"Bodyslick, sir. I'll call my man now. I'll tell him we'll pick up the heart."

"Not *we,* Jones—*you* will," Jacob said, smiling. The elevator doors opened. "Let me know something soon. In seventy-two hours the heart-lung machine will start to damage the oxygenation of the boy's blood."

Jacob tapped the button for the garage.

"But I'm sure you knew that already."

The elevator doors closed, leaving Jones alone in the hallway.

Chapter 2

Sharen Kemsley walked to the window of her Lake Forest mansion. A bright sun slowly lit a pristine blue sky, and a hot May summer afternoon came into being. Her five-year-old son and six-year-old daughter stared at her back, wondering what their mother was looking for outside.

The doorbell chimed. Sharen glanced at the door's vidscreen and found large pairs of eyes staring back at her.

"Can Danny and Sarah come outside and play?" a large mouth on the vidscreen pleaded.

"It's too hot today," Sharen replied. "Why are you outside? Don't your parents realize they're endangering your health?"

She switched to the wide angle lens and found their mouths were surrounded by faces painted blue, red, green, and black beneath sprouting tops of blond, brunette, and red hair.

"We took melanhue baths last night," said a small girl with a glimmering black face.

"But did your mommy and daddy tell you that the cream is only good for heat in the lower nineties?"

"What did you say?" asked a baffled boy with blue skin.

Sharen's own children tugged on her plastic pants.

"Mommy, we want to go outside!"

"Danny and Sarah can't come outside today!" Sharen said as she shut off the vidscreen.

"It's so boring inside, Mommy!" Danny whined. Sarah was

already looking mournful. Sharen bent down and grasped both their hands.

"Do you remember Carol who died from the sun's rays last year?" she asked softly. They both nodded their heads. "Do you remember Marie, your cousin? Jeffrey, her brother? Your daddy's boss, Mr. Olson? Remember your friends at the day care center, Sarah? Remember what happened to David, Jennifer, Janice, and Samantha? I'm sorry but I don't—"

She stopped. There was something on Sarah's neck. She snatched her daughter up to her face. It was brown; a spot with a scaly surface and a reddish base.

"Sarah!" The scream jumped out of her.

"What's wrong?" Danny asked. Sarah looked mortified.

"For chrissakes!" Sharen shouted, as she grabbed Sarah around the waist and ran into the kitchen. "Dr. Sanslow!" she barked at the voice-activated vidphone.

Dr. Sanslow's secretary morphed onto the screen.

"Dr. Sanslow's office, may I help you?"

"This is Sharen Kemsley. This is an emergency. Is Dr. Sanslow in?" She didn't give the secretary time to answer.

"Dr. Sanslow was selected as one of the doctors for the new colony on Mars," said the secretary. "He is going through training at NASA."

"I don't care where he is. I think my daughter has . . ." Instead of finishing the sentence she clicked off the vidphone, knowing the words would have brought her to tears.

The phone reset itself.

"Call me a taxi."

"It will be here in approximately eight minutes," the phone reported.

Sharen held Sarah tightly as she ran into the bathroom where there was more light. She sat her down on the toilet stool and brushed back her hair.

It was a hard dark lump. Quarter inch thick. Ulcerated, waxy. As if an insect was incubating deep in subcutaneous fat. She knew it was a UV nodular melanoma, the most lethal. She had seen too many in her life not to recognize one. She probed it with her thumb and felt her gut quiver, as blood crawled out of it. Maybe she should have invested in fertilized eggs, frozen in reserve, so if something like this happened, identical twins could have been made.

"Don't cry," Danny said, trying to act like the man of the house since his father died. She gazed hopelessly at him and wiped tears from her eyes.

"Danny," she said, trying to catch her breath, "I want you to go back in the kitchen and tell the vidphone to hurry up with the taxi."

"Okay," he said and ran back down the hallway.

It wouldn't matter. She knew it was too late. Too late for Janice, Carol, Mr. Olson, David, Jennifer, Samantha and, probably now, Sarah.

She heard the cab's horn.

Chapter 3

He glanced at his watch.
Game time.

Malcolm "Bodyslick" Steel pressed a tiny button on his watch that remotely activated his HVS (Holographic Viewing System). Instantly the lights started to dim. A panoramic screen surfaced from the jaws of the apartment. *Whoosh.* Like an exploding star, a three-dimensional stadium surrounded him. A crowd's roar rocked the walls, and he breathed in the air of the giant arena. A leg brushed against his neck—a spectator in the row behind him searching for his seat.

Good evening, folks. Welcome to the 2031 International Basketball Association Series Finale. But first, a word from some of the sponsors of tonight's game . . .

The first of a series of commercials began. Malcolm pressed his watch again and the cement stadium floor became his five-inch deep Berber carpet, African-Benin sculptures twisted up from disappearing hotdog vendors, and the mirrored blinds that a moment before reflected thousands of chanting fans now reflected his own image. He never watched commercials.

The vidphone rang.

Displayed across its screen was a mix of ethnic traits—white face, blond hair, blue eyes, surgically enhanced lips, ringed septum, gold-trimmed ears.

"What's up, Snow? Everything cool?" Malcolm asked, already guessing the answer to his question from the tick in Snow's left eyelid.

"We got problems. Big problems, homeboy!"

"Like what?"

"Like we gave the girlfriend of Willie D. Lloyd, the biggest drug kingpin on the South Side, a fuckin' junkie's kidney!" Malcolm laughed.

"Straight up," Snow said nervously, "the girl is probably in withdrawal right now—hey, this might be funny to you but remember *I* delivered the kidney. Slovik musta picked the wrong one at the depot in Robbins."

"Snow . . . this ain't good business protocol."

"If we don't get another kidney, I'm a dead man walking. *Me quieren matar eso pinches putos culeros.*" (They're going to kill me, those fucking asshole bitches.)

"Don't worry about Willie Lloyd. I'll call him. He owes me some favors. But I want to know why Slovik, who I pay a lot of money to manage LL&T, is mixing up something as central as ID tags. Snow, I want you and Geronimo to go out to the facility and check it out."

"We'll make him give us a tour of the place!" Snow said arrogantly.

"But I want to know who wasn't doing their job. The ID tags must have gotten mixed up at the storage facility."

Snow's face flickered strips of neon. He had the game on at his apartment too. Malcolm could see fans cheering around him. Snow looked like a ghost in the stadium, a pale cadaver around an army of colorful faces.

Snow had always been sickly. Malcolm's Uncle Will had been coming home one night after a late dinner with one of his girlfriends. He found Snow in the alley of Cabrini Green with a portion of his jaw broken. Snow had tried to rip off the local craps game—nothing elaborate, just a simple grab-the-cash-and-run plan. After chasing him down, the players took turns beating Snow against a dumpster. The only likely reason that the craps players decided to spare his life was that he was nine years old at the time.

Snow turned his attention from the holographic game and leaned into his vidphone.

"If we don't grab another kidney, Lloyd's henchies will be coming after my white ass. You know them clown niggas are primitive. We are on Mars, and they're still carving up people with butcher knives."

"I'll take care of it tonight. In fact, I'll contact the coroner at the morgue to get a fresh one. What's her blood type?"

"O."

"All right, it's a done deal. Call me after you inspect the facility because we got a shipment leaving this week for Virginia Anatomical Services. No room for mistakes in this order. Talk to you later!"

"Sooner better than later." His image decrystallized on the screen.

Within a month of Snow's jaw healing, Uncle Will had started to teach him the advantages of shaved dice. *Fear, gives you a license to do what other men only dream of.* It was a line Uncle Will would use again and again while teaching the boys how to read other players, slide dice rolls across the floor, make the odds bend in their favor. A year later Snow was one of the best dice throwers in Cabrini Green. Malcolm would tag along to games at the end of the month when assistant checks were distributed.

That was when everyone would lose big. Malcolm would stash the large bills in the collar of his uncle's pit bull, Ming. Usually that was enough. *Get the money out of their sight as soon as they lose it.* But the few times players refused to part with their cash, Malcolm could persuade them otherwise. Even at fourteen he was bigger and faster than most of the people on the block. And for the few players who still had an edge on him, there was always his half brother, Bubba. No one was bigger than Bubba. The three of them played

Cabrini until it was dry. Then they branched out: west to Chinatown, south to the Mexicans in Pilsen, and even far north to the Pakistanis on Devon. It didn't matter the neighborhood or the language. Snow could adapt and win.

Malcolm considered turning the HVS back on, but Snow had wiped out his taste for the game. Besides, he told himself, he had no good reason to delay further what he had planned. He picked up a newscube from the coffee table.

In the center of the palm-sized crystal, a crisp font scrolled upwards. Malcolm knew every line. He read out to refresh his memory.

Timeline for Brinks armored truck robbery,
October 5, 2010.

5:30 p.m. Two undercover state police detectives pull over a Brinks armored truck for speeding. Truck flees south on the Dan Ryan Expressway when officers exit their vehicles.

5:40 p.m. Truck arrives at Chatman Shopping Mall, East 87th Street. Driver fires at police in pursuit.

5:45 p.m. Driver, Shannon McGrady, and partner, Malcolm Steel, abandon truck and enter grocery store. They are seen carrying a large brown attaché case and two pistols. Incident is upgraded to hijacking.

6:30 p.m. Police initiate standard negotiations with gunmen. Gunmen refuse to surrender or release hostages.

6:35 p.m. Police discover two drivers naked and duct-taped in the back of the stolen truck. FBI agents arrive on scene.

7:00 p.m. Examination of armored truck's route reveals it was transporting $100,000 cash to Federal Reserve Bank.

7:30 p.m. FBI deploys remote-controlled surveillance robot into grocery store.
7:40 p.m. Gunmen are spotted in food storage area.
8:00 p.m. Agents and officers enter through loading
dock in rear of store and arrest gunmen without incident. Attaché case is not found.

Malcolm remembered certain images more than others. The
truck's worn brakes. The screaming 300-pound driver. The
grocery shopper holding his son's hand, both of them staring
at the guns. Snow falling over a cereal display. The police
robot turning the corner into the meat locker.

Reviewing the timeline was a ritual he repeated once a
month, every month, since his release from prison. He would
re-imagine the moments of his crime—the chase, the standoff,
the arrest and even the prison time—until he would again sit
before Warden Goring and plead his case for parole.

Warden Goring was a neckless bulldog of a man with an
immense bald head. He would seat himself at the middle of a
long table and read through the files of various inmates, his
eyes twitching behind tiny round glasses that could have been
swiped off his grandmother's nose. The parole room itself was
a windowless corner of the prison that stank from the sweat of
previous inmates under review. The board was comprised of
other men and women, but as hard as Malcolm tried, he could
only remember Goring sitting in front of him at the table.

"Malcolm Steel." The warden always began in a command-
ing tone. "As you know, you are due to be paroled. That is, of
course, if we determine you are psychologically rehabilitated
enough to re-enter society. This review will not last long. You
do understand our intentions, Mr. Steel?"

"Yes I do, sir."

Malcolm could hear a man begging piteously in an adjacent
room. It sounded like Snow. He was due to be paroled the
same day.

"I will begin with your initial psych evaluation when you came into our system."

A screen descended behind the warden. Undercover surveillance images of Malcolm flashed across its face. He wondered if the board had already made up its mind.

"*Bodyslick* is your street moniker, a reference to your alleged talent of selling human body parts."

The screen changed to a police photo of a repossessed human heart packed into a cryonic container.

Warden Goring cleared his throat.

"*Slick* is a nice addition, considering you were elusive enough not to get caught actually selling organs."

The warden looked up for a reaction, but Malcolm remained expressionless.

"You were raised in public housing with your mother, brother, and sister after your father was killed in the second Iraq war. Your mother used crack to soothe her chronic depression and was admitted to the county hospital when she tried to quit her addiction and suffered a nervous breakdown."

"I don't understand why we're talking about my mother."

"Perhaps that is why you are here, because you never took the time to understand," the warden retorted. He returned his gaze to the file display in front of him. "In your father's absence, your ruthless, hoodlum of an uncle, William Steel, became your mentor. We have gigabytes of material on him alone."

Malcolm was surprised to see images of Will on the screen. The photos spanned at least two decades, chronicling his transformation from a handsome, muscled teenager to the gaunt man with paper-thin skin that Malcolm now knew. He was surprised to see him look directly into the camera and start talking.

"Yeah, I taught him. I taught him two things. Power and fear. Those are the quickest ways of getting rich. You tell me that's not true."

The video clip froze Will's face in an angry contortion as he spat the last few words.

"Your Uncle Will believed that racism contaminates every fabric of society and narrows black men's choices, that an already corrupt system makes crime justifiable. Do you agree with him, Mr. Steel?"

"I didn't come from an environment of doctors, lawyers, and scientists. I came from a society where becoming a gangster was normal. I walked over dead bodies on my way to school."

"That sounds like an excuse. You could have chosen an education."

"No one gives a shit about E=MC² in my hood."

"Watch your language, Mr. Steel," the warden commanded.

Malcolm shifted in his seat and restarted.

"One of my friends could paint so well you swore he could see every molecule of what he was looking at. He was so gifted he won a full scholarship to college then went to an Ivy League school for a masters degree. His mother used to brag about him to all of us who stayed behind. Then one day she stopped talking. Couple years later I saw him outside an all-night diner. He was mumbling to himself and pissing down his pant leg."

"I warned you about language."

Malcolm could not discern if the warden had a problem with his word choice or his story.

"My meaning is, sir, academics was not going to help me find food for my brother and sister. My Uncle Will gave me another way. He saw what I was good at."

"Heartbreaking, it really is." The warden nudged up his glasses, but they were too tight to budge. "Tests here show your I.Q. is nearly genius. You excelled at math, languages, and athletics. You could have found other means of providing for your family. Instead you chose the streets. You became just another talented, gifted thief."

POWER 4 FEAR

He let these words linger in the air for a few moments before asking his final question.

"Why should I believe you won't use your talents the same way you did before, if I give you your life back?"

Malcolm considered lying, dropping to his knees and pleading like Snow in the next room.

"I read something about an Indian mathematician," he said instead, "who could never adjust to wearing English shoes. But he still wore them even though they hurt his feet. He did it so he could do what he was good at and stay at the best schools."

The warden cocked his head slightly, as much as his stout neck would allow.

"What's your point?"

"My point is, sir, if you give me my life back . . . I'll wear those shoes."

The warden tapped his touchscreen file display. The monitor overhead rose into the ceiling.

"We'll make our decision a week from today."

Malcolm remembered leaving the room with a backward glance, thinking he had failed when he heard Snow shouting deliriously in Spanish from the adjacent room.

"*No mas!*" he shouted. "*No mas! No mas!*"

It was a piteous cry; it was mournful, like the screams after the death of a loved one.

"*No mas!*" Snow yelled again and again.

"Your grandfather, Timothy McGrady, was killed by British troops in a conflict called 'Bloody Sunday' in Northern Ireland, when gunshots killed him and twelve other marchers in Derry in 1972. He was considered a ruthless tactical genius by Sinn Fein, the bloody political wing of the Irish Republican Army."

"What has my grandfather got to do with my parole?"

"Let me finish," Mr. Oslo said as he cleared his throat. "As a penal psychiatric administrator I have to establish a root cause for your antisocial behavior. Is it cultural? Societal? A dysfunctional family? We need a psychiatric profile to find out if you have been reprogrammed enough to re-enter society. Now let me continue.

"Your father, Shawn McGrady, was not only a skilled assassin for a military splinter group of the IRA called NIRB, the Neo Irish Republican Brigade. He was also a gifted linguist fluent in French, Russian, and Chinese. Is that how you inherited your linguistic skills, Mr. Shannon, aka 'Snow' Mc-Grady?"

"*Div leng lei!* (fuck you)."

"I'm not going to ask you what that means, but it sounds Chinese."

"Good," Snow said icily.

The large flat screen on the wall in back of Mr. Oslo's desk flickered an iridescent blue light, which reflected on his egg-white bald head. His long cadaverous face was oily. His huge macaw nose dominated his face, making his tiny rodent eyes seem devoid of humanity. He looked like a vulture sitting behind his desk.

"I never met my father. He was killed in a shoot-out with the FBI. I was only five years old at the time."

"And your father's death obviously had no impact on you, because you are standing here being evaluated for parole?"

Snow gazed at Mr. Oslo's rodent eyes. Hate consumed him. He was glad his hands were cuffed because he would have impulsively leapt for Oslo's throat and torn out his jugular. His left eye started to twitch.

"I like to think of my father not as a criminal, but as a political man, a revolutionary who died because of his ideology."

Suddenly, the huge screen beamed a picture of his dead father. The terror of his father's frozen face assailed him: black streaks of crusted blood snaked out of his nostrils and clung to his mustache and lips like a death mask. Blood oozed from Snow's lower lip as he bit down on it. Memories of his fatherless childhood clung to him like blood sucking leaches. Sorrow filled the chambers of his heart. His voice resonated pain.

"I thought I was here for my parole review, not to be tortured about my past!" he shouted. "My father was a man of principle. He died for what he believed in . . ."

"Mr. McGrady, lower your voice!" Mr. Oslo demanded as he pecked on the keyboard imbedded in his desktop. His mother's alabaster face crystallized on the screen. Her coal black hair glistened as if wet; her face was stenciled with lines of stress, worry, and pain. The white of her blue eyes had a jaundiced glow.

"My mother is a good woman. She did the b-best . . ." he stuttered, "she could to raise us."

"Agreed, but your father was a bank robber, kidnapper, and freelance hit man for the mob. Your mother met him in Washington, D.C., just before he and members of The Legion of White Angels, a home grown terrorist group, were killed plotting to blow up a British consulate with ammonium nitrate, fertilizer fuel oil, and blasting caps."

A frozen image of Snow selling the galactic drug *Martianzeeg* to an undercover NARC agent morphed on the screen. Snow felt anger surge through his body. He struggled to contain his rage. His heart felt like it was going to burst out of his chest.

"Why do you keep lying about my father? You got something against Irish-Catholics?"

"No, but you should get down on your knees every night with a rosary and thank the Catholic Church for saving your wretched life!"

"Why? What are you tryin' to say? Stop beatin' around the bush, man!" Snow said angrily.

"To some degree your father believed in the sanctity of the unborn. If he hadn't threatened to kill your mother if she aborted you, we would not be having this conversation."

"I said he was a man of principle," Snow said defiantly.

"Well," Mr. Oslo said as he tapped a key on his desk and the screen went blank, "why didn't he leave your mother some money to raise you, your brother, and sister, huh? Why did he

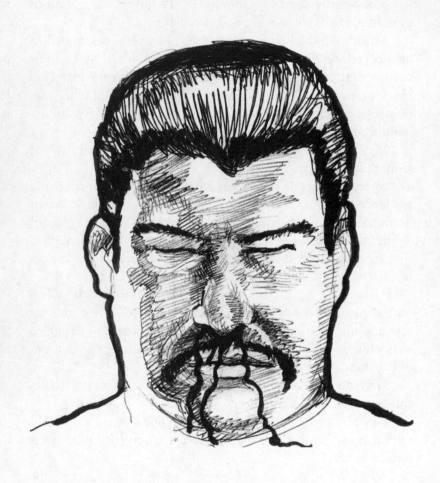

leave your mother in total poverty? You defend a father that left you to grow up in a squalid Indiana trailer slum like human sewage?"

"He did what he had to do. He sacrificed us for a greater cause," Snow said almost tearfully.

"He was a sociopathic killer!" Mr. Oslo shouted while banging his fist on his desk. "Yes, he had principles all right—just like Heinrich Himmler, the head of the Nazis SS had principles, as he exterminated millions of Jews!"

"Look, I know where you're going with this," Snow said confidently. "You want me to break down and lose control. Try to attack you, so you can have an excuse not to parole me. Well, it's not going to work. I'm not falling for your game. Can we move on to the next psycho test?"

The monitor screen turned black.

"You will hear from us within a week," Mr. Oslo said, as the guard escorted Snow out of the room.

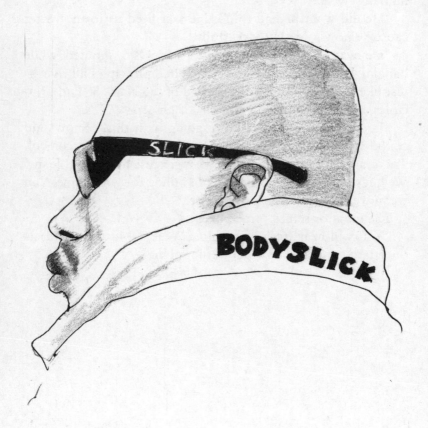

Chapter 4

Bodyslick's thoughts silenced as he heard a loud thump at the door. He tossed the newscube onto the couch. He quickly grabbed his 9 mm laser pistol from atop the table. He glanced at his watch wondering if Malanna was playing some kind of joke on him. She was late. He gazed through the peephole. Silent. Empty. Nothing. Nobody. The entry/exit video screen above the door was blank.

He cocked his laser pistol with his right hand as he braced his back against the door and slowly opened it with his left. The pungent odors of reactants: ethylene and nitrogen trifluoride stung his nostrils, as it wafted from the barrel of his pistol. He heard paper rustling against the bottom of the door.

Bodyslick swung the door open and slid into the doorway. A small gift wrapped box sat at the bottom of the door. He peered down the hallway. Not a soul. He picked up the box, walked back into his apartment, and put it on top of his kitchen table. He read the note taped to it:

TO BODYSLICK WITH ALL MY HEART! TWOC

Had Malanna put the box there? She never had done that before. If so, why would she not give it to him personally? And what did TWOC mean? Was it a bomb inside? He glanced at his watch dial. If it flickered *red*, it was a bomb and jammers would be activated to block a signal to set it off. There was no change. *I'm just paranoid*, he thought.

He slowly unraveled the blue ribbon. He impatiently tore off the paper. The brown cardboard box sat on the table. It looked like a small shoe box. It had the same type of lid. All he had to do was lift it. He gritted his teeth and opened it. Instantly, his vision was blurred by squirting *red . . .* blood. It flowed down his forehead into the cavity of his eyes and dribbled down into his mouth. It was human blood, although it was not his. He knew the taste of it. He had been in too many fights not to. Salty human blood.

He grabbed a towel and wiped his face. Large blotches of blood covered his white shirt. He peeped inside the box. There was a small plastic container inside. Within the container was an organ. A human organ? A freshly carved out human heart. He could tell that it was less than an hour since it had been snatched out of someone's chest. Who would do such a hideous thing and why?

There were two tiny copper filigreed wires attached to the heart: one was attached to the *sino-auricular-node*, which is the pacemaker of the heart, via a small square piece of carbon. At the end of the other wire was a clamped piece of *zinc*, imbedded deep into the muscular tissue.

Bodyslick had sold too many human *hearts* not to be familiar with its internal anatomy. He observed that the heart was still sheathed within its tough sac, the *pericardium*. Barely noticeable, slithering underneath it, was a third copper wire that was plugged into a small, round, silver 1.5 volt cell battery, which probably triggered the bio-electric currents in the organ. He thought, *The lid somehow was used as the switch, because the minute I opened it about an ounce of blood squirted from the contracted heart into my face.*

Bodyslick smiled at the comic aspect of it. It was a deathly joke. A joke that cost someone their life. Or was this just a healthy cadaver's heart sent as a message?

The old high school Luigi Galvani observation who observed that a frog's leg would be made to twitch if copper and iron, attached to a nerve or a muscle, was brought into con-

tact. Only this time a human heart was used. How hideously macabre. How ingenious. How insane!

He was drenched with blood. It was bizarre. For a fleeting moment he wondered if this was some mad, tormented nightmare. But the light, incessant laughter floating from the flickering holoscreen echoed reality. He looked at his blood-splattered carpet. *Why?*

He was consumed with murderous rage. Malanna? She still hadn't called. *Dammit,* he wondered, *was this her bleeding heart?* He rushed into his bedroom and called her. It *rang . . . rang . . .* and *rang.* His imagination went wild with images of some mad pervert slicing her heart out. He could hear her cries of agony, then the deathly silence. He could see glassy staring dead eyes. Was it her heart? He slammed down the phone and started to take off his clothes for a shower when the vid-phone rang. *Malanna?* He picked up the phone, and her beautiful caramel face metamorphosed on the video screen.

"Hello . . . love!" And like the sweet sound of a bird's song he heard her voice. "Bodyslick, you look depressed. Is anything wrong, baby?"

Darkness settled on his soul. His body was pungent with the stale rotting odor of dried blood. Some stranger's dried blood. He could feel his dull mind trying to pay attention to her words.

"Bodyslick . . . are you all right . . . huh? You act as if your best friend has died."

There were certain things he would never tell her. There were certain things she didn't need to know.

"Yeah . . . I'm all right. I just thought something was wrong because you hadn't called. I thought you'd have been over here by now."

"The Maglev train had some kind of mechanical problems on the way from the loop. Is that blood on your shirt, honey? Did you cut yourself?"

"Yeah, I cut my hand trying to fix something. It's okay though." (Sometimes a lie was appealing.)

"I got you a present," she said excitedly, "I'll bring it over tonight . . . and I'll make up for lost time. . . ."

He smiled. Sex with Malanna was so good it could make a blind man see. It could make the crippled and lame walk. Just the thought of making love to her made him sweat.

"Just call before you come. Because I got to make a few runs. I've got to take care of some business. I'll call you back when I'm done . . . be careful Malanna. I love you. Bye!"

"I love you, too. I'll see you tonight." She puckered her juicy lips and sent him a telepathic kiss.

He took off his blood-drenched clothes and tossed them into a nearby hamper. Then he quickly opened the bathroom medicine cabinet and found a bottle of nerve ease tablets and took two. He turned on the shower until it was almost arctic cold. His mind was now as calm and as peaceful as a grave. He clenched his teeth fiercely as muscles knotted in his jaws and icy daggers stabbed his skin. He shivered in nakedness as he glanced at the mirror on the bathroom door, which reflected the bloody box on the kitchen table. He felt intuitively, that impending danger was near. His body shook from the icy cold water. In his business, death was an everyday thing. His life-style depended on it. In his racket *death* was a certainty due to the vast amount of quick money that could be made. The vid-phone rang as he turned on the light in the bathroom. The walls glowed with speckled gold white tile, the mirror on the door and above the sink lit up, with borders of tiny twinkling lights. The marble countertop on the sink was splattered with blood from the heart. He spoke into the voice-box on the wall.

"Who is it?"

There was no image on the screen. All he heard was heavy breathing. A man's heavy breathing.

"Who is it . . . dammit!"

Then a deep baritone voice spoke. "Did you get your gift, chump?"

"Look, muthafucka, if and when I find out who you are, yo ass is mine!"

"Shut up, punk, and listen up—that heart belongs to Bubba Green, your main lackey."

He shut off the shower. *Not Bubba*, he thought. He hit the shower wall with his fist till his hand became bulbous and red. The voice rumbled on.

"The heart is a message from *TWOC*. You've got competition in Chicago now. In fact we're taken over. Watch your back, *ruffiano!*" The phone shut off.

Ruffiano? What the fuck does that mean? The voice was definitely Italian. He couldn't believe Bubba was dead. His main soldier. Maybe this TWOC was bluffing. Maybe, just maybe Bubba wasn't dead. Ruffiano? He would have to ask Snow what it meant.

He toweled himself dry and put on his boxer shorts, lightweight ostrich black shoes, and his dark-brown khaki summer jumpsuit. He then grabbed his shoulder holster from a hook on the back of the bathroom door. The German-made 9 mm laser pistol with its special made perforated silencer was in the holster. Bodyslick smiled as he put his arms through the shoulder straps. Only a select few could own such a weapon. A weapon with a detonating burst of intense white laser heat that was like a series of tiny nuclear pellets of hydrogen blowing up inside you. The old nickel-plated barreled pistols were archaic beside them. That was why laser weapons were illegal except for special branches of the U.S. government.

He went back into the kitchen and picked up the bloody box then opened a small garbage door in the wall adjacent to the refrigerator and dropped the box down into the incinerator. He then walked into his bedroom and reached for his leg knife-holster with its long serrated stiletto switchblade. He bent down and snapped it on.

His vidphone rang. Snow's pale white face gleamed on the vidscreen.

"You know what *ruffiano* means?" Bodyslick asked.

"Yeah, it means pimp in Italian!"

"Pimp!"

"Yeah, you got some sweet *baldracca* callin' you that?" Snow laughed facetiously.

"Hell no! Some nut with an outfit called TWOC called claiming they killed Bubba and they're gonna take over our business, blah, blah, blah! Sounds like a bunch of shit to me. What do you think?"

"Bad news!"

"What?"

"They found Bubba's body in an alley on East 43rd. The *bagaseias* (bitches) cut out his heart, Slick!" Snow said piteously.

"Shit, man!" Bodyslick moaned as he shut off the vidscreen.

He then walked to the other side of the bed, picked up an opened package of Marygold marijuana seagarettes (U.S. government approved) from a lamp table, took one out, lit it with his gold initialed lighter, inhaled deeply, and sat down on the bed. Thoughts started to dance in his head. He bared his pearly white teeth, with the one gold crown, in restraint as he tried to drown the pain of Bubba's death. He didn't even cry at his grandmother's funeral. But he now sat alone in his bedroom, and tears dripped from his face. Bubba Green, Shondell Williams, Geronimo Johnson and Shannon "Snow" McGrady had been friends since grammar school. They were tight as fish pussy, which is waterproof. They had fought together. Fucked women together. Traveled together. Bubba was his half brother. The kind of brother Bodyslick had always wished his own brother had been like. Bubba was second in command of The Bodyslick Salvageable Organ Company.

Bodyslick picked up a towel and wiped his face. He then walked over to a small arc-fan atop a mahogany dresser and turned it on, stirring up the pungent odor of marijuana. He sighed as he thought about how he would have to take care of Bubba's cremation (he wanted his ashes dropped into the Atlantic Ocean), and make sure his wife and young daughter received all the money and assets Bubba had invested in their Real Steel Chicken franchise. He would call his accountant

and make sure he contacted Bubba's widow so she fully understood all of the financial options that were open to her.

His vidphone blinked on again. Snow barked, "You don't
fuck with family—they gotta pay, man!"

Bodyslick stood up and brushed the ashes off his suit.

"Whoever killed him will be dead within 24 hours," Snow
continued angrily.

Bodyslick squashed out the joint in an ashtray; he started to
recite part of a street rap he had learned while in prison. Snow
joined in:

*"I was weaned off the tit of a wild boar, and I cut my
teeth on a Colt .45.
I can be mean without even trying. I'm a bad
muthafucka, and I don't mind dying.
I walked a thousand miles through the sunny South. Just
to punch one jive muthafucka in the mouth.
Human blood is my food, poison is my wine.
When I wake up evil, I dare the sun to shine.
I've handcuffed lightning, shackled thunder, walked
through a graveyard and made the dead to wonder.
I've fucked a she-lion, dared the he-lion to roar, and
fucked him in the ass when I felt like more.
If I catch you fucking with my body organ trade, I'll dig
one more plot in my private graveyard for your ass to be
laid."*

Chapter 5

The whining siren of the ambulance sent a cold chill down his spine. It always affected him that way. For most people, the sound imbued a feeling of deathly gloom, a feeling of man's mortality, but to Bodyslick it was the sweet sound of money. But he wondered *if it was money this time that would be made from Bubba's body?*

He quickly grabbed his nightvisors, slid open his ceiling-high panoramic window, and walked out onto the balcony. He inhaled the Lake Michigan flavored air deeply. He beamed the infrared lens into the teeming streets of East 57th, when flickering red lights caught his scan. It was a car accident. The gawkers, from his view, looked like tiny red ants milling around the remains of a member of their own species. Fusion jazz blared from neon-lit lounges. Shrill voices screamed. Tires squealed. A crowd started to mill around the accident victim. Horns blasted from the traffic jam.

He watched the ambulance attendants pick up the limp body of a young black man, then he saw Toejoe, face black as creosote, with thick fleshy lips. His bald head was gleaming from urban neon haze. He seemed tentative, nervous, as if the very sight of death repulsed him. Bodyslick sensed that he didn't possess the unflinching coldness that was a necessity for the trade.

Bodyslick squinted his eyes as Toejoe merged back into the

large crowd. He scanned the people again. He knew that Toejoe would make his move any moment now. Bodyslick wiped
his brow with the back of his hand as he thought about a
means of execution for Toejoe's violation of his turf. Did he
send the human heart? Was he responsible for Bubba's death?
Chicago was Bodyslick's territory. Anyone who was not approved by him was subject to die. The attendants slowly put
the body in the ambulance as Toejoe leaped from the curbside
and put a hundred dollar bill in the attendant's hand. The
man's face lit up like a firefly's glow with joy. Toejoe quickly
grabbed the corpse's limp hand and pressed a button on a
wafer thin black square box, which beamed arctic cold light
from the bottom of it, branding a stamp on it, which said in
large bold letters: OWNED BY THE TOEJOE WILSON ORGAN
TRANSPORT COMPANY. TWOC.

Bodyslick angrily turned from the window, while throwing
the nightvisors on a nearby couch. He grabbed his black summer jacket and two small boxes of portable disguises, out of
the closet, and hurriedly walked out of his swanky Hyde Park
apartment. His vidphone rang as he strolled away.

He waited for the elevator as globules of sweat formed
across his wrinkled forehead. He wondered was the air on. He
patted his 9 mm laser pistol as if it was a baby. The hallway
was empty. Suddenly, he heard the *buzz* of a magnetic mortise
lock and the screech of a door. As it swung open, blue light
smoked through.

He gazed at a tall, casually-dressed black woman wearing
an ivory white blouse, pink shorts, and bright pink Roman
sandals with straps that wound up her large ebony legs. She
was so black she seemed blue. Her skin reflected colors like an
artist's pallet. It was as black as bituminous coal. Her mammoth liquid cat-gray-eyes were highlighted with sky-blue eye
shadow. She beamed a sensuous smile at him that revealed
teeth that were as bright as *vampire* fangs. Her small pug nose
accented large lips that seemed as succulent as the meat of a

watermelon. She was healthy, fleshy, and had plenty of breast, ass, and thighs. She was sensuous. Soft. Malleable. Cushy.

Bodyslick's dick started to poke out of his pants. He quickly stuck his hand inside his jumpsuit pocket trying to conceal it. Her luminous eyes fell on his crotch. He gulped in embarrassment. The cobra had locked eyes with its prey. He grimaced as his penis started to throb with pain as he gazed at her huge *Hottentot derriere*, sculpted like chocolate in her skintight shorts. She smiled wickedly as a faint, funky odor wisped past his nostrils. He started sniffing the air like a dog smelling a bitch in heat. It was a glandular musky odor from sweaty sex that you would smell in an airless locked room. Was it pussy?

As she pushed her ID key into her magnetic lock with her free hand, she whispered quietly into the apartment as she pulled on the choke chain leash.

"Come on . . . Hodari! Come on, Kasi."

Bodyslick listened to the distant sound of an ambulance siren. *Where was the fuckin' elevator?* he wondered. He could hear from a nearby apartment the muffled trumpet solo of Miles Davis merging with the siren. He heard a loud playful bark come from the woman's apartment, then a distant growl? He wondered what was on the end of the choke leash. Some new gene-spliced creature? Bodyslick licked his dry lips with disbelief as a giant white two-headed, red-nosed pit bull romped out of her apartment. A couple of flies *bzzzzzz* past him as if in total fear. He knew the dog was a product of genetic engineering. In 2031, a hydra-headed guard dog was quite common. Greek mythology was real; the language of DNA molecules containing instructions for creating chimeric creatures had finally been cracked.

The woman unconsciously flicked her y-shaped tongue at him sensuously. She slowly walked toward him. Ropes of gold hung from her neck and arms. The dogs suddenly started sniffing the air and growling at him menacingly. The woman started to scream at the dogs while pulling tightly on the leash.

"Stop, Hodari! . . . Stop, Kasi! . . ."

Her distressed eyes shone like stolen emeralds from some
ancient Ethiopian Pharaoh's tomb. The beasts started to bark
and growl fiendishly. Their eyes were like hot red rivets. He
could hear the metallic churning of the choke chains as the dogs
pulled the woman at will toward him, while bared canine teeth
gleamed from the hallway light. Their dog collars, studded
with diamonds and red rubies sparkled blood-red. He wondered why the elevator was so slow. He patted his 9 mm laser
pistol nervously. The woman screamed at him.

"They must smell the reactants from your gun. I can't hold
them! Take the emergency stairway! Run!"

The dog wheeled and broke away from her. Bodyslick
quickly opened the nearby exit door and ran down the stairs.
He could hear the murderous growl and scratching of metal,
as the beast viciously banged against the metal door. He
thought as he breathed heavily, while opening the stairway
door to the lobby, *Mizz Luscious won't have to worry about
me knocking on her door for sugar, as long as she owns that
monster.*

"How you doing, Mr. Steel?" asked Chan Lee, the person-
able Chinese security guard.

"Cool, Lee, but I want to ask you a couple of questions," he
said, trying to catch his breath.

"Shoot, Mr. Steel. I'm all ears."

"In the last two hours were there any deliveries on my
floor?"

"No," Chan Lee said confidently, "but Otis Elevator Service
Company did some repairs about two hours ago."

"This late?" Bodyslick asked while glancing at his watch.

"Yes, but they are always on call twenty-four hours. Didn't you
take the stairway because of the elevator problem, Mr. Steel?"

"No, but if I hadn't, a huge two-headed pit bull would have
mauled me to death."

Chan Lee cleared his throat and smiled while waving at the
woman with the two-headed dog as she alighted from the elevator.

"Uh, uh, uh, Lawd have mercy, that's Miss Luscious with that beast . . . right there," Bodyslick said excitedly.

"That's Roseberry Star," Chan Lee said passively. "Her street moniker is 'Star.' She is one of the most expensive call girls in Chicago. Those are real diamonds and rubies in that dog collar. That two-headed pit bull is trained to attack when it smells the gas that seeps from a laser gun. Dogs detect laser weapons because the odors are imperceptible to humans."

Bodyslick whispered in Chan Lee's ear, "How's the organ business in Chinatown doin'? You know I pick up my money on the first."

"Not good, Mr. Steel, the Hip Hop Sung Gang has stopped buying and selling body organs . . . for now."

"What do ya mean . . . for now, Lee? That means a lot of fuckin' money, man!" Bodyslick said impatiently.

"Not good to talk out here. Let's go inside the security booth."

They walked into a glass-enclosed, soundproof booth that was located at the top of the first floor stairs. Bodyslick looked at the maze of video monitors as they all blinked images of every possible location in the apartment complex. Bodyslick sat down on top of a nearby desk. Lee angrily told a mean-looking Chinese teenager to leave. Bodyslick gazed at a blue and red equilateral triangle tattoo on the youth's forearm. He had seen it before, but he couldn't remember where.

"What's goin' on?" Bodyslick asked, as Lee closed the door. "We been makin' good money together. You are my main man in Chinatown. Let's keep it like that."

"Mr Steel, the leader, Choi Tse Tong, believes that his niece was raped and murdered by two men in your organization or the Mafia."

"But, Lee, why me? Talk to them, they should know you are my only link in Chinatown. Mr. Tong has been doin' business with me exclusively since my Uncle Will had a stroke last year."

"Mr. Steel, the girl was blindfolded and kidnapped. The semen DNA is European. Members of the Hip Hop Sung believe this barbaric act is a slap in the face to all people in Chinatown. The honor of the leader, the people of Chinatown, and his brother-in-law's family has been shamed."

"But, Lee, I don't have any whites workin' with you in Chinatown."

"I know, Mr. Steel, but this is a very grave matter in Chinatown, until the animals who attacked the woman are captured and punished . . . no organs."

Bodyslick glanced out the security room window at the Chinese youth who had his black hair combed back and tied into a ponytail. He knew that was the way the Hip Hop Sung members wore their hair.

"Lee, can you set up a meeting with Mr. Tong, so I can talk to him about this problem?"

He laughed. "I wish I could, Mr. Steel . . ."

Bodyslick interrupted him. "Will you call me Bodyslick? I don't like using my real name when discussing business."

"Bodyslick," Lee smiled, "if it was that simple I would . . . but this is the first time that something has happened in Chinatown that has caused such enormous unity. The Flying Dragons . . . the Ghost Shadows . . . and the murderous Rat Tat Tat Tongs have all come together in the name of honor for vengeance because of this hate crime."

"I know for a fact that the mob's not only angry over the Triad musclin' them out of almost eighty percent of the heroin trade by importing their cheap heroin from Asia and lowering the price, but also because of them not buying their cocaine or somellow from them . . . plus I've got the organ business sold up."

"You are probably right, Bodyslick, but just let things simmer down. Let things go their course. Wait till the girl's rapists are punished. I can assure you the Triad, at this very moment, is on the verge of resolving this matter."

"Any serious problems, contact me by the secret code."

"Gotcha!" Chan Lee said, as he started to walk out the security room with Bodyslick.

"One more thing," Bodyslick said, as he grabbed the doorknob, "Lee, lemme see your forearm?"

"Why? What do you want to see?" As he rolled up his shirt sleeve, he said, "This is what you wanna see?" Lee smiled as he only confirmed what Bodyslick already suspected. "Bodyslick, if you can imagine all the black gangs coming together for one singular nationalistic political purpose, such as a revolution to overthrow America, but failing because of Uncle Tom traitors, causing all the revolutionaries to be incarcerated and killed. And those that survive creating a secret society whose main purpose was to continue the revolution; you have a Triad. The three points on the triangle . . ." While Bodyslick squinted as he looked at the symbols, Chan Lee cleared his throat and continued, ". . . mean heaven, earth, and man. Unless you are a Triad member in Chinatown you are doomed to a life of working in some restaurant making sissy ass fortune cookies, especially if you come from a poor family like me!"

Bodyslick confidently patted Chan Lee on the shoulder, as he opened the door.

"All right Lee, but will you at least try to set up the meeting with Mr. Tong?"

"No problem," Lee said, as he rolled his shirt sleeve back down.

Bodyslick waved at Lee as he leaped down the stairs. The youth quickly ran back into the booth and picked up the phone.

Chapter 6

The name Triad bounced in his head as he deeply inhaled the putrid Lake Michigan breeze, as it swirled around him like a banshee's scream. He gazed at a skull-white moon casting its glow on the rectangular urbanscape, as tiny stars twinkled down on him, seemingly mocking at man's puny quest for immortality.

Triad. The word caused a blood-curdling fear to flood his body. He could feel the short hair on his back rise. He remembered when he was only six years old, how his Uncle Will, along with four other leaders of Chicago's top gangs, met in a secret place in underground Chinatown called Head City, which was directly in back of Hip Hop Chop Suey on East 23rd Street. The restaurant was merely a front for the Hip Hop Sung Gang's drug network. The city was about four city blocks long and three miles wide. It was used up until 1997 as a huge prostitute and tourist area. It was one of the most densely packed areas in Chicago. After the British crown colony of Hong Kong began its Communist Chinese government in 1997, almost a quarter of a million gangsters from who knows how many Triads, departed from Hong Kong. New York and Chicago were where the two most popular bases were located.

His mind remembered the stench of human piss, ammonia, rat, cat and dog dung mingled with the hot odor of fried egg

rolls. His mind whirled back in time as he remembered Uncle Will, Snow, and himself being led by a Chinese guide through a rat maze of underground tunnels, alleys, a tiny restaurant, two flights of stairs, a dark cavernous hallway, a small vestibule, a laundry, a black tunnel—then suddenly light revealing a ceiling and wall that turned into a cul de sac. A street light cast an eerie yellow light on a tall wooden gate with round shapes on top that were hidden in shadow.

The Chinese guide had pulled a pen-sized flashlight from his pocket. He had clicked it on and pointed at the round objects on top of the gate. He then turned and smiled at them, revealing fang-like teeth, as if he expected them to run with fear.

"Lawd have mercy! Not Johnny boy!" Uncle Will had shouted, as he wiped his eyes with disbelief. I had started to scream as the Chinese guide quickly covered my mouth with his hand. My six-year-old body had become delirious. My little heart felt as if it was going to leap out of my chest. I peed on myself. My whole body trembled like a junkie that had shot up acid-laced heroin. It was the first time that I had sensed terror in my uncle.

"So that's why they call this place Head City," Uncle Will said to the guide.

Uncle Will had picked me up as we walked past the five heads on top of the gate. One black, who was Johnny boy, one white, one bronze, one olive, one yellow. All male. Eyes opened, staring with surprise and disbelief. Uncle Will told me that each head was from one of the five gangs that were meeting with Choi Tse Tong, the infamous leader of the Hip Hop Sung, the main Triad in Chicago's Chinatown.

"This entrance to Head City. Leave weapon here. Follow me!"

We held up our arms and stretched legs, as our guide shouted at a young boy, no more than twelve, to search us. He had taken Uncle Will's .38 with a six-inch barrel, my switch-blade and Snow's ivory handled razor, and then wrote a blue chalk mark on them, and tossed them into a box full of weapons. Smiling, he then opened a small door built in the gate.

"We must hurry . . . Lao Yeh will kill me if we late. Time velly important. We must hurry!"

"Who is Lao Yeh?" Snow asked.

"The master is called many names. Tong is Lao Yeh. Master!"

It was pitch black, and the odor of pungent warm meat wafted past my nose. I could hear the distant pleading-like howl of dogs, cats, pigs and ducks, as they rammed their wire cages as if conscious of their butchered fate.

The mournful yelping of the dogs kindled hideous images of Lassie, Rin Tin Tin, and Benji being dispassionately eaten at a Chinese dinner table.

Rats scampered over garbage and refuse without fear. Strange voices bombarded my ears: Cantonese voices, Shanghai voices, Mandarin voices. The voices were blasting from made in Taiwan television sets.

A huge gray, steel door loomed in front of us as we exited the alley. The guide knocked on the door. A tiny video camera's red eye beamed at us. A voice spoke in Chinese from a tiny speaker made in the door. The guide reached inside his shirt pocket and pulled out a magnetic card and stuck it in a slot. The door swung open. The guide motioned for us to take off our shoes before going inside. The ceiling was so low and flat that Uncle Will bumped his head as he stooped over entering the small office.

A fat Buddha-looking Chinese man, immaculately dressed in a pin-striped dark blue suit, sat behind a huge mahogany desk carving up a steak with a diamond encrusted fork and knife. Two huge, stoic Chinese bodyguards dressed in black ninja costumes stood next to him like museum statues. The guide closed the door and was gone. The fat Chinese man gestured toward a leather couch directly in front of his huge desk. Between the couch and his desk was a small smoked-glass table. On top of it were faint black and white carved chess-

Lao Yeh

board squares. Tall black and white wooden dragon figures sat on each square. A huge Chinese painting of a blood-red serpent hung on the wall in back of him.

"I am Choi Tse Tong. I am the reason those decapitated heads were on the gate," he said, as he violently stabbed the knife into the steak. "I have already talked to two of the five street gang leaders of Chicago that were a part of this meeting—two of them fled after seeing the heads of their gang members. I see you and the little guys could stomach it."

"*Lay go yeun tsi leng sin!* (you are fucking crazy)," Snow said loudly.

I hid behind Uncle Will's leg as Tong stared at Snow with surprise and disbelief at his stinging Chinese. Images of the heads danced in my fearful mind.

"*Hai yeung!* (cunt face)," Tong snarled viciously. "No need for interpreter. What I have to say to Will can be easily understood in ghettonese rather than Chinese!"

Uncle Will rolled his eyes at Snow signaling him to keep quiet.

"Nobody sells somellow, Martianzeeg or heroin in Chinatown without my consent. Not a nuthin' huckin' ting without my okay, me make self clear, Mr. Will?"

A low ceiling fan cast whirling umber shadows on his pudgy face as blood dripped down the side of his mouth from the almost raw steak. He looked like a Chinese vampire. A huge diamond ring gleamed from his fat finger. Uncle Will silently nodded his head.

"Johnny boy's head is on that gate because he, along with the others, deserved to die because they were renegade shitheads who violated our treaty. If we hadn't killed them, I'm sure you guys would have."

"True!" Uncle Will warned Tong, "But don't you step over the fuckin' line either. If you ever try to sell that Chinawhite dope on the South Side of Chicago to my people, I'll come down so hard on your rice eatin' ass, that you'll want to swim back to China!"

"I don't like disrespect. You must watch your mouth, Mr. Will," Tong said as the veins on his temple writhed with rage. I wondered if Uncle Will was losing his mind. Had he forgotten the heads on the gate?

"Tong, nobody intimidates me, you fuck wid' the South Side and your forefathers in China will hear your bones rattle!" Uncle Will said defiantly, as Tong's bodyguards pulled huge, gleaming machetes from waist holsters.

"Do you want to sell your drugs and buy organs in Chinatown, Mr. Will?"

"Yeah, that's one of the reasons I'm heah!"

"Well, calm down! Mr. Will, be cool!" Tong said, as he gestured to the bodyguards to put their weapons away. I watched Uncle Will show no fear even as he realized that his threats could mean instant death.

"Give him the cocaine, Malcolm!" I nervously walked over to his desk and put a plastic bag of a half a kilo on top of it.

"That's yours if you lemme be your supplier in Chinatown." I smiled with pride as I watched Uncle Will stand his ground, unflinchingly, against the powerful Chinese leader.

"I like your guts, Mr. Will—you see we Chinese honor strength. We are taught from an early age to never show fear or pain. We fight to the death. You have proven your character is strong enough to be a business partner."

Bodyslick's mind snapped back to reality as he watched the serpentine movement of the Maglev train as it came into view. The coils echoed a howling sound as it generated a magnetic field down the suspension rail.

He remembered riding the old screeching, noise-ridden electric El when he was young. Now, he thought, instead of churning on metallic wheels one actually glided on air which created a floating, levitative glide. A ride of noise-free, friction-free, pollution-free, karma. In the old days it would take about 40 minutes to get from his apartment to the county morgue. But now with a 300 mile linkage in Chicago, the same route takes less than 15 minutes. With trains traveling at 400 mph in

2031, there was no real need to drive anywhere in Chicago. It was an A train which would take him west.

As he walked down the aisle searching for a seat on the sardine-packed train, snatches of conversation floated toward him:

". . . Lawd dat mannn waz killed gurl!"

". . . Somebody gottah stop this killin' of our Black leaders . . ."

". . . He died of a massive heart attack which was a by-product of obesity coupled with an unhealthy lust for fatty foods . . ."

". . . The stress of racism killed that man . . ."

". . . He was murdered because he was becoming too powerful . . ."

The cacophony of voices slowly ceased as the train doors swung open; eddies of wind rushed in causing bottles and cans to move on the floor. A tall, sinister, light-skinned black man stood majestically in the doorway of the train. He was dressed in a quasi-military black suit. His oval glasses gave him a studious air. He wore a red, green, and black cap, which he had often seen new-age Muslims wear. He held a thick black book in his hand and began to speak in a deep bass voice:

"My name is Hasheem X, and I'll only need a few minutes of your time."

Bodyslick knew he was a member of NAM: the radical New Age Muslims who wanted a separate state for black Americans because, they believed, there would never be total freedom for minorities in North America.

"Mayor Darold Mannington was targeted for assassination. His political enemies killed him . . . just like they did Richard Wright, Fanon, Padmore, Malcolm, King, Bekoe, Kennedy, Tupac, Shabaka and Huey P. Newton . . ."

Bodyslick sensed that the people on the train were listening attentively. Hasheem X only reinforced what they already suspected.

"He didn't die of no heart attack. The media is actually try-

ing to convince us that barbecue, greens, and hamhocks killed him. They want you to actually believe that his diet killed him. Well, that's just not true, brothers and sisters!"

The white passengers suddenly seemed extremely nervous. A metallic female voice bellowed out of the Maglev train's speakers. "According to code 10A of the Chicago Maglev Authority there will be no political speeches on the train. You cannot use this train for political purposes."

"Shut up and let the brother speak," a short black man screamed. "Go on, brother!"

"The FBI records, which our organization NAM has obtained under the Freedom of Information Act, state that before Darold was assassinated his life was threatened by a politically-motivated conspiracy. His stance on the have nots. His prominent role in trying to get the humanzee rights act passed: an act that would ban the use of chimpanzees, with human brain genes, as guinea pigs for human biology and disease experiments because they can think, feel, cry, and even love like us. His position that the profit motive in the donor organ underworld would enable only the rich to live. In short, brothers and sisters, he was a powerful black mayor. A black mayor who had the potential to become a world leader. But he was snuffed out! Murdered. Assassinated. How long are we going to stand passively by as our leaders are killed?"

The train's magnetic vibrations whooshed as it neared the next stop. Hasheem X turned toward the exit and shouted as the doors opened. "Make a change!"

Bodyslick had once met Mayor Darold Mannington after he had made a speech in Washington Park at a political rally celebrating his election as mayor of the city of Chicago. He could still remember the powerful hypnotic chant of the huge crowd as the mayor walked to the podium.

"We want Darold! We want Darold!"

Mayor Mannington grabbing the microphone and shouting in a deep baritone voice, *"You want Darold? Well, hereee's Darold!"* He raised his hands quieting the crowd. Cleared his throat. Poked the mike and said, *"And to paraphrase Theodore Roosevelt...'There is no room in my administration for hyphenated Americans. We are one nation. One people. We believe in one God!'"*

The mayor struck Bodyslick as a powerful and charismatic politician with controversial ideas that Chicago's conservative power brokers feared would create a balkanized city. A city of tribes all loyal to him. They called him a nativist because he believed the American national identity was inextricably linked to the philosophy of Lincoln, Roosevelt, Kennedy, M. L. King, Malcolm X, and Cesar Chavez. He believed fervently that America should nationalize before it naturalized. He embraced an American ideology that transcended race. His death seemed unnatural and more like a massive cover-up. But was he merely paranoid? Didn't Darold's lifestyle point to an unhealthy body? Wasn't his heart three times the size of an average man's because of his weight? On the other hand would the U.S. Government have a *real* need to assassinate him? He was no real threat in the international political arena. His political philosophy was more steeped in the doctrine of help for the urban needy here. Maybe it was his outrage against galactic drugs or his massive investigation into the illegal donor organ crimes, which could affect a billion dollar a year underground business.

Bodyslick's thoughts vaporized as he wondered if the pretty woman train attendant sitting across from him was human or a cyborbot. It was hard to tell because the new cyborbots being tested were so human-like it was virtually impossible and sometimes embarrassing, to discover they weren't. He wondered if those were human eyes monitoring the train or metallic-sensors. He looked at her painstakingly, hoping to find some obvious sign that she wasn't human; a waxy complexion, pupils that wouldn't dilate, a programmed set of responses. She was dazzlingly beautiful. Her hair was coal black. Her ethnicity was deliberately neutral. He laughed inwardly to himself because his dick was throbbing, possibly over some-

thing non-human. Something created from malleable non-organic plastics, a complex duodecahedral skeletal system, incalculable amounts of electronic circuitry, and a positronic brain capable of computing seven trillion computations per second. He had to find out before it was too late. Then she suddenly looked him straight in the eyes with a mechanical stare. Was she human? He felt nervous. He wanted to move. His eyes drifted distractedly out of the window over the neon glimmer of a Chicago urbanscape. He longed desperately to be near her. Or it? She suddenly made a quick glance at him; eyes fluttering. She was starting to stand up. A fierce rush of activity bounced in his skull. He rose up out of his seat as the county morgue loomed into view. He quickly walked toward her as she stood near the exit door.

"Excuse me, miss, but will this train stop at the county morgue?"

"Yes, in approximately . . ."—she mechanically gazed at her wristwatch—"three minutes and twenty seconds."

Bodyslick gazed at her slant shaped eyes that were as blue as the sky. Her waxy almond skin color. She was beautiful as the urban lights from the window caught her long wavy black hair. Her lips were juicy . . . succulent like the pink meat of a melon.

Bodyslick watched her prove what he felt intuitively all along. But he wanted to make sure. "What's your name?" He touched her hand. It was cold. Pulseless. Cadaverous with rose-colored fingernails.

"My name . . . Esha . . . and yours?"

"Malcolm Steel, but my friends call me Bodyslick." He heard neo hip rock booming from another train car.

She laughed mechanically. "How did you get such a name? Bodyslick? Meaning?"

"I have a slick body," he lied. "Where do you live, Esha?"

A mechanically-timbered voice whispered, "Live?"

"Yes, like home, apartment?"

"I live here on Maglev A-train 20018-1A. This, Body . . . slick, is my home."

His eyes glued on her round, taut, full breasts and her large pretty legs, momentarily forgetting he was talking to a cyborbot. He noticed she didn't breathe.

"Your stop is now approaching. Your exit ticket please, Bodyslick."

He reached into his coat pocket and gave it to her. He realized without it the cyborbots were programmed to restrain you.

He looked at her again, and again and again. Was science going mad? She was gorgeous. She was more beautiful than any human female he had ever seen. A creepy sensation blanketed his being. He tried to block out the hideous thought that haunted him. Beads of cold sweat started to form on his body. His dick throbbed. He slyly farted. His eyes became foggy. His breaths got shorter. He felt a volcanic lust surging through his being. His throat was dry. His scrotum pulsated with pain. The cavity of his skull heaved as desire oozed through his being.

"Bodyslick, I have subjected you to a holistic bodysensory-scan, and I sense a change in your metabolism?" She stood closer to him and secretly rubbed his throbbing penis, unconsciously igniting millions of sex waves.

He sighed with disbelief. He growled with lustful pleasure. She slowly released her sensuous grip. Had they actually programmed cyborbots to perform sexual acts? After all, she was an experiment. He knew friends who had gone to the *Robot-Erotica Spas* in Somellow Town, and they said that sex with a robot wasn't like sex with a real female. It wasn't remotely human. But it certainly came in a close second.

"Esha . . . you understand my feelings?" he asked, as a ploy to get more information from her. He marvelled at how her brain was merely a bundle of manmade synthetic convolutions which controlled her positromotive movements while working on the train.

"I represent a new generation of cyborbot which have positronic personalities that enable me to mimic human behavior in every phase including the rituals of sex . . . yes, I understand your needs as a human male."

Thoughts and sensations rushed through his being: *Here is my heart, a piteous offering for such a voluptuous creature. Here is my soul. Here is my power. Here is my will. Here! Here! Here! Here bitch! Here you metallic slut. Here!*

"Listen, Esha . . . I want to see you again."

"Why?" She stooped down, facing him as their noses touched. He could hear the *whir* of gears inside her head. "This is my home. This is my matrix. I am not human. I am a slave. A prisoner. I am an illusion, a simulacrum. I am merely a mental construct of what you would like me to be!" She quickly grabbed her pen out of her coat and started scribbling. "Here, Bodyslick," she tore the note off the pad, and handed it to him. "This is your stop."

She kissed him on the cheek before the door slammed shut. He wiped a sticky substance off his cheek where she had kissed him. It had a syrupy texture. He glanced at the note:

Maglev A-train 20018-1A is my home
ESHA

He threw it away and stepped off the train, walked across the street, and stepped into the vestibule of the morgue.

Chapter 7

He wrinkled his nose as the smell of chemicals and death whooshed past his nostrils. He put his ID card into the slot next to the elevator; the door opened. He walked in, jetted up to the sixth floor. A large gold plaque on a wall read:

DR. JONATH WEINER
COOK COUNTY MEDICAL EXAMINER
ORGAN PROCUREMENT DEPARTMENT

His eyes stung as he stepped off the elevator, causing him to bump into a gurney with a body on it that was angled against the corridor wall. The sheet fell from the head of the corpse. Bodyslick nervously looked at the head of a young white woman about twenty-two. He gazed closer. Closer. He felt nauseous. The top of her head had been sawed away. She was brainless. Her dead blue glassine eyes stared fearfully at the ceiling as if it was falling on her.

He knocked on the door. It buzzed. He slowly walked in. Immediately a small gray-haired white man with a large hook nose and tiny amber eyes stood over a naked black man's body. A number of metallic tools on a tray jutted out from the side of the stainless steel gurney. He peered at Bodyslick with puzzlement and confusion, while gesturing with his hands to keep quiet.

Bodyslick swayed frozenly in the autopsy room as Dr. Weiner spoke into a microphone attached to his blue, blood-spotted, mock jacket: "The body is that of a 65-year-old black male politician measuring seventy-four inches and weighing 270 pounds."

Bodyslick looked and looked. Was that Darold Mannington, the controversial mayor from the fourth ward? His ward? The mayor who supposedly died of a mysterious massive heart attack, just before revealing his findings on illegal donor organ crimes in city government? He listened as the doctor droned into the microphone. The doctor picked up a laser scalpel, pressed a button and a tiny razor sharp blue light beamed from it.

"I will now start my internal dissection."

He was petrified with disbelief. Recent memories of the late mayor assailed him. The voices on the train re-echoed their ghastly message: *. . . Lawd that man waz . . . killed, gurl! . . . Somebody gottah stop dis' killin' of black leaders . . . Dem' white folks killed that man! . . . The CIA killed him just like . . .*

He gazed at the body again. Yes, it was "Darold" as they used to call him in the streets. It was Darold Mannington, a black mayor who had single-handedly revolutionized Chicago style politics. A revolution that had brought forth fairness in city government; a totally multi-racial composition in the political arena, and most importantly a new feeling of racial harmony in the city. He peered at Dr. Weiner then back again at the body. Yes, it was him. Bodyslick felt momentarily dazed. To see, laying on that cold steel slab, the only man who ever made him give a damn about Chicago politics; a man who caused him to vote for the first time in his entire life; to see him dead caused a rupture in his conscience of unimaginable terror. Yet, he thought, he had come to this ghoulish place to see Dr. Weiner and not to view Mayor Mannington's body.

Beads of sweat started to form on Bodyslick's face. His heart started to *thump* loudly. The whirl of the fans built into the autopsy table caused the stench of humid, decaying, sulphur-like odors to sting his nose.

He watched as Dr. Weiner made a Y-shaped incision, beginning at the right shoulder, and moving directly to the left; then making a deep vertical cut down to the genitalia. Rib-boning clouds of bluish smoke circled the cuts from the hot laser scalpel. He felt sick as the neck and rib cage opened up. He watched nervously as the doctor extracted all the body organs that seemed a healthy color: the tongue, larynx, trachea, lungs, kidney. He gently placed them in a large greenish liquid-filled plexiglass tank that sat in a stainless steel pan at the foot of the gurney on a nearby table. A morbid smile appeared on the doctor's face as he glanced at the mayor's heart.

He slowly spoke into the microphone again. Only this time more clinically. More detached. "The size of the heart is one and a half times that of a normal man. It weighs . . ."—he paused as his assistant came in the room, put on his surgical gloves, grabbed a laser scalpel, and helped the doctor cut the heart out of its cavity—". . . 400 grams. The coronary and pulmonary arteries are in bad shape. All of the intricate cardiac musculature is in a state of atherosclerotic deterioration, but I have seen worse."

Dr. Weiner spoke with dread into the microrecorder. "It is my preliminary conclusion that Mayor Darold Mannington died of a massive heart attack probably caused by a clotting of the coronary arteries. Although there is no discernible evidence of foul play, all specimens will be taken to toxicology for further analysis. In addition . . ."—the doctor cleared his throat—"despite his heart condition I will not rule out the use of *Rauwolfia Serpentina* and *potassium chloride* both poisonous chemicals used by the CIA and the FBI as a means of toppling hostile foreign governments and to assassinate radical black leaders in America. The chemical mimics a massive heart attack and then becomes undetectable in the system. Of course, this is only speculation. Jonath Weiner, Chief Coroner, 2200 hours, May 2, 2031.

"Wilson, make sure those specimens get to toxicology. I want you to hand carry them. You certainly realize the importance of their results . . . and I almost forgot, make sure my speculative comments are deleted from the report."

The black assistant nodded with respect. He realized how important it was to ease the black community's mounting suspicion of foul play.

"I will, Dr. Weiner. Expeditiously."

"Good, I will leave now. I have an important visitor."

Bodyslick followed him out of the autopsy room; sadly glancing back at the body of a great civil rights leader. They quickly walked into Dr. Weiner's office. He turned to Bodyslick angrily.

"Are you losing your fuckin' mind, man? I told you don't come here. Your goddamn organ business can be dealt with elsewhere. Use some discretion. If this thing leaks out, everything I've accomplished the past twenty years will be snuffed out!"

"Doc, I thought we had an agreement that I would give you five thousand dollars cash for every corpse with healthy organs that I sell!"

Bodyslick glanced around the doctor's office: a huge sarcophagus-shaped desk piled high with decorative plaques, a yellow-tinted human skull, a sign that read "Let laughter flee. This is the place where death delights to help the living." Large holographic color plates of bodies glowed from the pale walls.

The doctor nervously spoke. "Mr. Bodyslick, do you realize that there are sixty-thousand deaths in Chicago each year? And do you also realize I have a staff of one thousand eight hundred? Considering that—then you should also understand that there is a lot going on that I can't monitor. Everybody realizes there's money to be made in the organ parts business. At this point you and I have got Chicago sold up. But do you honestly think that will last forever, now that organized crime and others are discovering how lucrative the organ business is?"

"That's not the point, Doc, we have an agreement," Bodyslick said angrily. "You sell me the bodies, we split the cash. I saw Toejoe Wilson put his stamp on an accident victim's body on 57th and King Drive about four hours ago."

The doctor took out a package of seagarettes, extracted one and, while trembling, tried to light it. Bodyslick knocked it out of his hand.

The doctor said fearfully, "Mr. Bodyslick, I am aware of our agreement. And I don't know any Toejoe Wilson. If someone is trying to move in on us, it's happening in the transportation department." The doctor walked toward the door. "Let's go downstairs to admittance and take a look at the body."

They walked out the office and got on an elevator. Their ears popped as the elevator descended down to the basement and the doors opened. The doctor seemed totally unaware of the sea of dead bodies on gurneys, as he and Bodyslick walked down the long cavernous hallway.

A green-frocked attendant approached Dr. Weiner. "Can I help you, Doc?"

"Yes, I'm looking for a young black male who was admitted about three hours ago. The cadaver had been transported from 5700 South near King Drive. The victim was fatally hit by a car."

The attendant flickered through his compu-clipboard and said unemotionally, "James Tyler came in at 1900 hours in room 14C, Dr. Weiner."

"Thanks . . . good work, David."

As they entered 14C, a bespeckled Asian attendant walked toward them.

"Got a minute?" The oriental glanced at Dr. Weiner's badge and nodded with enthusiasm. "Your name, son?"

"Lee . . . Lee Wong, sir."

He was short and stocky and had an almost feminine face. Bodyslick wondered if he was a secret member of one of Chinatown's many Triads.

"I'm looking for an accident victim a . . . James Tyler, and will you find out if he had an organ donor card on him?"

"I'll check. He is over there on gurney Al." The attendant pointed to the body of Tyler which lay in a corner of the autopsy room bathed in the glare of ceiling lights.

Dr. Weiner gazed at the accident victim. Bodyslick stood there shivering in the refrigerator-like cold. The doctor picked up the man's limp wrist: OWNED BY THE TOEJOE WILSON ORGAN TRANSPORT COMPANY. TWOC.

They looked at each other. The doctor cleared his throat and said, "Bodyslick, once it is found, especially in accident cases, that the deceased died instantaneously, and it is established that he wants his organs given to science, then it is now perfectly legal for a private organ transport company to take the body, once the death is recorded and the next of kin notified. This stamp certainly isn't a threat to us. He is hustling bodies on a street level. You have the massive power of my office on your side. He might conceivably get five grand or more for the organ parts that have already been removed."

The attendant walked urgently toward them with a pink sheet of paper flapping in his hand. "Here is a copy of his organ donor card, sir."

"Thank you," Dr. Weiner said as he pushed his glasses back over the bridge of his nose. "Look at this!" he said arrogantly. Bodyslick took the card from him and read it.

ORGAN DONOR PURCHASE CARD

James Tyler

Print or type name of donor

in the hope that I may help others, I hereby make this anatomical purchase if medically acceptable, to take effect upon my death. The words and marks below indicate my desires.

Sell   (a) __X__   any needed organs or parts
       (b) __   only the following organs or parts
       (c) __   only organs

Specify the organ(s) or part(s) for the purposes of transplantation and sale.

       (d) __   liver

Limitations or special wishes if any: all monetary proceeds go to my wife and son.

Signed by the donor and the following witnesses in the presence of each other.

James Tyler   4/3/2000
Signature of Donor   Date of Birth of Donor

3/21/2031   Chicago, Illinois
Date signed   City & State

Witness   Witness

This is a legal document under the Uniform Anatomical Purchase Act or similar laws.
Donor, P.O. Box 28010, Chicago, Illinois 23228 (800) 24-donor

"That card is why I don't understand your rash impulsiveness. Now, what is it man? This proves our agreement is still intact! Why, I have two cadavers in excellent shape available for you now."

"Fuck what you don't understand, Doc! My best friend's heart was cut out and sent to me in a gift wrapped box. This is far more sinister than it seems. Doc, don't play games with me. Those ambulance drivers work for you!"

Bodyslick could feel his heart pounding in his chest cavity. A business that had taken him seven years to build was slowly eroding before his eyes. It was a lucrative hustle. Even after he paid off Doc, he was walking away with ten thousand dollars in clear profit for prime body organs and parts.

He had risen from the impoverished streets of Chicago's seedy West Side ghettos to a posh condo overlooking Chicago's magnificent skyline. He would die and kill to maintain his hard-earned status quo.

"Doc, I saw Toejoe Wilson at the scene of a car accident today, and he put his stamp on this victim's hand. Doc, those ambulance drivers work for you—now, you tell me what's up."

Doc said soothingly, "Bodyslick, it's not me. Apparently, my drivers are up to something mischievous. Either they aren't reporting all the fatalities or there is a payoff involved. I'll get to the bottom of this. Just you wait and see."

Bodyslick gritted his teeth. He grabbed the small doctor, knocking his spectacles onto the floor. "Doc," he said, "if you're trying to run some kind of con game on me, I'm going to see what I can get for your old organs!"

The doctor looked in astonishment at Bodyslick. He trembled. Sweat poured from his wrinkled forehead. The doc looked up into Bodyslick's angry eyes. "Listen, Mr. Bodyslick," said the doc. "I have nothing to gain deceiving you. Body snatching is illegal. I could go to jail. I swear I'll find out what's happening!"

Bodyslick put the small man down. He straightened up the

doctor's mock jacket then said coldly, "Lemme see the two bodies you got for me!"

The doctor frowned and turned toward him while pointing his finger into his chest. "Now look, I'm a powerful man. You are nothing without me . . . but a street hoodlum. I am only doing this out of greed. You, Mr. Bodyslick, are doing this to survive. Keep your black hands off of me and don't press your luck!"

They walked quietly back to the elevator and rode back up to his office. The doctor walked quickly to a panel of buttons and pressed an orange one. A large rectangular screen jutted from the ceiling. He pressed another button, and a young Caucasian woman's purplish-red face crystallized on the screen.

"How did she die, Doc?"

"An overdose of valium, heroin, cocaine, and alcohol. The heroin is what killed her," the doctor pointed at tiny needle marks on her neck. "The heroin level in her blood was 120 micrograms-ml, almost one hundred times a fatal dose. Her body is still young and in prime condition. Most organs are virtually flawless. You should get excellent profits because of her high market value. She was not a junkie. This was a suicide."

"What's her blood type?"

"O!" said Dr. Weiner eagerly.

"I need her liver. Snow will be by to pick it up."

"It will be available whenever he gets here."

They watched the figure slowly disappear. The image completely faded; then a new image metamorphosed on the screen.

"Doc, you know I can't sell anything but human organs, but what the hell is it? A xenomorph?"

"You remember the dead piglet-human-embryonic types years ago on television?" Bodyslick nodded his head. "This one . . ."—Dr. Weiner pointed proudly at the image—"is an example of how little we know about cross-species genetic engineering, and most importantly what can go wrong. We call them pigmanoinks—you know, oink, oink!"

They gazed at a pinkish-white, blond-haired eight-year-old boy who had the eyes, nose, and ears of a pig. The other parts of the body looked human except for the mutant pig feet. Its dead blue eyes glowed with an emerald iridescence.

"We are still reeling from the human-pig-chimeras created in 2018. We did not expect that these creatures would be born from injecting human stem cells into pig embryos. As you can see, the child possesses hybrid cells of both pig and human. They only live about eight years, and then they die of the PERV virus."

"PERV virus?" Bodyslick asked inquisitively.

"It means porcine endogenous retrovirus, a virus that is not uncommon in pigs but fatal to humans." He clicked off the image and one just as horrific beamed on the screen.

"What happened to him, Doc?"

"He got shot from very close range with a .357-caliber Magnum. Eighty percent of the head destroyed. A pity, too. He was a star athlete. Kidneys are in excellent condition. Some punk gang member claims he shot him accidentally. We found the victim's murderer by protein-enzyme analysis of a piece of hair found at the scene. Through neurochemical studies of the deceased we found he was gifted—intellectually, physically, and had the kind of ambitious temperament needed to make it in modern society. What a waste."

Bodyslick looked at the young black athlete's face. The small mouth was frowned. Eyebrows strained. Total expression was one of surprise and disbelief. Doc clicked off the screen.

Bodyslick said, "I'll check with my clients tomorrow, Doc."

Doc said meekly, "All right. I'll see you. We will discuss money matters then, Mr. Bodyslick."

Bodyslick nodded. "Be cooool . . . And you better get your drivers in order, Doc!"

As he walked into the elevator, he thought about how the dead were enabling him to live a fantastic lifestyle. Bodyslick loved the money his organ company supplied. But because of his Baptist upbringing he could never quite accept organ trans-

plants as normal. He always viewed it as a sin to tamper with God's most glorious creation, and yet he felt intuitively and factually that it was saving a lot of people's lives.

Why, people who would have died were now living normal lives because of his body parts business. His organs had been transplanted into at least five thousand people. They had received heart valves, livers, lungs, eyes, bones, kidneys, pancreases, and even human tissue. Was it his fault that the Anti-Organ Transplant Act banned profiting on the use of human organs? Was it his fault that the Washington bureaucrats, with their restrictive federal laws, had driven thousands of desperate, sick people with degenerative organs, to underground businesses like his very own which procure and sell organs and reap a huge profit.

Didn't the idiots that created these laws realize that the potential profit of illegal organs trade was enormous and that very soon it would be an untaxed billion dollar a year business.

Bodyslick wondered why there was such a high demand for organ transplants. In 2031 there were 50,000 organ transplants a year, and that was in the United States alone which didn't include the so-called secondary transplants like tendons, cartilage, bone, corneas, nerves, and even skin from advanced aborted fetuses.

Why just one healthy cadaver's transplantable organs could easily translate into $25,000 to $50,000. Especially if it was a Caucasian. Bodyslick smiled inwardly, at how ironic it was, that even at near death, some races preferred organs from their own kind. Sometimes out of rage he would purposely give them Chinese, Mexican, or black organs, after their petty racist request. He wondered what were these racists going to do when cephalic-transplants had been perfected, which was the removal of a human's head from one body to another. Would they reject a healthy donor body because it wasn't white? There were already a huge batch of moral, ethical, and life-enhancement questions created from basic organ transplants. Wouldn't racism only worsen the problem?

He remembered how in the '90s there weren't enough organs around. So, while in prison, he met Hector, who was
serving time for shipping body parts from Panama to clients in
the U.S. He got busted when an infant torso's blood seeped
through the UPS package. Hector helped him create his company, Livers, Legs & Thighs, as a major organ-import business
for Fortune 500 companies that needed fresh corpses for surgical and cosmetic experiments. His business flourished because
he was buying pre-cut body parts from Hector in Panama and
shipping them to his warehouse in Robbins, Illinois. Because
of a loophole in State of Illinois and Federal law, which did not
regulate non-transplant organ tissue banks, his business was
legit. But the FDA forbids the shipment of cadaver parts from
overseas, which was illegal.

A full body in the U.S. would cost a maximum of $5,000.
He was getting them from Hector for $500 a pop. The Catch-
22 was that they weren't prime organs like you get in the U.S.
because of the poverty in the Third World. They had to be
minutely searched for diseases. But he was still getting $2,500
for a white torso, $1,000 for a white head, and only half that
for non-white body parts.

Even in jail he perceived that there were millions of people
in poor countries who would sell a secondary organ for what
an American would laugh at. His business flourished even after
the drug *misoprozatal*, which eliminated immune-rejection and
was a sort of synthetic version of a natural body chemical, was
developed. It reduced by eighty-eight percent the body's natural attempt to reject donor organs. It also improved the
health and reduced the infection rate that plagued so many
organ transplant patients. It virtually eliminated the use of *cyclosporine*, the immunosuppressive drug used in the '70s and
'80s. And it did not affect the International Organ Procurement
Act, which allowed the sale of non-transplantable foreign cadaver organs for research. But the moralists and the ethics
were the majority in congress, and the president was against
(as he called it), "the wholesale butchery for a privileged few."

Chapter 8

As he walked out of the morgue, Chicago's famous wind engulfed him. It hissed through the concrete and steel skyscrapers. It hissed through the alleys and streets. He glanced at his watch: 1:37.7 a.m., May 3, 2031.4.

He was hyper. Fidgety. Toejoe Wilson was now a marked man. Bodyslick knew that there was not enough room on the South Side of Chicago for more than one body hustler. Suddenly, he heard the light incessant squeak of rubber shoes. He nervously glanced around the street. It was dark. Quiet. Desolate. He patted his gun out of habit. Then he heard another set of footsteps much heavier and louder than the first. Bodyslick's hand automatically went inside his pocket. He tightened his sweaty palm around the butt of the pistol. His finger felt numb. Cold.

He mumbled between his teeth. *"Come on mutha'... come on out in the open like a man. Come on, you stinkin' coward punk!"*

A car *zoomed* past. Nearby, he heard the *tat tat tat* of a woman's high heels; the jangle of keys; the slam of a door. Unexpectedly, he jumped, as a huge alley rat scampered over his shoe. He shook his pants leg. His heart pounded. And then, abruptly, he heard a voice inside his head. A woman's voice. A voice that was as sweet as a bird's song. It was Malanna's voice: *"I'll always remember the good you have done, and so will God.*" For a moment he felt a blanket of sorrow. Why hadn't he been more understanding of her love for Jesus? Why did he poke fun of her belief in heaven and hell? Why did he constantly make a mockery of her God who was pure and good? Why did he fall in love with a poor naive Christian black woman who actually believed in angels and being saved?

He was a sinner, after all. He shook his head hard as if to crush his wicked deeds against her.

Again he heard the *pitter patter* of rubber shoes. From the corner of his eye, Bodyslick could see a long black stretch Mercedes Benz limo draw abreast of him. He panicked. The car lights went out. He frantically looked around the desolate street; looking for an escape route; an alley; an abandoned building; a tavern; the police. He desperately looked up and down the street, then he saw a mangy dog run out of a nearby alley across the street. He pulled his laser pistol out and cocked it, as he again heard the gritting shoes behind him. He thought, *Is this the way I will die? On a dismal street, near the county morgue? Alone? Except for the mutant alley rats that will be baring their fangs, to fight over my dead carcass, like sharks in a feeding frenzy?* He mumbled to himself, "I can be mean without even tryin'. I'm a bad muthafucka, and I don't mind dying . . ."

His mouth shut tight as he felt ice cold steel on his neck, as the barrel of a .357 Magnum nudged him toward the limousine. The man's hot breath made the hair on his neck bristle.

"You no make problem! You no die! Git in the car!"

As the back door of the limo swung open, the man quickly snatched his gun.

"We must hurry . . . Git in car!"

Bodyslick glanced in the car. There were three Chinese men dressed in black ninja uniforms. A huge, old, grotesquely fat Chinese man, who was immaculately dressed, sat alone on one side of the limo, eating a small pizza. Bodyslick slid next to him. The ninja, who had accosted him sat next to him while shoving the .357 deep into his side.

Bodyslick knew that the fat Chinese man, ravenously eating the pizza, was the infamous Choi Tse Tong, the leader of the Hip Hop Sung, the most powerful Triad in Chinatown. He hadn't seen him since he was six years old.

"Your Uncle Will told me to keep an eye on you, Malcolm."

"Bodyslick, Mr. Tong . . . My name is Bodyslick!" he said arrogantly.

"I say Malcolm. You have a problem with that?"

The muzzle of the .357 Magnum was jammed harder into his side.

"Naw, man!"

"Malcolm, did Lee explain to you the rape and murder of my niece in Chinatown?"

"Yes, but I couldn't believe that you would think that I . . ."

"Quiet, Malcolm, I have something to show you!" Choi snapped an order in Chinese and pointed at a portable freezer on the floor of the limo. "Show him the head of the *gwai hem gat san* (good for nothing shithead)." The ninja servant opened the top, dug deep down to the bottom of it, rattling ice, as if the object being lifted out was clutching it.

Bodyslick momentarily gazed out the window, as the car sped down Harrison Street. He peered at the millions of twinkling lights of the Loop, which created a surreal, hypnotic urbanscape: a creation that easily hid the corruption, murder, and filth that lurked deep within the belly of the pulsing beast.

"What the hell is . . . ?"

He blinked his eyes in disbelief. Panic seized him. The roots of his hair tingled. Street lights sliced through the car window for a fraction of a second, allowing light to emerge from the darkness a decapitated human head, as if painted by the Italian master, Caravaggio. Then the head would submerge back in darkness, as the limo sped past pulsing neon light. The street lights created an eerie, hideous, flashing image of depravity. He lowered his window and stuck his shivering head out for fresh air.

A light rain had started to fall. He glanced at a bumper

sticker that read: JESUS IS MY FRIEND. He heard loud laughter within the limo. To them looking at a human head was no different than looking at the head of a goat, dog, or monkey. He had seen too many decapitated heads to get squeamish. He showed no fear. Suddenly, he felt the icy cold flesh of the man's face licking against his arm; his cold nose; his icy lips; his frozen hair was tangled up in thin clumps like stalactites. The ninjas were toying with his emotions; they were trying to trigger absolute uncontrollable fear.

"That's him," snarled Tong's graven voice from the blackness inside the limousine.

The severed human head rekindled memories of an incident that happened during his gangbangin' years in high school. It was after school when Cochise, his homeboy, and he had left the safety of the West Side and traveled out south to rendezvous with *Maddog*, an old boyhood friend who had moved from Cabrini to the South Side after his mother had hit big in the lottery. Maddog was a dope fiend. He knew where all the dope houses were located at on the South Side. Bodyslick's mind could remember how they sat in the car at the McDonald's parking lot on 57th and Cottage Grove, eating hamburgers and fries, while they waited for Maddog to arrive, so they could split the money from a recent crackhouse bust. But he realized he couldn't show any quantum of fear or trepidation to Cochise, because that would crush their mutual respect.

As Bodyslick gazed out the limo at the passing cars, he wondered if the grotesque image that haunted him all these years would ever be forgotten. It happened in such lightning speed: He remembered he was taking a bite of his Big Mac and Cochise was laughing, while munching fries, about how scared the dope fiends were when they had busted in on them. A rival gang assassin coolly crept up to the car on the passenger side, stuck the cold nickel-plated muzzle of a .357 Magnum to Cochise's temple, pulled the trigger, and then ran down a nearby alley. Bodyslick remembered first the thunderclap roar, then the blinding flash that went off from inside Cochise's skull,

and he could actually feel the *whiz* of the bullet as it swept by a hairsbreadth from his chin. The suffocating air inside the car was smoldering blue-gray from cordite fumes, tinged with molecular blood particles. Bodyslick stared in horror at the bone-white pieces of skull, cartilage, and bloody pinkish-gray, noodle-shaped brain tissue as it covered his entire body. Pieces of brain clung to his hair, eyebrows, inside his nose, and the corners of his mouth. His blood froze as he recalled the salty, mushy taste of human brain. He leaped out, pushing Cochise's heavy body off of him, and he started tearing off all his clothes in the midst of his nausea and wretchedness.

A passing siren jolted Bodyslick back to reality. A couple of minutes had passed. The rain had started to fall heavily. His face was dripping with water. He wondered why they thought a man in the body organ business would react squeamishly to a human head? Was it the surprise element? Or the shock? He sat back down in his seat. Lightning started to zigzag across the rainy sky. The street lights, neon signs, and passing car lights started to become a whirling glimmer on the wet hood. Thunder rumbled distantly through the milky black sky. The gods were fucking.

"Are you okay, Malcolm?" Tong asked with a corrosive smile.

"Who is he? He looks like a mob boy to me. Maybe one of Luziano's soldiers?" Bodyslick asked curiously, after lighting a seagarette given to him by one of the bodyguards. He gazed again at the severed head of the dark-haired white man. Italian? The ninja held the head up by its hair, just over the freezer opening. The head's face was a hideous white, his lips were bared back from his teeth with an expression of horror and disbelief. Tong ordered the ninja to put the head back into the freezer.

"I cannot reveal his identity, Malcolm, until we catch the other animal, hopefully in the next 48 hours. You were never a suspect, Malcolm. I just wanted to halt all external business in Chinatown for a week, to assure my people that vengeance will be mine. And until the heads of the culprits are on the gate of Head City so all my people can see the punishment of outsiders who dared to commit barbaric acts against our women, there will be no organs, drugs sold, or special favors!"

"I remember when my Uncle Will showed me the human heads on top of the gates at Head City. It's a sight that I will never forget," Bodyslick said while flicking the seagarette butt out the window.

The limousine slowly pulled off from the curb. Tong gulped down another drink. He looked to be about seventy or eighty years old. Bodyslick wondered how he could eat and drink with such wild abandonment at his age.

Tong cleared his throat and whispered to Bodyslick, "We can make a lot of money together once we cut off the other one's head." He smiled as he looked at the portable freezer.

"What? I get a bigger chunk of the somellow sold in Chinatown?" Bodyslick asked eagerly.

"No bigger than that. You see, Malcolm, during the Lunar New Year in China is when thousands of Chinese prisoners are executed in Beijing. Their kidneys are sold abroad."

"Are they screened?"

"Yes, they must be at a price of $10,000 in China and $100,000 a kidney here!" Tong said, pouring another drink.

"Sounds good, Tong, but that's a touchy international human rights issue, and it can get real ugly if you get busted. Besides, how would they get transported here? My black ass ain't goin' to China to get 'em!"

"Your clients can fly to China and get the oper—"

"Whoa! Whoa, no flying . . . gots to get them right here!"

"Well, transatlantic cargo shipments in cryonic freezers delivered to your warehouse."

"How soon?"

"Maybe two weeks."

"You know we're talkin' a million fuckin' dollars!" Bodyslick said ecstatically.

"I want half," Tong said, as he belched after gulping down the drink.

"What about a third?"

"Half or no deal!"

"All right, as long as you are responsible for the delivery and the quality."

"It's a deal. But just remember," Tong snapped, "this is a deal I worked on with your Uncle Will before his stroke. We will take you to the Maglev train stop now," Tong said, as he wiped his mouth with a napkin. "Before I left Hong Kong in 1996, a year before the Communist takeover, I was one of the leaders in Shanghai's old Green Gang. I was served fresh fried monkey brains with scrambled turtle eggs every morning."

A galaxy of neon lights flickered on Tong's old face as the limousine sped down the street. Bodyslick smiled as he thought about how he used to poke fun at his Grandma Malone for eating chitterling, pigfeet, hognuts, and neckbones.

"Malcolm, I once had a coolie servant named Sammy Wong in Hong Kong, who could cook dog meat, civet cat, and monkey brain with marvelous seasoning. Oh, how I miss that coolie's cooking."

"What's a coolie?"

"Malcolm, a coolie is to China what an African slave was to the United States: cheap labor. The difference is that during the early 1900s, the starving Chinese who indentured themselves to foreign labor camps had a contractual agreement for a limited amount of time."

The meaning of Tong's words vaporized as Bodyslick glanced out the window and saw two black Mercedes, with their lights out, cruising alongside the limo. He pressed his face against the rainy window, straining his eyes to see the occupants in the two cars. The two ninjas quickly grabbed MAC-10s from underneath the seats. Bodyslick snatched back his .45-caliber laser pistol. Tong barked orders to the ninjas as he pressed an orange button on the arm of the door. Long curved petal-like blades jetted from the sides of his seat—slowly closing around his entire body like some kind of ravenous metallic crustacean.

Suddenly, the two black Mercedes pulled up closer on each side of the bulletproof limo. *Bammm!* They battered the rear doors. The Chinese driver frantically put the pedal to the metal and roared down Harrison Street. The two ninjas and Bodyslick lowered the bulletproof windows about four inches and rapid fired at the cars leaving strings of laser tracers. Bodyslick leaped to the front of the limo and caught a MAC-10 that was thrown to him from the ninja in the backseat. He shot at the driver of the Mercedes.

"All right, muthafuckas you done fuck wid' the wrong nigga, tonight!" Bodyslick shouted with glee.

Bam bam . . . rat tat tat . . . bam . . . rat tat tat. Bam ba . . . ba . . . bamm.

The Mercedes quickly caught up with the limo. The sunroof top opened, and a white man wearing a black fedora opened fire at the limo with an Uzi.

"Ahhhhh!" screamed one of the ninjas, as he dropped his MAC-10 and fell back dead onto the seat. Blood gushed from his eye socket. Bodyslick no longer had to guess about their identity. White faces. Mean faces. Dago faces were trying to kill them. *Bam. Bam. Bam.* Bodyslick ducked as the bullets from the semi-automatic ricocheted off the bulletproof window. Silver glass fractures zigzagged across the window. Bodyslick fired at the driver with the dead ninja's MAC-10; red heat spat at the car like hot rivets. He ducked as bullets *whanged* against the door. Bodyslick lowered his window a few inches to get a better aim at the driver. He listened as bullets from the Uzi *banged* on the roof of the limo.

The Chinese driver swung the limo into each Mercedes like a pendulum knocking the mob henchmen shooting out the sunroof to the floor. One of the Mercedes skidded to the curb on the rain swept street and crashed into a fire hydrant and exploded.

The ninja looked at Bodyslick and shouted, "Numba fuckin' one!"

The other Mercedes slowed down and drove in back of the limo. The sunroof top opened. The limo lurched forward, but it couldn't race with the Mercedes. The ninja quickly stood up and snatched open the limo's sunroof and fired at the mob assassin as bullets whizzed from the Mercedes. A spat of blood spread like cancer across the mobster's face as bullets from the MAC-10 silenced him. The Mercedes then turned down a vacant street, ducked through an alley, and sped away into the night.

Tong whispered to his driver as his armored seat unfolded like petals on a flower revealing a tiny red screen inside, which enabled him to see everything going on inside and outside the car. He patted the hand of the dead ninja beside him as the other ninja closed the rooftop and gazed menacingly out the limo while reloading the full metal jacket of the MAC-10.

"Life is so fragile, Malcolm," Tong sighed, as he lit a seagarette and blew smoke rings to the ceiling of the limo. "We will take you to the Washington Maglev Station downtown," he said as the driver bulldozed his way onto interstate 290 North.

"You do realize that those were mob hit men in those Mercedes, don't you?" Bodyslick said curiously.

"Look, boy," Tong shouted angrily, "while you were wearin' huckin' pampers and smackin' your lips on Gerber baby food, me and your Uncle Will were fightin' street wars. So don't insult my intelligence . . . You fuckin' right I know it was the Mafia! I got one of his boys' head in that freezer. Who the fuck' else could it be? Vinnie Luziano threatens my life daily. We are at war with the mob, and so are you." Tong blew smoke in Bodyslick's face and smiled. "But you fight with the same wild abandonment as your uncle. He should be proud. You are a real warrior."

"Thanks . . . but don't ever call me *boy* again!" Bodyslick snapped.

"Malcolm," Tong paused as his driver spoke to him then continued, "business will continue as usual with us. As soon as the other rapist is punished."

"Well, here is my stop, Mr. Tong, good to see you again, and it's good to know our business is still solid!"

"Malcolm, there were two rapists and murderers. They were *gweilo*. White men. To be specific, Mafiosi. We will behead the other rapist in public, in Head City, when we catch him. Would you like to come, Malcolm?"

"No thanks," he said, as he grabbed the doorknob. He could hear the distant howl of the Maglev train.

"We Triad have our own codes, rites, and traditions. A possible war with the Mafia is only one penalty for violating a Chinese woman of my niece's age and stature. She was a fourteen-year-old virgin, and her young life is ruined!" Tong said acidly.

A pulsing red traffic light glowed on his face revealing wrinkled skin that made him look like some embalmed Asian mummy. His right epicanthic eyelid ticked, revealing tiny lavender veins.

People ran past the limo hurrying to catch the approaching Maglev train. Bodyslick glanced up above at glowing blue light from the electric currents in the reaction rail; the levitating train reminded him of a snake floating on air.

Suddenly, two cops with a huge rottweiler stopped in front of the limo. It was a huge black dog with a tan patch across a muscled chest. Its head was massive. The dog's fiery eyes started to gleam, as it raised its head as if sniffing the wind. It started to bark voraciously at the limo, while pulling desperately on its choke-chain leash toward it. Tong became nervous and mumbled something in Chinese. His ninja bodyguard quickly grabbed a MAC-10 submachine gun from underneath the seat. Bodyslick wondered, *Did it smell the stench of the human head? Or the dead ninja in the backseat?* The dog continued to growl maniacally. Its claws scratched the sidewalk as it lunged toward the limo.

As the dog's handler restrained it, the other cop walked over to the limo, crouched down, and tapped on the darkened window. Tong let it down about two inches. Sky blue eyes curiously gazed at him. "Everything all right in there, buddy?"

"No problem officer," Tong said consolingly.

"But those are fresh bullet holes in your limo. Where did you get shot at?"

"We Chinese take pride in takin' care of our own squabbles!" Tong said arrogantly.

"But we can run a report on . . ."

"Maxwell! Somebody just buzzed the alarm on the Maglev platform. Let's go!" the other cop said, as a woman's scream from up above echoed from the noisy platform. The cop swerved from the limo and ran through the turnstile behind his partner and the dog.

As Bodyslick climbed out of the limo, Tong grabbed his forearm and whispered to him, "Malcolm, watch yourself and always remember that I owe your Uncle Will a favor. He once saved my life. Contact me through Lee if you ever need help."

"I will, *Lao Yeh*. Master," Bodyslick said, smiling as he alighted from the car and watched it screech off into an unknown destination.

Bodyslick stuck his Maglev card into the slot and rushed through the turnstile as the howl of the train neared the platform. He quickly ran up the moving escalator stairs so he would not miss the approaching train. He saw the same policemen and dog slowly going down on the opposite side of him. His heart started to pound as the dog barked at him viciously, within the seconds it took to pass him. Bodyslick lunged back as the beast jumped at him, baring its razor-sharp fangs.

"You! Hold up! We want to talk to you!" the cop with the dog shouted.

Bodyslick leaped up the stairs, two at a time, not looking back.

"Sic 'em, Tor, restrain him, Tor!"

He glanced over his shoulder as his right foot planted firmly on the platform floor. The train was coming to a screeching stop. He only hoped, as he ran down to the last car, that the doors would open quickly. His hand became clammy as he grabbed the butt of his laser pistol. He could hear the clawed feet and jingling chain as the dog slid on the slippery concrete floor. He turned around, almost running backwards, aiming the pistol between the dog's blazing sapphire eyes. The door swung open. The two cops had just reached the platform. The doors slammed shut. The dog pounded on the plexiglass window of the door. Maglev lights slathered on huge canine teeth. Its claws scratched into the metal. The train started to move. The dog wheeled and fled after the train barking.

"Next stop Roosevelt Road," the loudspeaker announced.

Bodyslick smiled as the cops ran toward the door with their guns out. He winked at them as they became a tiny blur. The Maglev train shot away at bullet-like speed.

Chapter 9

The ivory white moon seemed to follow him. The car was empty; they always were late at night. He wiped sweat off his forehead with the palm of his hand as he slid into a seat near the door. He inhaled deeply trying hard to catch his breath. It was good he was still in excellent shape (all that weekend boxing had paid off). Puddles of sweat dropped from his bald head and snaked down his neck. His window started to rattle. A sense of apprehension heaved through him. A sense of the unknown. If he had been *seconds* slower, the dog would have got him, and if he had shot it the police would have caught him at the next stop. He didn't need that type of action.

He shook his head as he closed his eyes wearily and the image of the severed head and dead ninja danced in his mind. He smiled thinking that Tong was actually doing him a favor killing the Mafiosi, because Luziano had sent an assassin to kill him. He only wished that he would exterminate all of them.

"Roosevelt Road. Last stop before thirty-fifth and State." The voice sounded like the cyborbot attendant Esha. He craned his neck glancing around the train for her. Her name unleashed a tidal wave of lust in his being. He amusingly wondered if there were any books on human/robot relationships.

He glanced out the window. The darkness ebbed. The doors slid open, and a group of weirdly dressed white youths walked on the train. The five boys had on short leather black biker

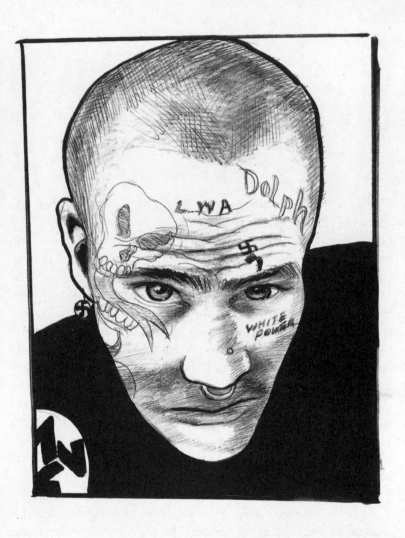

jackets. Three of them had skinned heads. The other two had mohawk haircuts. The five girls all had bald heads and wore weather-beaten, raggedy jeans with black sequined vests that covered pink T-shirts. A tall mohawked blond boy walked over to Bodyslick and sat down in front of him then swerved around in his seat and snapped his fingers. The rest of them fanned out around him.

"Sir, are we going north?" a menacing voice hollered at him two seats back.

The girls' laughter floated past him. He pulled himself up in the seat. He brushed his hand against his laser pistol confidently. His eyes latched on to the blond kid's eyes.

"Why you askin' me a stupid ass question like that?"

A boy behind him yawned. The girls continued to giggle.

"Look, mister . . . I'm asking you one more time. Is this train goin' north?"

Bodyslick shook his head with wonder. Hadn't he just seen a severed human head? Had a shootout with the mob? Hadn't he just narrowly escaped a police dog? He wondered when would this nightmare end.

"You lookin' for trouble, kid?"

The white boy's face was sharply chiseled, his nose had been broken, his blue eyes were huge; a wild stare beamed from them as if he were high on something, maybe Martian weed, somellow, or arti-coke. A tiny gold swastika earring dangled from his ear lobe. Bodyslick's eyes raced across some of the other hate-ridden white faces; all of them wore the same earrings. They were members of some sick, misguided hate group. He noticed the boy in back of him had freckles and a tattoo over his left eye. He could feel his hot breath on his neck.

"Are you deaf? Dolph asked you if we goin' north?" A pale hand reached around Bodyslick's neck, tiny freckles lay in red hair, as a twelve inch knife glimmered in his eyes.

"All right," he said nervously, "no, the train is going south," Bodyslick said, realizing he could kill them all in a millisecond.

"Funny how fear can get information ain't it, Dolph?" the redhead belched out. The girls started to laugh hysterically.

Dolph stood up nodding his head walking toward him. His steel toed boots thumping on the floor in a military cadence.

"I told you, dammit, it's goin' south . . . Now I'm warning you to chill out 'cause you obviously don't realize who you fuckin' wid'!"

The boy in back of him started to gently stroke his throat with the gleaming blade.

"You know," Dolph said, "you're a pretty arrogant nigger to be in the situation you are now in." He poked his tattooed HEIL HITLER fist in Bodyslick's face. "Wrong, this train ain't goin' south. This train mistah is goin' to hell! You see, LWA thinks you niggers, tacos, camel jocks, towel heads, and hymies are the cause of all this great country's problems. We spend so much money trying to keep you freeloaders civilized, to keep you from retreatin' back to your savage ways here, that it has literally broken the system and made it into a colony of the third world!"

The girls' laughter got drowned as a Maglev train zoomed past going north. Frowning, Dolph pointed his finger at Bodyslick's eyes.

"Nigger, your civil rights agenda is why white boys like me grow up and can't get good jobs because we aren't bilingual. We are the new minority! Why? Because your civil rights movement mutated into a bastard concept which helped open America's door to global human sewage, investing our white blood with preying, mongrelizing foreigners. Making our system immoral, sick, and bankrupt!"

"Lemme tell you about this savage *shit*!" Bodyslick replied as he felt the cold steel of the knife against his throat. "We were kidnapped. We were slaves for four hundred fuckin' years. Your forefathers arrived at Ellis Island voluntarily, mine were hostages! We didn't exactly come here first class. Besides, poor blacks have always been treated worse than foreigners, even though our ancestors were here before the pilgrims!"

"As I was saying," Dolph continued, totally ignoring what Bodyslick had said, "because of this government multicultural civil rights agenda, look what's happen!" He pointed to two men hugging and kissing each other near the exit door.

They turned and looked at him then yelled, "We're married!" One of them pointed to a gleaming diamond ring.

"Shut up, bitches!" Dolph yelled. Two of his members with dyed blond and orange spiked hair walked over to them and slapped one of the men.

"Look what has happened since the taco wetbacks have come like roaches across the border! Even though it's laser-gated now, there are almost as many of these cockroach fuckin' Mexicans as white folks! Hispanic foreigners and Jew-controlled media makin' this country mulatto. No other government does this. Not in Japan, China, Korea, India, Spain, or Germany—only the weak-kneed government of the United States has become a dumping ground for human sewage.

"That is why our own white god has sent us a legion of white angel patriots to strike terror into the weak souls of you traitors. It is our god, our covenant compelled LWA to seek out and cleanse the system of waste like you!"

He coughed, gazed out the dark windows, and continued, "And we will use any means necessary. Even secession, which the Aryan Brotherhood is fighting for in Montana. We are American patriots, and we believe an ocean of blood will spill from the belly of the beast before we get our white America back!"

Bodyslick wondered if he could reach these sick minds with rational thought. Could his words affect their perverted and racist indoctrination? Could his words have meaning to only one of many white racist youth movements who felt that their futures had been "sold out" by a deficit caused by social spending on minorities? A group who believed immigration is a luxury, not a necessity; that in 1965 America was 90 percent white; in 2031 it was less than 20 percent?

The kid blinked his blue eyes at him as if he was waiting for a reason to justify his actions. Bodyslick suddenly grabbed the boy with the knife's hand and bit down on it to the bone. The boy screamed in pain and dropped it. Bodyslick quickly pulled his .45 laser pistol from an inside coat pocket and swerved out of the seat, stabbing the barrel of the gun into Dolph's temple. He noticed a small red and black tattoo of a swastika over a hatchet above the boy's left eye.

"What's the hatchet suppose to mean?"

"It means, in order to earn the tattoo, you must have lynched a nigger, shot a Mexican, bombed a Muslim, and killed a Jew with a hatchet!"

Clacccck! The clash of flesh, bone, and metal quieted the train as Bodyslick bitch-slapped him with the barrel of his gun.

"If you say *nigger* one more time I swear I gonna put a bullet in you that's gonna make you squat when you piss! You understand me, muthafucka?"

Dolph stiffened. He spat bloody saliva from the corner of his mouth.

"Yeah . . . I understand!" he moaned as he rubbed his swollen jaw.

His gang looked sad, lost, and alienated. It was the helpless-piteous look that hyenas have when they watch one of their own being devoured by a lion.

"My father died a hero in the Iraq war, a war he never should have been in. My poor mother used to cry over how vile army skinheads, KKK, and racist punks would treat them on base. But my father still gave his life for so-called American democracy. My mother, after his death, had a nervous breakdown . . . Maybe like my father you should give your life for what you believe in, huh?" Bodyslick's finger tightened on the trigger.

"Listen, spook!" Dolph snarled. "Ahhh Jeeesus!" he cried out in wrenching pain while bending down holding his side after Bodyslick's knuckle punch. "Goddamn you . . . fuckhead! But you can't kill the messenger with pain," Dolph said as he tried to hold back tears. "We are a part of something bigger than me. I'm just a pebble on the beach. Unlike you jigaboos, I'm ready to die for my cause! Shoot, nigger!"

Bodyslick, consumed with rage, pressed the barrel into his

temple realizing that it would take more than a bullet in the head to change racists like Dolph.

"Kid, you think because you are white you have the right to determine my destiny. The right to play God!"

Dolph's face turned pale and flushed red. He whispered, "*Nigga, Nigga, Nigga on the wall, ain't the white race the smartest of them all!*"

"Dolph, let's get outta here. We can change for a train goin' back north here. Come on, we're heading for the South Side. The jungle side! Niggaville!"

Bodyslick laughed. He felt the redhead's switch blade snap closed as he stood up and walked toward the exit door. The girls followed behind him. So did three other white boys.

The beaten gay men scurried to an adjacent car door. One of them screamed, "You're all fuckin' monsters. I dare you to try to legislate love. What are you goin' to do . . . kill everybody that don't think like you!"

Bodyslick grabbed Dolph by the shoulder, and pulled him down on the bar of the seat while putting him into a half nelson. "You see this!" Bodyslick screamed.

Dolph nodded as strings of gummy saliva seeped from the corners of his mouth. "We weren't going to hurt you. We were just scarin' you," Dolph said almost tearfully, as he looked at the large gleaming hole of the .45 caliber laser Colt barrel pointing up his nose.

"Yeah, sure," Bodyslick said sarcastically. "All of a sudden you've become a good Christian, huh?"

The girls and boys at the door started to scream hysterically. "Let him go, pleassse!"

"Esha!" Bodyslick moaned, as all heads turned toward the rear door.

"Bodddd—dy . . ." Her metallic eyes pulsed red as the big spiked-haired redhead boy deftly sidestepped her and locked his arms around her neck and stuck a .38 snub nose with a perforated silencer attached into her temple.

"Don't do that!" Bodyslick said compassionately momentarily forgetting she wasn't human.

Whooooosh! The bullet burst through Esha's head pulverizing her positronic brain. A dark gray fume spurted from the gaping hole as she fell to the floor shaking spasmodically. A yellowish oily substance (tears?) trickled from her eyes. Her body randomly twitched and shook like a novice driving a stickshift for the first time.

"Goddamn you!" Bodyslick murmured, as the girls laughed while pointing at the shaking de-charged cyborbot.

Dolph said nervously while gazing at the laser pistol, "The sentence for killin' one of them fuckin' robots is ten year imprisonment at Solstice Galactic Prison." He glanced at his watch. "Security will be at the next stop . . . they'll get you for accessory to the crime . . . Now lemme go, nigger, 'cause time is running out!"

Bodyslick gazed down at Esha, as her eyes shimmered from the ceiling lights in the train. He shook his head mournfully. He jammed the barrel of the pistol harder into Dolph's head.

"Punk," Bodyslick said quickly, realizing that security would be at the next stop. "My father died for this country, and to hear you call me nigger and say my people are the cause of all this country's problems really bothers me!"

Dolph sighed. "Jesus, that's what I was taught. That is what the leaders of my organization are teaching. Crime, immorality, rioting, and societal disruption are attributed to niggers!"

"What did you call me?" Bodyslick asked, as he clicked the trigger on his laser pistol while leaving the safety button on.

"I mean minorities . . ."

The train slowed.

Bodyslick quickly tucked the gun away. As he released his grip on him, Dolph raced to the door with the others. His pants were soaked and dripping a trail of urine.

"Po boy, such a sissy coward he done peed on hisself," Bodyslick said with contempt.

Embarrassed, Dolph turned around beaming a scalding look

at Bodyslick. Red and blue sconces of light from the Maglev platform shone on their white skin demonically.

"My white pee is more purer than your nigger blood!" The stench of the puddle of steamy urine near Bodyslick's shoes wafted past his nostrils.

"Dolph?" he angrily shouted, "all of you are a bunch of xenophobic cowards scared shitless of anybody non-white. Your enemies are the corrupt bureaucrats at the top who are using a bankrupt capitalist system to fuel a racial war. They are the ones advocating a newer, cleaner Buchenwald with high tech ethnic weapons instead of gas ovens!"

"Listen, nigger, if I ever catch you up north, I'll kick your black ass . . ." Dolph fearfully raved, as he pushed the emergency stop switch. The Maglev train screeched as it stopped abruptly.

"You better get your smart ass off the train before I bitch slap you and make you piss on yourself again—tell the attendant we need a mop if you see one!"

"Bye, nigger!" Dolph waved, as the door opened and his gang quickly ran out the car.

Bodyslick walked over to Esha and knelt down and picked up her limp, cold hand.

"Esha, this is Bodyslick. Can you hear me?" he asked, hoping she still possessed some quantum of being. Her eyelashes fluttered. And a red light pulsed like a dying heartbeat from her eyes.

Her mouth twitched as she spoke. "My name Esha . . . Maglev A-train 20018-1A is my home! . . . My name Esha . . . Maglev A-train 20018-1A is my . . . my home! My name . . ."

Bodyslick stood up as the train started to move. He shook his head dizzily as he took one last look at her and then gently stepped over her, opened the rear door and walked into the next car.

He sat down. Tired, weary. Fatigued as he reached the last car. His whole body trembled with exhaustion. He bit his lower lip savagely as he glanced out the window at a city that seemed irrevocably lost forever in darkness.

He pressed the button on his wrist phone to check for any

recorded messages from his apartment. He quickly read the words as they raced across the screen: ". . . I'll contact you as soon as I arrive in Chicago. Have a good heart, and I'll call you. It's urgent!"

He knew that Doc always spoke in codes. He needed a donor heart. Just like last year he needed lungs, kidneys, livers, and a host of other vital organs. He would wait until he arrived in Chicago to get the specs on the heart rather than return his call. After all, Doc was one of the special few who had his secret phone code. He would wait.

He thought of Dolph, as he gazed out the window at a neon-infested cityscape that disguised an environment seething with fears: chronic food shortages, unemployment riots, racial division, and a new non-human cyborbot underclass who thought they were humans and were using violence, sit-ins and marches to gain their rights. He smiled as he recalled them singing "we shall overcome" on the news.

The doomsayers of the early '90s had certainly predicted it: The stock market crash in 2020 was so devastating that the country was still reeling from it in 2031. If only the corrupt leaders had harnessed the spiraling deficit in the early 21st century. If only they had listened to the voices that had screamed, "You are mortgaging your children's future!"

He remembered how, in his youth, America showed compassion for the maimed, insane and misfortunate through social programs like welfare, general assistance, food stamps and Medicaid—all that was now gone. Abolished. Along with Jesse Jackson's plea for hope, optimism and faith and the nation's first black president's plea for unity. There were fifty million homeless in America in 2031. The problem was so pervasive that no one could avoid it: from Madison Avenue in New York to Robbins, Illinois.

New York was a case study of what economic chaos could lead to. It was under Martial law because anarchy was rampant. Nobody cared. The citizenry had lost faith in a bankrupt system. Politically, America had been splintered by the centrifugal forces of various right and left wing factions which had caused catastrophic political consequences for the nation: revisionists, anarchists, socialists, Maoists, NAM (New Age Muslims), LWA (Legion of White Angels), Voodnarfs. The days of two-party centrist politics had vanished with the hopes, dreams and aspirations the people had cherished before the catastrophic crash in 2020. The collapse of the economic system had spawned a host of changes; changes that were nurtured by corruption, social irresponsibility and failed leadership of the ruling class.

"Fifty-seventh Street next stop!" The Maglev train howled hideously as it swerved south on the air cushions. He could hear the squeal and moan of air resistance as it approached 350 mph. The sound was so abstract that it was reminiscent of the muffled, staccato burst of sounds from the trumpet of Miles Davis.

A shaft of light cut across his face as he thought about what had happened to the America that his father gave his life for; an America of many problems, but a country where hope served as a collective panacea for the millions of dispossessed.

"Fifty-seventh Street!"

As he alighted from the train, he hurriedly walked east on 57th Street. He listened to a cacophony of street sounds; sounds he loved—sounds and smells that had convinced him as a youth that he wanted to be a street hustler. Voices came from a gang of homeless children. Voices of desperation. Voices of poverty. Voices that no longer were heard by an abolished Welfare system. Voices of children who looked at garbage as a source of nourishment. Their stench made him reel.

A little mixed-breed blonde girl with blue melanin lotion on her face walked up to him in a raggedy dress and tugged on his pants leg. She gave him a note that read:

> *I am willing to sell one of my kidneys to help someone's life in exchange for money. My family is homeless.*

He could see her mother and two small brothers crowded in a nearby building doorway. He dug into his pocket and gave her a hundred dollar bill. He shook his head as he walked away because he had seen the same faces in the slums of Calcutta, the favelas in Brazil, the barrios in Mexico, and in his warehouse in Robbins.

Bodyslick, I wanna be jest like you!
Bodyslick, how much that ring cost?
Bodyslick, teach me the keys to the game, mannn!

He started humming a street poem that had been penned for him:

I play it cool, snatch 'em quick,
That's the reason they call me Bodyslick . . .
My motto as I watch and wait
Is look out for the ambulances, then stalk and take!

After taking a long drag off of a seagarette, and coughing simultaneously, he traversed west toward an alley, which was a shorter route to his apartment.

As he walked through the alley, his senses were dazed by the foul odor of garbage and litter. There was a beer can that still bore the imprint of someone's shoe; there were scattered green-tinged Martian reefer butts; there was a broken shooter that some frustrated junkie had probably used and broken while trying to get a hit.

O sinner! Consider the path of death you walk.
The flames of divine wrath are upon you.

Bodyslick listened as he passed the rear of a Baptist Church. He listened as he was bathed in the glare of the alley's lights. He listened as rats and mice scampered over rot and refuse. He listened as a choir sang a hymn, in a soulful a cappella.

*Amazing Grace, how sweet the sound, that saved a
wretch like me.
I once was lost, but now ummmm foun,
wazz blind but now I see!*

His mind whirled back to when his mother would send him
and his brothers and sister to church. But she never, ever went
herself. He remembered the blind fear of seeing a 250-pound
woman possessed by the Holy Spirit. Possessed to the point
that it would take five or six men to wrestle her down.

His thoughts were broken by a deep bass voice echoing
from inside the church: *"The mighty spirit of God can make
you become reborn again, brothers and sisters. If Lazarus
could be raised from the dead, then so can you and I."*

"Amen! Preach, brother. We listenin'. Praise the Lawd!"

*"His wrath toward sinners will burn like fire. You know
what a sinner is?"*

"Teach us. Amen. Go onnnn . . ."

*"Now the sinners are discovering that no matter what they
do to extend life, it won't work. You see, a sinner is a person
that believes in man's knowledge, not God's. Are you listenin'
tah me?"*

"Yessah. We listenin'."

"A sinner believes that science not God is their Savior."

"Amen! Preach."

*"A sinner believes he can buy a heart, a liver, a kidney and
defy death . . ."*

Bodyslick couldn't accept the Reverend's archaic notions
about life and death. Hadn't mankind traversed the stars?
Hadn't primitive forms of alien life been discovered? Were not
scientists now discovering cures for lethal diseases in plant
species from other galaxies? If there was a God, why was life
so barren and squalid for some solar systems and not others?
And if the universe was created by some omniscient God, why
was life so imperfect here on earth? Why the food shortages,
racial wars, bio-chemical warfare? Why was the history of the

planet riddled with the carcasses of those who believed in some divine deity who never intervened on their behalf?

Bodyslick shook his head as he thought about the slaughter and evil that existed in the world, which proved there was no perfect being and also proved there was no morality in the universe, but just a vast, cold region of blackness and impartiality. Didn't those Christians realize that scientists had discovered that the universe is teeming with life? Didn't they realize that if there is a God in the universe, that He uses the same physical laws that govern life on earth for other planets? Were the problems on this planet universal? Or were earth's problems of war, races, and weaponry constants in the universe?

Bodyslick felt it was a profound mistake for minorities to think that their Christian God would eliminate the poverty, despair, and sense of powerless that plagued their wretched lives. He disagreed with their naive concept that a white man's God would have a divine purpose for the downtrodden. Didn't they realize that the men who bought the slaves were Christians? Wasn't Jesus the name of one of the slave vessels? He couldn't swallow the notion that God was choosing, directing, and making miraculous interventions on the behalf of any particular race of people; especially American blacks.

He patted his inside coat pocket for his .45-caliber laser Colt which was his god. He hurriedly moved on. The ivory white moon seemed to follow him. As he watched it, he thought about how he had once read in prison that the moon is actually a part of the earth. A binary planet. A double planet that the earth is linked to. Without it all life would die. All the oceans would be stagnant. No pissin', no fuckin' in them at the beach. The oceans would become a gigantic static cesspool. Ain't that a bitch!

"Comrades, this system is rigged against the political, economic, and cultural interests of the working-class American community! Profit-hungry global capitalism is also the reason white children have to stay in the house during the day because of the fear of UV rays causing skin cancer!"

Bodyslick slowed. Watched. Listened as he walked past a political rally. He could feel the unrest of the multi-racial crowd, as a medium-sized white man with a large protruding forehead, a wizened walnut-colored face, chiseled nose criss-crossed with broken spider-like purple veins, blazing red hair, and Johnny Walker red eyes stood on a moving dock area across the alley. He wore an old fatigue coat and tattered jeans. His green eyes seemed to ignite with excitement as the orange sunset cast an eerie shadow over his pale white skin. He nailed up a small poster and pointed at it.

"Malcolm X once said, 'A chicken cannot lay a duck egg because the chicken's system is not equipped or designed to produce a duck egg.' "

The sky was almost dark. Groups of pigeons blotted the horizon, looking like hundreds of black ants. A storm was brewing. A sense of change blanketed the crowd.

"My name is Elijah Brown, and I am a member of ARP which means the American Revolutionary Party. My pet will be passing out a pamphlet to you that explains how ARP will get a new social contract for all Americans through revolutionary agitation. My brothers, you must stop killing yourselves. Crime and drugs are not the answer. We can change the political balance of power in this country. We can change this capitalist democracy! We can make a difference. That is the only way we can make this chicken system produce a duck egg. A revolutionary egg. Only, my brothers and sisters, by a long, bloody protracted revolutionary struggle!"

Americans are scared of revolution! Bodyslick thought, shaking his head with cynicism. He wondered when Elijah Brown would give up; after all he had been preaching the same rhetoric for almost twenty years in Chicago.

Suddenly, he felt a tug on his pants leg. He nervously looked down. He was momentarily frozen with disbelief. Huge iridescent, vulpine eyes stared up at him. The creature had a platypus-like nose. A rat-like mouth was making a grunting noise. Huge monkey-like, cauliflower ears twitched as if waiting for him to say something. It had dark brown fur and long thin bird legs. It looked part baboon and vulture. It was a zenomorph: a man-made thing created by splicing the genes of various life forms together for experimental reasons. Most of them died at birth.

A leaflet flapped in its three-fingered grip (fingers that looked more like octopus tentacles). Bodyslick snatched the leaflet from it, and the creature scampered to the next person. Bodyslick stuck it in his back pocket and trudged on down the alley looking for a dark corner to piss in.

"Bodyslick! . . . Bodyslick!" A distant voice. A familiar voice. It was the voice of Elijah Brown as he bulldozed his way through the applauding crowd.

"Bodyslick," he said pleadingly, as he tried to catch his breath, while looping a friendly arm around his shoulder, "you're a revolutionary not a body snatcher. Leadership is in your blood. I've known it since you were a kid. I knew your father, we grew up together. He was an honest, decent, and courageous man who gave his life for this country. He was a leader, son, just like you. He believed in democracy. He believed in the American system, but unlike me, he wanted to change from within, which I don't believe will work, but both of us always believed that it does need change.

"Help us change the tide of history. Help us rekindle the revolutionary spirit of our forefathers, Malcolm. Abandon your worship of material trinkets and perishable goods—instead, embrace something that will have an everlasting effect on future generations. Embrace something far more meaningful and spiritual than immediate, shallow, hollow material goals. Join ARP and help create revolutionary change!"

Bodyslick smiled at Elijah Brown. Smiled because it was white men like Elijah Brown who stirred thoughts about the fanatical white abolitionist John Brown who his great grandfather used to talk about as if he were a messiah. A constant reminder that *all* whites weren't racist devils out to destroy the black race. He had for many years toyed with the notion

of joining Brown's ARP movement, but because of his fanatical love of money he never took the thought seriously enough. "Elijah . . . one day. One day I'm gonna join you. And when I do lookout 'cause umma be a *baaad* revolutionary!"

Elijah Brown patted him on the back and gave him his business card. "Stay in contact, Bodyslick!"

"I will, Elijah, I will."

The leaflet read:

Somellow (Volcanix)
  Generic Name: Somellow Tripelennamine
  Drug Family: Galactic Antihistamine
  When Prescribed: This drug is a powerful non-earth antihistamine discovered inside the great Martian Shield Volcano, Nix Olmpica in 2020. When used under medical supervision, it lessens the likelihood of seizures occurring.
  Precautions and Warnings: Patients using one pentazocine with somellow can increase seizure activity. The euphoria (well being) effect of a non-earth antihistamine dominates the dysphoria (bad feeling) effects of pentazocine. In many cases causes the illusion of levitation.
  Side Effects and Adverse Reactions: Nausea, blurred vision, tumors, chills, respiratory failure and cardiac arrest.

A dog howled piteously from afar. He walked to a hidden corner of a building and started unzipping his fly when he glanced at a *somellow* junkie as she crouched in an adjacent dark corner in the alley. Her once pretty golden face was now sucked ashy and cadaverous from years of vampiric drugs. Soft yellow moonlight bathed long purple claw fingernails as she beckoned to him.

"Lookin' fa sum fun? Git me high an um yours!"

As Bodyslick zipped up his fly and hurriedly walked on, he caught a glimpse of her demonic sapphire eyes as she licked her long dragon red tongue at him like a serpent.

The alley was dead quiet. As quiet as the dead. Not a piece

of paper moved. Even the rodents were quiet out of fear. He slowly walked down the alley when a tall, bald African-robed black man with a simian face, smiled a snaggle-tooth grin and held out a leaflet as he approached him. The man started to bark like a dog. It reminded Bodyslick of how fans used to chant at old Chicago Bear games when they got charged up.

"AAARF . . . AAARF! . . ."

He snatched the leaflet from the man and continued to walk. He read:

SQUIBBOTT TIMELINE

2023:   Squibbott introduces XAIDS drug which includes vorire.

2025:   Squibbott introduces Zarvorire. Internal documents about Squibbott pharmacists discuss using

2026:   South Africans to pre-test drug.

9/2028:   FDA approves drugs for 100mg dose pill.

11/2029:   Squibbott sales hit billions globally.

12/2029:   School girl from Oprah Winfrey Leadership Academy in South Africa writes newspaper essay exposing how Squibbott used poor South Africans as guinea pigs and harvested the bodies of those that died from the drug.

Bodyslick threw the leaflet on the ground with disgust and guilt as he thought about how he profited from the deaths of thousands of South Africans with the spread of xeno-acquired immune deficiency syndrome (XAIDS), a global epidemic in 2031 that had spread from North America to Asia, Europe, Australia, and South Africa. A disease caused by contaminated pig cells genetically engineered to produce human growth hormones, which infected the human immuno-deficiency viruses (HIV). By 2030, 20 million people had been infected with XAIDS—one person every seven seconds. Squibbott Laboratories increased its global sales to $2 billion a year by using poor South Africans as guinea pigs to pre-test its new drug Zarvorire, a protease inhibitor that is considered a possible cure for the disease. Bodyslick made a huge short term profit by setting up a small OHS (organ harvesting shop) near the Squibbott plant in rural South Africa and agreeing to dispose of the *dead* that died from the drug. In return he could *harvest* their healthy organs for free. Business did not last long after Squibbott was exposed by a school girl who wrote a riveting newspaper article about how her 15-year-old male cousin died from the drug and how his body was *dumped* into a *cadaver pit* with thousands of other unknown victims. Because of the global outrage over her article a lawsuit had been filed in the U.S. District Court and the International Court of Law by global government investigators into the illegal use of Zarvorire and the harvesting of body parts from those who died from the drug. The case will go to trial in March 2031.

Suddenly, as Bodyslick neared the alley exit, a short bald pygmy man with huge bird eyes ran toward him. He had on nothing but boxer shorts, a T-shirt and holey socks. Blind terror was on his face. He scampered behind Bodyslick. He was trembling like a junkie in a poppy field. His ellipsoid mouth opened wide enough to hold an ostrich egg.

"Mista' she gonna key-ill mee!"

"What's up man?" Bodyslick asked in confusion as the man peeked from behind him. "Who's goin' to kill you?"

At that moment, a mammoth black woman appeared at the end of the alley. She weighed at least four hundred pounds and had arms like tree trunks. She was as black as coal. Her eyes beamed a dazed blue contact marbleized glow. A deathly glow. She wore a cheap blond wig. Her lips were huge and as red as newborn mice. She was an original. The original motha. She was Lucy. She had on a flowered cotton dress and was bare-foot. Her toes looked like snarled tree branches. Primitive. She was breathing so heavily her nostrils flared as if she was trying to blow fire. She started walking toward Bodyslick with a de-mented smile and a gleaming ice pick in her hand.

"Dah Lawd know's I wasn't playin' roun' on yah, Hattie!" The man pleaded in a falsetto voice, as he fearfully crouched behind Bodyslick. With a crazed, deranged look on her face, Hattie raised the gleaming ice pick and started toward them.

"You don' fuck wid' de wrung bitch dis' time, Orvill!"

A raucous crowd started to gather. A woman's voice wailed from the crowd. "Kill the chump, Ice Pick Hattie!"

"Pleas sah don't let her key-ill mee!"

The crowd started laughing as she raised the ice pick as if it was an axe and walked defiantly toward Bodyslick.

"Miztah, um warnin' yah . . . dat dis ain't cha buznis . . . naw git de fuck outtah mah way!"

She slashed the gleaming ice pick at him. He felt a *whoosh* of hot air against his neck as he leaped back almost tripping over the fearful man. Hattie backed up again and charged again like an enraged bull elephant, while slashing the ice pick again, again, and again. Bodyslick instinctively ducked. Dodged. Danced as he moved around her like a boxer. He sidestepped as she slashed wildly with her left, and he undercut her swing with his right fist then hit her with a hard left to the jaw. Hat-tie slumped back seeing whirling stars. She was dazed. Dizzy. He then grabbed her left arm and locked the ice pick between his right arm and body. Simultaneously he bent her elbow at an inverted angle until he heard the snap, crackle, and pop of bone; then he released her. There was a loud thump on the ground as she fell on her back kicking and screaming.

"Jesus. . . Lawd knows 'n heven all you niggas want tah do is fuck ovah a black woman! Don' broke mah urm! Usah dead nigga naw!"

The crowd became silent. Bodyslick glanced around daring anyone to challenge him. He brushed off his clothes. Hattie

made a convulsive effort to get up but fell down again. Her face looked like some grotesque African mask used to ward off evil spirits. Bodyslick hurriedly moved on. He approached the edge of the alley. Bright neon lights pulsed like a dying heart as he neared 57th Street. He wondered if that was the infamous "Ice Pick Hattie" who had stabbed her two husbands in the hearts with a dagger sculpted of ice. It had melted, preventing her from being convicted for the crimes because there was never any evidence found.

Suddenly his special wristwatch beeped. Bodyslick knew it was important because only a very select few knew his secret code (check it out) which activated the voice transmissions.

"*Check it out*. Malcolm, this is your sis . . . sis . . . ster . . . Pe . . . Pea . . . Peaches."

"*Check it out*. This is your brother. Anything wrong, sis?"

He listened intently because from childhood she'd had a stuttering problem that became pronounced when she was nervous or fearful of something. He could hear her heavy breathing. He could sense something was wrong.

"Malcolm, Uncle Will had . . . had . . . a . . a . . . heart attack . . . this . . . this . . . aft . . . after . . . ter . . . noon!" she stammered.

"What?" Bodyslick shouted in disbelief.

"I don't know how ser . . . ser . . . severe it is . . . but he wants to . . . to . . . see you!"

"Is he in the hospital?"

"No . . . he . . . he . . . is at home with Aunt Eltha. He didn't want to stay . . . for some reason. So . . . you bettah go on over there because Aunt Eltha say he really wants to talk to you and she said he . . ."—Peaches started to cry—"that it don't look good at all, maybe that's why he didn't want to stay in the hos . . . hos . . . hospital."

"I'm going over there right now," Bodyslick said nervously. "How long you think it will take you and Raog to get here from Waukegan?"

"About two hours, flat!"

"Okay, I'll see you then, and thanks, Peaches."

Chapter 10

The jet black Cadilectro's hydrogen engine shut off as the GPS guidance system's screen faded and the mechanical voice ebbed into silence.

"This place looks like a graveyard," Geronimo moaned to Snow, as he strained to get his lanky 6'7" body out of the car.

"Yeah, wouldn't be a good place to bring a date."

Both men wore green safari jumpsuits with epaulets. Green meshed with Robbins' dense foliage. Snow liked the way his .45-caliber laser pistol nested in the large pockets. They slowly walked toward a warehouse building that was totally hidden by tall weeping willow trees and an old equipment yard filled with bobcats, bulldozers, and scrapers that looked like exoskeletons of alien creatures.

Three eighteen wheelers were docked in the shipping area with the red and white heart-shaped logo LL&T pasted on them. A black and gold hearse was parked next to the trucks. Snow could see the glimmer of the copper casket inside it.

"Snow, try one of these." Geronimo took a filtered seagarette from a white and gold pack labeled HydroGold.

"No thanks. I never liked water-grown grass, and I don't like the smell."

"Yeah, I forgot you like that alien shit somellow and Martianzeeg," Geronimo said, as he inhaled deeply on the joint while coughing convulsively.

"G, somellow and zeeg highs are out of this world, and I do mean out of this world!" Snow laughed.

A sign over the entrance read: LIVERS, LEGS & THIGHS, INC.

"Snow, what kinda name is that?"

"What name?"

"That." Geronimo pointed at the sign.

"Come on G," Snow said, "what's your fuckin' IQ, sixty-five? What you want Bodyslick to name it? Human Parts, Inc.? With neon lights around it? LL&T is discreet. Sounds sorta like his chicken business."

"Chicken?"

"Yeah, chicken—he wanted it to sound like a chicken factory."

"Instead of chicken wings." Geronimo laughed as he exhaled the smoke stinging his now-bloodshot eyes. "Human arms and legs."

"Yeah, G, you're not as dumb as you look." Snow peered at Geronimo's high cheekbones and wavy hair; traits from his black father and Apache mother. His moniker on the basketball court was G because of his gee whiz moves. He was almost drafted by the NBA, but his timing was awful because genetically engineered athletes were now replacing normal players.

Suddenly thunderstorm clouds started rumbling over the dark, sorrowful sky. Flashes of lightning carved the clouds. Blackbirds flew overhead. From nearby, some dogs started to bark and howl piteously, as if something unholy was near. The sky became pitch black.

They hurriedly walked to the building entrance as raindrops started to pelt down on them. Snow lowered his head so the camera could make a retinal scan of his blue eyes. The twelve-inch-thick door was reinforced with three inch concrete and molybenum steel alloy cord. It slid open.

"I bet even nitro wouldn't dent this door!" Geronimo said with amazement.

"It's probably got built-in thermostats, so if you try to torch it, a coolant would be released," Snow said.

They gazed into the vast 30,000 square foot warehouse.

"Damn, man," Geronimo said with disbelief, "this is huge!"

"Yeah, Bodyslick must have sunk millions into this. It's totally automated."

Hundreds of robot pickers zipped around on forklift like chassis and two-wheeled carts following orders from a centralized computer. Snow gazed up at a ceiling of bar joints that looked like triangular-shaped spider webs. Structural columns jutted upward, and hundreds of horizontal interlocking shelves crisscrossed them. Twenty-foot high rows of neatly stacked four by four vats of liquid green nitrogen tanks were marked RESEARCH ORGANS, with size, blood group, and type labeled on them. Human heads, arms, livers, vaginas, penises, legs, feet, hearts, lungs, and kidneys floated in nitrogen well below zero degrees to keep the organs free of infection. Blue phosphorous serpentine hoses linked each tank like Siamese twins.

SECTION VII
SPILL OR LEAK PROCEDURES
STEPS TO BE TAKEN IN CASE LIQUID NITROGEN
IS RELEASED OR SPILLED: VENTILATE AREA, ONLY
USE MAINTENANCE ROBOTS TO DISPOSE OF WASTE.

The robots were hauling the large tanks to the shipping docks where the deep freezer eighteen wheelers were parked. A morgue-like chill blanketed the warehouse. As Snow pressed the intercom button, the faint smell of feces wafted past their nostrils.

"Snow!" Slovik belched out, "come on in, make a sharp right, and go down the corridor to aisle three. I'll be waiting for you!"

Aisles one and two were strewn with broken liquid nitrogen tanks, empty pallets, packing material, robot parts, and maintenance tools. A dark carmine red liquid substance started to stick to their shoe heels. Was it blood? A rotten smell was thick and suffocating.

Beep! Beep! Beep!

Geronimo nudged Snow to move quickly as a robot whizzed past. Its grim reaper metallic face looked like a human skull as it turned and gave them the finger. The plate on its back read: HONDA INDUSTROBOT Ser. 893JL.

"Snow, this is some creepy shit." Geronimo pointed to a block long translucent nitrogen container. It reminded him of a huge fish aquarium, but there weren't any fish floating. Instead they saw hundreds of human thoraxes, heads, arms, and legs all neatly hung in rows by hooks. Each one had an ID tag on it reading: African, Caucasian, Mexican, Chinese, etc.

As they entered aisle three, they were assailed by an overpowering stench. Geronimo pinched his nose. Snow covered his nose with his hand. They gazed down the aisle at heads, arms, legs, and skin strewn across the floor.

The lightning, the roar of thunder, and the beating rain upon the roof sent an unspeakable terror down aisle three. Snow tried to leap over the body parts only to slip and fall near a three-year-old girl's head; face ashen gray, lips purplish, blonde hair stiff like a mop. Her frozen hazel eyes stared at him. And yet on her tiny face Snow thought he saw a smile . . . a ghastly smile filled with the thawing vapors of liquid nitrogen.

"I can't take this shit, man!" Geronimo hollered, as he leaned against a steel beam to get his bearing. He looked down with nausea at the squashed gray convoluted human brain he had stepped in up to his ankles. He could feel the coldness as three pounds of it slithered up and down his socks . . . dripping inside his shoes. He vomited until it seemed as if he would rupture his insides.

"Goddamn, Slovik!" Snow shouted, as he came from around a corner and he helped Snow to his feet. As Snow stood up he accidentally kicked the little girl's head. "Don't you have any fuckin' respect for the dead? This place is an abomination!" he said almost tearfully, gazing down at the girl's head.

"I'm sorry, you just came at a bad time. One of the fuckin' robot pickers dropped a couple of tanks . . . don't forget this is how we make our money. Don't get soft on me."

"Jesus Christ, man! You should still treat the dead with respect." Geronimo rushed Slovik and grabbed him around the neck choking him. "I should break your fuckin' neck, bitch! This shit is sacrilegious! Ain't nobody soft, we just human!"

Slovik's face turned purplish as Geronimo tightened the hold to his neck stopping the flow of air. His feet twitched in the air as Geronimo's 6'7" frame held him up.

"Let him go, G! You'll kill him before we get our tour," Snow said, smiling.

Slovik dizzily reeled and swayed as Geronimo let him go. He coughed convulsively. "*Bychara*, will you tell that *chernozhopyi* to leave me alone!"

"You callin' me a redneck and Geronimo a nigger, you *zalupa* (dickhead)?" Snow yelled.

"You callin' me a nigger, you Russian vodka-drinkin' bitch?" Geronimo lurched toward Slovik. Snow held his arm between them.

"*Vebitsche* (freak), I'm going to tell Bodyslick about the mess you got here!"

Slovik Wishnafski's sixty-five-year-old bald head reflected the green translucent tanks. His small rodent eyes and coarse features twitched nervously as he fearfully watched Geronimo. His skin was as pale as a corpse, and the smell of vodka oozed from his pores.

Geronimo stooped over again, holding his stomach like he was vomiting maggots.

"Well tell him, dammit!" Slovik yelled, "and let him bring his ass out here and work with the dead! You think I'm a fuckin' necrophile? You think I like defiling corpses? You think I like looking at the heads of cute little girls floating in liquid nitrogen instead of being buried because some doctor

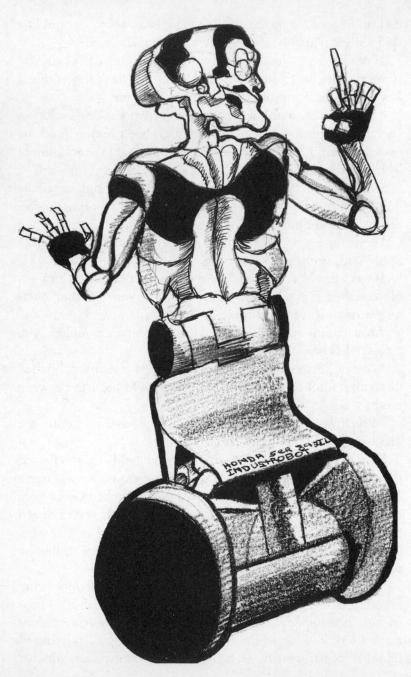

wants to use a new surgical tool on their brains? You know what that little blonde girl's head will sell for?"

"How much?" Snow asked.

"It will sell for about $1,500!"

"I can't take this shit!" Geronimo moaned. "I'll wait for you outside." He started swaying back and forth as he walked back down the aisle toward the exit.

"Where is he going?" Slovik snapped.

"He's all right. Just needs some fresh air. This ain't exactly a place for normal people."

"Well, just so you don't get the wrong impression of me, years ago I got my degree in anatomy at the University of Chicago. I was also adjunct professor of cryonic science for ten years before my divorce. When Marge left me, my whole world crashed. You know the story . . . drinking, drugs, attempted suicide. I even had a nervous breakdown. I just couldn't accept losing everything I had worked so hard for. But I digress . . . that's another story."

As they walked down the aisle, Snow heard a weird sound: *Oinkahhh, Oinkahhh*. "What's that noise?"

"What noise?" Slovik asked.

"Listen!" *Oinkahh, Oinkahh*.

"Oh, that's Helen and George," Slovik said with a laugh, "they must be at it again."

"Helen and George?" Snow asked incredulously.

"We're almost there. Seeing is better than words."

Snow became nervous as he heard the loud rattling of a metal cage. Something huge was banging inside it. The smell of shit blasted his face as they walked toward a five foot high cage. He could see it tilt and slam in a seesaw motion from the weight inside it. It reminded him of the type he used to keep his rottweiler locked up in.

Slovik abruptly stopped and whispered, "That's Helen bent over in the doggy position, and that's George on top fuckin' her brains out."

Snow squinted with disbelief. He saw two hairy, pinkish

brown creatures with pig-like heads, human noses and arms, and knees inverted like a dog's. They were huge. He watched as the male plowed his huge, horse-like, red serrated-serpent dick into the rear of the female.

"*Oinkahh . . . Oinkahh*," the female moaned deliriously. The male peered at them with its beady red eyes and kept on stroking.

Snow smiled and said, "I wish G would have stayed and seen this shit. He's doing some serious fuckin'. What the fuck are they?"

"I bought them when they were just pups . . ." Slovik gestured, lowering his hands. "From an Australian genimorph zoo after they were banned because of cross species viruses. Helen and George have the genes of an Australian wombat, a pig, and human embryonic stem cells. They have the IQ of a chimp. They are the last of their kind because they are sterile. Bodyslick let me keep them because he was hoping they could breed and produce transplantable organs."

Snow walked up some stairs into a large brightly-lit office. It looked like a loft with its high ceiling, floor, and Plexiglas windows. He could see the entire warehouse operation. He glanced at a large liquid nitrogen tank filled with tiny mutated fetuses. Slovik gestured for him to sit down in a nearby chair. Computers clicked. Monitors blinked. A large GPS map linked colored lights on the wall designating delivery and truck locations. The sound of an alto saxophone floated through the huge office workspace.

"He died on July 17, 1967. He was only forty-one," Slovik said matter-of-factly.

"Who?"

"John Coltrane."

"Never heard of him."

"Says a lot about your MS education. You heard of Jimi Hendrix, right?"

"Yeah, 'Purple Haze' . . . who hasn't?"

"John Coltrane was the genius who influenced Hendrix

along with the rest of the world! Want a drink?" Slovik asked, as he poured vodka into a glass full of ice.

"No, too early for me."

"Coltrane was a bonafide genius like Einstein, Picasso, and Steven Spielberg," Slovic said, as he sipped the drink and wiped his mouth with his hand. "He was about the harmony of life. His music was healing. Magical. Spiritual. He tried to capture the essence of God with his horn. When I think about my legacy . . ."

Snow cut him off. "Coltrane's legacy was his music. Your legacy will be that you were *too* drunk to do your job! Was Coltrane a nigger *shithead* like Geronimo?"

"No, I'm not a drunkard and I do my job!" Slovik said with guilt.

"I didn't come here to listen to you talk about Coltrane and you moaning about your legacy! Bodyslick wants you to give me a tour of this place!"

"You already had it!" Slovik laughed as he gulped down the vodka and poured another.

"Dammit, man!" he said with a slur, "buildings fall down, stars burn out, fuckin' eggs break, and so do machines. This place operates very efficiently considering it's completely automated. In any warehouse where you have robots instead of people there are going to be glitches. This is a very dangerous, hazardous place. A pin-sized drop of liquid nitrogen will eat through your entire body! We have over a thousand body organs leaving here weekly, with deliveries nationwide. There are only four humans who work here: myself, Silas, the warehouse engineer; Willie, the mad butcher—he programs the robots for organ cuts—and Han Wah Choi, who keeps the robots running. They are made by a Jap company."

"Bodyslick is concerned about the shipment to Virginia Anatomical Services. Lately there has been a rash of mislabeled organs shipped out of here. Why that kidney you gave me was from an alcoholic. You didn't screen it. It was diseased. I could have been killed by Willie Lloyd's henchmen over that mistake!"

Slovik stood up, reeling as if he had lost his sense of balance. He seemed inebriated. "Well, mistakes happen. Ever heard of Murphy's law? If the cheap bastard can hire someone else to do this graveyard shit—" He belched. "So be it. But let's . . ." He fell back down into the chair in a drunken stupor.

Snow called Bodyslick.

Chapter 11

Bodyslick slowly walked up the screeching stairs to Uncle Will's third floor apartment at the Saint Booker Hotel on the corner of East 47th Street and Cottage Grove. He rang the bell as the stench of human urine and rat, cat, and dog dung stung his nostrils. He wondered why his uncle chose to live in such poverty with all the money he had.

A leery woman's voice moaned through a peephole. "Who are you? And what d' yuh want?"

"It's me, Aunt Eltha, Malcolm."

There was silence for a moment. The terse trumpet of Miles Davis's *Porgy and Bess* assailed his ears from inside the apartment. "Look, ain't no Jesus-lookin', long-haired white boy with beads and a robe on gonna make me believe he is Malcolm? Naw go away cause I don't know whut you up heah foe. I will call the po-leeeese!"

"Aunt Eltha, I'm just in a disguise—ask me something about my family . . . anything. I have to wear a disguise because my life is in danger."

"Awright, you say you Malcolm Steel, what's your street-name?"

"Bodyslick."

"What's your mamma's name?"

"Mattie B. Steel."

"Your sister?"

"Peaches is her nickname, and Bernita Steel is her maiden name."

"Your young brother?"

"Kenny."

"Your nephew?"

"Pumpkin."

"You got two daughters, what's their names?"

"Michelle and Brittany."

"What's they mother's name?"

"Deanna."

"What public housing did you live in Chicago?"

"Cabrini Green."

She looked through the peephole for a long time then moaned and the door swung open. "Lord have mercy on mah soul. You really is Malcolm. Lordy Jesus, I would swear you was one of them Krishnas, or neo-hip-hop-rockers. Well, have mercy, chile, what will they come up with next?" She closed the door and just laughed and shook her head.

Bodyslick stepped into the apartment and peeled off the dermo mask. Aunt Eltha stiffened with astonishment. Reverend Clyde Taylor, Uncle Will's pastor, was sitting on a nearby sofa. The reverend stood up as Bodyslick walked over to him and shook his sandpaper rough hand.

"We will talk a bit once you visit your uncle, okay, son?"

"Sure, Reverend Taylor."

"Malcolm," Eltha said with a serious scowl, "I begged your uncle to stay in the hospital, but he wouldn't listen to me or Reverend Taylor, so the doctors released him and hooked him up to their online home-care diagnostic computer at the hospital. The nurses are monitoring him by transmissions sent from the computer in his room and a medichip in his chest. So if there are any problems the ambulance will be here in five to eight minutes flat. Ain't God good, Malcolm?"

She held his hand tightly as they walked down a long cavernous hallway. The wooden floors tweaked under their weight. As they entered Uncle Will's room, she clutched his hand tightly, fearfully. The room had a lot of oriental rugs, teakwood dressers, Asian sculptures, and Chinese paintings. Bodyslick quickly fixed his eyes on a large photograph of Uncle Will shaking hands with Choi Tse Tong, the leader of the Hip Hop Sung Triad in Chinatown. Aunt Eltha pulled a perfumed handkerchief from her robe pocket and dabbed at tears from her eyes. Bodyslick felt a deathly chill as he gazed at blinking visual and audio transmissions, screens, a pulsing digitalized image of his uncle's weak heart on a computer screen, and the myriad tiny wires implanted into his chest and arms.

Bodyslick slowly walked toward his bed. He studied his uncle's face. Intensely. It was ashen, and his once fleshy cheeks were now shrunken and hollow. He looked like a corpse. He was lying supine in the bed. His once-hypnotic, wolf-grey eyes were now filmy, slit, and glassy from medication. He had the stare of a dying beast; yet, when he saw Bodyslick, his eyes seemed to flicker a glint of hope. Life.

Aunt Eltha stood attentively at the bedroom door with her arms crossed defensively. Her cheeks were shiny from tears. The hot smell of sizzling collard greens, sweet potatoes, corn bread, and ham hocks wafted through the apartment. The *whong whong* of a distant siren bounced off the walls of their hotel. The ghostly wail of the siren sent a deathly chill down Bodyslick's and Aunt Eltha's spine. She was Uncle Will's third wife and the most loyal.

Uncle Will gave Aunt Eltha a feeble wave to leave. She grabbed the doorknob and whispered to Bodyslick, "If he needs anything, Malcolm, I'll be in the livin' room."

As Bodyslick sat in a chair next to Uncle Will's bed, he could feel his piercing eyes as he gazed at him with a sudden burst of energy. Uncle Will grabbed an old crumpled letter from beneath his pillow and gave it to him.

"Read it!" he said uncompromisingly. With leaden fingers, Bodyslick took the letter out of the old tattered opened envelope and started to read with astonishment.

Sergeant Malcolm Henry Steel
24th Infantry Division
U.S. Army
December 24, 2003
  Son, about an hour after I . . .

"Malcolm!" Uncle Will snapped feebly, "I want you to only read the last paragraph of that letter, which is on page five at the bottom!"

"But Uncle Will, this is the same identical letter that I have been keeping all these years. How did you get . . . ?"

"I'll explain all that after you read the last paragraph . . . Naw go on, boy . . . read!"

  One last thing. Do me a favor and stay clear of
  your Uncle Will when I'm gone. I'll sleep better.
  Trust me, I do need my sleep.

"Uncle Will, why did you want me to read that to you right now? Haven't you had enough pain in one day?" he said, as he folded the letter and put it back in the envelope and set it down on a nearby table.

"Stay clear of your uncle . . ." Uncle Will moaned with a twisted, almost painful grin as if the words scorched his brain like hot bullets. There was a moment's silence. Bodyslick looked down at him as a flickering silk-shaded lamp cast a pale yellow light onto his gleaming jet black skin. The corneas of his eyes were a dark umber. Enamel-like. His skin was smooth as a baby's booty. He had a pronounced, chiseled, Roman nose. Thick, fleshy, African lips. He had a huge domed forehead. His hair was nappy and gray. A furrowed brow which issued a sense of thoughtfulness. Meditation. The structure of his head and face reminded Bodyslick of a picture he had once seen in a book, of the Egyptian Pharaoh Merneptah's face, which was in the Cairo Museum in Egypt. A face that had once looked Moses in the eye and said, "No!" A face that worshipped the ancient Egyptian sun god Ra and renounced Moses' Christian God.

Uncle Will coughed, then snorted and said, "Your father was a good nigga, Malcolm. He actually believed in the American dream. Just like Martin Luther Queen," he giggled. "Both of them were good law-abidin', Bible readin', flag wavin', nonviolent, good niggas that actually believed they could teach the white man how to love!"

"Look!" Bodyslick barked viciously, "Naw don't get outta' line, Uncle Will, because I have killed men for talkin' about my dead father. I respect you. But you must"—he pointed his finger at his uncle—"and I mean it. You must respect my father. And the man's name was King, and he was a great leader."

Uncle Will cleared his throat and continued. Cautiously. "That's why he despised me. Hated me. Cursed the ground I walk on. Don't get me wrong. Your father was a good, honest decent square. He was a born military man and was one of the best because he gave his life for his country. But what he didn't understand"—Uncle Will pointed at a glass of water next to his bed and took a few gulps after Bodyslick gave it to him, then continued—"is that even a crook like me has feelings," (Bodyslick laughed) "has compassion. He never could see me beyond my brushes with the law. My only regret, Malcolm, is that you didn't take heed to his words! He hit it on the money when he said I was a crook because I have been one all my life. Every detective in the union knows about the escapades of Uncle Will! And it seems," he said with a strained chuckle, "I'm goin' to die a crook!"

"Uncle Will," Bodyslick pleaded, "we all have flaws and regrets. You didn't put a gun to my head and make me become what I am. I chose a life of crime—because since a child I never could reconcile why black people, no matter what they do for this country, are treated like niggers, expendable beings."

"Give me a seagarette, Malcolm . . . they're in that drawer."

Bodyslick snatched open the drawer and wondered if it would be wise to give him a seagarette after his heart attack.

What if the seagarette triggered another attack? He hesitated, staring frozenly at the package.

"Okay, don't, dammit! But just listen to me!" Uncle Will said with anger scratched across his face. Anger that had cost the lives of countless men who hadn't taken heed. "Malcolm, I want you to get out of the fast lane. I know what you're sayin' about racism and prejudice and all them other 'isms', but there is another way to change the system. You can't go through life with a grudge against this capitalist system. All man made social systems are corrupt. *Power* corrupts, son. I didn't realize that when I was younger . . . when I was teaching you how to survive. But now near death," he coughed with agony, "I realize that corruption, racism, and human brutality are not just confined to America, but are rampant across the globe. That's why we don't have a United States of Africa, because each little gang wants its power base. Malcolm, look at how this country treats *genigs*. Everybody hates them because their heads are twice the size of a normal person's. Their skin is a pinkish-blue because of what scientists called a lightnin' bug gene. They look like Japs. Noses like Jews. Lips like blacks. Tall as fuckin' pygmies. Yet most of them are smarter than us. They come from families that could afford engineered babies. Families that wanted perfect blonde, blue-eyed kids. But it backfired. They have no common sense; they can't tie their shoes, pay a bill, drive a car. They think so deeply, they can't focus on normal stuff. Now we got millions of them demonstrating, rioting, marching, singin' 'We shall overcome' so they can get government aid and public housing. That's why they are being targeted for violent hate crimes . . ." He coughed.

"All social systems change or perish . . . America is no different. Now listen because I'm your old hoodlum uncle on his deathbed," he grabbed Bodyslick's hand, "and um beggin' ya to let the blood money go. Get an honest job—you're a smart guy. Marry that nice girl Malanna, and make her a decent husband. I am a no good scoundrel, but it's not too late for you to change. Get out of that filthy organ business, son, before it's too late. Don't end up an old broken down crook like me. Don't let racism be an excuse for failure!"

"How did you get that letter, Uncle Will?" Bodyslick asked, as if his uncle's plea for change was meaningless.

"Well . . ." Uncle Will gestured for some napkins on the tabletop. Bodyslick gave him two, and he wiped his sweaty brow. "When your father sent you one, he sent me a duplicate. I guess he wanted me to know how he felt about me lookin' out for ya. But I swear, Malcolm, when you were young you reminded me so much of myself. It was unbelievable. Also, I guess because I never had a son of my own, that I know of." He laughed. "I started to look at you as my son. You were always so quick, so smart, good with your fists . . . so . . . so . . . much like I was when I was young."

Bodyslick gripped the sides of his chair to smother the grief, the sorrow of his dying uncle's words. His piteous plea for him to change his lifestyle; to do something that was honest and decent shook his soul.

Suddenly, he heard the barefoot steps of Aunt Eltha as she walked down the wooden hallway toward the bedroom. She strolled into the room and quickly started tidying up his bed as Uncle Will sleepily closed his eyes.

"He needs his rest, Malcolm!" Aunt Eltha said in a gravely voice, as her tearful eyes bore into him. She whispered, "Come on, Malcolm, and let your old sick uncle sleep."

He stood up and walked over to her, kissed her on the cheek, looped his arm around her waist and sneakily tucked three thousand dollar bills into her robe pocket. They walked down the hallway toward the living room door. He squeezed her reassuringly. The faint saxophone solo of "My Favorite Things" by John Coltrane sounded from an old CD.

Aunt Eltha was sixty-something. A well-shaped yellow woman with striking long curly red hair. She had a white father. She taught twenty years in the Chicago public school system. She retired as principal. People said that in her youth she was the "hostess with the mostest" when she worked at the

Cotton Club on South Michigan. She had big chestnut brown eyes, freckles, juicy melon lips, and a long gazelle neck. She wore a tight red satin robe which revealed big, pretty legs.

Aunt Eltha sat down beside Reverend Taylor. Bodyslick sat in a chair directly in front separated from them by a cocktail table. He glanced at a large book on the table. He squinted his eyes as he read the bold title:

AUCTION

His eyes froze when he read:

At the Same Time I Will Sell My
6 NEGRO SLAVES

The black and white cover of the book shocked his senses:

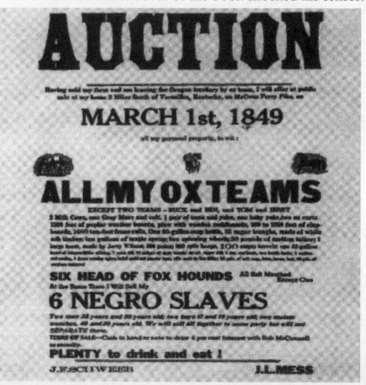

"What are you goin' to do, Malcolm?" she asked, as she clicked on a nearby lamp.

"About what?" he asked, puzzled, as he picked up the book and flicked through the pages.

"About your sinful life!" Reverend Taylor said in a booming Howlin' Wolf raspy voice.

"Don't be judging, Rev, because you think you gonna get your wings," he snapped acidly.

"A lot of people love you, Malcolm," Aunt Eltha said passionately. "All of us have been pleading with you for years to stop profiting off the dead! Are you going to change, son? Haven't you made enough blood money from death?" There was tough love in her voice. "Malcolm, I used to teach American history in grammar and high school. Did you know that slavery was the vilest example of 'body ownership'? Even in death their body parts could be sold for profit."

"No, I didn't, Aunt Eltha, but we are living in 2031, not 1831. Why are you talkin' about something that happened centuries ago? Something that happened even before you were born!"

"But you're missing the point, Malcolm. The issue is you are still doing it today. Slave cadavers were harvested and sold by grave robbers to medical institutions illegally, like the Universities of Michigan, Georgia, Mississippi, and Louisiana. They pillaged our cemeteries well into the twentieth century, Malcolm. Your slave ancestors were easy targets of grave robbers by whites and blacks!"

Bodyslick cringed as he thought about all the thousand dollar kickbacks he had paid black funeral homes for body parts. "Look," he said, trying to hide his guilt, "I didn't come here for a lecture on black history, I came here to check on my sick uncle. Not to talk business!" He slapped the book closed and shouted defiantly, "I'm saving black lives. Do you know how many black Americans are alive and healthy because of free kidney transplants I have supplied? Thousands! Nationwide! The rate of death has dropped because of this so-called sinner's compassion!" He looked at Reverend Taylor harshly.

"Nobody is saying you haven't done any good, son," Reverend Taylor said in a fatherly way. "We are just trying to put an historical perspective on the organ trade. Put a black face on it!"

"Look, I have had enough of this! Time is money." He stood up. The reverend and Aunt Eltha stood up also.

"Respect your elders, Malcolm, and let me finish! It won't take long!" Reverend Taylor said sternly. "I realize you have saved black lives. But the bulk of your profits come from whites, right?"

"Yeah, and your point, Reverend?" Bodyslick asked as he glanced at his watch.

"As a pastor, as a Christian, I see a profound link between the body and the soul. The whole idea of organ transplantation comes from the white man's belief that he is God! The human body is viewed as a machine that you can salvage parts from like a hydro-car. We no longer view the dead as sacred, but as a profit source. Medicine now sees replacing body parts as a cure all. What's next? Pig organs? Our faith in science has eroded our faith in God."

Bodyslick stood up again. "Reverend, at this very moment we are terraforming Mars's atmosphere. Galactic drugs are saving lives . . . will you stop living in the past!" He could feel their critical eyes on him. They knew their comparison of slavery and the selling of organs both stemming from capitalist greed was weak. The calculated reaction Aunt Eltha hoped to evoke from the book's grotesque images of slavery did not work either.

"Aunt Eltha, Reverend Taylor. It's too late for me. I'm a crook like Uncle Will. A hoodlum. An organ broker. A man who makes his livin' outside of society. A lone wolf. Just like your husband."

A window curtain started to flap. A cat meowed outside the door. He heard a man screaming at a child in the apartment below.

"You love Uncle Will even though he has been a crook his entire life . . . right?" She nodded her head. "I'll check on you and Uncle Will. Just give me a call and keep me abreast of his status. You need more money for anything, just call me."

He waved at Reverend Taylor as he put back on his dermo-mask, opened the door, and walked into a pitch black corridor. *Why was the hallway light out?* he wondered. He quickly pulled out his .45 laser. He crouched down listening, watching as one hand felt along the wall to find the banister that would lead him down the stairs. A constellation of thoughts bounced in his skull. Was he walking into a trap of some kind? Had Toejoe and the mob followed him here? How did they know he had on a disguise? He froze, as the staccato barks of an old gas engine drove past the hotel. He grasped the smooth wooden banister rail. He took his first step down the stairs. He listened, straining his ears for a clue, a sound, a shadow—anything that would give him an edge.

And then, suddenly, he was *whacked* across the head from behind. It didn't hurt. He heard a panting sound. He wasn't sure if it was human or animal. His heart thudded loudly. Relentlessly he cocked his pistol as he swerved around in the darkness. If this was a trap he certainly was the prey, he thought as he gritted his teeth. He could see nothing in the milky blackness. Beads of sweat formed on his nose. Uncle Will's words echoed ominously: *Get out of the fast lane.* He bit down hard on his lower lip as two large lime-green eyes stared face to face at him. His finger slowly hugged the trigger.

Suddenly, Uncle Will's door screeched open. Pale light poured on the source of his terror.

Meowaff . . . Meowaff . . .

"Come on, come on, Sadie, come on in the house," Aunt Eltha purred to her large black dat. She laughed at Bodyslick as he stood holding the banister with his gun out.

"The children are always bustin' that stairway light. Did Sadie scare you?" He shook his head, smiled, and tucked his pistol back inside his robe. He watched as the genetically spliced cat-dog leaped into her arms and licked her face. "Take care of yourself, Malcolm," she said, as she closed the door.

He was back in darkness. He started to walk down the stairs when he heard the sound of shuffling feet, the jangle of keys. A door slammed on the first floor. He could see nothing. Suddenly he saw a shadowy figure approaching the stairway. It had a long object under its arm. Was it a gun? He snatched out his laser pistol from his leg holster and aimed it at the shadow as it started to climb the stairs. A flash of light beamed into his eyes making him squint in the darkness. He slowly squeezed the trigger.

"Don't shoot, sah, po-leeese? Um James da' janitor heah." He was a small fragile man with huge owl-like eyes. His skin was as black as coal. He nervously licked his lips. His nappy hair seemed to stand on his head like iron filings to a magnet. He trembled uncontrollably. He clicked off the flashlight. He had a small ladder and a light bulb in his free hand.

Bodyslick ran down the stairs noticing a puddle of pee where the man stood. He laughed. And walked out into a neon jungle.

The cool city wind felt good blowing off Lake Michigan on the hot dermo-mask. That sense of dread he'd felt with Uncle Will and his wife was slowly dissolving. He could not shed who he really was any more than a leopard its spots. He was a crook. A crook to the bone. To the marrow. He had been weaned, nurtured, and schooled on the streets. He was a bonafide, resolute citizen of crookdom.

As he walked down the street he thought there was too much at stake to turn back now. Suddenly, he felt a sense of imminent danger.

Chapter 12

The cry of a whining siren caught his attention. He noticed a mass of people as they gathered in front of a lounge across the street from him. Bodyslick started running toward the scene. He heard a woman scream. The sound crackled like the recoil of a whip through the musky night air. He listened.

"Why don't our leaders stop the flow of extraterrestrial drugs?"

As Bodyslick neared the mass of people, he saw Toejoe Wilson talking to an ambulance attendant. Toejoe saw him and ducked around the van. Bodyslick quickly sought cover behind a nearby aero-car. He felt the hot beam of a laser pistol as it carved a hole in the aero-car's bumper. The crowd panicked and started running, hollering, and screaming.

Bodyslick bit down on his lower lip. His hand became wet, as perspiration meshed with his laser pistol. He wondered how ironic it was that the fear of death was echoing through every atom of his being; yet his very survival depended on it. Toejoe Wilson fired a flurry of flaming white laser beams. Bodyslick ducked. He fell on his knees and started crawling to the front of the aero-car. The howl of laser beams, as they tore through the wind, made him overly cautious. As he crawled, the laser bursts sounded like maniacal demons hooting and screaming for his death.

The streets became empty. Quiet. Desolate. The ambulance

attendants had run into the lounge. Bodyslick could see the overdose victim's body as it lay limp and twisted near the rear ambulance doors. The dead man's glassine eyes caught Bodyslick's attention as he watched Toejoe's movement from underneath the car. The dead man's eyes glistened in the moonlight. White laser bursts hissed in the wind. Bodyslick's eyes latched onto Toejoe's slow movements underneath the ambulance. It was time for him to make a move. A death move. One of them must die. Bodyslick crawled to the very front of the car; his eyes glued on Toejoe's lower body. He smiled. He was a sitting duck. Bodyslick rose off his knees and scrambled half erect. The whining siren of a distant police car echoed through the night. It was now or never. Time was running out. He cocked his laser pistol. Beads of sweat crisscrossed his face. The bright neon signs reflected off the metallic aero-car's door—amber, blue, and carmine red lights—bounced onto the dead man's skin every thirty seconds, creating an eerie, immobile sculpture on East 47th Street.

Bodyslick lurched from the front of the aero-car, darted across the street and knelt at the rear of the ambulance van. He peeked around the corner. He could see Toejoe at the front of the van. He was only fifteen meters away. Toejoe smiled as he aimed across the street at a non-existent foe. His ivory white teeth gleamed in the darkness. His eyes shone like silvery metal. His mouth grimaced with the anticipation that the hunted was on the brink of killing the hunter.

A restive wind caused brown paper bags, beer cans and shattered wine-bottle glass to glide in the street. The street seemed to shimmer with blinking pastel-neon lights and the flashing signs of the urbanscape.

Bodyslick slowly, quietly, cautiously, turned toward Toejoe. His sweaty finger hugged the trigger. He had killed before. He wondered why he could always remember the stare, the horror, the disbelief that shone in the dead men's eyes after he had killed them. The whining siren came closer. Toejoe quickly ducked into the lounge. Bodyslick ran through the crowded door while holding his laser pistol in his coat pocket. He peered around the lounge. It was dark. Pastel blue. It was packed. Was Toejoe alone? He couldn't risk shooting anyone accidentally for it would cause too much pandemonium. He looked. And looked and looked. It would be impossible to spot him in this weird crowd. He peered at the bar and laughed to himself as he gazed at a group of men or were they women prancing through the door.

As he thought back, he remembered that every Wednesday night at Satan's Den was Gay Night. The transvestite entertainers came to the lounge to put on a show. It was a night when drag queens would get more attention than real women and sometimes look just as real. He glanced around as he stood near the door. Looking. Searching for Toejoe. Then the blinding stage light shone on a person who had on a glittering G-string. He began to dance, shaking his narrow ass while erotically flicking his hands at the rowdy crowd. His crooked blond wig was flecked with glitter. He had huge owl eyes, and his eyebrows were plastered with silver. He grinned, showing front teeth crowned with tiny gold stars. Strands of phony diamonds glittered from his huge neck. The music was burlesque and funky. He bellowed in his high falsetto voice.

"Oh . . . yeahhhh . . . this is Wednesday night, Laydeeez and Gennnemen and In-Betweens . . . Ha. Ha. Yeah! This is the night anything can happen, ya'll. This is the night when the women act like men, and the men act like women . . . I ain't lyin', ya'll. Why . . . why . . . you might even see . . . yo grandmammy in drag . . . ohhhh yeah, chile. So just lie back and buy a lot of that Alpha Centauri wine . . . and have a good time while I introduce the sensuous, or should I say infamous, Bertha 'the butt' Jones . . . Let's hear it for Bertha!"

What he heard and saw in the lounge made him think these people were mad. they were actin' like they are the happiest mothas in the world, when they didn't even have the vaguest notion about their political situation. Did they even care that Mayor Darold Mannington was lying dead and rigid on a slab of icy steel at the county morgue? He sensed in them an ingenious ability to blind their minds to the causes of their squalid and narrow living space. A sense of futility heaved through his being.

He again glanced around the lounge, as the patrons loudly applauded the entrance of a 400-pound man dressed in a lavender bikini prancing onto the stage. Then suddenly, the blinding light of a laser pistol shot from the corner of the stage. He ducked. Cries of terror and fear echoed from the audience.

A woman screamed at the door as someone hollered, "She's been shot!" Another series of blasts shattered the mirrors in back of the bar. People were clutching their heads, hiding behind chairs, or lying prone on the floor with their arms covering their faces.

The crowd was like stampeding beasts running toward the door. Laser pellets spat into the walls. Bodyslick could see Toejoe now. He was near the glowing red exit sign adjacent to the stage. He fired at Toejoe. He answered. Their laser pistols created hot crisscrossing strings of heat and death. Toejoe blasted the exit sign light with a shot and burst through the door. Bodyslick jumped over prone customers as he rushed after him. He slowed down as he neared the exit door. He leaped through the door and rolled onto the refuse-ridden alley ground. The asphalt exploded along with beer cans and wine bottles, as staccato bursts of laser pellets streamed at him. They came from a black sedan electro-car as it sped down the alley. He quickly stood up and fired. And fired. Then a loud voice hollered from the car.

"Remember Bubba, chump!" Bodyslick was tired. He was sore. Pain shot through his entire body. Maybe Uncle Will was right, he thought. Maybe it was time for him to take his money and re-invest in his fast food business and get out of the fast lane before it was too late.

He had cut his leg. He could feel a geyser of blood as it

poured into his shoe. Every time he took a step he could feel the spongy, bubbling sensation of blood. Was he shot? The pain spread through his thigh. He braced himself against a nearby fence. He felt his leg. It was a deep cut. He limped down the alley. He would take a taxi to Malanna's apartment. He needed her now. More than ever.

The phone chimed on his watch. Snow's face slowly crystallized on the tiny screen.

"How was the tour?"

"Fucked up! Slovik is an alcoholic and a racist. He was totally drunk when we left there. Good thing that system is automated, or we would be fucked up."

"What about Virginia Anatomical's order?"

"He was too drunk to talk about the order!"

"I'll call Silas to check on it while I find a replacement for Slovik. How did Geronimo like the place?"

"He vomited the whole time we were there. The warehouse is fantastic, but Slovik has got to go!"

"I was at Coroner Weiner's office earlier, Snow. He has a fresh Type-O liver waiting for you to pick up. When you do, I'll arrange for Willie D. Lloyd to get it, okay?"

"Yeah, I'll pick it up, but I want to check out the corpse's feet."

"Why?"

"Because this will be my second delivery to Willie, and this liver has got to be good."

"Don't worry . . . it's fresh."

"I'm still going to see if the feet are scaly and have a lot of skin, which would mean it's another alcoholic's liver."

"While you're there, Snow, check to see if she has any corns on her feet," Bodyslick said sarcastically.

"Fuck you! Like I said, this is my white ass they coming after! I'm on my way. I'll contact you when I pick it up."

"Snow?"

"Yeah."

"Some heat's getting ready to jump off. I need Shondell, you, and Geronimo to be ready for backup."

"Just tell me when and where!"

"I'll call you when I want you to rendezvous with me at Malanna's house."

"What time?"

"As soon as I give you the spot to drop off the liver. Talk to you later."

"Be cool," Snow said.

Chapter 13

Malanna was sprawled in the bed nude when Bodyslick walked in the bedroom.

"What's happening, angel?"

She jumped out of bed and threw her arms around him tightly. Passionately.

"Baby, I've been worried sick about you. Why didn't you call? Don't I deserve that much? You could have at least . . ."—she started to cry—"since Bubba's murder I've been so worried about you!"

"How did you know about Bubba's murder?" he said with astonishment.

"Honey, they found his body under the Maglev stop on 43rd Street. I heard about it on the holoset while coming home from work . . . why honey, didn't you know?"

"Yeah, baby, I knew."

"Not only that," Malanna said with uncontrolled horror, "someone . . . had . . . had . . . cut the poor man's heart out!"

He consoled her. He whispered in her ear. "Everything is being taken care of, honey. All of his business and funeral arrangements will be handled by me. His wife and child are financially secure for life."

She glanced at his bloody pants leg. "You've been cut! Oh, my God! Let me dress it for you." Quickly, she scampered out

of the bed and went into the bathroom to get some gauze, cotton, tape, and alcohol.

He grabbed a nearby remote and clicked on the holoset. A male news anchor nervously spoke.

> *"Tomorrow morning, at nine o'clock, the city's Chief Coroner, Dr. Jonath Weiner, will release his controversial autopsy report on the late civil-rights activist, Mayor Darold Mannington. As you know, the cardiologist, James Kilmora at Northwestern Hospital, has already stated that the mayor died of a massive heart attack, but because of the blacks' suspicion of foul play, an autopsy was demanded . . . Joan . . ."*

"Isn't that horrible about Mayor Darold Mannington, honey?" Malanna said, as she stooped down on her knees and cut the torn pants leg off with scissors then inspected the leg. Bodyslick sat coolly on the corner of the bed.

"Malanna . . . easy, baby," he moaned as she applied alcohol to the large open gash. His attention again shifted to the news on the holoset:

> *"A 6-year-old Chicago girl, Mary Sullivan, who would had died yesterday due to the lack of a donor liver, is now recovering from seven-hours of transplant surgery today, after receiving an anonymous donor liver. The liver arrived at the emergency room early this morning in an electro igloo cooler. A large yellow ribbon was tied on the cooler with a get well card attached that read: To Mary Sullivan from a friend . . ."*

"Bodyslick," Malanna said anxiously, "did you have anything to . . . ?"

"Shush . . . I've got to hear the rest of this."

> ... *"I'm Mrs. Sullivan, Mary's mother, and I just*
> *want to thank you from the very depth," she started*
> *to cry, "of my heart. Not just me but my husband,*
> *sons, and daughters. We don't know who you are,*
> *but thank you ... for saving little Mary's life. Our*
> *daughter will now live a normal life thanks to you.*
> *May God bless you."*

Bodyslick proudly smiled. He had saved a child's life. She had received the healthy liver from his donor organ storage facility in Robbins, Illinois. At least, even in a business that made its profits off grief, he was supplying a vital service. A vital need. He smiled again as he gazed at the Irish family as they sat next to the bed of a giggling healthy Mary.

"Honey, that was so sweet of you," Malanna said almost tearfully.

"Thanks, baby ... I just wonder if anyone besides you and me will ever really remember the good I've done."

"I'll always remember, honey. I'll always realize the good you have done, and so will God. Bodyslick, good is always remembered. Why, that's how legends and heroes are made," she said, while kissing him on his forehead.

"Thanks, Malanna ... I really needed to hear you say that."

"Bodyslick, your only problem is you're helping other people but tearing up your own body. You're just fortunate it wasn't a laser pellet that got you. It looks as if you fell and hit your leg on a real sharp object. You need sutures. I need to get you to a doctor."

"No, Malanna ... just do the best you can ... I just need some rest, okay?"

"All right, this is going to sting as I wrap it up. Finished." Malanna rose up, slightly dizzy from bending her knees so long. As she stood up her navel was directly in front of his lips. She looked down at him as he gazed up at her large voluptuous breasts. She placed her hands on his shoulders and gently pushed him back on the bed. She pressed her soft ebony cheeks against his mouth. He clicked off the holoset. He kissed her. Again and again.

He peered at her fearful feline eyes and said, "Listen, Malanna, I want to stay with you a couple of days until things cool down. I can't stay at my place until I figure out what the hell is going on. I can't afford the risk right now. I . . ."

"Sure, baby . . . but don't you realize there's more to life than money and power? Bodyslick, sweetheart, don't you realize I love you?" She straddled him and pulled his head against her stomach. "Bodyslick, what will your baby do if you get hurt . . . huh?"

He nervously pondered Toejoe Wilson's next move.

The phone rang. Malanna hurriedly picked it up and gave it to Bodyslick. "It's Shondell, honey."

"Bodyslick, they took out Bubba, man . . . you know we got to get some revenge. I been trying to contact you all day. You got your watch activated?"

"Yeah, but I'm having problems with the audio switch. Look, I'm taking care of all the arrangements with Bubba's next of kin. I want you to contact Snow and Geronimo for a meeting at the Chicago City Gym tomorrow at about six o'clock. That way we can get in a little boxing and get our strategy together for dealing with this war we are about to engage in. Leave your phone on because I might need some help tonight."

"Will do. Did you say war?" Shondell said incredulously.

"I believe"—Bodyslick flinched as Malanna started licking his navel—"that Toejoe has hooked up with the mob to try to muscle us out of business . . . you know what um sayin'?"

"I'll be there at six, and I'll tell Geronimo and Snow when I see them tonight. You might need some firepower! Damn, every time I think of what they did to Bubba, I go crazy. All right, I'll see you at the gym at six. Watch yo' back, man."

Malanna kissed him on the forehead. He smiled. He looked at her body in the mirror. He saw a tall, healthy, girlish body of a twenty year old. He saw a dark ebony woman with long flowing Indian-like hair implanted on a brickhouse frame. He pulled her soft naked body on top of him. He placed his hand between her legs and brushed his knuckles softly against her vulva. She smiled. She sighed. She moaned. She frantically unzipped his pants pulling his ramrod out. She unbuttoned his shirt, and helped him pull it off. She started to unsnap his special watch. He stopped her. She pulled down his pants carefully, avoiding the cut. His drawers. She quickly pulled off his socks. He was nude, naked; she smiled. He lasciviously smacked his lips. The taste of bile came into his mouth. The bed sheet had a stain on it. He wondered if it was his stain. The bed started to sag with their weight. A film of sweat glistened on her body like one of Rueben's voluptuous maidens. Her dark eyes became hazy and bulbous.

"I am yours forever and ever, now love me, Bodyslick. Love me like I remember. It's been so long!" she said sensuously as she took him in her mouth.

His pelvis churned. His rod became a gyrating piston in her mouth. He panted. He sweats. He cried out in delirium.

"Ummmmm . . . commmin'!" His vision fogged. He farted.

Her eyelids fluttered. His seed burst forth in a torrential flow. She sucked. He gasped. She sucked. He panted. She sucked. He sighed.

He bellowed out, "Malanna, you're so good tah meee!"

He pulled his dripping rod out of her mouth and listened to her lips as they smacked at the void.

"Turn back over, baby!" He quickly mounted her. He thrust his rod into her hard and sensuously. Her fat ass became hot against his fingertips. She screamed deliriously.

"Ohhhh, that's so . . . so . . . good!"

As I made love to Malanna doggystyle I started to see and smell grotesque images of Doctor Weiner fiendishly pointing at four female torsos on the autopsy table. Probably pointing the same way the Jivaro people of Ecuador did as they gave the Spanish traders shrunken heads as gifts.

A rotating ceiling fan cast dark shadows on the putrid flesh of black, white, Spanish and Asian women butchering bodies.

"The breasts," he grabbed the large breast of the black woman and squeezed it lustfully, "vaginas—the uterus and Fallopian tubes already are being used for a womb transplant. All the remaining organs are in excellent condition. Tragically, the young college bound women were killed in a car accident traveling to school."

Dr. Weiner smiled morbidly as he poked and wiggled his finger inside the vagina orifice of the white girl probing inside as if it was a Thanksgiving turkey.

"This one should fetch a great market price—just look at how firm," he spreaded them with his fingers, "the *Labia majora* is."

I couldn't shake those images as I gazed down at Malanna's glistening body as I made love to her. Suddenly, my mind started to play tricks on me. She became the black torso. I felt unclean. Vile. Nauseous. I thought about the bodies of all the women I love—were their torsos just commodities also? Were the young women torsos any different than human heads being sought after trophies by New Guinea tribesmen? Has global capitalism turned human bodies into commodities? Under the guise of "a gift of Life"? Are human body parts any different than shrunken heads? Hell *muthafuckin'* NO!

He quickly disengaged. Angrily shouting.

"The stench! Sometimes the stench of death clings on me!" Thoughts of vaginas floating in liquid nitrogen containers waiting to be shipped to a gynecology seminar danced across his mind. Sometimes the odor of organ-rot seemed to sweat from his pores.

"Did you say stench of death?" Malanna asked with disbelief from her doggy position.

Ziiinnng . . . zinnng! The doorbell rang.

She quickly leaped from the bed and reached for her robe then dashed down the stairs inwardly mad because the interruption had stopped her orgasm. Bodyslick mumbled to himself as he started drying himself off. Face covered with chagrin, he thought, *Forget about power and money, and maybe that stench will disappear.*

Suddenly, Malanna screamed with agonizing fear. "Run, Bodyslick, run!"

He quickly put on his clothes, grabbed his laser pistol out of his shoulder holster and locked the door. He dashed over to the bed and beat the pillows into a human shape, covered them up with a blanket, and jumped into the closet. Malanna had shown him a long time ago his escape route for a situation like this: inside the closet was a shelf that she kept her church hats on. Three feet above the shelf was a trap door. All Bodyslick had to do was climb up to the shelf and use his head to bump the trap door open leading to the attic and roof.

But he would wait on the shelf with his .45-caliber laser pistol cocked till the time was ripe to save his beloved Malanna. He knew it would only be minutes before the assassins burst through the door looking for him.

He could hear her tearful scream downstairs as the clap of a hand slapped her face.

"Sammy, hold her down here while me and Pumpkin check upstairs," Toejoe snapped.

Bodyslick listened as the clatter of their shoes thumped on the hardwood stairs. The bedroom doorknob slowly turned. He had turned off the lights so the shape they saw in bed would suggest that it was him.

There were a few seconds of silence.

Then there was the menacing *hissssing* sound of laser pistols with silencers, spewing white and blue heat, crisscrossing the bed like a laser show.

Then there was silence. A flashlight cut across the scorched bed and pillows.

"Is he dead, Toejoe?" Pumpkin asked.

"He escaped! Let's get outta here!"

Bodyslick watched them as they ran back down the stairs. Then he heard the soul-wrenching cry of Malanna again.

"Malcolm, help me! Don't let them . . . them . . . take me!"

It was time to make a move, Bodyslick thought, a death move:

I was weaned off the tit of a wild boar, I cut my
teeth on a Colt .45.
I can be mean without even trying. I'm a bad
muthafucka, and I don't mind dying!

He recited it to himself as he climbed through the trap door to the attic. Crouching down, avoiding the rafters, he raced to the window that he would open and climb onto the roof. As he poked his head through the attic window, gazing at the shingled roof, his body trembled with fear as he heard the *whir* of an electro car's ignition; then the *whiz* of the engine as the powerful voltaic batteries triggered the motor.

He crept along the rooftop while peering down at Toejoe, Pumpkin, and Sammy, a black hoodlum. Lurking out the right side of his peripheral vision he saw shadowy movement. Human. White. Hiding in some shrubbery next to a junk car. He squinted in disbelief as he saw a lone white man crouching down. Italian? Was it Snow? Or a mob boy? He hid in the shadows, but his white skin stood out like an addict in a poppy field. It was blurred, but Bodyslick watched with amazement as the white man stooped down trying to avoid contact with Toejoe, Pumpkin, and the lackey. Was he a lone assassin sent by the mob to kill him?

Toejoe walked behind Pumpkin, while the hoodlum pushed a defiant Malanna toward the car. It was now or never, he thought. He crawled through the attic window and started scooting on the slippery roof, using broken shingles as leverage until he could get to the chimney that he would use as a shield. He clicked his .45-caliber laser pistol on automatic. He had only one nine-round magazine left. Each detonation had to count. He quickly grabbed his regular Colt .45-caliber out of his ankle holster. Only six rounds. He farted. Quietly.

Bodyslick could feel the adrenaline coursing through his blood. His lips became desert-dry. His cold, grey, wolf eyes sharpened on the predators down below. It was good no man could gaze into his icy soul and see the naked savagery and abominable hate he felt.

His fingers nestled on the icy cold triggers of both weapons as he watched his precious Malanna kick, twist, and scream in cold defiance.

"Let her go! Now! Or each one of you punks are goin' to get a bullet with your name on it shot into your rotten hearts!"

Toejoe and his lackeys looked around nervously, wondering where the disembodied voice came from. The white man saw him, and for a microsecond they gazed at each other eye to eye. Cold rage heaved through every atom of Bodyslick's being. The white man's eyes told him he was there to kill him. He moved back into the shadow. A dog barked from a nearby yard. Then another. It was a full moon. The stars were twinkling overhead. The lunatics were out. The goon still wrestled with Malanna while trying to open the car door. It was now or never.

Bammmmmm! He shot the short, black hoodlum, Sammy, in the face as he opened the driver's door. Brain matter and blood splattered on the windshield. His head had exploded into a bloody fire of laser heat. Toejoe ran to the dead man and tossed his limp body on the ground.

Pumpkin started firing an M-16 at the rooftop with one hand, as he pushed Malanna into the backseat. Bodyslick squinted his eyes as the bullets hit the roof lifting up the shingles. He could feel the hot heat, as the bullets blasted the chimney bricks. He shielded his eyes from the dust.

He fired as Toejoe leaped into the driver's seat. A distant siren meant the police were on their way. Lights clicked on in the many neighborhood tenements. A cacophony of fearful voices echoed.

Suddenly, there were bullets ripping at the chimney from the opposite direction. The direction of the white man. Bodyslick watched the mobster tensely, as he ran toward the two-flat. He was moving closer. Bodyslick fired and fired.

Then he tossed the .45 away because he was out of ammo. Luck was running out for him. Bodyslick shot bursts of laser heat at the white assassin, as he fired at him with his semi-automatic. Relentlessly. He watched helplessly, impotently, as Toejoe and Pumpkin wrestled Malanna into the backseat of the car and got in. He fired again at the white assassin, making him duck for cover in a nearby junked car. The police siren became louder. Closer. As Toejoe swerved the car onto the vacant street, Bodyslick desperately leaped from the two-story building, rolling with the impact of the fall to minimize the injury to his gashed leg. He ran like a wounded beast after the car. He glanced back over his shoulder to see if the white gangster was following him. He was. Bodyslick felt the hot whoosh of laser pellets as the assassin followed him. He quickly dived into some shrubs.

Bammmm! He felt the heat of the red pellets as they zoomed past him. He stood up again. He patted his pants pocket for his other magazine. Dammit, he had dropped it! His leg was throbbing with pain. He hopped on one leg. He fell down. He thought of his beloved Malanna, now wearing only her robe and nightgown, with that hideously smiling Toejoe Wilson inside the car. He stood up again. He ran with all the energy he could muster. He fired and fired, until the car vanished. He prayed that Malanna would stay alive. He stopped, as pain tore through his lungs. The assassin was near. Deathly near.

He ducked into a nearby alley and squatted behind an old electro car silently in darkness. He could hear the *thump* of his assassin's shoes. His footsteps perforated the silence. They stopped. He held his breath. Terror raced through him as if he was a junkie who forgot his shooter. He could see the silhouette of the man as his back faced him. He seemed confused in the thick darkness, like a bee buzzing around a plastic flower. When a cat suddenly leaped from underneath the car with a fiendish screech, the man turned and fired nervously. His face was lit by a nearby window light. Its rays danced on his blank face as he searched blindly for his prey.

Thoughts were popping in Bodyslick's mind like a rag snapping on a clothesline: *Should he make a move? A death move toward the assassin and shoot him with his .45? Or should he wait, like a lion, for his prey's most vulnerable moment and only injure him? Then attempt to get some information on this nightmare.* He was conscious of the terror that lurked within. The terror of error. The terror of missing his prey and getting killed in the process. The haunting presence of death blanketed his being. The assassin turned around again with his back toward Bodyslick. Bodyslick sized him up. They were almost equal in height and weight. The assassin turned around. And around again.

Finally, Bodyslick saw his full face. It was pale pink. He was a white man. His thick raven black hair, his dark eyes hooded by bushy black eyebrows, signaled Italian ancestry. An Italian? Questions bounced in his skull. Would Dr. Weiner pay to have him executed? Wasn't that an Italian voice he'd heard on the vidphone talking for TWOC? He thought it was unlikely the doctor would want him dead—they made too much money together. His blood froze as the man started to crouch and walk around the car. It was unreasonably windy and cool. A pale moon glowed death gray rays.

Bodyslick suppressed the nervous grating of his teeth as the assassin slowly neared him. Instantly, the warrior within him awoke from a dormant sleep with murderous rage. He grabbed a nearby brick, and with all the energy he could unleash, he whacked him in the kneecap. When the assassin heard his patella crack, he cried out with horrific pain and dropped forward. Bodyslick stood and smiled as Snow and Geronimo walked toward him. The would-be assassin lay curled up like a fetus. Snow snatched his .45 out of his inside pocket, bent down, and aimed the muzzle with its perforated silencer between the assassin's eyes.

"How's your knee, bitch!" Snow snorted.

"*Caccati in mano e prenditi a schiaff!* (take a shit on your hands and hit yourself)," the hitman yelled then spit in Snow's face.

Snow tightened his finger around the cold trigger and slapped him in the face with the gun. His head snapped back on the ground, and he shut up.

"*Ciucciaml il crazzo!* (suck my dick)," Snow screamed as he started to unzip his pants, pointing the .45 between the man's eyes.

"Look, you don't have to die now," Bodyslick said, pushing Snow back.

"*Stronzata!* (bullshit), this punk fucking spit on me!"

"Slow down, Snow, maybe he wants to live. Who sent you, man?"

Snow jammed the .45 into the man's balls. "Yeah, he gonna live, but he's gonna squat like a *bagaseia* (bitch) when he takes a piss!"

"*Stronzo di merda!* (fucking bastard), white trash nigga lovin' *finocchio* (faggot)! If I could, I'd cut your balls off and stuff 'em down your moolie girlfriend's throat!"

"That hurt you, guinea bitch?" Snow snarled at the man as he rammed the muzzle harder into his balls. Snow turned his head as the assassin spit at his face. He tightened his finger around the cold trigger.

"Look, you don't have to die now . . . Are you with the mob?"

"Nigger, if I could I'd cut your fuckin' balls off and stick 'em down your stinking throat!"

Snow reacted before he was conscious of it. He started to pull the trigger.

"Snow!" Bodyslick hollered. "You know how much his organs are worth, fuckhead? Geronimo, take care of him!" He walked over to the assassin, quickly grabbed his head and twisted it, snapping his neck instantly. The body shook in convulsions for a moment. One eye stared open, frozen, reflecting the sodium-illuminated alley.

Geronimo stooped down and searched the man's pockets. The smell of his feces seeped into their nostrils. Bodyslick watched him bring out a wallet, his rental car keys, a 9 mm Beretta and a claim check for Midway Airport. He searched his wallet. His New York driver's license proved what he had suspected all along. The Mob. The *Mafioso*. His name was Antonio Villichi.

"A mob boy, huh?" Snow said, not surprised.

"Yeah, looks like the mob wants me dead, along with a whole bunch of other goons. They imported a hitman to take me out. But it just don't add up. Why would they send a white assassin to kill me? Are they that stupid, or was he really after Malanna?"

"He probably was after Malanna then got sidetracked when Toejoe showed up. Look how he's dressed. Like a fuckin' insurance salesman!" Snow said sarcastically.

"Chicago is my turf," Bodyslick said arrogantly. "Blood is going to flow like Lake Michigan before we give it up. Toejoe is just a lackey, a frontman for their organization. That's where you come in, Snow."

"I already know where you coming from," Snow said, as he held the dead man's Beretta up in the air against a full moon's light.

"What?" Bodyslick asked eagerly.

"You want me to infiltrate the mob, right?"

"Yeah, we need you inside to kill them from the outside, Snow. We will get into the details later."

"His 9 millimeter is a work of art," Snow said gleefully. "All right, how you want me to infiltrate these punks?" He took off the dead man's expensive Zotex watch.

"Like I said, we'll discuss details tomorrow at the Chicago City Gym—about noon. Who's driving?"

"I'm driving!" Geronimo said while staring down at the broken neck of the dead man.

"You can drop me off at my apartment."

"Let's get out of here. The cops are still searching Malanna's house," Snow said impatiently.

Bodyslick suddenly turned around and walked back over to the dead man.

"I thought we were leaving, man?"

"This won't take long, Snow. Just be cool."

As he neared the body, he pulled out a flat black aerosol can from his coat pocket. He stooped down to the head of the dead man then sprayed gray spider-like foam from the man's head to his waist. The spray quickly formed a cocoon, covering the corpse's head and thorax then disappeared. He then stuck a small black wafer-thin card inside the man's belt.

Bodyslick stood up and clicked on his phone as he walked back toward Snow and Geronimo.

"Shondell?"

"What's up?"

"I need you to get the portable cryonic cooler, the surgi-set, and perfusion fluids to keep the organs fresh. I just sprayed the body with a reanimate cryonic spray. That should hold off decomposition for a minimum of four hours. I need you to get over here as quick as you can."

"You got the GPS chip on the body, right?" Shondell asked.

"Yeah."

"One second," Shondell said, "the GPS locator has just pinpointed the body location on my watch at 41° 48N 87° 36W."

"Good, Shondell, call me once you've taken the organs to my storage facility in Robbins. We only want the major ones, okay?"

"I'm on my way now!"

"Shondell?" Snow clicked on his three way line.

"What?"

"Check the dead man's feet for excess skin!"

"Fuck you! You gonna have to pay me a lot more dollars for rubbing dead folks' feet!" Shondell said playfully. "Okay, Bodyslick, I'll give you the specs on the organs tomorrow at the gym." He laughed then said, "I almost forgot . . . and the feet!" *Click*.

"All right, let's get out of here. You realize how much money we can harvest from that guy's organs?"

"If Slovik's drunk ass doesn't mislabel them!"

"Geronimo's right, you need to fire that alcoholic quick! You've got too much money invested out in Robbins!"

"I can't get my mind off my baby, Malanna. If them punks harm her it's gonna be a massacre. I'm going to scorch this city looking for whoever harms her!"

"They're only using her as a hostage, Bodyslick," Snow said confidently, while patting him on the back. "They're using her to gain leverage. She is more useful to them alive than dead."

"My lectro is parked down the street," Geronimo said.

Chapter 14

Bodyslick wondered if anyone would recognize him in his *coolie* disguise as he slowly climbed the stairs to the second floor of the Chicago City Gym. He inhaled deeply the smell of disinfectant, liniment, and stale cigar smoke. As he stood at the entrance of the gym, he gazed at the two small rings, each about fourteen feet square, which were the centerpieces of the place. He smiled as he thought about the many years he had spent sparring in those rings.

It was a small gym with old, worn, and beaten equipment like the heavy punching bags that dangled from squeaking chains. There were speedballs at the opposite end of the gym. The wooden floor was painted green for money and was full of scuff marks from the thousands of fighters that had skipped rope on its floors. Eight yellowish fluorescent lights beamed down on the rings giving them a spectator quality. The gray painted walls of the gym were peeling. Old torn posters of Muhammad Ali, Mike Tyson, Evander Holyfield and Riddick Bowe covered the tattered walls.

"What do you want here, old Chinaman?" Gerry Collosi barked.

"It's me, Gerry, Malcolm," Bodyslick said, as he pulled off the dermo-mask.

"For chrissakes . . . it looks so real. I mean it's unbelievable."

"Feel it, Gerry." Bodyslick gave him the mask.

"It feels like real human skin," Gerry said with astonishment.

"That's because it's plantopermis, which is human skin that is grown by genetically tailored plants."

"You mean plants with human fuckin' skin?"

"That's right, Gerry."

Disgusted, Gerry gave him back the mask. "Malcom you have always been a little weird, but don't you think you takin' this organ business a little too far?"

Bodyslick looped an arm around Gerry's shoulders.

"How you been, Gerry? How is the boxin' business treatin' ya?"

"Not bad, but the kids that come in here now just don't believe in the system like they use tah. They have turned into cynics. It's getting harder and harder to reach 'em, Malcolm."

Bodyslick smiled because here he could be himself. Here he was not Bodyslick, the organ hustler, but just another guy in the gym to work out. Of course everyone knew how he made his living. Why, he had even given Gerry money to help with his "Youth Boxing Program."

"Well, anything I can do to help, Gerry. Just let me know!"

Gerry grabbed him and hugged him tightly.

"You've practically subsidized this place, Malcolm, already . . . But I'll always keep that in mind," Gerry said, as he slapped him on the back.

"By the way, Malcolm. Shondell, Snow, and Geronimo told me to tell you if you get here first to let you know they're on the way . . . look, if you guys want to use my office to talk business or somethin' jes lemme know, awright, Malcolm? Jesus, that disguise musta' cost you an arm and ah leg . . . ha . . . ha. That was a joke . . ."

"Yeah, real funny, Gerry."

"Lighten up, Malcolm. Always remember, son, this is home. It's not us that's fucked up . . . it's the world."

Gerry Collosi was a sixty-year-old Irish Catholic who had known him since Bodyslick was in grammar school and his family had moved to the Cabrini Green housing project. Bodyslick got involved in the gym early in life because minors with felony records had to serve time at the gym for community service work. Gerry had always felt that Bodyslick was special because he had a jab and a right hook faster than a blink. He felt sad when he thought about the number of brilliant kids who had come through those doors with hopes and dreams of being somebody who ended up dead over nonsense like the color of a hat, gym shoes, jackets, gang signals, and drugs. Gerry smiled at Bodyslick as he climbed the stairs because there still was a chance that he might go legit and leave that body hustling alone.

The *whappity-whappity* echo of the speedball as Bodyslick punched it sounded good to him. *Whappity . . . whappity . . . whap . . . whap . . . whappity . . .* He thought about his beloved Malanna. Was she still alive? Had Toejoe and his goons raped and tortured her? And why would the mob send a dago hitman into his hood to kill him? He hit the speedball even harder as he thought about Bubba's heart.

Bodyslick listened to the trainers as they barked their commands.

> *"Don't forget your uppercut . . ."*
> *"Make openings from yo' blows . . ."*
> *"Use the ring to your advantage . . ."*
> *"Goddammit, while you were sucking your mama's tits and wearing pampers I was fighting terrorists in Somalia . . ."*
> *"Now listen to me . . ."*

Bodyslick moved from the speedbag and put on his holo-head gear, touched a button near the visors then climbed into the ring. In thirty seconds, he began to dance around, ducking while bobbing and weaving his head as three dimensional images: Ali, Frazier, Louis, and Tyson threw seemingly real upper-cuts, right and left jabs that *whizzed* through the air.

"You think you tough, slick!" Someone tapped him on the shoulder and turned off his holo-head gear. "'Cause yo' sister show is a soft bitch . . ."

Bodyslick pivoted around while cocking for a right jab. He fired. Geronimo smiled as he offered his head as a target. A group of old black and white men started to gather around the ring ropes—anticipating a little excitement.

"Don't ferget ya left, boy!" one of them shouted with a to-bacco stained grin.

Geronimo quickly fired rapid, stinging body blows as Body-slick let down his guard for a moment to gaze at the ringside. Geronimo then started to pound Bodyslick with hard punches to the head and body.

"Come on Slick. You gotta concentrate, block out every-thing else, remember you said we were preparing for war!"

Shondell's bright, shovel-encrusted gold teeth gleamed while he leaned on the ropes looking at Bodyslick and Geronimo as they exchanged punishing blows.

"Geronimo, use your uppercut, he's wide open, man!"

Geronimo was part Apache and part black. People on the street gave him the moniker Geronimo because in his youth, before a fight, he would put war paint on his face. Bodyslick realized early in life that you can't go alone. You had to trust someone. Since grammar school those someones were Geron-imo, Snow, and Shondell.

Bodyslick winced as Geronimo shot stinging left and right jabs into his stomach then threw an uppercut that cocked back his head. Bodyslick dizzily grabbed him tightly in a clutch as he tried to regain his composure.

"Don't let up, G-man," Shondell hollered from the ringside. "Don't let up!" *Whack!* Stunned from a sharp uppercut, Geronimo lowered his guard. Bodyslick, sensing his weakness, backed him into the corner ropes. He quickly fired a flurry of hammer-hard body blows to his chest, arms, and ribs. All were pounded with unrelenting power.

"*No mas*!" Geronimo shouted, as he struggled to take cover from the ferocious blows.

The two clinched and hugged then climbed out the ring exhausted. A geyser of sweat drenched their bodies.

"Let's . . . Let's . . ." Bodyslick wheezed while struggling to catch his breath. "We can use Gerr . . . ry's office to talk."

They walked down the long hallway toward his office quietly, as sweat from their bodies pelted the tile floor.

"I thought Geronimo had you for a minute, Slick. I swear I did," Shondell said, as he walked behind them taunting Bodyslick.

"You doin' all that talkin' Shondell. When you gonna get in the ring, huh?" Bodyslick snapped.

"I'm a player not a fighter, besides, my hos would kill you if you messed up this pretty face."

They all laughed as they stepped into his office, and Shondell closed the door.

Bodyslick sat on Gerry's desk while wiping the sweat off his face. Geronimo and Shondell sat down in portable metal chairs. Gerry's office was small and sparse; a big metal desk with an old phone on it dominated the room. There was no window. On the walls were various photos of Gerry with celebrities, ex-champs and even one of him hugging Bodyslick.

"And where in the hell is Snow? Anybody know? Dammit, he would be late for his own funeral," Bodyslick barked.

"Bodyslick, Snow is really getting big on the concert scene. His rap style is catching on like fire. Why I heard through the grapevine he has been offered a lucrative recording contract. But he said he would show, and his word is gold," Geronimo said confidently.

"Shondell, how's business on the East Side since Bubba's murder?"

While Geronimo was the muscle of the outfit, Shondell was

the type of guy that, if you listened to him for just one hour, you would believe anything he said. He was a master con man, pimp, and hustler. He sat in his chair in his green plastic suit and alligator shoes. His tiny diamond earring reflected the light from the ceiling of the room. When he opened his mouth to speak all of his teeth covered with 14K gold would make a cat burglar nervous. He was medium height, banana peel yellow in color, and his hair was sandy brown. He sat there like he was too cool to move.

"Business is sparse. Most of the East Side organ business is based on retrieving healthy organs from the young, who die from lethal doses of galactic opiates, somellow or electrode-induced stimulants. I'm averaging about ten deaths a month with salvageable organ parts. So far there have been no reports of Toejoe and the mob from my people on the streets."

Bodyslick nodded his head as Shondell finished.

"What about the West Side, Geronimo?"

"Now that our organ storage facility is in full operation in Robbins, we're making more money. Even though Slovik is an alcoholic, we still have had a good year. Before I had to sell the organs in twelve hours—now we don't have the problem of preservation and transportation. Now we have long term maintenance of organs. And with the high homicide deaths on the West Side, we should make a killin' this year . . . if just a small percentage of the organs are healthy."

"Anything else, Geronimo?"

"Yeah, I almost forgot to tell you that Yuripov Vassokef, the Russian mob boss called. Says he needs a kidney for his wife like yesterday."

"How much is he willing to spend?" Bodyslick asked, as he tapped his finger on the metal desk.

"I told him one hundred thousand, but . . ."

"But what?" Bodyslick asked impatiently.

"Yuripov says he has some info from his old FSB comrades that is worth a free kidney."

"You tell Mr. ex-FSB that I need one hundred thousand dollars if he wants a kidney!"

"You can tell him . . . he's going to call you tonight." Geronimo glanced at his watch. "It's 9:30 now, I told him to call you at 10:00."

"What's his wife's blood type?"

"O positive," Geronimo said confidently.

"We got one last night!" yelled Shondell gleefully. "Mr. FSB's wife is going to get an Italian hitman's kidney."

"Good work, Geronimo and Shondell. Now, listen to me closely." Bodyslick stood up and put back on his Chinese dermo-mask.

"What's up . . . brothers? You realize you are lookin' at a star? A white shining muthafuckin' star!" Snow said, while slapping Bodyslick, Geronimo, and Shondell's hands in high fives. "Now Slovik is messing up big time at the warehouse." He pointed toward Geronimo who nodded his head in agreement. "I say we take care of him because he has too much info on us and replace him with Silas," Snow said, as he sat down in a nearby chair.

"I agree. I want you and Geronimo to handle that as soon as you can," Bodyslick replied. "I'll call Silas to get an inventory of the warehouse."

"It's a done deal!" Snow said.

"Things are hot right now. We got the mob, their lackey Toejoe, and his boys—all tryin' to take our business in Chicago. You know that last night they kidnapped Malanna and almost killed me." He wiped sweat from his brow. "We were all in kindergarten together," Bodyslick moaned.

"They dead men!" Shondell said as he rose up defiantly out of his chair.

"They all gonna die!" Geronimo shouted.

Bodyslick slammed his fist onto the desk with rage. "If she is dead or not I don't know. I hope, for their sakes, they just want to see if she has any info about us!"

"Did you take any of them punks out?" Geronimo asked in bewilderment.

"Sammy is dead. I got him with a laser burst to the face. I could have taken out Toejoe and Pumpkin, but . . ." He angrily paced the floor.

"But what?" Shondell asked.

"But I had to also deal with a Mafia assassin. Man, I was being blasted from every conceivable direction just before you guys showed up!"

"You mean the mob sent a white man to get you in Malanna's hood? That just don't make sense!" Shondell said incredulously.

"We got the bitch though. He won't be eatin' any pasta and wine where his punk ass is!" Snow said venomously.

"You check out his ID?" Shondell asked.

"Yeah, he was from New York, one of Vinnie's hitmen!"

"See, fellas," Snow said, smiling wildly, "that's where my white Irish ass comes in. I can infiltrate their circle. Then we can kill them from the inside out!"

"But right now we got to concentrate on finding Malanna. And when you and Geronimo get a chance, get rid of Slovik. After that Snow is going to join the mob." Bodyslick laughed.

"If there's anybody that knows where Toejoe is at, it's that faggot-flamer Tootie Baker. He mixes up their somellow for them!" Shondell said angrily.

"All right, let's make his drug house our first stop. Let's move!" Bodyslick ordered. The minute Bodyslick put his hand on the gear shift to back out of the parking lot of the gym, his vidphone screen clicked on.

Geronimo and Shondell waited behind him to make a right taking the Stoney Island artery to Tootie Baker's apartment on East Colfax. Bodyslick and Snow watched patiently as the LCD began blinking. Then it slowly crystallized into the pale peasant face, with a square jaw, hazel Asian eyes, and silver-grey hair of Yuripov Vassokef, the Russian mob boss.

"Snow, activate the scrambler!" He pressed a tiny orange button on the console which would eliminate retrieval of the communication.

"I need the kidney," a thick Russian accented voice said piteously. "My wife won't live another twenty-four hours without it!"

"We have the kidney. The issue is *do you* have the hundred grand?"

"Yes, I have it. Just give me a time and delivery location to pick it up!"

"I'll call you back tonight. Now what's this info you have for me?"

Snow lit up a Martianzeeg, and the thick green fumes engulfed the car. Both of them started wheezing and coughing uncontrollably.

"Dammit, Snow, will you put that shit out? Don't smoke that crap in here! You can't get that alien stench out of the car!"

Snow angrily tossed the joint out the window.

"The info I have is from a KGB friend of mine who was a chief of security during the operation in Saratov."

"Saratov?" Bodyslick asked.

"They had to pick a hidden place in Russia with a good technological infrastructure and air transportation. Too risky to do it in the US."

"They?" Snow yelled, "Will you get to the fuckin' point? Didn't you say your wife was dying?" Snow was frustrated because he couldn't smoke his Martianzeeg.

Yuripov cleared his throat and continued. "An American neurosurgeon has performed a successful head transplant in Russia, without even our government being aware of it. He was sneaked in, in complete secrecy with the help of rogue FSB agents who, unlike the old KGB, will do anything for good old American money. You see, a rich quadriplegic American CEO paid a total of $5 million for it."

"You're wastin' our time!" Snow bellowed out. "Doctors been trying to do that for years, but they can't sew the head back to the spine!"

Bodyslick made a swift left turn onto Colfax.

"The point here," Yuripov continued with irritation, "is that he has created a successful way to reconnect the head to the spine. In other words, a body transplant would eliminate the need for separate organ transplants. Your business will eventually crash!"

"Why don't you get your dying wife one then?" snapped Snow.

"Be realistic . . . and watch your smartass mouth, lackey, for when I was FSB warden at Lubyanka I tortured, executed, and cut the tongues out of dissidents who even frowned at me! There are still tortured inmates in the 'cellar' or basement of the new high-tech Lubyanka Prison Complex in Moscow that shit and piss on themselves when they hear my name. Bodyslick, we are talking hours before my wife dies. We got a deal?"

There was interest in the tone of Bodyslick's voice now. "Yeah, he's got a point, Snow. Why keep fixin' a used car when you can trade it in and get a better one?"

"Too bad the doctor doesn't realize that there are fatal consequences for messin' with our business!" Snow said viciously.

"You must have a solution, eh?" Yuripov asked slyly, revealing his capped teeth.

"Is the doctor still in Russia?" Bodyslick asked impatiently.

"For more information I need my fifty percent discount."

"All right . . . all right, go on!"

"His name is Dr. Jonathan Graham. He is a neurosurgeon and professor at the University of Chicago. You're in luck because he even lives in the Hyde Park neighborhood. I have his address. You ready?"

"Go on!"

"He lives at 5234 South Blackstone. It is a two-story, Victorian, gray stone. Stays there with his wife. No pets. Children are grown. He will be giving a lecture at the University of

Chicago this Friday at 8:00 p.m. Now, what time can I pick up the kidney?" he asked.

"I'll call you tonight. Just sit tight and have the $50,000 cash when I call you." The screen flickered off.

"Snow," Bodyslick said, as they parked in front of Tootie Baker's building. "Make sure the doctor doesn't make any more body transplants!"

"No problem. Geronimo and me will give the doctor a house call."

Bodyslick, Snow, and Geronimo listened as Shondell beamed the white heat of the torch at the lock. They burst through the door and walked into a somellow house; a house where addicts of all types could inhale, ingest, shoot, or toot any drug imaginable for a cover charge. Bodyslick glanced over the dark room looking, searching for a face, a clue, anything that would help him find Malanna.

"All right, everybody get up. Take off yo clothes and stand next to the wall with yo hands behind yo backs. Hurry naw 'cause we ain't got all day!" Geronimo barked, waving the mini-Uzi at the drugged crowd.

"Where's Tootie Baker?" Bodyslick shouted, as he gazed around the pastel red and blue light as the pungent medicinal odor of various drugs wafted past his nose.

"You boys lookin for me?" A jet black, fat, effeminate man with long dreadlocks, long flapping eyelashes, bright pink lipstick, and a lavendar robe on darted his reptile tongue out while smacking his thick lips as he walked out of a small candlelit room.

Bodyslick walked over to him and stuck his .45 laser pistol at his pudgy nose.

"Look *flamer*, I ain't got no time fah games. Now tell me where I can find Toejoe! Now, faggot!"

"My, aren't we rough? I like a rough man," Tootie said, while smacking his lips and rubbing Bodyslick's chest passively.

Bodyslick nodded at Geronimo. He fired the Uzi at the

walls, tables, and ceiling. A table full of drugs ignited into dust.

"That was a thousand dollars worth of drugs," Tootie moaned.

"Where is Toejoe?" Bodyslick demanded.

Bodyslick glanced around the decadent house. Dirty mattresses lay strewn on the filthy floor. Women with uncombed hair and dirty clothes seemed immune to the gunfire as they smoked on glass pipes. The dark room must be like hell Bodyslick thought, as he gazed at the bright red fiery light that pulsed from the hundreds of glass pipes throughout the room being inhaled on by the addicts.

"Look, I ain't got any time to waste with yo punk ass . . . now where is he?" Frustrated, Bodyslick punched him in the stomach.

"Ah right, jest don't hit me!" Tootie wheezed. "Toejoe was here yesstidy, he stocked up on somellow and cocaine. He's probably at his flat on South Ellis."

"All right, punk," Bodyslick said, as he released his grip on Tootie's collar.

"Let's leave," Shondell cracked, as they walked toward the door almost tripping over the stoned bodies as they lay like zombies on the floor.

Chapter 15

Dr. Jonathan Graham woke up as the Hydrostream VIII private jet hit pockets of wind turbulence. He looked out the window at the vast Black Sea as it stretched across the horizon. The jet started to descend and dovetailed into Saratov. He could see the twinkling urban lights of Moscow and the skyscrapers of St. Petersburg igniting the milky black Russian sky. He sat back in his leather seat coolly at latitude 51° 30W, Longitude 45° 30E. He listened to the screech of the landing gear as it unfolded like eagle talons. Ten minutes later the jet's thrust reversers activated, and the jet came to a grinding halt.

After the plane landed, the famous Russian neurosurgeon Dr. Krutosov rushed over and shook Dr. Graham's hand. He was flanked by two huge Russian Air Force generals and two smiling FSB operatives. Dr. Krutosov pointed toward one of the three open-door shuttle buses.

"How was your trip?" Dr. Krutosov asked in a thick Russian accent as he sat down next to Dr. Graham.

"Fine. I slept most of the way. No problems with security, huh?"

"The five million dollars is relatively cheap for the security, the medical facility, and the healthy donor body your American client is buying."

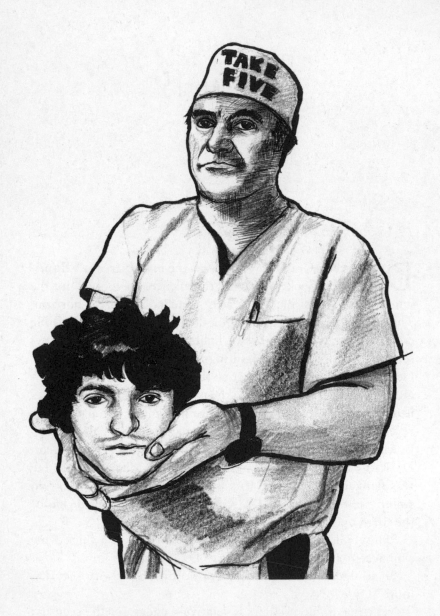

"How old is the donor?"

"Thirty-five years old."

"How did he die?" Dr. Graham asked.

"He was a soldier in the KGB Army, shot in the head in a skirmish with secessionist radicals in Belgorod. He is a perfect brain-dead specimen for a historic operation of this magnitude."

"Historic, it certainly is, Dr. Krutosov. It's definetly not like the primitive monkey head transplants I did years ago."

"The difference, Dr. Graham, is this will be the first body transplant," Dr. Krutosov whispered.

"Without it the forty-year-old corporate CEO, William Gleeves, will die from failing organs like his kidneys, liver, and lungs! He is bankrolling this entire operation and wants his identity to remain secret an entire year until we are absolutely certain the operation is a success."

"How did he sever his spinal cord?" Dr. Krutosov asked curiously.

"A kite surfing accident."

"I remember." Dr. Krutosov coughed and cleared his throat. "Years ago when I did the first head transplant with a dog, we called the dog Frankenhound."

"Frankenhound?" Dr. Graham laughed loudly.

"Yes, because Frankenhound was a dachshund . . . you know, they look like what you Americans call hot dogs?"

"Yes, hot dogs!"

"Anyway, I succeeded, as you did, in transplanting the head, but Frankenhound was paralyzed from the neck down. At that point it was hopeless to connect a severed spinal cord."

"But look at how we have advanced," Dr. Graham said. "Now with embroyonic stem cell scaffolding, we can grow new cells on scar tissue and keloids. That, combined with transplanted motor neurons and nerve growth chemicals, has revolutionized cephalic transplants!"

"You Americans are very clever at creating original innovative ideas, Dr. Graham."

"Thank you, but you Russians were the first in putting Sputnik in orbit, and the first to actually perform a head transplant with a dog!"

The shuttle buses stopped outside a huge hospital complex. A black BMW stretch limousine opened its doors as they quickly alighted from the bus.

"This hospital complex," Dr. Krutosov pointed proudly, "is the best Russian medical science has to offer. The director is Dr. Ivan Kofpovotic, a top FSB organ transplant surgeon, who will assist in the surgery with us. He is fluent in English, French, and Chinese. He also has a doctorate in molecular chemistry. He is a fuckin' genius!" Dr. Krutosov said gleefully. "He was the chief surgeon for Premier Gerbgatrov's wife's kidney transplant. You must remember this whole secret operation has been given the nod of approval from the top of the Russian food chain, because all of us will split the five million dollars."

"But you, Dr. Krutosov, are not totally concerned with the money, are you?"

"No, but you must remember our economy has been hurt by the Chinese-African trade embargo against us because of the massacre in Belgorod where we had to kill fifty thousand radicals to restore order."

"Well, tomorrow is the historic day!" Dr. Graham said.

"Yes, and the limousine will take you to one of our finest hotels to get a night's rest."

Dr. Graham glanced at William Gleeves, the quadraplegic CEO, as his wife pushed him in his wheelchair to a specially equipped van.

"Tomorrow," Dr. Krutosov said, "we will defy God!"

9:00 a.m. Sunday morning, May 4, 2031

Doctor Graham walked into the operating room first. His tech crew of seven years followed behind him: Jack Hilton, the veteran fifty-year-old anesthesiologist; Ruth Sandiago, the meticulous Spanish scrub nurse; Janice Carr, a forty-year-old black circulating nurse; and Troy Smith, his black assistant surgeon. Troy was a thirty-year-old, single Chicago native, and a fellowship winner at the prestigious University of Chicago Hospital kidney transplant department. They all smiled and exchanged greetings with the two Russian surgeons: Dr. Krutosov and Dr. Kofpovotic. They also nodded and smiled at Dr. Graham's crew. The two nurses were visibly shaken as they looked at the faint neon-blue glow of the radioactive dye that was injected into the spinal cord of the donor on the gurney.

"The stem cell derived neurons," Dr. Graham said, "are scaffolding and integrating with the donor's nervous system a lot faster than we expected."

Everyone was glued to the huge electronic microscopic image of neurons on the holo-screen.

"Let's get started," Dr. Graham said, as Nurse Sandiago handed him the gleaming laser scalpel. The red pulsing light of the laser shined on William Gleeve's deathly pale neck.

"Put on my Dave Brubeck 'Take Five' HCD, Miss Carr." The music quickly changed the mood in the room. Everyone seemed calm, relaxed. The jazz had a spiritual quality to it.

"I never operate without listening to Dave Brubeck's jazz, Dr. Krutosov. I'm superstitious. Do you like American jazz?"

"We Russians like Miles Davis and Coltrane, but our favorite is Louis Armstrong. He is a god to us. What a genius, eh?"

"I agree. Turn up the music, Miss Carr. I love that song. 'Take Five' is a classic."

"What's the brain's temperature?" Dr. Graham asked.

"Thirty degrees Celsius."

"We need it lower and faster, Jack."

"Will do!" the anesthesiologist said.

"Regional cerebral flow and neuronal activity slowing down."

"Good. What about his FMRI reading?"

"Blood-oxygen levels good!"

Dr. Graham looked at the OCI monitor. It was scanning the brain with a resolution of 250 nanometers using an Optical Coherence Imaging on lightwaves to show an *in vivo* holoscan of a living brain.

"Another reading, Janice, of brain temperature?"

"Now hovering at twenty-five degrees Celsius."

"Good."

"Now twenty degrees!"

"We need ten to fifteen degrees Celsius, Jack, before I can make my incision!"

"We should be there . . ." Jack counted anxiously to himself, "One, two, three, right now! We are at ten degrees, doctor. You can operate!"

Doctor Graham looked at the CEO's serene face then at the nanoscreen showing brain scan data communicated by nanobots, the size of human blood cells scanning the brain's neural activity with wireless communication.

"Now we can suspend blood circulation to his brain," Dr. Graham said as the nurse gave him the laser scalpel.

The three surgeons watched intensely as the scalpel cut through fat, muscle, arteries, and the spine of the CEO. The suffocating, putrid odor of burning flesh and cauterized blood in the airless room was like being in a Nazi crematorium. There was a suction sound as the head disconnected from the spinal cord.

Dr. Graham looked at a wall clock. "In about fifty minutes we should be able to thaw the brain and attach the head to the donor body." He glanced at the strapping Russian on the gurney. Blond. Blue-eyed. Muscular. He was a perfect specimen like Doctor Krutosov said, yet, Graham wondered, was he a specimen from the old Russian Eugenics program where they established a colony and enforced selective breeding on couples to create a "Super Russian"?

The donor was draped in a blue sheet up to his neck. His face was peaceful. He did not seem dead. His breathing was rhythmic, his heart beat strong. His skin was vibrant and pink. His body warm. He was the living dead.

"Dr. Graham, the cold animative preservation fluids have been pumped into all his major organs," Dr. Krutosov said anxiously as he glanced at the empty bottles hanging from steel stands. "We can now remove the heart-lung machine from the donor. All organs in the donor are 'transplant cooked.' We are now ready to make medical history."

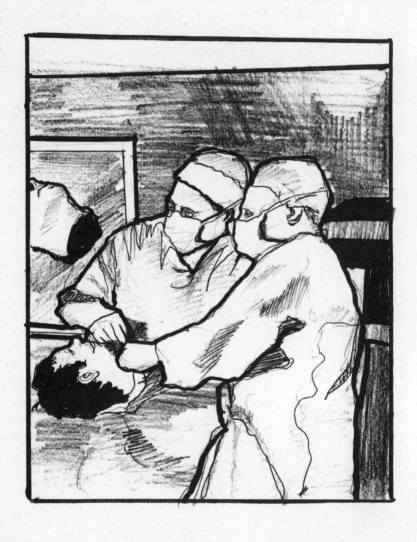

Chapter 16

"The guard shouldn't present any major problem. We might not even have to deal with him," Toejoe said. "What we will do is snatch her immediately after she gets out of her car. If my memory is correct, she should be driving a blue Fiat convertible. I was selling somellow out here only six months ago and saw her, so keep your eye out for that blue Fiat. And remember if we do this accurately, I mean without excessive noise, it will be easy and flawless. You know what I mean?"

"Yeah, but what if something happens? Let's say she screams . . . what then?" Pumpkin said with concern.

"Well, fah God sake don't panic. In the event that she screams we'll still continue with our original plans, because then it will be too late to turn around."

"I brought my piece with me." Pumpkin pulled out a Smith & Wesson .38 Special. "What about you?"

"Hey, guy . . ." Toejoe pulled out a 12-gauge Ithaca stake-out shotgun with a five-round magazine, an ivory white pistol grip, and a short 13.23-inch barrel, which was excellent for concealment under his seat. "And I don't play!" They slapped hands loudly.

"Okay, put on your ski mask!" Toejoe said impatiently.

* * *

Richard Stragenberg was just about finished reading *The Exorcist*. He was sitting on a sofa in the living room of his half-million dollar home. He rubbed his eyes. He was tired. Suddenly every muscle in his body stretched taut, as a woman's agonizing scream sliced the silence of his plush living room. Frightened, he peered at his watch. It was 11:55 p.m. He scurried to a window overlooking the street, hastening his steps as a second scream shattered the silence of the chilling May night. Peering through the curtains, he saw two men lunging over a huddled figure. A woman. A white woman! An old 2021 Chevy's headlights gleamed through the night, and the motor was running. The car was parked beside two figures. He wondered if the security guard was asleep.

Richard had read much about the roaming black revolutionary underclass and the now blatant terrorism against the wealthy. His being shuddered with the thought of have-nots with guns. But he'd never dreamed he would see this in Olympia Fields, a virtually all white wealthy suburb, so he wasn't about to sit around as a spectator and watch terrorist vandals assault one of his neighbors. He only wondered why Dr. Weiner, the coroner for the City of Chicago, would be so negligent about securing his own home. He tossed his book down and ran into his bedroom while hollering:

"Marge! . . . Marge! . . . call the police!"

"What's wrong?" she asked.

"Just call the police, dammit, and tell them there's two men in ski masks on Maple Street, at the coroner's house, assaulting a woman. Tell 'em I think it's . . . it's a kidnapping. They must have broken the gate security code! Now hurry, Marge!"

"Okay, but where are you going with that gun? Please, Richard, let the police handle it!"

"No, Marge, that's what's wrong with this world today—people are so fucking scared to help one another! Now look will you go call? Jeesus you're wasting time. If this double-gauge shotgun doesn't stop them black sons of bitches . . . nothing will!"

As he crossed his lawn he had a dim look at the two masked men. He saw one of the men moving the limp body of a blonde woman. As he approached them, both of the men quickly put the unconscious woman's body in the rear seat of the car. Then they furtively jumped into the car and drove off.

He hollered at them. "Stopppp . . . You stop or I'll shoot . . . stop!"

At that moment the security guard rushed from the back of the guard house and started firing. Richard Stragenberg anxiously raised the shotgun with the butt of the weapon nestled firmly in his shoulder blade and pulled the trigger.

Bammm! Frantically he pumped then pulled the trigger again. *Bammm!* He hit the trunk of the car. He started trotting after the car, but the wet grass hampered his movement. He then tried to decipher the license plate number, but it was too late. The car had vanished into the night.

Frustrated, Richard Stragenberg ran to his garage, pulled up the door, and jumped into his son's car. He immediately rammed the key into the ignition praying that it would start. He listened. *UGH . . . UHHHH* "Start, sucker!" *JJAAAAAAH . . . ZAHHH*—"Oh, Jeeesus!"   *PUET . . . PUET . . . PUET . . . ZAROO!* "That's it . . . That's it!" The car backed out, spattering pools of water. Once he had swerved onto the street, he proceeded after them.

"Toejoe, step on the gas, man, you know they got a lynch mob after us by now!"

"Shut up! Don't you think I realize that! She's waking up, man!"

"Please let me outta here! Please!" She screamed and frantically opened her door.

"Pumpkin, stop her . . . stop her!"

Pumpkin grabbed the woman by her hair and slapped her successively. "Now get back in here! You crazy? You realize that the impact of hitting the ground would kill ya? Look out the rear window!"

She intensely strained her watery eyes. She placed her hand on her swollen jaw and said, "Well, I don't see anything!"

"Bitch, are yah blind? You don't see that diesel back there! That's what would have squashed you to a pulp if you had leaped outta there!"

She started screaming again. "Please, lemme go! What do you want from me?" She was banging her fist on the car seat and kicking spasmodically.

Toejoe cleared his throat and said, "Organs! Lots and lots of organs!"

"Organ? No one plays an organ in our house!" she said.

"Idiot!" Toejoe yelled. "Human organs! Your father will understand or we'll be selling yours!"

"So that's it . . . well you guys really are barking up the wrong tree," she said. "My old man wouldn't give you shit. He hates me. If anything he'll thank you for taking his lesbian daughter away from him!"

Pumpkin bellowed out, "Well, we have really done it. I mean we have really done it, not only is the bitch worthless she . . . she's a fuckin' dyke!"

"Just lemme handle it! Be cool!" Toejoe said confidently. "Look, Miss Weiner, I don't know what kind of con you're trying to run on us, but it ain't working . . . I know for a fact that your old man will do anything for you. The deal is this . . . you're going to call him and tell him that you will be freed if he sells body parts only to TWOC!"

"Besides," Pumpkin said sarcastically, "taking your organs was a joke. Who in their right mind would pay to have organs from a scum-drugged-ass-freak-bitch-like you?"

Toejoe glanced around from the driver's seat again and said, "If you fuck up, bitch, we'll kill your family! If you think I'm playing, mess up! And also you goin' to tell him that unless he stops dealing with Bodyslick . . . the next time, someone in your family is going to die . . . you got that, bitch?"

Pumpkin peered into the rearview mirror and said, "That

car's been following us for the past ten minutes . . . man." Toe-joe nervously peered into the mirror.

The woman joyously looked out the window screaming, "That's Mr. Stragenberg!" She started waving frantically.

Pumpkin hit her in the eye hollering, "Shut up, beast!"

"We gonna stick tah our plans," Toejoe said confidently.

"Fuck, some plans, man! This dyke is dead weight. We gotta git her outta here. That's our only chance. If that dude hadn't seen us back there we might could have went through with it. Besides they probably got an all out area stop and frisk order on us!" Pumpkin said cautiously.

"But if we put her out and something happens . . . then we got a murder rap."

"Man, don't square up on me!" Pumpkin said nervously. "What in the hell is wrong with you? Right naw we've got a chance! Look, I see some lights down the road. I see some lights . . . let's put her out!"

She screamed. "I won't say anything! Just let me out! Jesus Christ . . . please!"

She was a short plump woman with a large hook nose and a mannequin face. Her appearance was that of a street walker.

"Look, bitch!" Toejoe grabbed her around the collar of her dirty sweater. "And listen good . . . if you tell the police 'bout what happen tonight you're *dead*! Not just you but your whole fuckin' family, you understand?" She shook her head fearfully. "But make damn sure you tell your father what I said."

The car slid as it stopped. Pumpkin jumped out the car and opened the rear door and dragged her out. Momentarily feeling sorry for her, he snarled, "Remember, if you talk, you're dead!"

Fighting dizziness and cold, she stood up where she had been abandoned and shuffled toward the approaching car. Shuddering, she waved frantically in her haggard dress, hoping the driver would stop.

* * *

"Toejoe, from here on out when you get any crazy notions about kidnapping leave me out of it, you dig?"

"Shut up, Pumpkin! Will you please just shut the fuck up! The dagos wanted us to shake up the girl, so that's what we did. A couple of hours ago you were drooling at the mouth about buying a hydro-hog once we sell our last kilo of somel-low like a typical ditch-digging Negro, so just shut up and help me find my way outta here. What's the quickest route without running into a lot of cops?"

"We could take I-57 to Robbins. I got a brother out there we can stay all night with, but we wouldn't have the mobility that we would have by taking these back streets and staying away from the main streets. Hey, if my memory is correct the best route . . . lemme see, I used to party out this way a lot and . . . yeah, I remember. You see that sign we are approaching now?"

"Yeah!"

"If you make a right, that back road will take us dead into Robbins. It's going tah be one hell of a bumpy ride though, 'cause it's really a railroad route. So don't get frantic if a train zooms past us."

"You are good for something, aren't ya?" Toejoe said.

"Look who's talkin'. If it wasn't for me you probably would go up into the police station asking for directions!" They both laughed.

The car slid on the rain as it stopped. Richard lunged over to the door to unlock it; then he got out of the car and ran around to the girl to assist her into it.

"What happened, young lady? Are you wounded or anything? Please, let me help you into the car."

After assisting the woman into the car, he turned the car around and started to drive back west.

"Look, young lady, you're Dr. Jonath Weiner's daughter . . . correct?" She nodded her head. "Please tell me exactly what happened. I just wish one of those hoodlums would try this with my daughter. Here put this coat on. What's your name, honey?"

"Shirl Weiner."

Richard smiled and patted her confidently on the shoulder then said, "Shirl, I don't understand. I just don't understand how your father, who has uncountable enemies worldwide, doesn't have added security for his own home! But, Shirl, exactly how did it happen? They must have been under concealment, because the guard didn't see 'em. And if I hadn't been in my living room I probably would have missed them . . . so how did they kidnap you?"

She thought about the gruesome threat on her family's life if she told the police anything. "Does it really matter how they did it, Mr. Stragenberg? I really don't want to discuss it . . . besides I feel a bit whoozy!"

"Shirl, do you understand the seriousness of this crime? I realize you're still shocked over this nightmare . . . well, just relax, you can tell everything to the police."

"Thank you. I am rather shaky!"

Richard's mind was full of paradoxes. He could understand that the girl was still in a mild state of shock, because she had reason to be; yet she seemed too alert for shock. She didn't show any noticeable signs of the aftermath of a serious rape. She seemed too nonchalant for that. His car pulled up into the police station.

A tall man with a news badge on his coat approached him with a querulous tone in his voice. "Mr. Stragenberg I presume?"

"Yes! . . . but no questions—please!" he answered, irritated.

"But sir, just one please . . . there are people begging for some information on this degenerating crime. Woncha gimme a break, buddy?"

At that moment, as he assisted Shirl out of the car, he signaled for a cop to help him with the inquisitive newsman, also to get a doctor for the young lady.

A tall young rookie cop approached him. "Mr. Stragenberg, the ambulance should be here any minute. You know, it's sickening that these paper tiger revolutionaries would have the nerve for something like this. Why we're trying to keep the people from getting guns and running into the nearby minority communities for revenge!" He pointed into the waiting room. "Let's wait in here till the ambulance comes."

A man who was about forty, rather short and stocky and with round shoulders, which made him look heavier than he really was, approached them. He wore conservative drab-colored clothes and looked like a corporation executive. His carriage was like that of a military general and his shoes were spotless. He had a wide yet angular face with solid protruding cheekbones and a very pale complexion. His wetted down hair was sparse and had turned a silvery gray. His thick beard was darker than his hair. His eyes were blue, displaying a shrewd calculating look. His lips were like a surgeon's incision, long and precise. He was a rather determined looking man.

The rookie cop quickly stood up, walked toward him and started talking while pointing at the two of them, then said, "Mr. Stragenberg, this is my boss, Police Chief Randol, best man in the business!"

The police chief stretched out his hand, with a very pensive demeanor on his face. "Mr. Stragenberg, is the girl seriously hurt or what?"

"No, she doesn't seem to be! Apparently she wasn't hurt. She certainly doesn't act like she was assaulted, but I can assure you she's in a terrible state of mild shock. I think it would be best if you delayed questioning until a later period. She needs rest."

"Er . . . yes, I'm sure she does. I agree with you," the police chief said impatiently. "But we have got to have a few questions answered, because they are our only leads. Are you sure her two assailants were Negroes?"

"Yes!"

"Can you give us a brief description of each one, assuming there were two, correct?"

"Yes, there were two. Well, my guess was that they were young, about eighteen to twenty-six, somewhere in that area. They seemed nervous, awful nervous, as though they weren't that confident. I couldn't see 'em that clearly. They had on ski masks."

Police Chief Randol sat down next to him and looked at the rookie cop then back at Stragenberg incredulously. "Did you say . . . ah . . . ski masks?"

"Yeah!"

"Look, Mr. Stragenberg, could you be a little more explicit? I mean, put yourself in my position. Now, what about height, weight and clothes . . . things of that nature?"

"Well, I really wish I could tell you more, but the rain compounded with the dark made everything seem blurry, you know? That's why I'm so vague."

"Now, Mr. Stragenberg, this is a very serious accusation you have made here . . . about seeing two blacks kidnapping this girl . . . and yet you are now telling me they had on ski masks. Are you an idiot or just damn crazy?"

"Neither! I think they were black!"

Randol looked at the girl then angrily back at Stragenberg. "What's the kid's name?"

"Shirl. Her father is Jonath Weiner, the coroner of Chicago . . . you know . . . the city morgue."

Chief Randol questioned her. "Shirl?"

She looked up at him coyly with Toejoe's words ringing in her consciousness. *If you fuck up, bitch, we'll kill your family! If you think I'm playing, mess up!*

"Shirl?" He waved his hand in front of her face and repeated, "Shirl Weiner?"

She looked at him and bellowed out, "I can't . . . I can't!" *If you tell the police 'bout what happened tonight you're dead! Not just you, but your whole fuckin' family, you understand?*

"Okay, here's the ambulance," the rookie cop announced.

"Okay, take her away, 'cause she's really in bad shape, I don't know what they said but it sure stuck." Chief Randol waved at the rookie cop. "Come on, I want you to drive me to the hen house!"

"My daughter, where is she? Is she hurt? Please, I want my daughter!"

The nurse at the registration desk peered at the woman with apathy. "You're Mrs. Weiner?"

"Yes . . . yes for Christsakes, where's my daughter?"

"Mrs. Weiner, your daughter is in extreme shock at this time, and we think it would be better if you came back at a later time."

"What the hell do you mean a later time? Why the nerve of you! My daughter has been molested by some degenerate perverts, and you have the nerve and audacity to tell me to come back. Well you can kiss my . . . ass!"

At that moment two of the male attendants came to help the nurse calm Mrs. Weiner.

As they roughly grabbed her she screamed, "Please . . . please, all I want is to see my daughter! Is that asking too much? Please, just let me see her."

The two attendants wrestled with the woman, and then a tall Nordic looking, heavyset man with blond hair, a blue medical jacket, and stern eyes approached them.

"What's going on here? This is a hospital, isn't it? Let her go immediately!" They quickly let her go.

"I've had just about enough from you interns!" the nurse bellowed out. "You come in here and you act like you're God's gift to the earth. Well, you just remember, buster, that you're not a full fledged doctor yet, and secondly, on this shift and on this floor, I'm chief!" Nurse Hawkins stood with her legs spread. She was a stout middle-aged woman with large puffy pink cheeks. Her blonde hair was shaped like a beehive. Her face twitched spasmodically. She stood defiantly with arms folded.

"In case you've forgotten, Mrs. Hawkins, I'm the head doctor on this shift," the doctor reminded. "Consequently, I would imagine that would mean I have some power in the discernment of how to treat people who frequent this medical institution. Now, what's going on here?"

Mrs. Weiner mournfully cried out. "All I really want is to see my little girl. Is that asking too much?"

"I understand perfectly well what you're asking, Mrs. Weiner. Your daughter is in a mild state of shock at this time, but you can see her." As Nurse Hawkins' eyes darted evilly at her, the doctor continued, "But please refrain from talking to her . . . that would only magnify her condition. I'll show you to her room."

When they entered the room she started to cry. The intern attempted to calm her. Her daughter slept silently.

"Mrs. Weiner, I understand how you feel . . . but please refrain. It will only make your daughter's therapy less effective."

"I know, doctor, but—"

The intern escorted her out of the room; patting her on the back, hoping that it would mollify her grief. Once they had reached the registration desk, he signaled for the male desk attendant.

"Mrs. Weiner, do you think it would be advisable for you to drive home with this on your mind? If you would like, I could have Ed here to drive you home?"

"That's quite all right, my chauffeur is quite capable, besides I have to meet my husband at O'Hare at . . ." She glanced at her watch. "Oh dear, I'm late . . . well, doctor, was Shirl sexually assaulted or not?"

"No, our test indicates no such assault. Only a couple of minor lacerations and a slightly fractured hand. That's all Mrs. Weiner, no need to fret."

"Well, thank you, doctor, that's a relief."

"Toejoe, park the car in the garage. It wouldn't be smart to leave it out in the open!"

"Yeah, good thinking. I got to think of a good excuse to tell Fred for those bullet holes in the car," Toejoe said with concern.

Pumpkin mumbled while putting the key into the back door, "My brother must be outta town again. He's a salesman." He swung the door open to the tiny studio apartment. Toejoe walked in.

"I'm going to check a chick out. I'll be back later," Pumpkin said, as he closed the door. He then ran down the street to Hamlin Avenue and through the back yard of one of his neighbors who had vicious doberman pinchers. He hoped they were in the garage. They were. As he entered her apartment building, he wondered if he would have enough energy for sex. As he knocked on her door he could hear the radio. He listened to the pitter patter of her feet as she walked to the peephole.

"Special report... This is Ted Shannigan here at the Olympia Fields. We have just been informed that in this wealthy suburb, a young white woman by the name of Shirl Weiner, daughter of Joseph Weiner, coroner for the City of Chicago, was the victim of a ransom attempt by two alleged black men wearing ski masks.

"The police are trying every possible lead in order to capture the assailants. Authorities are speculating that this might possibly lead to retaliatory action from angry white neo-Nazi groups in nearby communities. The police are trying to establish whether or not there is a possible linkage with the crime and the work of a revolutionary militant subversive group called ARP, the American Revolution Party that have been associated with kidnapping the rich... Now on the national scene... NASA has successfully landed an unmanned robot on Mars that will release chlorofluorocarbons into the Martian hemisphere to push the temperature above freezing. Scientists state it will take eight million tons to create a greenhouse effect on Mars. This is the first stage of NASA's "terraforming" project on the planet."

Pumpkin smiled. Their threat had worked. The Weiner girl
hadn't said a word, or had she? The radio commentator re-
sumed.

> "We have an update on the Olympia Fields at-
> tempted kidnapping . . . Ted?"
> ". . . This is Ted Shannigan here at the Olympia
> Fields Police Station with Police Chief Jacob . . .
> Chief, can you give us a brief summary of the search
> for the kidnappers . . ." "Well, at this point we
> don't have very much to go on. But we are doing a
> lot of clinical investigation; checking virtually every
> possible lead. When the girl recovers from her mild
> state of shock, the case will be hopefully solved". . .
> "Thank you, Chief Jacob, and this is Ted Shannigan
> reporting . . . back to you, Walter."

RINNNG! The phone rang shattering Toejoe's thoughts.
"Hello . . . Toejoe . . . who is it?"

"This is Pumpkin, man . . . you check out the news yet?"

"Yeah, listening now! Where you at? Why you leave me
alone over your brother's house?"

"Hey . . . I got a little chick in Robbins I thought I'd give a
visit . . . you doin' all right aren't you?"

"Yeah, but that ain't the point."

"Look, Toejoe, I'll pick you up at about eight o'clock, man
. . . you hear what they saying about the ARP?"

"Yeah, forget that, Pumpkin, you should be happy that
Weiner girl is quiet. I was just thinking she heard us use our
names and everything!"

"Wow, I forgot about that . . . well, I guess you're right. Besides, like you said, they ain't got nothing on the ARP. But the
dame was lying, man!" Pumpkin said angrily.

"Lying about what?"

"It was just on the radio!"

Toejoe hurried over to the radio and turned up the volume; then he walked back over to the sofabed, consciously squashing a roach in the process. He said, "You mean about how she says her old man feels about her?"

"Yeah, they interviewed the guy on the radio, and he said that there wasn't a price he wouldn't pay for the freedom of his daughter!"

"Use your brain, Pumpkin, what would you had said? 'Tough luck.' He was probably lying, man. Anyway, for the next couple of days we had better take it easy, you know, maintain a low profile. Tell Fred it's my fault about his car, and when they quiet down I'll fix it. 'Cause I can hear his mouth already!"

"Okay, be cool, and I'll pick you up in the morning. Right now I got to make up a good lie to cover up for this botched kidnapping when Vinnie Luziano calls me!"

After hanging up the phone Toejoe yawned. He walked back over to the stereo and turned it off, simultaneously kicking off his shoes, then his dark T-shirt and grimy jeans. He jumped onto the loud yellow sofa, extended his arm to the light switch, and clicked it off.

He lay nestled on the large sofa, thinking about how the police probably were harassing the American Revolution Party over the erroneous assumption that they had something to do with the attempted kidnapping, but his brain was too fatigued to think clearly. Every fiber of his being ached with exhaustion; his body was swiftly growing weak and faint. Just as he was on the brink of falling asleep, he rose up from the sofa and furtively glanced at his feet. The skin was ebony and rough and there was a roach on his big toe. He kicked his foot against the arm of the sofa jarring the roach loose, he then yawned and rolled over on his side and fell asleep.

Chapter 17

Vinnie Luziano was happy as a sissy at Menard Penitentiary. He wasn't doing badly for himself. While in New York he had only been working for four years in the family's extortion operation and quickly rose to a *capo*, controlling his own group of soldiers. After murdering twenty men, he was exiled to South Jersey because of his ruthless and deadly temper. He became known in the *Cosa Nostra* as Vinnie "Lucifer" Luziano.

His five main soldiers had come to Chicago with him: Antonio "The Lion" Villichi; Gino Sartucci; Nicky "The Snake" Sigichi; Angelo Beresio; and Oscar "Pampers" Decarlo, who was the bad seed in the group. He would have left him in Jersey if the Godfather hadn't made him bring him to Chicago with him. He got a vile taste in his mouth every time he thought about how he got the street moniker "Pampers." He was arrested six times in Jersey for deflowering young grammar school girls. The only reason they tolerated his sick mind was because he was one of the best hitmen in the states.

When Vinnie first arrived in Chicago, the outfit was losing money because the goddamn *chinks* in Chinatown, the Ton Ton Disciples on the North Side, the moolies on the South Side, the Latin Kings in Pilsen, the Russians, Pakistanis and Colombians were controlling the distribution of heroin, cocaine and galactic drugs in Somellow Town. It was getting to

the point where the mob was looking like a bunch of school girls. Especially against the Triads, controlled by Choi Tse Tong, the undisputed ruler of Chinatown. He frowned as he thought about how much more difficult it had become since the arrival in the late '90s of almost a quarter of a million chink gangsters from Hong Kong, who were the most fearsome, ruthless fighters the mob had ever dealt with. The Triad, like terminal cancer, was slowly eating away at the world's most efficient crime organization. Every day, he thought, the mob was losing drug, extortion, and prostitution business to other crime groups. Especially the Triads. Not enough to worry about yet, but it was a problem. Since the Don had made him head of the Chicago La Cosa Nostra, the number of ruthless young soldiers being broken into the outfit had tripled. And money from the extraterrestrial drugs and Martianzeeg (which the mob monopolized) was phenomenal. Money from gambling, extortion, and galactic commodity swindles had also doubled. But what he wanted most seemed more and more elusive. He gazed around his luxury office and peered at the many photographs he'd had taken with some of Chicago's most respected leaders. He smiled as he thought cynically that they were all legit hoodlums. He only hoped Mayor Darold Mannington hadn't survived his heart attack because his investigation into the North Side body parts business wouldn't help the organization's expansion plans at all.

Vinnie stood up, walked to his bar, and made himself a scotch and soda. He wondered how Toejoe, his new black frontman for TWOC, the lucrative body parts business on the South Side, was doing. He should have heard from him by now.

Was Malcolm Bodyslick Steel history now? And if he wasn't, Antonio "The Lion" Villichi would make sure his girlfriend was dead. He'd been a hired assassin with the Jersey Mob for two years, and he had personally murdered two hundred men nationwide. He walked back to his seat while sipping his drink when the phone rang.

194 *John H. Sibley*

"Hello? This is Vinnie."

"What's up . . . man?"

"Look . . . Toejoe," Luziano said, while wiping his mouth with a napkin, "I think you better tell *me* what's up! Is he dead?"

"Vinnie . . . I had a shootout with him at a lounge unexpectedly, didn't have time to take him out . . . But it's just a matter of time . . ."

"Listen . . . I'm tryin' to let you black guys maintain some degree of control of the body business on the South Side."

"Yeah, Vinnie, but we . . ."

"Shut up, dammit, and listen. If Bodyslick ain't dead in 24 hours . . . We gonna do it our way. The Mafia will take him out and let you girls do something you can handle. Now I want you to know that I have already sent Antonio Villichi out South disguised as a salesman to kill his girlfriend, scan the area, and get some strategic info on Bodyslick's hood. If I don't have Bodyslick's freshly carved out heart on my desk in twenty-four hours, we will take him out the old-fashioned way. Do you understand where I'm coming from, Toejoe?"

"Vinnie . . . Vinnie, we won't let you down, man . . . I swear. Give us credit 'cause we did kidnap the coroner's daughter . . . and we caught Bodyslick's girlfriend, Malanna. You can recall your boy Antonio. But the bitch is square, a working girl. We've tried everything to get info from her. We even used a cattle prod up her cunt . . ."

"You moolies bungled that too, huh? Well, kill her then! Kill her in a way that will send Bodyslick a message!" His intercom buzzer sounded. "Wait a minute, Toejoe," he snarled then pushed the button.

"Vinnie here."

The voice was pained, and yet a sense of outrage barked through the phone. "Vinnie, this is Sal Ferlino."

He knew that Sal was his main informant inside the Chicago Police Department. If it was info he needed, Sal had access to it. Sal rarely called him unless something really important had happened within the outfit.

"Sal . . . how you doing?"

"Not good Vinnie . . . I got bad news!" Vinnie braced himself as the sad voice babbled on. "Antonio Villichi's body was found this morning in a South Side alley with a broken neck and a .45 bullet wound to the head . . ."

"Jesus Christ! Go on, Sal!"

"The fuckin' cannibals took his heart, lungs, corneas, liver, kidneys, and heart . . . they took everything but the man's dick!"

"You mean they found his body wid' no fuckin' heart?" Vinnie asked with outrage.

"He was murdered and cut up by these fuckin' cannibals for a reason, Vinnie. They trying to relay a message to you . . ." There was a nervous pause. "Are you with me, Vinnie?"

"Yeah, I'm witcha, Sal. I'm just numb over how they carved up poor Antonio's body . . . why, he has been with me since he was a pup. What am I goin' to tell his folks back in Jersey?"

"Like I said, Vinnie . . . he was cannibalized to relay a message to the outfit."

"I don't give a fuck about the fucking message, Sal! What I'm concerned about now is getting Antonio's body back and killin' the bitches that committed this unholy act!"

"You must've not heard about the rape and murder of Choi Tse Tong's niece in Chinatown this week, huh?"

"I could give a fuck! Those Chinese Triad gangsters refuse to do business with us . . . and what has that got to do with Antonio's death, Sal . . . ?"

"Nothin' Vinnie, if he ain't one of the two rapists. Gotta go now, Vinnie. I'll stay in touch."

"Take it easy, Sal."

"I'll take it any way I can get it, Vinnie."

Vinnie slammed down the phone and banged his fist on his desk. Then he punched Toejoe back on the line. "Toejoe? Forget about twenty-four hours. Antonio got murdered. I want to have a meeting with some of your boys tomorrow night at my lounge, The Wise Guy on North Avenue, at 8 p.m. You got that? And by tomorrow morning I want his girlfriend dead in a way that will let Bodyslick and anybody else know you don't fuck with the Mafia. I want her murder to make the front page of all the local newspapers! They found Antonio Villichi's body on the South Side with a broken neck, and the fucking cannibals took his heart, lungs. He was my most trusted *capo*. I'm very upset over this shit!"

"Sure, Vinnie. Sorry about Antonio!"

"Niggas and chinks!" he said in a disgusted voice then slammed down the phone.

He walked back over to his bar and made another drink, lit a seagarette and watched the lasso prongs of smoke whirl to the ceiling. He stirred his drink and walked over to the wall and stared at an old photograph of his great-great-grandfather, Giovani Luziano, who was one of the mob bosses in the billion-dollar Palermo organization back in the '80s. *Things were so simple then*, he thought.

Frowning, he walked back over to his chair and sat down. He knew that Antonio Villichi hadn't raped Tong's niece. So Antonio, without a doubt, was killed by Bodyslick. He remembered earlier in the week when he had sent Oscar "Pampers" Decarlo and Nicky "The Snake" Sigichi to Chinatown to talk with Mr. Lu, a snitch, who was trying to help the outfit infiltrate the Hip Hop Sung's drug network. Had they raped and murdered Tong's niece? If they had, no matter how much he would hate it, he would kill them. Or face a possible gang war with the Chinatown Triads, a secret society that was the most vicious and treacherous in the world. Sure, he wanted Tong dead, but he wanted him assassinated quietly. He gulped down the drink and lit another seagarette. He decided to keep quiet about the rape at the meeting tomorrow until he could get the *real deal* from Pampers and Snake. That way, he wouldn't make all the members of the outfit feel like suspects.

ANToNio Villichi

He smiled, slightly high, as he crushed the seagarette out and pressed down the intercom button.

"Gina, you seen or heard from Pampers or Snake today?"

"No, I haven't, but Angelo is in here. You want me to . . . ?"

"No, that's okay, I'll just wait. Will ya send Fanny in here because I need a massage; you know what I mean, sis?"

"She's on her way now, big brother."

"How is everything goin' in the lounge?"

"Good, Vinnie," she whispered, "but there's a hippity-hop rock boy in here. He calls himself Joey the Poet."

"Joey the Poet?"

"Yes."

"What does he want, Gina?"

"He wants to talk to you."

"What about?"

"About who killed Antonio . . ."

"Antonio?"

"Yes . . . that's not our Antonio Villichi, is it, Vinnie?"

"Yeah, Gina." He slammed his fist on the desk. "Some niggas on the South Side butchered him. He was a damn good soldier, too!"

Gina let out a loud wail on the phone, crying. The type of wail that only death can conjure up.

"Easy, Gina, I know this is tough. He was like a brother to us. Whoever did this, you got a front row seat when I cut off their balls! Now, have Angelo search this Joey the Poet character and escort him to my office. Tell them to make sure they blindfold him. I don't want him casing the joint."

"All right, Vinnie," Gina said tearfully.

As Snow marched blindfolded down the hallway with Vinnie's goons flanking each side of him, he hoped his John Travolta dermo-mask was convincing. It certainly was for the lounge crowd. Everybody smiled, pointed, and waved like he was the old movie star reincarnated.

Even the two goons had snapped, "Why you look just like . . ."

One of the goons tapped on the door. "It's me, boss, Angelo."

"Send him in."

A mahogany door squeaked open, and Snow was shoved into the room.

"All right, you can take off the blindfold."

Snow stood a few feet from the large mahogany desk. Vinnie had a headset on, a red Chicago Bulls jumpsuit, and black Solarbeeks gym shoes. A pack of fashionable seaweed seagarettes was on his desk. He gestured for Snow to sit down on a nearby couch.

"Joey the whatever you call yourself," Vinnie said, "what the fuck you doing here?"

"Joey the Poet."

"All right, what kind of info you got? Secondly, I don't know shit about your pedigree. Who are you?"

Snow locked eyes with Vinnie and said, "First, my real name is Joe Poetino. I was born and raised here in Chicago, the West Taylor area. A few people know of me that you know. At least their children probably know of me." Snow reached into his pocket and gave Vinnie his driver's license. Vinnie lit a seagarette. "I'm a hustler, Vinnie," Snow continued. "I'm also a rapper. I'm a versatile guy who can help you. My rap connection keeps me in touch with the crime on the South and North Sides. I know who killed Antonio Villichi."

"Who did it? Even though we already have got a pretty good idea."

"What's in it for me?"

Vinnie tapped a button on his console. "Sal, this is Vinnie."

"What's up, Vinnie?"

"Sal, I got a young Italian guy here who wants a job. You ever heard of Joey the Poet?"

"My son plays enough of his music. My understandin' is he raps in black, Italian, Chinese, and Russian. They say he's a linguistic genius. He's also . . ." Sal quickly tapped in the moniker Joey the Poet into his computer. "Yeah, he has a possession on him, which is only a misdemeanor, a few petty thefts and a coupl'a assaults . . . no felonies. And he's a dead ringer for a young John Travolta."

"Thanks, Sal!"

"No problem!"

"All right, Joey the Poet, my sources tell me you're fluent in languages, huh? They say you can speak everything from Nigganeese to fuckin' Chinese!"

"*Diu leng lei!* (fuck you). *Rompere le palle a gualcuno* (break someone's balls)."

"I hope you don't mean breakin' my balls!" Vinnie laughed loudly.

"*Non fare il pirla* (don't be silly)."

"Good Italian!" Vinnie said in amazement.

"*Ty mne van'ku ne val'aj* (don't pretend you don't understand what I'm saying)."

"*Me vale madre!* (I don't give a fuck)!"

"*Chingalo!*"

"Don't that mean 'fuck it' in Mexican?"

"Sure does!"

"All right, already, you've convinced me. And you are given me a fuckin' headache. Angelo will find something for you to do." Vinnie stood up and gestured for a handshake. Snow slowly walked toward him. "Listen kid, I've killed over fifty men in my life. You fuck with me, and you'll be number fifty-one. Now get outta here!"

Snow smiled and said arrogantly, "Um down wid' ya! OG!"

"What's that?" Vinnie asked.

"That's just a taste of Nigganeese!"

"All right, and don't you ever fuckin' forget that I am an original gangster! Now put back on your blindfold and go start workin'." Vinnie pressed his intercom. "All right, Angelo, come and get Joey. Start him off as a valet . . . parking cars."

His intercom buzzed as he let Angelo in to escort Snow out of the office.

"Yeah, what's up, Gina?"

"Speakin' of the devil, Oscar is on the phone. He says it's an emergency."

"All right, lemme speak to 'em."

"Vinnie?"

"Pampers, what the hell is goin' on. I send you and Nicky out on a simple job, to get some info from Mr. Lu, and now we might be on the brink of . . . look, you tell me what's goin' on?"

Vinnie Luziano opened his drawer to make sure his .38 Smith & Wesson was in there. He angrily rose from his chair, and cracked the venetian blinds and looked out his window as rain started to pelt it.

"I'm waiting, Pampers, and where's Nicky?"

Pampers' tongue cleaved to the roof of his mouth, with just the anticipation of Vinnie's wrath once he revealed what had actually happened. A blanket of helpless fear wracked him.

"We fucked up! We fucked up real *bad*, Vinnie!"

Vinnie picked up his glass and noticed his hand trembling. His heart started beating rapidly. "Tell me what happened, Pampers?"

Pampers started to speak slowly, tentatively. Fearfully. "We met Mr. Lu at the Green Tea Restaurant in Chinatown like you told us to. He was munching on boiled dog and rice as he told us it would be very difficult to sell somellow in there without the Hip Hop Sung Gang finding out. So we were on the verge of leaving until Mr. Lu told us that Tong's niece had just came into the restaurant, to pick up something. I ain't gonna lie to you Vinnie, Nicky and me were high as fuckin' kites: Litup off of cocaine and somellow. And Tong's niece was *fine*. Curves like a goddamn violin. Not only that, Vinnie, we started thinkin' that we could get some info from her about the Triad. So we paid Mr. Lu and followed her out of the restaurant and kidnapped her. We had parked in an alley so it wasn't noticeable. The bitch couldn't even speak English. Like I said we were super high. So we raped her and dumped her in the alley. We thought this would be a good way of showing the gangster chinks that they better do business with us, or else."

Vinnie was silent. Frozen with disbelief. He lit his last remaining seagarette to calm down. He could feel the short hairs on his back rise.

"Vinnie? What should I do? Nicky panicked and is on his way back in a taxi."

Vinnie spoke to him with loathing, his mind raced over the most hideous means of executing them.

"Come on back. We will deal with the details when you get back, Pampers, okay?"

"Thanks, Vinnie. I figured you would understand."

A nauseating feeling crawled over Vinnie as he hung up the phone. He had always hated rapists and freaks. He had felt intuitively, that Pampers would eventually mean trouble. He looked at men who preyed on hapless young girls as lowlifes who should be castrated or killed in the vilest method. His thoughts vaporized.

A tall curvaceous blond walked in his suite wearing a blood red sequin dress that was as tight as a glove; her legs were big and she had on silver high heeled shoes. She locked the door, and started taking off her clothes.

"Fanny!" he said as he snatched off his clothes. "It's good to see you!"

Chapter 18

"I don't trust that fuckin' dago, Toejoe," Pumpkin snarled with apprehension, as they sped north on North Avenue in their jet-black aero-car. "Why we got to meet them on their turf? Luziano wants Bodyslick's girl mutilated . . . Well, we gonna do that. He will even get her stinkin' heart. But now because one of his punk wop soldiers has been murdered he suddenly wants to talk with us! I tell you, man, I smell shit, and it stinks!"

"Pumpkin," hollered Toejoe authoritatively, "look out the rearview window and tell me what you see!"

He craned his neck and glanced at a shiny, new, fiery red Mercedes Benz.

"Yeah . . . a new Benz . . . so what?"

"That car has four Ton Ton Disciples in it that are freelancing for me as assassins. They are carrying . . . wait a minute I'll let big Jake tell ya." He pressed a button on his large watch, which served as a two-way intercom system.

"Jake, give me a rundown on your work tools to make my boys feel more secure!"

Big Jake answered in a deep bass voice, "No problem."

They listened to the clank of hard metal as Jake and his boys checked their arsenal.

"Listen up, Toejoe . . . we got one box of .38 special ammo, twenty rounds of 157 hollow head grain shells, fifteen boxes of .45 caliber Colt automatic-ammunition, and I have one M16 between my legs with a full metal jacket. Al is holding a MAC-10 submachine gun. Chris has got a Stevens 12-gauge pump fully loaded, and Willie has got an M79 grenade launcher with a 40 mm bore that he's holding like a baby. We've also got M61 hand grenades, one Beretta 12-gauge auto-shotgun. Unfortunately we didn't have enough room for the M72 light anti-tank weapon."

"All right Jake, any questions on what to do, huh?" Toejoe asked.

"We'll be waiting for your signal!"

Toejoe clicked off communication. Smiling confidently, he looked at Pumpkin from the rearview mirror. "I have instructed them to annihilate The Wise Guy Lounge upon my instruction." He held up his wristwatch. "All I have to do is press the beeper on my watch three times, and all hell will break loose. We are not walking into this meeting blindly. The only reason I'm dealing with Luziano and the mob is because of their strong organizational structure. Something we blacks are denied access to not because of inability but because of racism. They have assured me that once we remove Bodyslick from the lucrative South Side organ business we'll receive thirty percent of all body parts profits on the South Side.

"We can't be stupid, man. Look how much money we've been making with the somellow smuggling operation! We don't have access to that kind of drug. The mob has even got connections in outer space, man. Luziano has got a direct connection with a Martian colony where the drug is extracted from. We don't! As far as heroin is concerned, or crack, or cocaine, we don't need them for that because we can get forty-kilo deals with Colombian dealers in Miami. As it stands now they can guarantee us fifty kilos a month, which can translate into almost five mil a year.

"But this new galactic drug, somellow, that we're all hooked on, is the latest craze. Everything is taking a back seat to it.

"We are not boys,
We are men"

That's why I'm on the verge of starting a link with the Luziano Crime Family and our enterprise. Look at the figures. Last year we bought one million dollars worth of somellow from Luziano, and after we cut the shit with pentazocine, we made two million in gross profits.

"I'm telling you, if it wasn't for the dagos, you mother-fuckas would still be penny-ante niggas. If they keep supplying us somellow, we can all retire in a year. So they want a cut of our body parts business, so fuckin' what? It's a business association, man. You never will make any real big money with your racial hang-ups. It's about money and mutual respect. They need us, and we need them, and besides with the Chinese Triads only buying cocaine and selling organs to Bodyslick, we need all the help we can get!"

"Do you actually believe that, Toejoe?" Pumpkin asked with disbelief. "Are you that naive? If you are, I have a right to be suspicious of this meeting we're going to. Why do you think we can trust these guys? I haven't read anywhere in modern history where blacks and the Mafia have actually co-existed peacefully. They don't have a history of dealing with us fairly. Hasn't history taught us that power will only concede to power? I say we break off with the mob and handle the South Side on our own terms. This is a black thing, Toejoe, not a *Cosa Nostra,* and we don't need no fuckin' dago mobsters musclin' in on our space!"

"You don't know your history, man!" Toejoe shouted. "We been dealin' with the mob since the 1970s when the old *Mafiosos* were replaced with young ones who were more inter-ested in money than skin color. This new breed of mobster rec-ognized the huge amounts of money to be made in heroin, at that time the most-consumed drugs by blacks. Anyway, the mob realized it would be foolish to ignore that kind of money so they struck a deal, mainly in New York with the black drug kingpins, whereby the Mafia would sell the heroin to them and the black dealers would still maintain control of their turf. The mob were only suppliers. The blacks were the distributors.

Similar to our situation. Wake up man and realize it's about money!"

The bright red neon sign of The Wise Guy Lounge loomed into view. Darkness started to blanket the sky. A quiet suddenly hovered in the car. Toejoe now felt more apprehensive. More cynical. More doubtful about the Mob's real motive. He quickly turned into the lounge's parking area. Big Jake and his boys, in the backup car, continued to cruise down North Avenue. Toejoe turned around in his seat.

"All right, Butch, Pumpkin, check your work tools!"

Both Pumpkin and Butch pulled out gleaming Ruger Security-six .357 Magnums fully loaded with 158-grain jacketed hollow point rounds. Toejoe checked the safety on his .45 caliber Colt.

"Remember," Toejoe said with sternness, "we're in this thing together. If you want *out* now is the time."

"We warriors, man! Let's go," said Pumpkin.

Butch eagerly opened the car door and shouted, "Enough talk, let's deal with Mr. Luziano and the mob!"

Chapter 19

A flashing neon sign stung their retinas as they walked ap prehensively through the vestibule of The Wise Guy Lounge. They gazed around the large multi-tiered, spacious interior. A huge dance floor with a large revolving chandelier flashed colorful lights to the syncopated beat of Sinatra's "I Did It My Way," booming from giant loudspeakers hovering from the high ceiling. Mirrors from every conceivable direction bombarded the senses with the illusion of thousands of bright flashing carnival lights. The dance floor was empty. Surrounding it were tables half-filled with an early after work crowd. Barmaids, with long dark Sicilian hair and dressed in scantily clad sequined, red bikini, vested uniforms, stared at them as they stood casing the joint.

A giant Italian bouncer stood stoically at the entrance with his arms crossed defiantly, as he gave them a contemptuous nod to move freely in the lounge. Pumpkin stared at him menacingly, as he noticed a puffed lavender stitched scar that stretched from his lower right ear to his right lower jaw.

A beautiful Italian barmaid with coal-black hair and a huge bosom wiggled up to them sensuously. Smiling. Sonorously speaking to Toejoe.

"Mr. Luziano is expecting you. Please follow me. What would you like to drink?"

Butch cracked smoothly,

"There's just one thing I want and I'll give you a clue.
It's the best dish in the house, and it seems to be you.
You got eyes like diamonds, big, black, and bold,
and your smooth soft skin is the color of gold.
Your lips run like a cool mountain well
that show all the fire and brimstone of hell.
Your hair is black and long and shiny with a glare,
and you got a body that would make Beyonce stop
and stare.
Your lips, hips, and kiester are so shapely and fine,"

Butch went berserk and shouted, *"You gotta be mine!"*

"Listen here, baby, please tell me your name. My name is Butch, and rapping to pretty women is my call to fame."

"My name is Gina Luziano . . . this way please."

"You mean you're . . . Vinnie's?" Butch said with regret.

"Yes, I'm his younger sister. I am the manager of the lounge. Toejoe looked at Butch and shook his head with anger.

They followed her directly across the dance floor and crept down a narrow cavernous hallway. The muffled echo of a man's mournful scream reverberated off the walls. It was the wretched howl of a human being pleading for mercy from the depths of its soul. It was a blood-curdling piteous cry for life.

Gina Luziano acted as if she didn't hear anything, as a huge steel impenetrable door loomed into view at the far end of the hallway. Toejoe realized that The Wise Guy Lounge was a mere decoy for its main purpose, which was to serve as a base of operation for drug trafficking, illegal gambling, extortion, and hijacking. He instinctively patted his .45-caliber Colt inside his coat pocket, wondering would he have to use it. They gazed at hanging oil portraits of Vinnie, yellow-tainted newspaper clippings of famous mob murder stories, and black and white photos of Vinnie and some of Chicago's most famous politicians, many of whom Toejoe recognized.

Gina grabbed the gargoyle-sculptured doorknob and with a

ballet-like gesture said, "They're waiting on you guys . . . and see you around, Butch." She darted her viper tongue at him.

The room was spacious, but sparsely furnished with art deco furniture. The somber walls were filled with gold leaf framed pictures of Vinnie and his friends. A vast mahogany table stretched from one end of the huge room to the other.

A bald, old Italian man, who was about eighty and nattily dressed, smiled a toothless grin and pointed his cigar at them. Vinnie Luziano sat next to him in a Napoleonic-carved leather chair at the head of the table. He was immaculately dressed in a pinstriped gray suit, silver-gray shirt, and silk fox-gray tie. On his pudgy finger was a diamond, as big as a half dollar that shimmered from a ceiling light. His *capons,* Angelo Beresio, Gino Sartucci, and Nicky "The Snake" Sigichi sandwiched him. Four other goons sat alone. Gina reopened the door and brought a bottle of wine and glasses for them, then quickly walked out.

Toejoe was momentarily shaken by the cold eyes of Vinnie Luziano. Eyes that seemed to be lifeless. Non-human. The eyes of a tiger in the midst of stalking its prey. Eyes that displayed a ruthlessness he had only seen once before when Pumpkin had mutilated Bodyslick's girlfriend with the meat cleaver.

As Toejoe, Pumpkin, and Butch stood in the doorway, they could feel the suppressed rage of the Italians as tension crackled in the musky air.

"Glad you and your boys could make it, Toejoe," Vinnie said pretentiously.

"We are not *boys.* We are men, and all a real man has got is his word," Pumpkin said arrogantly.

The old Italian pointed his cigar at Pumpkin and stood up frowning at him as he snapped, "How coma you niggas sowa sensitive? Vinnie no maka fun of you. He no talka thingsa like that. Whatsa matta? You moolies gotta toilet tissuh feelin'? *Sono cazzate!* (that's bullshit)." The goons laughed loudly.

Pumpkin blew his top. "Who the fuck you think you talkin'

to, you old dago wop faggot! You better watch yoe fuckin' mouth, or I'll cut your goddamn *guinea* tongue out. We don't take that shit!"

Vinnie stood up and whispered in the old guy's ear hoping to quiet him down. Then Vinnie apologized for his behavior.

"Toejoe, this is Rufino Carillo, my uncle. He is just visiting us from San Luca, Italy. He now serves as a *consiglere,* an adviser for the New York, Boston, and Chicago outfits. But be careful what you say. The thought of disrespect gets these old dons fired up. Just ignore him."

Rufino Carillo again stood up, pointing another lit cigar at Pumpkin.

"Doncha curse thata way at me. I no lika that shit! I cut your nigga balls offa and stick um in your foula mouth. You showa respect whena you talka to ah me! Thatsa why you moolies donta havah any powah causa you donta showa any respect to anybody, *strunzo di merda* (fucking bastard)!"

"Yes, Uncle Carillo," Vinnie said impatiently, while reassuringly winking at Pumpkin. The old don sat down mumbling.

"I donta knowa why Vinnie needa dem niggas. Theysa crazy. *Fuori come un balcone.* All they wanta doa isa runna afta thesa white girlsa."

"Uncle Carillo is eighty-one years old, Toejoe. He's senile. But many years ago he was the ruthless boss of the 'Ndrangheta mob, Europe's biggest supplier of bodyparts, guns, and women . . . a $60 billion dollar operation worldwide. They make us look like sissies."

As Toejoe stood there, he started to feel droplets of moisture pelting his right shoulder. A steady stream splashed and slithered down inside his coat collar and zigzagged onto his spine. Another drop splashed onto the tip of his nose and dripped into the corner of his mouth. He wondered why Vinnie's goons hadn't fixed the leak. He also wondered why Vinnie hadn't offered them a seat. He realized they would never admit they secretly agreed with the old don, Rufino Carillo.

They sat there. And sat there. The old don kept mumbling, *"Me ne sbatto il cazzo* (I don't give a shit)," while staring at the ceiling, *"Nowa* respect." All of them stared at them, including Vinnie, as if they expected some kind of surprise. Toejoe quickly wiped the dripping water from the ceiling off his mouth. But it wasn't water. Water was not red. Water was not salty. But blood is red and very salty.

Suddenly the goons started pointing at the ceiling while laughing at them hysterically, especially the old don, Carillo. They slapped their knees with convulsive glee, as a rotten odor of death hung in the air. The three of them tried to fathom out what they had gotten involved in. A feeling of naked dread consumed them. They were stiff with terror.

Pumpkin gazed up at the ceiling, and so did Butch. What they saw made them recoil with horror. A white man's body swung slowly from a chained meat hook. They squinted as tiny drops of blood splashed onto their faces blurring their vision. The goons laughed louder. Pumpkin moved a few steps forward out of the path of the now steady shower of blood and again looked up. Toejoe stepped back. Then Butch. They all nervously peered up at a young Italian man in his boxer shorts swaying slowly, to and fro, from a meat hook hung from the ceiling by a chain knotted around a pipe. It stuck so deeply through the man's back that they could see the serrated bulge of the curved hook through his chest cavity. The corpse swayed back and forth like a pendulum. A ceiling light showed eyes gouged out with a corkscrew. Tiny rivulets of blood spilled from the dead man's gaping mouth and crisscrossed down his neck. Blotched dead blue coloration had started to cloud the man's skin. Rigor mortis had started to set in.

Suddenly, they jumped as the corpse expulsed air. Farted. Vinnie laughed with hysterics. Slapping his knees. Coughing uncontrollably. Tears started to form in his eyes. He was delirious with laughter. Vinnie took his handkerchief and wiped his rheumy vision.

"We don't think it's so funny, man. We come to your meet-

ing to find a dead man hanging from a meat hook in your con-
ference room . . . ain't too inviting," Toejoe said, without smiling. Pumpkin and Butch nodded in agreement.

For a blind moment they saw themselves as victims of one
of the mob's traps. They instantaneously pulled their weapons.
All three of them unflinchingly aiming their barrels at the
laughing mob. Pumpkin's left eyebrow twitched nervously, as
his finger tightened on the cold trigger of his .357 Python.

"Toejoe, you and your guys can put your guns away. There
is no need. The punk hanging over your head is an example of
what we do to stool pigeons. Nicky, you and Gino get him
down!"

They again gazed up at the twisting corpse, as a puddle of
blood had started to cover the floor underneath his body.

"One of my informants, in the Chicago Police Department,
told me this guy was on the verge of ratting on everybody in
the outfit. Joey was a sneaky weasel fucker who would rat on
his own mother for a price!" Vinnie said venomously.

The goons started to hoist the swaying body down. The old
don Rufino Carillo pointed at the dead man and snarled at
Pumpkin.

"*Testa di cazzo* (cockhead), see whata happen whena you
hava nowa respect!"

Once the body was on the floor, Gino and Nicky grabbed
dead Joey's hands and put them behind his back then tied his
wrists together with wire made into a Chinese knot. Then
Nicky forced his legs behind his back, sort of like an inverted
fetus position, and entwined his ankles together and pulled
that wire tight till it reached his wrists. Vinnie Luziano tapped
his finger on the table and gazed at his diamond-encrusted,
gold-nugget cufflinks and glimmering gold Baum and Mercier
wristwatch. His goons wrapped the body in a blanket and tied
it up, and Gino carried it out on his shoulder through a rear
door.

"Since you and your partners are going to be working along
with us on the South Side, there is a message you ought to re-

member from the dead punk carried out of here, but first, would it be asking too much of you dudes to put your weapons on the table? It would make me and Uncle Carillo less nervous!"

Toejoe gave the nod to Butch and Pumpkin to place their weapons on the table. Once his goons returned they also put their weapons on the table.

Vinnie lit a seagarette, cleared his throat, and spoke. "Okay, just remember, gentlemen, that we have a lot of respect for you. Let's keep it mutual. Don't violate us, and we won't violate you. If you screw over us, just keep in mind, there's absolutely no place in the U.S. that you can hide. We have connections in every public and private business in the world."

Vinnie pushed back his chair and stood up and began walking toward them.

"Nicky, take Uncle Carillo up front to look at the girls, huh? And where is Pampers at?"

"Ain't seen 'em since this morning, boss."

Nicky escorted the old don from the room as he kept muttering nowa respect.

"Now sit down, and enjoy the wine, we've got a lot to talk about. By the way, that wine you're drinking is vintage 1967 Lafite-Rothschild Pouliac. Who says wiseguys don't have any class?" Vinnie said, as he gulped down a glass of it and wiped the corner of his mouth with his suit coat sleeve. Some of his goons laughed.

"Shut up!" Vinnie snarled with embarrassment.

Toejoe, Pumpkin, and Butch cautiously sat down. Butch nervously gulped down a glass of the expensive wine.

"I am very upset over Antonio's death. It has caused me a lotta grief because he was such a good soldier. We know Bodyslick murdered him, but we will get to that later. First and foremost there is business. You see, my old uncle is so into being Italian that it interferes with him making money. I represent a new breed. I think that the old hatreds and prejudices are not good business concepts. I believe in diplomacy, and, Toejoe, since you have been dealing with me, you can vouch that I have been fair and square." Toejoe nodded his head with agreement. Vinnie continued. "There is more money to be made by us working together than killing each other. I'm your South Side connection. Martianzeeg marijuana gold. I hooked Toejoe up with the Colombian wholesalers in Miami. Since I've been laundering your drug profits, Toejoe, have you had any problems with the White Collar Crime Squad?"

"No problems, Vinnie," Toejoe said confidently.

"Besides, to the white man or to the white man's system, we are nothing but *wops* and *niggars* anyway, right?"

Pumpkin was momentarily stunned by Vinnie's honesty about racism in society. He started to listen more intensely.

"You made a minimum of two and a half million last year in somellow that we supplied you. You made close to a quarter of a million in the body parts business, while your rival Bodyslick and the city coroner split three million dollars between them minus payoffs for miscellaneous shit. Now that disturbs me. And what disturbs me even more is Choi Tse Tong's Hip Hop Sung Gang in Chinatown. Those chinks won't buy somellow from us, and they won't buy cocaine from us. So where are they getting the stuff?" Luziano asked, with an inquisitive look on his face. "Well I'll tell ya. He's getting it from Bodyslick. Not only that, they are letting this guy *buy* and *sell* organs there. This shit has gotta stop! What I want to do is combine our forces, using the power of the outfit and your organization, Toejoe, to form an alliance to take out the lone ranger motherfucker. But you will still maintain your territory. We only want a piece of the pie. Now the glues that will hold this coalition, if you will, together are the following: loyalty, trust and mutual respect. If any of those things are violated, the deal is off. And we don't need no gang war because then we'll be spending all our energy on killing each other rather than making money."

They all laughed. Nicky, his soldier, nodded at him as he walked back in the room and took a seat.

"Now, Toejoe, what are your plans to get rid of Bodyslick?"

"Vinnie, I have hired Ton Ton Disciple assassins that would kill their own mothers for an ounce of somellow. These guys specialize in murdering chumps like Bodyslick. His days are numbered."

"Toejoe, I think you're underestimating this guy." Vinnie paused for a minute as the crackle of thunder and lightning outside momentarily vibrated through the building. It started to rain as the flash of lightning became dimly visible through a nearby window.

"As I was saying. This guy ain't somebody we should take lightly. Look how he took out Antonio . . . so cold, clinical, and unemotional. I'm telling ya this guy is a dangerous man. A goddamn animal! I checked out his B-sheet from the Chicago Police Department. This man has got a record as long as this room: arson, attempted murder, robbery, loan sharking, drugs, and now *body parts*. We aren't dealin' with some amateur. We're dealing with a man who will do anything to maintain his power. A man who is skilled in weapons, self-defense, explosives, and one who's as cunning as a fox.

"Why, I heard that one time Bodyslick dressed up like a woman to kill a man. His weakness is that he is a loner. Bubba, who was his right-hand man, is dead. He is now nothing but a free-wheeling hoodlum that has got himself in a lot of trouble with some powerful people. Bodyslick isn't aware that there is strength in numbers. And very soon he will be taken out because of this!"

"Vinnie," Toejoe said impatiently, "I've known Bodyslick since we were kids living in Cabrini Green on the West Side of Chicago. We almost got busted once over a jewelry store heist on North Clark awhile back before he got involved in the body parts business. We also used to work the streets on the South Side together selling somellow. About five years ago, he took me under his wings and taught me everything you need to know about the body organ business. The only reason we split up is because he likes runnin' his own thing. He's a real loner. He likes to view himself as the lone rebel against society. He is a genius at discovering new, underground methods of making money. He has single-handedly made body parts a lucrative underground business for the straight world. He's making money out of supplying the living with vital parts from the dead for a price. And he is now trying to tighten his leash on his operation, because the word is out that there is more than enough business in Chicago for him to spare, but his greed won't let him. He's an independent loner with a small group of vicious assassins who work with him to protect his turf."

Toejoe coughed and continued. "We've already taken out Bubba, his main soldier. But Bodyslick has built a thriving business on death, so he is immune to it. Death to him is money. Just like it is to the undertaker. He is a treacherous, dangerous, and unemotional man. He will kill you for the slightest provocation. Or the slightest insult. A misused word can mean death . . . when dealing with him. Everybody on the streets is afraid of Bodyslick. He'll kill anyone who stands in his way. He once cut a petty hustler's hands off because he was trying to muscle in on his turf. Twenty people saw Bodyslick and Bubba cut the guy's hands off, but not one said a word out of fear!"

Vinnie poured more wine and nervously lit another seagarette. He cleared his throat and quickly gazed at his watch and said, "Look, we got this planned to a T, Toejoe. We're gonna supply the guns, the cars. We know the location for the hit and how you'll get out of there. Nicky, here, and Gino, who both are experts in any weapon you can name, are going to be involved in this. The outfit has taken care of everything. Even where we going to hit him at. Have you guys ever heard of Louis K. Vanderbilt?"

"Yeah, the billionaire publishing tycoon. He's one of the most wealthiest men in the world," Butch said confidently.

"Mr. Vanderbilt didn't become one of the wealthiest men in the world by being honest. He has other investments besides publishing. He owns a string of small casinos in Las Vegas. He got his start by selling large quantities of cocaine from South

America at discount rates and then laundering the money and reinvesting it in legit business schemes. He then parlayed that money into publishing houses, real estate, banks, and casinos. Now there is a reason I am telling you this. In Las Vegas, he and the State Commissioner of Gambling Licenses are good pals. Mr. Vanderbilt recently told him that his nephew is undergoing a heart transplant at Baltimore Memorial Hospital and how he is paying for a donor heart. So the wise guys in Las Vegas called me up yesterday because the commissioner got drunk and told them about the transplant, and since they understand how important the body parts business is in Chicago, they told me to be on the alert for someone to contact Bodyslick about a donor heart for old man Vanderbilt's nephew. Now, we have planted electronic bugs on Bodyslick's phone, and guess who called yesterday? Nicky, give me that machine."

Nicky quickly stood up and walked to a cabinet built in the wall, directly in back of the puddle of blood. He pulled out the drawer, grabbed the digital recorder and skipped over the blood.

"All right, listen to this!" Vinnie pressed the button on the digital recorder and fast forwarded some of it.

"This is Dr. Donald Jones. In case you have forgotten, in the neighborhood you used to call me Doc. I'll be in Chicago Friday. I'm now calling you from Baltimore General Hospital. I'll contact you as soon as I arrive in Chicago. Have a good *heart*, and I'll call you. It's urgent!"

"We have a special decoder that we use to tap into his transmissions. It's pretty obvious Dr. Donald Jones is coming to Chicago to get a heart for Vanderbilt's nephew. All we have to do is wait for his arrival. Toejoe, you, Nicky, and Gino and four other of my boys will be at the O'Hare Hyatt when he arrives. Once he arrives you guys will kidnap him and wait for my instructions. Angelo will hold down things here if I decide to visit you fellas."

Chapter 20

The intercom rang. The meeting was over. Vinnie felt a surge of confidence with how good it had went.

"What's up, Gina?"

"It's Pampers, Vinnie . . . It's . . . It's . . ." she cried uncontrollably. ". . . They cut him . . . Oh God, Vinnie . . . It's horrible . . ."

"Now calm down, Gina, all right?"

"Okay, Vinnie, okay, but it's so . . ."

"Who worked the door tonight?"

"Scarfo did."

"Tell him to come to the phone."

"Here he is right here, Vinnie," Gina said, confused.

"Scarfo, what happened?" Vinnie asked impatiently.

"Vinnie, them goddamn ninjas from Chinatown muscled their way through the door with Uzis and threw Pampers' headless body on the dance floor. Blood is everywhere. The crowd's going bananas. The women are hysterical!"

"Scarfo, did you and the boys get any rounds off?"

"Yeah, Vinnie, we wounded one, but it was very quick. The whole thing was over in less than three minutes."

"Dammit, you guys couldn't shoot an elephant in the butt with a shotgun . . . alright, Scarfo, keep everything cool. Start lettin' the people go home. Make sure you tell all of them to keep quiet about this. No police, Scarfo. We'll take care of this, ourselves. I'll be up front in a few minutes!"

"All right, Vinnie, I'll start talkin' to the patrons."

Vinnie opened his drawer and snatched his snub-nosed .38 Smith & Wesson out the drawer. *I figured that pervert would cause problems, I should have sent him back to Jersey.* He bit down on his lower lip. Everyone in the room stood up like soldiers waiting for his orders. "Shit!" he shouted, as he banged his desk with his fist. He stood up, straightened out his suit, nervously pulled on his neck tie then spoke.

"Them fuckin' Chinese gangstas have murdered Oscar 'Pampers' Decarlo. Yesterday Antonio's body was found on the South Side. We got enemies hitting us from all directions. Well, this shit's gonna stop! If these muthas want *war* they gonna git it. Are you with me?"

"We with you, Vinnie," Toejoe barked.

"We won't let you down," howled Nicky.

"These punks are dead, Vinnie!" Angelo growled.

"All right, Angelo, give Toejoe and his men back their weapons. Okay, we goin' up front and find out what the fuck is goin' on. Nicky, me and you have got to talk."

As Vinnie walked out the door, two of his henchmen approached him with guns cocked, running down the hallway.

"Vinnie, they really fucked over Pampers! The fuckin' Chinese have totally violated us, Vinnie!" the biggest one said, as he shook his head solemnly with disbelief.

"Where's the body at, dammit!" Vinnie snapped.

The henchmen pointed toward the lounge.

"Come on!" he barked to his men as he stormed down the hallway. He slowed his pace as he entered the chandeliered lounge. He heard a cacophony of ghastly voices echo from it. Uncle Carillo walked toward Vinnie with a vicious smile on his face. Whirling rings of cigar smoke trailed behind him. He angrily stabbed his finger into Vinnie's chest.

"Demma chinksah killa poor Oscah like-ah thisssah?" He

then gazed balefully at Toejoe, Butch, and Pumpkin. He accusingly pointed his cigar at them. "An demma niggas ah killa Villichi!"

Toejoe grabbed Butch as he lunged for the old man and whispered, "Chill out! Overlook him!"

The multicolored lights continued to spin, bounce, and reflect off the huge dance floor. Vinnie gritted his teeth and balled his clammy fist tight as he peered at Scarfo and ten rookie wise guys as they encircled the body on the floor. As he neared them he noticed a long twisting stream of blood crawling from a much larger puddle underneath the corpse. The men surrounding the body quickly grew silent, as all of them seemed to crane their necks simultaneously, studiously trying to size up Vinnie's mood. They had all learned that it could be murderous, lethal, and deady to miscalculate his volcanic personality.

Vinnie quickly realized that it didn't take a rocket scientist to see why Pampers' body was so close to the lounge entrance. He could easily imagine how his killers at gunpoint had caught Scarfo off guard at the entrance and threw the beheaded corpse on the floor.

Gina ran out her office crying, as he walked by. "Oh Vinnie ... they ... they ... how could they do that to poor ... poor Oscar?" She moaned tearfully while hugging him and pounding her tiny fist on his chest.

"Don't worry, sis, Vinnie will take care of things ... Angelo?"

"Yeah, Vinnie," boomed a voice from the rear.

"Will ya take care of Gina for me?"

"Sure, no problem, Boss."

He rushed to his aid and gently pulled her from Vinnie. Her behavior only affirmed what he had always suspected about her: that she didn't possess the unflinching, callous coldness that was a necessity to be a mob boss. He wondered why Vinnie refused to realize that despite the fact that she was his sister.

"Come on now, Gina ... Let me get you a drink to calm your nerves."

His men opened the circle as Vinnie walked up to them. Scarfo nervously approached him.

"Vinnie, it happened so goddamn quick," he said pleadingly.

Vinnie grimaced as he looked at Pampers' beheaded body. Years of bloody murders and grizzly deaths had not prepared him to look at a body of one of his own men.

"Nicky, come here!"

Nicky "The Lion" Sigichi was a nattily dressed small man in his mid-thirties with a beak-like nose, almond eyes, receding forehead, and a perpetual scowl on his face.

"Dem fuckin' chinks did this to Pampers!" Nicky shouted deliriously.

Vinnie snatched his snub nose .38 out of his shoulder holster and grabbed him by the neck. "*Sorca* (pussy), get on your knees!"

"Vinnie, don't kill me, I swear Pampers wouldn't listen to me . . ." Nicky exclaimed. "Pampers was just an animal! He couldn't keep his stinkin' hands off the girl!"

"But I thought I could trust you, Nicky. You've never let me down before." Vinnie pulled back the trigger. "You were in command, Nicky, weren't you?"

Nicky nodded his head solemnly.

"You and that filthy pervert raped a fourteen-year-old girl yesterday, didn't you!"

"No!" Nicky shouted.

"Why lie, Nicky? You got some of that young pussy, didn't you?"

"Hell no, Vinnie, I swear I didn't touch her!" Nicky sobbed. "But I wasn't goin' to leave Pampers in that car by hisself either. I knew the minute he pushed the dame in the car . . . that we were *fucked*, even if we didn't touch her!"

"Well, if you so fuckin' loyal, why didn't you stay in Chinatown with Pampers instead of runnin' back here in a taxi?"

"Look, Pampers wouldn't stop fuckin' the bitch . . . I mean girl . . . shit! If I hadn't . . ." He started to stutter as he looked

up at Vinnie from the floor as if he was praying. "I . . . I . . . didn't rape any goddamn girl. I swear, Vinnie, I didn't . . ."

"Shut down on that fuckin' whining, man! Just shut the fuck . . . !" Vinnie kicked him in the stomach. Nicky grabbed his belt as if holding his intestines inside. Terror scratched across his face.

"I swear, Vinnie, I didn't touch her." He glanced at the frozen faces of the men as they stood around him. Silent. Cold. And unmoved by his humiliation.

"Pampers raped and murdered her after I left," Nicky reiterated.

Vinnie made a disgusted face. "You realize what's gonna happen if I don't blow your fuckin' brains out right now, huh?" he said, as he poked the gun deeper into his temple.

"Let me kill the punk pervert," Angelo said.

"No," Vinnie said demonically. "Maybe that would be too easy. Maybe I'll just let you boys drop his rottin' ass off in Chinatown tonight and let Tong and the Hip Hop Sung Gang tear him apart like they did Pampers here."

Angelo laughed and slapped Vinnie on the shoulders approvingly.

"Now, Nicky, did you rape Tong's niece or not?" Vinnie shook the gun between his eyes. Nicky's gut cramped with unbearable pain. He farted.

"It was Pampers!" He grunted in scorching pain.

"Get the fuck up then!" Vinnie demanded.

Nicky held his stomach with one arm and pushed himself up.

"You don't have to worry about me, Nicky. You just better watch out for them fuckin' chinks!" Vinnie shook the barrel of the gun at him. "They some mean treacherous killers! Now clean up the mess, Nicky!"

Vinnie stormed back toward his office with Scarfo walking in sync with him as if he were a Siamese twin. Angelo, Gino, Toejoe, Pumpkin, and Butch filed behind them. Vinnie looped his arm around Scarfo's neck and whispered in his ear.

"Now, Scarfo, you gotta redeem . . ." He ceased talking. His outrage over Pampers' death had constricted his throat; it was becoming difficult for him to breathe. He cleared his throat as his rage abated. Scarfo nervously gazed at Vinnie's pulsing temple veins as they writhed like venomous snakes.

"You gotta redeem yahself. It ain't no reason them chink gangstas should had escaped without one death from this!" Vinnie snarled, as his dazzling, quarter-sized diamond ring gleamed almost hypnotically in Scarfo's eyes.

"Just tell me what you want me to do, Vinnie!" Scarfo pleaded.

"I want revenge, dammit!" Vinnie whispered in a slithering voice which made Scarfo feel like snakes were crawling on his neck.

"Lemme handle it, Vinnie. I swear I won't let you down. Just lemme take Angelo, Gino, Toejoe, and a couple more boys with me. I swear, Vinnie, by tomorrow mornin' dem Triad gangstas will understand the price you pay when you fuck with the Cosa Nostra!"

Vinnie turned the doorknob to his office. He felt enormous weight on him and the eyes of his soldiers tugging at him. He closed his eyes for a second and wheezed in strangled air. Then he turned around and pointed a finger at his men. Thunder rumbled outside.

"The Cosa Nostra has a code of conduct!" Vinnie's voice had a squeaky, morbid castrato tone to it. "I've ordered Scarfo to handpick some of you dudes to go with him to Chinatown. Your mission will be to show them fuckin' chink Triad punks that you don't kill one of us without a big payback! Your mission is to bring me back the chink head of Tong, the leader of the Hip Hop Sung Gang. If that's not feasible, then I'll settle for one of his soldiers' heads!" Vinnie gripped the doorknob, opened the door, walked into his office, and slammed the door.

Scarfo turned toward the men. He lit a seagarette. The building shook as lightning and thunder crackled outside. Scarfo stabbed the seagarette at them as he snarled wrathfully.

"This is the deal," Scarfo said, as he crushed the butt out in a nearby ashtray.

"Me, Angelo, Gino, and Toejoe along with twelve more of you guys are goin' to Chinatown tonight to git some *head*!" The soldiers in the hallway laughed convulsively, trying to abort the fear. The unknown rising from the ghostly image of Pampers' beheaded body.

"There will be four cars. I want Deno," he pointed at each one of them, "Salvatori, Palarsi, and Violani to drive. All of us are familiar with the layout of Chinatown, but before we get there we'll study our strategy for attack over a map. We will break up Chinatown into four intersecting coordinates. Jesus, I almost forgot." He held up a palm size, black, razor-thin cell phone. "Each of you will carry one of these for the unexpected—it's got speed dial settings for each one of you clowns! All right, enough talk. Let's do it!"

Chapter 21

A blood-red full moon gave the night sky a carmine darkness. A blackness that made the three shining black Cadilectros exiting Canal and turning right into 22nd and Cermak—the main artery of Chinatown—reflect the luminous green tea, red, and white lights that pulsed from its many pagoda-shaped restaurants.

"Remember our plans," Scarfo barked into the car's tactical radio-intercom. "Listen up, 'cause for Christ's sake there ain't no room fah mistakes!"

"Go on boss," one of his henchmen in each of the three rear cars said.

"Deno is going to make a left at Wentworth. Salvatori, you make a left at Princeton and you follow him. Palarsi, down to Alexander and make a left. Violani will then make a left at the stoplight going back east to Wentworth and make another left. This means all four cars will intersect with each other on the opposite sides of each street. I want you to shoot to *kill* every young male chink that looks over fifteen. And remember, if you get in a jam, speed dial any one of us. And don't fuck with women, children, and old people. Any questions?"

The night air was hot and humid. The streets of Chinatown were sparse. Quiet. Restaurants and buildings with Chinese temple motifs were pressed together. The façades of the buildings were colored in slate blue, sandy white, and grey. A crowd of men, women, and children, mostly white, streamed from various Chinese restaurants. The smell of egg foo young and dog meat wafted through their car windows.

"Yo Scarfo!" Deno called out, "any chance I can buy a couple of eggrolls first? I'm starvin' marvin'.''

"No, *dumbfuck,* we down here for one reason, and that is to get revenge for Pampers' death. Now let's move out!"

The three cars headed south to Cermak Drive at 22nd Street then turned west entering the main artery of Chinatown. Scarfo and his three henchmen put full thirty round metal jackets into their Uzis as they made a left at Wentworth.

"Slow down!" Scarfo yelled, as the Cadilectro slowly rolled to a stop in front of Hip Hop Chop Suey. Scarfo knew it was just a front for the Hip Hop Sung Gang's Triad empire. He looked inside the restaurant as a young Chinese man with a pigtail walked out with a pregnant Chinese woman. Scarfo scanned the street. It was relatively quiet except for some old *papasans* standing in front smoking long pipes filled with tobacco or maybe opium.

Scarfo pressed the down button of his window and gestured for Deno to slowly drive and follow the young Chinese couple. It was one of those hot May nights that intensified the odor of Chinese food spewing from the restaurants and the stench of garbage.

"Hey, you!"

The Chinese couple gazed suspiciously at the car. The male acted fearless. "*Gwai tsi leng sin!* (foreigners fucking crazy)," he mumbled as they kept walking.

"Look, I just wanna know where the Green Tea Restaurant is located?" Scarfo said, as the car stopped. He nudged Azensio and Gilberto to get ready to capture the couple at gunpoint. Suddenly, Deno sped up the car as the couple neared an alley and made a wild right turn into the alley opening. Scarfo and his two henchmen quickly leaped out of the car.

"Me don't know of any Green Tea Restaurant, mistah!" the Chinese youth said with a thick Cantonese accent.

"Get in the damn car," Scarfo barked, as the henchmen jabbed their weapons into their backs.

The Chinese girl started to cry. Lines of panic and fear crinkled around her slanted eyes.

"Let's go down the alley and park, Deno," Scarfo said, as he closed the door. The Chinese girl cried and moaned in Chinese. The Chinese boy uttered something to her that sounded suspicious. Everyone else sat there silent. A large fly whizzed into the car. Scarfo and the boy looked at each other. The boy took in the rough topography of Scarfo's face and the gleaming Uzi between his legs. He sensed that he was about to be a dead man.

The car stopped half a block down the alley. Scarfo smiled as he got out the car. He heard the distant *rat tat tat* of gunfire from his boys on their killing spree. He pulled a 9 mm Ruger Laser pistol out of his shoulder holster and gestured for the Chinese couple to get out the car on his side.

"Deno, you stay in the car!" Scarfo shouted, "Me, Gilberto, and Azensio can handle this."

Gilberto and Azensio quickly grabbed the sobbing girl. Scarfo looped his huge arm around the Chinese boy's neck and stuck the cold muzzle of the Ruger into his temple. The car's intercom clicked on.

"Scarfo, this is Savatori and Palarsi . . ."

Scarfo snatched the mini-intercom from his pocket. "How many chinks you kill?"

The gunfire from the cars crackled through Scarfo's intercom. Police and ambulance sirens echoed in the distance.

"Boss, the streets are full of dead bodies of Triad gangstas. Their blood, guts, and shit are splattered everywhere. This is one night they won't forget during the next Chinese New Year. You want us to rendezvous with you or go on back to the lounge, boss?"

"Good work . . . but you can go on back while we try to bring back Tong's head."

"You sure, boss? 'Cause the police and Terro-Swat team are going to be swarming this place like locusts real soon."

"Yeah, go on back, we got good concealment in this alley— besides we can always put on our chink dermo-masks!" The intercom clicked off.

"Pull up your shirtsleeve!" Scarfo screamed, as the captured Chinese youth's eyes darted up and down the cavernous alley. Searching for help. For his gang. For his pregnant wife. His arm trembled as he rolled up his shirtsleeve to his elbow. Scarfo grimaced with rage as he gazed at the blue and red three-pointed equilateral triangle tattoo that only the Hip Hop Sung Gang members wore.

"Why you scum-ass, rice eatin', dog meat lovin' scum-bucket!" Scarfo snarled, as he pushed the youth around and hit him so hard in the stomach with the pistol that tiny drops of blood started to string down the corners of his mouth.

"What's your name?" Scarfo yelled.

"*Diu leng lei!* (fuck you)."

"Bitch!" Scarfo slapped him so hard saliva sprayed out of his mouth like a water fountain.

"Yazoka."

"And is she your wife?"

"Yes . . . yes," Yazoka moaned, as he grasped his stomach as if his entrails were going to fall out. "Her name Mikome."

"Azensio, you and Gilberto take his wife and put her head on the ground beneath the front tire."

The two lackeys grabbed the kicking, moaning girl, gagged her mouth and dragged her over to the front tire of the car then pushed down her fearful bobbing head into the garbage and filth of the alley ground.

"Ready, boss!"

"Now, Yazoka, yo wife's head is goin' to pop like a balloon if you don't tell me where to find Choi Tse Tong."

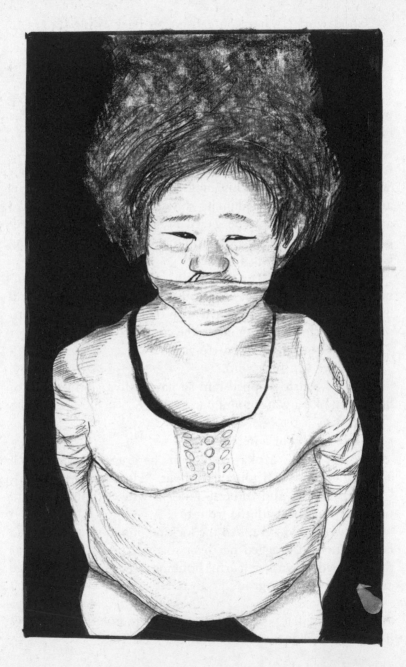

"Me don't know. Short time dis country. Me speak veddy little English."

Deno revved up the electric engine of the car and smiled maniacally at Scarfo.

Mikome's teary slanted eyes opened wider, as the vomit taste of saliva dribbled from her screaming open but gagged mouth. Muscles twitched in her face uncontrollably. Her hands were tied behind her back.

Scarfo slapped the youth in the head with the pistol knocking him to the ground. "Where can we find Tong?"

"Me don't know. Please no hurt wife. She pregnant," he pointed at her protruding stomach. "Baby *lo no* (mother) soon," Yazoka begged piteously.

"Alright, Deno, he don't wanna' cooperate. Kill the bitch!"

Deno again revved up the engine. The two goons had to bear down on the delirious pregnant Mikome. Blood, feces and urine started to form a puddle beneath her dress. Suddenly, as Deno put the car in drive, a baby's sculpted head protruded from between her legs. Azensio and Gilberto gazed at it with disbelief. Then a faint baby cry pierced the silence. A subtle moan. A wail crackled from her throat; then a loud thump hit the ground beneath her. A baby cried, its umbilical cord still attached to the handcuffed and gagged mother.

"Scarfo!" Azensio shouted squeamishly, "she done had a baby!" He lifted up her skirt and peered at the wailing infant.

"Deno, hold up!" Scarfo signaled, as he walked over to a dazed Yazoka. "Last time . . . where can we find Tong?"

"Tong leave country. He no in Chinatown. Please. No kill wife," he said, now on his knees as if praying.

"Deno, kill her!" Scarfo barked out menacingly while he snapped his finger.

As the tire rolled over her head it sounded like a dropped melon. Blood, brain, hair and white crushed skull clung to the tire wheel. Deno revved the engine and put it into reverse then rolled over her head again and again. Azensio turned away,

bent over, and vomited uncontrollably. Gilberto grabbed a screaming Yazoka as he jumped up and down deliriously.

"Shut him up!" Scarfo yelled, as he walked over to the woman's headless body and lifted up her skirt. He snatched the tiny infant from its dead mother's umbilical cord and tossed it up like a football then kicked it down the alley. He then looked down, shook his head, and said, "Will ya look at my new shoes?"

"Now it's your turn, Yazoka. Grab him!"

Scarfo, Azensio, and Gilberto surrounded him. "*Che jil ba dan!* (you will die now)."

Yazoka screamed as he threw a whipping roundhouse kick at the head of Scarfo who fell back. Azensio then lunged at him from the right. Yazoka twisted and kicked him in the ear causing him to drop his knife. Yazoka picked it up and carved into his heart.

Azensio stood up and ran toward him, madly slashing his knife. Yazoka leaped back and karate chopped Azensio's wrist with his knife. He then jumped on top of him and started gutting him with his knife.

Scarfo ran toward the car and got the Uzi. As he aimed at Yazoka, he felt the shadowy serrated blade of a machete as it sliced through his neck severing his head. As his head fell to the ground, he gazed up at the faces of Chinese men. He blinked his dying eyes as he listened to a cacophony of angry Chinese voices. Hip Hop Sung voices encircled him. He feebly looked at them as they trampled over his body then methodically cut off the heads of Deno, Azensio and Gilberto. Walking past him, they held them by their hair as if trophies. For a nanosecond his dying brain could hear the *swish* of blood on their shoes, as thick as car motor oil. A shaft of sodium alley light gave tiny ivory white fangs a vampiric sheen as hundreds of alley rats *slurped, lapped, licked, and gorged* on his blood, as it flowed into the sewers and potholes of an alley in Chinatown.

Chapter 22

The slammed phone echoed in Toejoe's ears. He looked at Malanna's naked body as she lay with both arms and feet tied to the four bedposts. Butch and Pumpkin stood menacingly over her. She stared at the ceiling with terror.

Malanna's whole life flashed before her. Images of her three aborted fetuses flashed through her mind. She should have listened to her mother's warning about the risk involved with Bodyslick's lifestyle. Was this a payback? And where was Bodyslick? She could feel her wrists and ankles growing numb with pain. She prayed for God Almighty to save her. She glanced around the tiny room. The fetid smell of rot and drugs engulfed it.

She listened to the three as they injected the galactic drug somellow into their veins with a shooter, which looked like a small caliber laser hand gun.

"Pumpkin, my shooter is clogged up . . ."

"Man, nobody uses my shit but me . . ."

"So . . . mellow . . . I feeeel it . . . oh yeaaah . . . shiiit . . . this is so good . . . !"

Toejoe stood there with a shooter dangling from the pit of his elbow as tiny filigreed lines of blood oozed from it. He wondered what would be the most heinous means of killing the girl. He glanced at his watch. It seemed a mile away. He ground his teeth as he felt the medicinal taste of the drug coursing through his being, igniting millions of impulses in his pleasure zone. The feeling of levitation started to affect his senses. He peered at Malanna. She was tied to the bed, and yet with each second she seemed to be drifting away from him. He fanatically snatched the shooter out of his armpit. His sense of balance was gone. He was in a state of limbo. Gravity now had no effect on his consciousness. He gazed at Pumpkin and Butch. They too, seemed to be struggling to maintain their equilibrium. Then suddenly the sensation dwindled. It was like snapping out of a bad dream after experiencing the jolt of plummeting from high elevation.

"Listen up . . . Antonio Villichi was killed yesterday on the South Side and Vinnie Luziano wants us to make an example of this woman. He wants us to cut her up into tiny little pieces and then gift wrap her remains in a box and send it to the newspapers. And he wants her heart on his office desk tomorrow morning to sell to a rich donor client."

The two men looked at each other with indifference while struggling to shake the hunger for more somellow.

"Why don't we use this?" Pumpkin asked, while smiling wildly, insanely, as he pulled a shiny new meat cleaver from his inside coat pocket. "After all, I worked three years as a butcher."

Malanna panicked. Her heart pounded with blind fear. Her eyes became bulbous with terror. Meat cleaver? Would God let her die like this? She closed her eyes as the images of a butcher carving meat sent shivers through her being. She twisted. She farted. She gagged as fibers from the cloth tied around her mouth became soggy with saliva. She lost control of her bodily functions. She felt the wetness of her own urine and shit as the meat cleaver neared her neck.

As Pumpkin raised it over his head, Toejoe and Butch grimaced, trying to hide their nausea at the barbaric act. Shock had rendered Malanna unconscious. With one swift, rhythmic motion he dropped the meat cleaver. Bone, cartilage, and the flesh of her shoulder cracked with a mushy *thump*. A geyser of blood instantly splattered the walls as Pumpkin again held the meat cleaver over his head. Then, with a demented gleam in his eyes, he aimed at her other shoulder. Toejoe and Butch walked to the door, trying to hide their disgust at Pumpkin's homicidal glee as he slammed the meat cleaver again and again. He carved Malanna's body up as if he were a butcher and her body was merely one of many carcasses he had dismembered in the course of a work day.

"She's dead, man! I just know she is dead!" Bodyslick moaned, as they looked at the dried blood that covered every inch of the bed in the tiny kitchenette apartment.

"Look!" Shondell shouted, as he walked out of the bathroom holding a small red and blue electric cooler. He walked over to Bodyslick while rattling the ice inside it. "Look, man! Look inside!" Shondell whispered.

Bodyslick clenched his fist in fear and terror that what was inside the cooler would be one of Malanna's body parts: her head, her eyes, her hand. He was frozen with immobility.

Geronimo sensing his fear grabbed the container and gazed inside. "Jesus Christ!"

Two brown, filmy, glazed eyes stared at him. Dead eyes. Eyes that beamed unspeakable terror and pain. It was Malanna's decapitated head inside. Only her ice-speckled face showed through the ice. Her hair and ears were covered with ice. Only the eyebrow to the upper lip was seen. Geronimo quickly snapped the lid shut and locked it.

"What's inside, dammit!" Bodyslick hollered fearfully.

"Something we won't let you see, maan. Something that could drive you insane." Geronimo winked at Shondell as he handed him the container to put back in the bathroom.

Bodyslick bent down near the bed and picked up a gold ring with dried blood on it. "This is my baby's ring. I gave it to her . . . on . . . her . . . birth . . . day. Oh God . . . why . . . why?"

Both Shondell and Geronimo grabbed him by the arm and escorted him out of the apartment. Bodyslick openly cried as he left the blood-spattered room.

"I swear, Malanna, they goin' to die for this! I swear, baby, they are *dead men*!"

Bodyslick shook his head mournfully as if trying to shake the gloom and horror of Malanna's death, as he stepped from the vestibule of the apartment building into the sweltering May heat in the sodium lit alley where Geronimo had parked the car.

Bamm! Bammm! Ba bammm! He winced as a bullet whanged an inch from his face as it carved into the building's brick wall. Bodyslick ducked down behind a garage wall. He swept his laser pistol left and right gesturing for Snow, Geronimo, and Shondell to spread out. Snow bent down while running across the alley holding both hands on his .45-caliber Beretta. Bullets banged the concrete of Snow's steps as he leaped behind a parked car. He squinted his eyes in the alley darkness looking for the source of the gun shots. Bodyslick caught Snow's attention and pointed at the shadow of an automatic weapon on the alley wall three meters down the alley from them.

Bodyslick watched the shooter's shadow movement. He aimed. He calibrated his shot against the movement of the shadow. He pulled the trigger. *Bammm! Ba bamm!* It was a surgically clean hit. Bright carmine blood exploded from the shooter's head giving the shadow a bloody crimson tint.

"Cover me!" Shondell whispered. The *rat tat tat* of bullets peeled up the concrete behind his feet as he ran across the alleyway while aiming his .38 at the source of the automatic gunfire. He fired. And dived, rolling on the alley floor underneath the rear of the hydro-car next to Snow. He could feel the blood oozing down his pant leg from the fall.

Snow nudged him as he pointed at the metallic gleam of another gunman's weapon in the alley corner. Both of them fired a fusillade of bullets. They heard the *ting* of his weapon and cartridge case as he moaned, falling to the ground dead. A zigzag stream of white and blue muzzle flames crisscrossed the alley from exchanged gunfire.

A large, mutant, alley rat *hissed*, baring his tiny fangs while leaping out of a garbage can in back of Geronimo. He shot it with his .44 Magnum. He could see a faint silhouette of a gunman hiding behind a nearby doorway. He slowly creeped up on the assassin who was holding an Uzi. The gunman saw him and panicked, aiming wildly. Geronimo extended his long arm and stuck the barrel of the .44-caliber Magnum to the man's temple and pulled the trigger. Blood, skull, and brain matter splattered on the door like a Jackson Pollock canvas.

Bodyslick's laser pistol *whoozed* a bright China-blue muzzle flash as it hit another gunman in the back, but he kept running. Bodyslick mumbled in disbelief, "The muthafucka has got to have body armor on!"

Snow crawled from underneath the hydro-car and ran to the rear of the garage wall. He peeked around. He could see the white of the eyes of the gunman's blank, cold face. He yanked his gleaming dagger out of his Velcro ankle holster. He smiled. He liked nothing better than stabbing his hand-forged, twelve-inch, Damascus blade into the gut of an assassin. He had killed fifty men with his dead father's dagger. A dagger his father had killed one hundred men with as a soldier with NIRA. Now there would be one hundred and fifty-one notches on the mammoth ivory and turquoise handle.

He slowly crept to the back of the gunman. Silently. In a split second their eyes locked. Snow quickly collared him around the neck with his left arm and slashed his carotid artery with his right hand. Blood gushed from his throat like an opened fire hydrant. The gunman dropped his Uzi 9 mm submachine gun while clutching his bloody throat and fell forward dead. Snow smiled, savoring his kill while wiping the dagger on his pant leg.

Shondell hopped a fence and ran through the backyard of a building. A small dog started to bark, nipping at his ankle as he leapt out of the yard. He slowed down as he heard the *clang* of a cartridge magazine falling to the ground. He peeked around the garage wall. He clicked the safety off on his .45. The man was standing next to a black Cadilectro truck. He probably was the driver. Shondell stealthily walked up to the gunman and put the cold steel muzzle of his gun to his temple. The gunman dropped his gun and put his hands on top of his head.

"How many more with you?"

"There are only five of us including myself."

Shondell noticed the sound of his voice had a metallic timbre to it; like the *twang* when you hit metal. He reached down and picked up his 9 mm Beretta.

"Lay down spread eagle on the ground so I can search you!" The gunman's coal black face gleamed under the full moon. It shocked Shondell how reflective it was. It was like looking at a grotesque African mask.

"Shondell, is that you?" Bodyslick asked as he, Snow, and Geronimo walked around the car with their weapons drawn.

"Yeah, it's me! Now stand up, asshole!" Shondell hollered at the driver as he dusted himself off. "Your four partners will be helping dandelions grow. You wanna end up like them?" Snow said as he poked his finger into the man's chest. "This bitch thinks he's in church. Get up off yo' knees. Didn't I tell you to stand up! Do I look like Jesus to you?" Shondell shouted.

They laughed as they looked at the driver's cold, lidless reptilian eyes; his shiny, froglike, amphibian face; wide simian mouth; and the synthetic snot that snaked from his nose.

"Look, mistuh," he said as he stood up shaking uncontrollably. "I was just doing what I was told to do. I was told to drive here."

"Yeah, to kill me, right?" Bodyslick spat at him. A gob of saliva whizzed past his head.

"No, suh . . . no names mentioned. I'm just a driver. I didn't get hired to kill anyone!"

"Then how did you know who to kill, moron?" Shondell said while looking at his dummy-like face.

"We had pictures, and a GPS chip was implanted in your car."

"Who sent you to kill us?" Bodyslick asked viciously, "and how did you get those laser holes in your clothes? You the fucker that I was shootin' at with the body armor on, huh?"

Whaack! Snow bitch-slapped him with his gun. "He asked you a question, asshole!"

"It was . . . it was . . . it wa . . . was . . ."

"Stop stuttering, fool!" Bodyslick said impatiently.

"It was Willie Loyd. His girlfriend almost died from that diseased liver you sold him." The side of the man's head swelled up like a grapefruit. It had a faint neon-like glow to it.

"Call him up! Now!" Bodyslick snarled as he handed him his phone. He pinched his nose at the putrid odor of garbage, feces, urine, and rat offal that blanketed the alley.

The driver was trembling so hard he couldn't punch the keys. Bodyslick snatched the phone from him.

"What's the number, asshole?" He dialed the number and a ragged voice that sounded like he had drank drain cleaner when he was a child answered. It was a voice Bodyslick knew instantly.

"Sam, I told your ass not to call me unless . . ."

"Unless what, asshole?"

"Who is this? What's goin' on, Sam?"

"I'm your worst nightmare, Willie."

"Who the fuck are you, and how did you get my number?" Bodyslick gave the phone to the driver.

"Willie, this is Sam!" he said while wheezing and holding the side of his pulsating head. A yellow oily substance seeped from the side of his head. A darker oily substance started to leak from his nose and trailed into the corner of his mouth.

"Did you kill the muthafucka?"

"Hell, no, I'm the only one here. Everybody else is dead!" he said, his hand trembling like a plucked violin string.

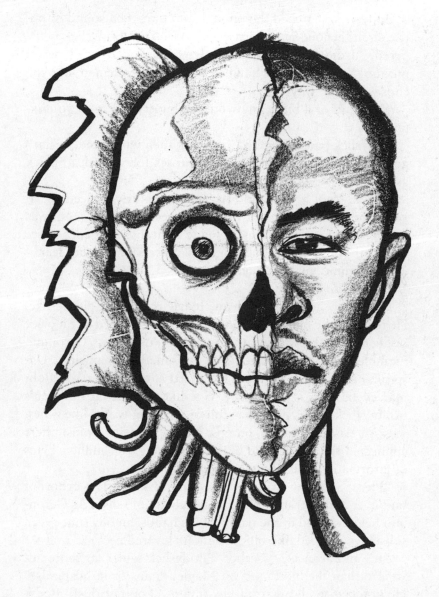

Bodyslick snatched the phone from him. The sound of police sirens echoed in the distance. "Asshole," Bodyslick whispered, "I didn't intentionally sell you a bad liver; it was a mix-up. You could have handled this like a gentleman. But you chose the thug way!"

"You son of a bitch, my woman almost died from yo mix-up!"

Bodyslick paused, waited a second, then whispered, "That's good because she gonna be buying roses for your dead black ass!" *Click!*

"Look, I got a wife and four kids," the driver pleaded. "If you lemme go I swear you won't ever see me again." Sam was crying, wimpering, sniffling. It made Bodyslick nauseous to see a man about to die without dignity and consumed with fear.

"Geronimo, make it quick!"

"*Please* don't kill . . . !"

Geronimo grabbed his head. It felt cold, oily, plastic-like. He torqued the man's neck 360 degrees. It snapped like a piece of fiberglass. "Holy Jesus, this fucker ain't human," Geronimo mumbled as if he were looking at something nameless. Unspeakable. Vile and unclean. He gazed at one of the 3-D globular eyeballs as it hung on a vine-like cord from the man's orbital socket. His head was full of writhing worm-like tubes, sensors, elastic actuators, pumps, pistons, and nanotransmitters connected to a positronic brain containing 100 million bytes of information in its digital library.

"Please . . . don't kill! Please . . . don't kill!" The cyborbot said over and over again like a scratched holo-disk. As Geronimo held the head in the palms of his hands, an oily snot-green substance dripped like blood from its severed neck.

"It's an advanced cyberbot," Bodyslick said, "far more advanced than the kind used on Maglev trains or in hospitals!" He grabbed the head from Geronimo. "Look at this!" Bodyslick pressed down on the nose and watched the skin and bone reshape back to normal. "The skin is so human-like that when

Snow slapped it with the pistol, it could detect the type and force on it and react like normal human skin would!"

Snow reached down and pulled his dagger out of his ankle holster. He made a vertical slice down the middle of the forehead, nose, mouth, and neck. The black plastic-like skin snapped loose like a tight rubber band in opposite directions.

"Look at that," Snow said with astonishment, "they made the skull, lips, teeth, eyesockets, vocal cords, and tongue out of rubbery plastic. It's like looking inside a real human 'cept there ain't no blood!"

"It has self-awareness. It knew it was in danger. It was programmed to react to any threatening situation. I remember Esha, a cyborbot attendant on the Maglev A train 20018-1A. She was drop dead gorgeous. She was the finest female, including human, I have ever seen. My dick still gets to throbbing every time I think about her!" Bodyslick said passionately.

Snow, Geronimo, and Shondell started to laugh uncontrollably.

"You are one sick fucker!" Snow said, laughing so hard he was almost in tears.

Bodyslick watched the headless cyborbot's body jerk spasmodically on the ground. It seemed to whisper faintly, "Please don't kill . . ."

The sound of encroaching sirens broke the silence of the night air.

"Let's get outta here," Bodyslick said. "We can't salvage any organs from Sam the cyborbot."

"Bodyslick," Snow said, "you mean you would have fucked Esha? A damn robot?"

"Hell, yeah, and you would have too if you had seen how fine she was!"

They all laughed as they walked down the alley toward Shondell's hydro-car.

Chapter 23

"Malanna was a good girl. A Gawd-fearin' girl. A girl who did not deserve such a diabolical death. May the Lawd up in heaven cast His mighty wrath down on the sinners who committed this crime!"

"Amen, praise the Lawd!"

The Reverend pointed his huge hand at Malanna's relatives and trumpeted. "It was divine providence that caused her death. It was the will of the Almighty Gawd!"

"Praise dah Lawd!"

WOULD JESUS WANT A TRANSPLANT?
*Come out next Sunday at 9:30 a.m. and hear this
inspiring sermon by Pastor Taylor.
Mount Olive Sanctified Church*

Bodyslick frowned, wondering if the poster was aimed at him. As he walked into the small storefront church, a sea of faces turned toward him from pew-like rows of seats. Faces full of disdain, hatred, fear, nausea and revenge stared at him. The glares felt like daggars stabbing him. The funeral had just started. Bodyslick's eyes flicked about the crowded church and caught on a sculpture of a blond, blue-eyed, crucified Jesus hung high above the fat, darkly-robed Reverend who was about to start his eulogy.

The smell of stale roses and funky perfume wisped past his nose. It was a "sanctified" church. Better known in the ghetto as a *"holy roller"* church where obese women and effeminate men often rolled on the floor possessed by the Holy Ghost. This dismayed small children, who often got stepped on, crushed, or injured in the wild spiritual abandonment.

Bodyslick grimaced as mournful, piteous notes echoed from the organ. Two young boys started to warm up on tambourines and drums. Fat women ushers in white blouses and white gloves stood like African statues at the back of the church waiting for someone to start speaking in tongues. He noticed the paint on the wall was peeling and the plaster was showing through. The metal chairs seemed worn and beaten. As he glanced around at the church's meager contents, he realized there was no room here for ostentation. He wondered why his beloved Malanna would choose such a poor church. Yet there was a high voltage energy that seemed to pulse through the poverty. An energy that made the hair on his neck rise.

A large holographic picture of Malanna hovered over a shiny, copper, closed casket. The church choir, in long flowing red robes, seemed to gasp with anger as he swaggered down to the front pews. He walked over to Malanna's mother and other relatives and briefly gave his condolences. He then sat down behind them.

Her young brother turned around in his seat, pointing his finger at him while gritting his teeth and mumbling, "Umma git you fah dis, man!" Bodyslick sat motionless in his chair and lowered his head. He felt a current of hatred surge at him from the people in the church.

A beam of sunlight was shining through a bright multicolored diamond gothic stained window onto the flock.

The Reverend Clyde Taylor was a big man, 6'2", with huge hands and a fat, porcine face. He was handsome in the sense that an English bulldog is handsome, but it was his bass voice, that could make grown men cry and old women talk in tongues, that was his unique gift. He cleared his throat while icily glancing at Bodyslick.

"After living in a troubled world. A world filled with *godless*, money hungry people. A world where people openly profess to be atheists. A world where some people advocate disbelief in Christianity. A world where getting on your knees in prayer to *God* is an abomination. After living in this troubled world, Malanna is finally at peace in body and mind."

Bodyslick cringed at the thought that he was responsible for her death. Was the price of his success a naive Baptist girl's life? Did his lifestyle encourage Malanna to prepare for blood and suffering?

"What legacy did she leave?" the Reverend asked pleadingly. "How did she affect all of us? She will always be remembered by me as a young woman who loved her neighbor. She had trust in the God of Jacob. She had trust in the God of the fatherless. The God of a poor and despised people who are forbidden by the system to rise, to soar like a bird to their highest glory!"

Malanna's friends started to shout, scream, and cry. Feet stomped. The choir mourned. Hands clapped. The tambourines and drums thundered. A baby's cry accented the commotion. Bodyslick could *feel* the power the church held; it became a living, pulsing thing. But something prevented him from feeling what they felt. He wondered if it was the idea of a white savior?

"*Jesus, Gawd Awlmighty, you done took mah baby!*"

Her mother stood up, arms flailing, and leaped up and down as if possessed by some spirit, some other world force. Two sister ushers rushed toward her. The organist hit the keys, and suddenly everyone started to sing.

*"Precious Lord, take my hand and lead me on and
let me stand."*

It was an eerie feeling, Bodyslick thought. It was as if some powerful force like lightning was charging the air.

"Malanna was a good girl. I mean she was the kind of daughter any man would be proud of. Can I get an Amen on this?"

"Amen!"

"Amen . . . Hallelujah!"

Bodyslick felt a shiver run down his spine. His thoughts wandered over space and time. Malanna's smiling face crisscrossed his mind. Was it not his cowardice, his money-hungry selfishness that had prevented him from being killed like her? Or could he vindicate himself by admitting that she "played" blind because of her love for him? She refused to believe that his lifestyle was treacherous and dangerous. Should she share in the responsibility for her death? To some extent, he was to blame for her death, but should he be blamed for surviving in a system that violates and disrespects a man because of his skin color? Should he be blamed for trying to get enough money so Malanna could live a decent life? Should he be blamed for makin' it in a system that seems to rob young poor men daily of jobs and self-respect? Should he be sorry for surviving by any means necessary in a system that didn't believe that his beloved Malanna's womanhood was as sacred and precious because of her poverty?

It is a system, that is partly responsible for her death, because it is just as cruel and devilish for poor people to be trampled on under the class notion that they are not as valuable as the well-heeled. If institutional racism, classism, and ageism can be rationalized, then so can crime against the state, Bodyslick thought.

Reverend Taylor raised his hands to quiet the emotional congregation. He pointed his finger at them accusingly and moaned: "Malanna's favorite biblical passage was in Psalms.

"But their idols are silver and gold, made by the hands of men. They have mouths, but cannot speak; eyes, but cannot see; noses, but cannot smell; they have hands, but cannot feel;

feet, but cannot walk; nor can they utter a sound with their throats. Those who make them will be like them and so will all who trust in them.

"Malanna's body will be laid to rest, but not her unwavering spirit. A spirit that believed that life is governed by some inexorable logic that defies man's logic."

Bodyslick scooted over as a white man sat down next to him. He quickly moved back over as a huge black man plopped down on the other side. Bodyslick's head was lowered as if in prayer. He only looked at the men's hands. But he could feel pulses of rage as it surged at him from the black man. He looked at him. It was Detective Tank Morgan on one side; on the other was Detective Olerhy.

"In closing, Malanna, from childhood, loved life passionately. She loved life with a fervor and lust that maybe was her undoing. You see, there are a lot of young women like her. I only hope that young women in here will learn *something* from her horrible and senseless death. Maybe you young women should be extra careful about the type of men you get involved with. Maybe the spirit of Malanna is beckoning you all to not drink out of the same cup of *hemlock* with a man, just because it is made of shiny gold, encrusted with diamonds, and lined with silver."

The quality of Reverend Taylor's voice suddenly changed. It went from a high octave to a wrenching, *bluesy* bass. From silk to sandpaper. From gospel to Howlin' Wolf. The words became almost incomprehensible. Pleading. Tearful. Angry. Slurred like he was speaking in *tongues.*

Bodyslick could feel the tormented words stirring his soul. He fought back tears as a suffocating spiritual presence seemed to haunt the church. Sweat dripped from his forehead as Reverend Taylor shook a thick Bible accusingly at the mourners and whispered piteously.

"I prayed all night fuh Malanna and duh night befoe ... And I *feeeel* I want tuh pray some moe!"

"Amen ... Hallelujah!"

"Ohhhhhh, prayin' is duh thing that will take her tuh heaven . . . I'll be prayin' in duh church till duh clock strikes eleven!"

"Amennnnn . . . Reverin'. Amen!"

"Are you reaaady tuh meet the Lawd?"

"We red-day Reverin'!"

"Is you reaaady tuh stop sinnin'?"

"We reaaady."

"Tuh stop thinkin' a puny man can conquer death!"

"We listen' tuh yah!"

"Tuh stop thinkin' the nightlife is a righteous life!"

"Amen. Praise duh Lawd!"

"De Lawd say yo' clock is gonna run out just like Malanna's."

"We ready!"

"OOOOH GOOOD GAWDAH MIGHTAY, you don't heah me!"

"We listenin' Reverin'!"

"Is yuh ready tuh walk down tuh duh pearly gates?"

"We ready, Reverin'."

"You might be ready, but is the Lawd gonna let you in like Malanna?"

"Let us in, Lawd!"

"Lawd have mercy on dis poe chile's soul and de monster that murdered her!"

"Amen. Hallelujah!"

"Rest in peace, Malanna!"

Bodyslick stood up to leave as the pallbearers carried her casket down the aisle.

Her brother lunged for him. "Punk, you killed my sister! Umma git you, man!"

Bodyslick snatched the boy's grip loose from his suit coat. "I didn't kill your sister! The *mob* killed her! Them goddamn niggas and dagos killed my woman!" Bodyslick shouted so everyone in the church could hear. He fought back tears as

Malanna's mother grabbed him by the arm as she walked past him down the aisle.

"Malcolm, I believe you. I believe also that Malanna did not die in vain."

She seemed bewildered as he stuck a sealed envelope in her hand that contained a fifty thousand dollar cashier's check. He kissed her on the cheek. She patted his hand. Her young son frowned at him.

"You fuckin' body snatcher, um watchin' you. If you take a shit too long, punk, umma come lookin' fah ya!" Tank whispered as he walked behind him.

"Bodyslick, remember you are still a suspect in her death," the Irish detective Olerhy, said as he walked beside him.

"Will you lemme mourn in peace? She was one day goin' to be my wife," he said piteously.

As he walked out the church he glanced up at a dark cloudy sky. A mournful sky. He glanced back, looking desultorily for Olerhy and Tank who'd threatened him.

Tears made the lashes of his eyes glisten. He watched as the long convoy of limousines slowly moved toward her final resting place.

"I'll kill all of them for you, baby!"

"You all right?" Snow asked as he patted him reassuringly on the back.

"I'll be all right once I avenge her death!"

"You ride with me. Snow will come back later and pick up your car," Geronimo said with concern.

Chapter 24

"**I**n closing, I have not only transplanted a human head on a donor body, but actually made it totally mobile. The difficulty was, of course, the reconnection of the head to the spine. It took me years to find the solution. I had to experiment with at least a thousand combinations of transplanted embryonic stem cells before discovering the right recipe!"

Snow and Geronimo sat in the third row from the front, in back of the press section in the packed auditorium. They were dressed in dark blue corporate suits with phony HUMAN-SOURCE ID tags on them. Snow and Geronimo wore horned rim glasses to give them the appearance of intellectuals.

"All of you realize that, by cooling the brain to a very low temperature . . . ten to fifteen degrees Celsius, we can suspend the circulation of blood to the brain . . ." As Dr. Graham talked, a large screen jutted down from the ceiling. The lights dimmed. A holographic image of a human male's head, clamped with a myriad of tiny hoses to arteries, lay on the steel gurney. ". . . thus never depriving the human brain from its circulation once it is re-warmed. What you are viewing is the brain temperature being lowered."

Snow peered at the short, thin man with close-cropped, grizzled hair, and glasses with bifocal lenses. He had a domed forehead and large cauliflower ears. He wore a wrinkled dark brown suit.

"That was the easy part!" The image faded. The audience seemed to collectively cringe in their seats. "Another holo-image, please."

The auditorium was deathly quiet. A blanket of fear seemed to be hovering over them. The professor's voice became hoarse, loud, and rasping. With the stealth of a cat, he walked while swinging his arm in a theatrical gesture to a hologram of a man that appeared on the podium. The lower half of his pale white face was covered with a mask. He wore only green patient pants. The audience squirmed as the image of his sutured neck was blown up. The man walked slowly with a slight limp toward the audience. In the deadly silence you could hear mice fucking.

The professor approached the hologram and spoke. "How do you feel?"

A surgical mask covered the man's face from his nose to his chin. The mask shook from a slight twitching of the mouth. "Good."

"How does your new body feel?" the professor asked.

"What new body?" the man asked, not realizing that he'd had a successful body transplant. His body was that of a healthy, thirty-year-old, white male.

"This will wipe out our business!" Geronimo whispered.

The holographic image disappeared, and the lights popped back on. A cacophony of voices echoed through the auditorium.

"The days of suffering for body organs are numbered. Now you can trade in your whole body. Any questions?"

"This body transplant could increase the theft of human bodies rather than organs," a newspaper reporter stated. "If there is a shortage of healthy livers and kidneys, where are you going to find healthy donor bodies?"

"My dear fellow," the professor replied, "it is easy to raise these *micro* issues. But if we look at the *macro* long term value . . . why at this very moment genetic engineers are trying to eliminate imperfections of the human body as evolved by nat-

ural selection." He cleared his throat and continued, "For example, the donor body used for this transplant died in an accident causing brainstem death. Just imagine if he'd had small extra lungs, with a tiny heart and blood vessels in his throat to keep the brain oxygenated in an accident. Why, he would still be alive! And in some major countries, they are experimenting with genetic engineering techniques that could design human bodies without heads . . . a body farm. We now mass produce chickens without heads or feet. Why not humans? One more question." A student raised her hand. "Your question?"

"What method, Dr. Frankenstein . . ." The audience laughed.

"You can call me Dr. Graham," he said, smiling.

"What method did you use to reconnect the spine and the head?"

"The method is right here." He pointed to his temple. "What I can tell you is that morphed human stem cells are part of the equation. And on that note, I want to thank all of you for coming out tonight!" Dr. Graham received a ten-minute standing ovation.

Snow and Geronimo walked out of the crowded auditorium to wait for the professor to walk home. They sat in their car two houses down the street from his home, waiting quietly.

"Jesus, am I hungry!" Geronimo said, as he sat frozen behind the wheel. "Hey, Snow, why don't we go get a Polish real quick? The professor's got a nice walk to get here."

"That's him coming now!" Snow said.

"Drive around the block and lemme out behind him. You can pick me up in ten minutes. I'll be walking east toward Stoney Island on this street," Snow said, as he slammed a ten round clip into his .380 with the attached perforated silencer. "Where's the derma-mask kit?"

"It's right there in that gold and silver box on the backseat."

Snow walked toward Dr. Graham, extending his business card. His Brazilian dermo-mask felt natural on his face. "Sir, I'm affiliated with Humansource . . ."

The professor stopped for a minute, peering cautiously at Snow as he held his attaché case tightly.

"Look, I am very tired. If you'll just give me your . . ."

Bam! Ba bammm!

Snow shot him two times with his silver muzzled .380-caliber gun; once in the head and once in the heart. The professor dropped to the ground. Snow took his attaché case and started walking east for Stoney Island.

Chapter 25

Bodyslick sat alone in the almost empty holo-theater. Alone and suspicious. A kaleidoscope of images and sounds bombarded his senses. Images that weren't real but seemed three dimensional. It was called holovision. He remembered how his grandfather used to tell him about the old 3-D glasses. Times had certainly changed, he thought for a moment, as the gangster movie caught his attention. He squinted as seemingly real bullets flew at him from a submachine gun. But it would take more than an optic trick to erase the blind pain of Malanna's brutal death. And the pain of Malanna's brother blaming him for her death.

Every time he thought of Dr. Weiner showing him her butchered body that was found in a garbage bag with the acronym TWOC scrawled on it in her blood, he felt wretched. Nauseated. His whole being trembled with disbelief. Blind terror stabbed his heart. Nothing in his fast-lane lifestyle was as devastating as Malanna's mutilated body.

Suddenly he became tense. He had always possessed an uncanny sense of impending danger. He craned his neck and gazed down both aisles. There was no one else sitting in his row. It was the last movie, and the theater was nearly empty. A creeping feeling of apprehension gnawed at him. He narrowed his eyes with icy terror when he saw, approaching him from both the right and left aisles, two men in long gray trench coats and black fedoras. Were they cops? Or were they assassins? One of the men was black. He beamed a tiny flashlight into his face as he walked slowly down the narrow space between the seats toward him.

Bodyslick was momentarily seized with hot panic. It became a tight knot in his throat and raced through his blood. He told himself to be cool. The side that was the least emotional usually won the battle. They neared him. The white man started to reach into his inside overcoat pocket. A gun? Cold fear sliced into his being with such overwhelming power that he felt immobile. Stiff. Granite. He attempted to stand up before the two men were upon him. The white man had a red mustache and he was slowly pulling his hand out of his pocket. It was now or never. Do or die. He thought if he had to die, let him die like a man. Let him die like a warrior. Let him die not whimpering and begging for mercy, but fighting and defying his foes till death ended his battle. They were nearly upon him. It was time for a death move. He reached inside his coat pocket for his laser .45-caliber Colt.

Just as he had grabbed the smooth pearl handle, the white man shouted, "No need for that, Bodyslick! We just want to talk with you." The black guy shone the flashlight on the white man's leather fob containing his shield, as he pulled it from his inside coat pocket. They sat down on either side of him.

"Bodyslick, you remember us. I'm Detective Milton Olerhy, and my partner here is Detective Joe "Tank" Morgan."

There was no need for a formal introduction. There wasn't a criminal on Chicago's South Side streets who hadn't heard of their legendary ruthless salt and pepper escapades. He had heard that the 250-pound, muscular, black guy sitting next to him, "Tank" as they called him in the streets, was just that, a human killing machine. A black detective who had absolutely no remorse for shooting a fifteen-year-old black youth for letting his two-headed pit bull loose on him.

He knew how both Olerhy and Tank felt about his body

parts business. He knew they hated him more than the drug pushers, prostitutes, and gangsters. In reality, all cops hated "body snatchers," as they called them. The reason was because they viewed the selling of human organs as one of the most parasitical crimes a person could commit. To treat a dead human being as if they were butchered meat and to argue and kill over their organs was incomprehensible.

"Bodyslick," Olerhy said compassionately, "the word on the streets is that the mob has got a quarter of a mil contract out on your ass because of the murder of one of Vinnie Luziano's main *capons*, Antonio Villichi!"

Tank Morgan nodded his head in agreement and said angrily, "Look, scum, we are obligated to read you your rights . . . so listen up."

"Skip it . . . I already know the spiel."

Tank continued in a monotonous bass voice. "In keeping with the 1966 Supreme Court decision in Miranda v. Arizona, we are not permitted to ask . . ."

Bodyslick's mind raced over recent events. Bubba's gift wrapped heart; the kidnapping of the coroner's daughter; the mutilated death of Malanna; the killing of Antonio Villichi; and the recent murder of Dr. Jonathan Graham. Lingering guilt gnawed at him. The notion that he hadn't done enough to rescue Malanna was driving him insane. He snapped out of his thoughts as Tank hollered at him.

"Do you understand your rights?"

"Yeah . . . yeah I understand."

"Will you answer our questions now?" Olerhy said.

"Yeah," Bodyslick said anxiously, "anything to get this over with."

"You know anything about Villichi's death, Malcolm Steel?" Tank Morgan asked in a resonating bass voice.

"No, I don't know . . ."

"Malcolm, did you know that Antonio was sent by the mob to kill you?" Olerhy asked cynically.

"No, I didn't think I was that important! And call me Bodyslick!"

"Listen, you body snatching slime," Tank said menacingly, "Malcolm Steel is your name . . . that's what I'm going to call you. Anybody that makes a living from the dead . . . from the grave . . . from dead human remains, ain't got no respect as far as I'm concerned. And you better understand, sonofabitch, that I have a personal interest in Malanna's death because her mother is a close friend of mine. How do we know you didn't chop her up in a fit of rage, you lowlife . . ."

Bodyslick pulled out a stiletto so fast that it caught Tank off guard. He held the knife at Tank's pulsing jugular vein as the blood-red holo-colors gleamed on it from the movie screen. "Listen, you ass kissin', tom-ass, Uncle Remus ass nigga!"

Olerhy screamed at him as Tank cocked the .357-caliber Magnum at Bodyslick's temple. "Put the knife down, Malcolm . . . put it down . . . now!"

"Listen, man, she was my future wife, and I'd kill for her. And I will kill because of her!" he said, as he closed the knife and put it back in its holster inside his pants leg. He trembled with murderous rage as he tried to regain his composure.

"Malcolm," Tank said, as his baseball glove sized hands grabbed Bodyslick's throat, "I've killed punks like you fah lookin' at me the wrong way . . . don't ever do that again or you'll end up at Restville Cemetery!" He released his grip from around his neck leaving his handprint on it. Bodyslick coughed and gagged.

Olerhy, more compassionate than Tank, displayed concern. "Malcolm, you play straight with us, and we'll play straight with you. Okay?"

"I didn't kill her, man!"

"What about Antonio Villichi?" Tank asked with intimidation in his voice.

"I don't have anything to do with that, either!"

"Come clean with us, Bodyslick. Make it easy on yourself.

You dropped your gun running from the house, but we know Villichi died because of a broken neck," Olerhy said with sympathy.

"You're wastin' your time with me. The mob killed Malanna. And how do you know Antonio wasn't killed by Vinnie Luziano's own soldiers and just dumped on the South Side to make you think what you're thinking? Or better yet maybe the Hip Hop Sung Gang in Chinatown did it."

"And why would Vinnie do that?" Tank said derisively. "And you have heard about Tong's niece, huh?"

"Maybe he was a threat to Vinnie's empire. Why don't you go ask him? And everybody on the street knows about the rape of Tong's niece."

"Malcolm, we would like for you to take a ride with us to the prosecutor's office for some more questioning," Olerhy said, as he and Tank stood up.

"Malcolm, you're safer with us than in the streets . . . 'cause 225Gs is a lot of money. And believe me I know a lot of dudes that would take a punk out like you for less than that!"

"Fuck you, yo daddy's a punk . . . !" Bodyslick said maliciously.

"Why you . . ." Tank grabbed Bodyslick by the neck and lifted him out of his seat.

"Let him go, Tank," Olerhy said pleadingly.

"Look, Uncle Remus. No man grabs me like that and lives. You got a payback coming. I fear no man. Violence is a part of my business! Let's go!" Bodyslick said confidently.

Chapter 26

Bodyslick glanced around the small room. He listened to a cacophony of voices outside. A sign over the door read: THIRD PRECINCT INVESTIGATION UNIT.

It was a typical interrogation room with the trick windows which enabled the cops to watch you from outside without being seen. There were snot green file cabinets; a peeling, cracked ceiling which squeaked loudly from traffic above; two metal desks with small computers on them; and long clipboards; wanted posters; bulletin boards; and a torn *Playboy* centerfold on the walls.

He sat on a small, wooden, three-legged chair in the middle of the room. An intensely bright light glared down on him causing him to perspire. The door opened, and Detective Olerhy walked in holding a brown folder. Tank, holding a black cup of coffee, and a uniformed cop followed behind him. They grabbed two chairs and scooted them next to him. The third cop stood at the door as a sentry. Olerhy cleared his throat while rummaging through the folder and mumbled as he pulled out a long yellow computer B-sheet.

"Malcolm Steel . . . alias 'Bodyslick.' Place of birth Chicago, Illinois. Did time in 2011 for an armored truck robbery, sentenced to three years at Menard Penitentiary. 2016, a year probation for possession of the galactic drug somellow. 2017, illegal transportation and selling of human body parts . . . what we call body snatching. Etcetera . . . etcetera."

Olerhy tossed the B-sheet to Tank and nervously cracked his knuckles. After glancing at it, Tank angrily threw it on the floor, stood up, crossed his arms behind his back, and paced the floor. He walked back over to Malcolm and scooted his chair closer to him, then sat down and hollered at him.

"Malcolm, did you kill Antonio Villichi?"

"No . . . I told you already. I had nothin' to do with it!"

"Where were you that night?"

"I visited Malanna for a few hours at her apartment."

"Is her address 5119 S. St. Laurent?"

"Yes."

"What time did you visit her?"

"About 8 p.m."

"Did you all have an argument?"

"No."

"Was anybody else there?"

"No!"

"Did anybody see you en route to her place?"

"Not that I can remember."

"Think man!" Tank said.

"No . . . no, I don't think so!"

"What did you do while over there?"

"That's personal!"

"What did you do?"

"We fucked!" Bodyslick said arrogantly.

"How is your leg feeling?" Olerhy said sarcastically.

"What about my leg?"

"You were at Satan's Den that same evening, weren't you?"

"Just answer the question," Tank shouted.

"Yeah, I was there . . . so what!"

"So why the shootout with Toejoe?"

Bodyslick became quiet. Cautious. Apprehensive. He didn't want to implicate himself so he would play it by ear. He wouldn't volunteer any information.

"The only Toejoe I know of is dead. He was the Jap general in World War II."

"Listen, smartass," Tank snarled, as he balled his huge fist at him. "I ain't in no mood fah games!"

Olerhy restarted the questioning. "Okay, what about Willie T. Wilson, alias Toejoe?"

"Yeah, I know the runt. So what?"

"Look punk, everybody in the damn lounge was ducking laser blasts from your gun exchange . . . so come straight with us. Why the shootout?" Tank asked.

"You got my fuckin' folder. You know what kind of business I'm into . . . so cut the bullshit, man. You know damn well why we had a shootout and don't be calling me no punk, you big sissy!"

"Malcolm, we got a warrant for your arrest stemming from the damage accrued and the disturbance caused that evening," Olerhy said confidently then shook a pink sheet of paper at Bodyslick.

"I know the owner. I'll pay for all damages in cash!" Bodyslick snapped.

"But that's secondary . . . our main concerns are the whereabouts of your co-partners, Bubba's killers, and what you know about the kidnapping of the coroner's daughter and the deaths of Antonio Villichi and Malanna Thompson," Tank said emphatically.

"Bubba was murdered by Toejoe Wilson."

"How do you know that?"

" 'Cause me and Toejoe go back to childhood, man. He is a loser. And all his damn life he has been tormented by the fact that he will always be a nickel and dime hustler. He used to work for me. I gave him the keys to the game, and now he's trying to take over."

"Keys to the game, huh?" Tank asked curiously.

"Yeah . . . you haven't been *tomming* so long that you have forgotten how black folks talk."

"Why you scum-ass!" Olerhy grabbed Tank's hand as he started to swing at him.

"Go on!" snapped Olerhy.

"I heard it through the grapevine that he has hooked up with the mob to increase his power base. Toejoe is a spineless punk that needs an army to do what a single individual could do with guts!"

"Is that why Luziano sent Antonio after you? We know about the assassins that Luziano has brought to Chicago with him," Olerhy said.

"I don't know nothin' about that. What I do know is that they're out to get me."

"Like they attempted at Malanna's apartment?" Tank said derisively.

"Yeah . . . Toejoe kidnapped her there. And then they murdered her. But you can bet your last dollar they all gonna *holler* over her death!"

"That's not your job. We get paid for that. We don't need your kind helping us do anything. The only thing you can help us with is quit fucking with the dead!" Tank said.

"We know that Toejoe, Pumpkin, and Butch were at the apartment. And people in the neighborhood described Antonio to a T," Olerhy said.

"Why shouldn't they have?" Bodyslick mumbled, "He was like a speck of white flour in black coffee!"

"Steel, we don't have enough on you to hold you," Olerhy said with regret, "but we will let you hang yourself . . . besides, whatever justice you're supposed to receive, I'm sure Toejoe and the mob will succeed at it. So we're going to let you go. Because even with all your money I don't think there is any place on the planet where you can hide. Now you do have a choice. We can put you under our witness protection program and no one can touch you. You'll be safe for life. We will change the way you look. We will change your whole identity, and you will have a monthly stipend the rest of your life. Just give us the information we need about the body parts network that you're involved in nationwide.

"How about your old somellow connections? You have information about Toejoe and his somellow connections with the mob that would enable us to put all of them away. All we need is cooperation, Steel." Olerhy lit a seagarette and offered Bodyslick one. He shook his head rejecting the offer.

"What you trying to say in a nice way is you want me to be a *rat*. You want me to be a paid, protected stoolie. Well I'd rather die first. I ain't no punk ass snitch. I'll fight my own wars. I didn't get this far snitchin' on people. I can deal with whatever the Mafia and Toejoe got. I thrive on a challenge. I am at my finest when death is just around the corner."

"All right!" Tank said impatiently, "we don't need no Napoleonic speech."

"Steel, come on . . ." Olerhy said, as if they were friends, "can't you drop that tough braggadocio guy mask for a while? We know what you did for that little Irish girl, Mary Sullivan. We know you gave her that anonymous liver. Steel, I'm Irish . . . and let me tell you, man, it was the most heartwarming thing I've ever seen. My wife cried like a baby over it. Now we know you got a heart. And I don't mean someone else's."

Tank laughed hysterically.

"Steel," Olerhy said almost pleadingly, "this offer is for right now. The minute you walk out that door . . . no deal. Eventually we're going to find out which one of your henchmen broke Antonio's neck. Once we do, you going to be in deep trouble in jail with all those wiseguys. I'm trying to give you a break like you did for little Mary Sullivan. Help us and you don't have to worry about anything."

Tank nodded his head in agreement with a vile look on his face.

"Look, man," Bodyslick said almost mournfully, "I come from a poor home. All my life I've struggled and fought for everything . . . this suit is tailor made, and it costs five hundred dollars. My shoes are handmade. My fucking underwear is made of Thai silk. Listen, Olerhy . . ." Bodyslick stood up brushing off his suit. "Your offer would be appealing for someone else. But I will survive Luziano's outfit and thrive! The market is growing every hour for hustlers like me. At this very second, someone's life is dependent on a donor organ. The appetite for my business is insatiable. There is a *price* for everybody, even you and Tank."

The door opened, and a tall blond man in his early thirties and a shorter Hispanic man, both dressed in plain dark blue suits, walked into the room.

Bodyslick could sense that they were federal agents. He nervously wiped sweat from his forehead. Detectives Olerhy and Tank acknowledged the two men and exited the room. The tall blond agent introduced himself in a no-nonsense voice.

"Malcolm 'Bodyslick' Steel, my name is Ben Wilson." He reached in his inside suit pocket and opened his wallet showing his gold badge and his ID card. He then gestured to his comrade. "Emanuel Gomez is my partner. We are with the FBI and we have come here to investigate improprieties in your income. We want to talk to you about your financial disclosures, and I hope we can resolve this matter quickly."

Bodyslick's blood raced to his head and seemed to burst with pressure because, at that moment, he had no idea how much information the bureau had about his illegal activities and he was in no hurry to find out. He decided that it would be best for him to seem cooperative rather than defensive. After all, his money was invested in legit businesses. He sat back down in the chair.

"I would like to verify some data about you." Agent Wilson sat down and opened up a black attaché case on his lap that quickly turned into a mini-computer system. He started pecking at the keys.

"You were born in Chicago, Illinois . . . correct?"

"Yes."

"When?"

"January 2, 2001."

"You live in Hyde Park in Chicago, correct?"

"Yes."

"Are you married?"

"No."

"How far did you go in school?"

"Completed high school while in prison, and got two years of college credit."

"How long was Willie 'Bubba' Smith co-owner in your Real Steel Chicken franchise on the South Side?"

"Maybe two years. I started it, and Bubba wanted to invest in it."

"How many of them are in operation presently?"

"One."

"How many have you owned at one time?"

"Six."

"What happened?"

"We sold out."

"Why?"

"Why would any businessman sell out? We sold them for double their original price."

"How much money was originally invested in the franchise?"

"About fifty thousand dollars."

"Who loaned you the money?"

"Some friends."

"Drug friends?"

"Just friends," Bodyslick said unflinchingly.

"According to our computer checks we have absolutely no records of you filing income taxes, either federal or state, between 2025 and 2027 for Real Steel Chicken. Also, no records of your utility bills, organ sale receipts, business insurance, or organ inventory data from 2027 to 2030 from Livers, Legs & Thighs Inc., your organ storage facility."

"I can supply all that information."

Bodyslick peered at Ben Wilson's pale white skin with contempt. As a white man, Ben hadn't been discriminated against because of his color; his mother hadn't raised him in the infernos of public housing; he hadn't slept as a baby with rats and roaches crawling around him; he didn't know what it was like to see his mother exploited and abused because she was black and poor. He wondered, as he stared at his white hand pecking the keys on his computer, if he had the faintest notion about the environmental forces that had helped shape and mold who he was. Didn't Agent Wilson realize that he was interrogating a *victim* of his lily white institutions? Didn't he realize that he was taught from youth that it was public policy to *deny* black men power, prestige, and wealth?

Didn't Agent Wilson understand that the way the white man governed the existing system made black men rebellious, dishonest, and corrupt? Didn't he realize that being good, honest, and Christian hadn't worked for black folks in America?

Bodyslick could taste hate and disgust as it rose from the pit of his stomach and flooded his being, as Agent Wilson continued his interrogation.

"Do you know anything about why Willie 'Bubba' Smith was recently murdered?"

"No, I don't."

"Mr. Steel, you were a business partner and close friend weren't you?"

"Yes, but he had his own personal life. He had a wife and children that he loved. It wasn't all business."

"But his death now makes you the single owner of all Real Steel Chicken's assets?"

"And also liabilities. We had our problems and disagreements like any business partners," Bodyslick said emphatically.

"Did you have anything to do with Bubba Smith's murder?"

"Hell no! He was my main partner. We were tighter than fishpussy, and that's waterproof. We were friends since childhood."

Agent Gomez laughed loudly. Wilson continued.

"Are you still in the illegal drug business?"

"No!"

"What about your retrieval organ business?"

"What about it?"

"According to your 2029 tax forms . . . you're doing damn well in the organ business."

"Once you get the consent of the deceased relatives to sell the organs at a fair market price," Bodyslick said defensively. "Of course, this is only done after verifying the validity of the donor organ card. It's really quite lucrative, and I'm helping a lot of people who would otherwise be dead. It's all legit."

"According to your tax information your Real Steel Chicken franchise was worth, last year, in claimed assets and liabilities about a half million dollars. Is that figure correct?"

"Minus Bubba's fifty percent. Yeah, it's reasonable."

"What we are puzzled about is how you have failed to leave a paper trail for us to catch you."

"I'm doing nothing wrong. All my investments are legit! I also own five mutual funds worth $50,000 to $100,000."

"When I say puzzled, Mr. Steel, this is what I mean. We know you made almost $700,000 in organ parts in 2029."

Bodyslick was cool. He knew what they were fishing for. That one mistake. That one error.

"For instance in 2029, from the sale of your five chicken franchises, your corporate checking and saving accounts were worth almost a million dollars. You realized you couldn't withdraw that amount of money without causing unwarranted attention. You are sharp enough to realize that any currency transaction higher than ten grand requires notification to the FBI. We realize that you were merely using your chicken enterprise as a means of converting the money you had laundered illegally via your organ business back into hard cash. We are attempting to uncover how you did that."

"You guys get paid for that."

Agent Wilson stood up and angrily started pacing the room with his hands behind his back.

Agent Gomez said, "Mr. Bodyslick, it's just a matter of time before we will have stiff indictments against you. Some of the charges will be tax evasion, drug dealing, the illegal selling of body organs, and the first degree murder of Bubba Smith. If you would cooperate with us now, we could make things a lot easier on you."

Ben Wilson reassuredly patted Bodyslick on the shoulder as he said, "We could cut your galactic prison sentence in half. I'm sure you've heard the horror stories about being an inmate at Solstice Galactic Prison, which is where you will be going. Why, you won't see a blue sky again for the rest of your life."

"Just cooperate *bro*, we can talk to the judge and reduce your sentence," Gomez added. Bodyslick realized they expected him to break. Crumble. Most people did. But he figured by the time they had their indictments, his business complications would be totally coordinated and organized.

"Look, man, I have nothin' else to say to you," Bodyslick said arrogantly. "For any further questioning I'll have to talk to my attorney for consultation."

"All right, Mr. *Slick*," Agent Wilson said facetiously, "we will indict you under 848 for continuous involvement in criminal acts. Also, we believe your company LL&T is perfect for a RICO prosecution."

"I once knew a guy named Rico," Bodyslick said solemly, "who wiped his ass with toilet paper soaked in nitro glycerin; the heat from his ass served as a trigger . . . KAPOOOW!"

Gomez laughed loudly.

"The RICO we are talking about," Agent Wilson said icily, "is the powerful racketeer influenced and corrupt organizations statute that allows us to go after organized criminals who use loopholes to hide their criminal activities from existing laws. We also use it for galactic drug trafficking, illegal organ sales, murder—you name it!"

"I felt sorry for poor Rico. What a horrible death. To get your ass blown up like that!"

"We will see how funny it is when your wise ass gets sentenced to life at Soltice Galactic Prison with no hope of parole, and you don't see a blue sky the rest of your life. But I'm sure you've got hoodlum friends up there!" Agent Wilson impatiently slammed his briefcase closed.

"See you round, *bro*," Gomez said with regret, as they walked toward the door.

Bodyslick abruptly stood up and ran up to Agent Wilson. Ben's blue eyes became bulbous. Fearful. His pale white skin became livid. His thin body suddenly became stiff, rigid, almost frozen under the blanket of hate that beamed from the demented black man's eyes. He felt lightheaded. He locked eyes with Emanuel Gomez for help. Gomez stood there indifferently.

Bodyslick grabbed Wilson by the collar and knocked over tables and chairs as he pushed him up against a wall. Ben Wilson's body sagged under his blind fury. He tried to reach for his laser pistol that was in a clip-on holster on his belt, but the weight of Bodyslick pressed him too tightly against the wall.

"Why don't you ask me about how I feel about my father dying in your muthafuckin' Iraq War!"

"What has that got to do with all this? And get your *nigger* hands off of me!"

"It's got a helluva lot to do with my life. He died for this country, and his children ended up living in abject poverty because he was just another *nigger* that died for the flag!"

"That's not our concern. We came here to question you . . . Gomez, dammit, don't just stand there, get this punk off of me!"

"As long as he don't pull a weapon, it's you and him, man!" Gomez said sternly.

"Why haven't you mentioned my father, Army Sergeant Malcolm Henry Steel, who got a purple heart in 2004 posthumously for his role in your stupid war in Iraq?" Bodyslick asked, as his hands trembled with anger.

Agent Wilson attempted to break loose from Bodyslick's hold. But it was like lifting a car off his chest. He worked up a gob of saliva and was on the verge of spitting on him. Bodyslick continued to scream at him in a fanatical rage.

"I am a product of a fatherless home. Because my father died in a stupid war, on the front line, along with a disproportionate number of other black troops. If he hadn't," Bodyslick said almost tearfully, "maybe my life would have been different."

"At least," Agent Wilson said angrily, "at least he died with honor. At least he had *beliefs, valor, patriotism.* I would imagine he would turn over in his grave with agony, if he realized that his death has produced a dope dealing, body snatching, conniving, hustlin' nigger son . . ."

"Fuck you, man!" Bodyslick said as his words stabbed at his heart. "I do what I have to do. What did it get my father's family for him dying with *honor* in Iraq? What did it get my family for him giving his life to protect America's vested oil interest in a country ruled by a dictator who didn't even believe or give a shit about so-called democratic values. I'm still treated like a *nigger.* I'm ashamed to tell anyone my father died for this country!"

Agent Wilson swallowed the saliva and nervously said, "Look, a single individual can't change the system. Your father will be remembered as an honorable man. The name *Steel* will be remembered in the annals of military history with courage, bravery and respect. Now if you want to live, get your fucking hands off me, now!"

Bodyslick shifted his feet for balance as he held the agent against the wall. Then he loosened his grip.

"Besides," Agent Wilson said mournfully, "I'm a Jew, dammit . . . and my people are experts in bigotry and suffering!"

Bodyslick looked at the man, straining his eyes. Searching. Staring for some obvious physiological sign of his Jewishness. He certainly didn't have the familiar features. He let him go, reasoning that Jews were also members of a despised race.

"You're a Jew, man?"

"Yes, my real name is Benjamin Wilson Levine."

"Levine?" Bodyslick said incredulously.

"Yes, I dropped the surname. I also have had cosmetic surgery. One of the reasons for the changes is that the anti-Semitic forces in this country are alive and growing. Believe me I haven't had it easy. Sadly, Mr. Steel, there are still people in this country who hate Jews more than blacks. Both you and I are products of a deranged society. We have merely chosen different methods to deal with it."

Bodyslick found himself tongue-tied. "Well," he was at a loss for words, "*you* should be more sympathetic toward me since you are also a member of a persecuted race. Just keep in mind Mr. Levine, that only six million Jews died in the Nazi holocaust while almost a hundred million Africans died during the four hundred years of slavery!"

Agent Wilson brushed off his clothes and angrily stared at Bodyslick.

"Mr. Steel, don't take this personally but you're a *nigger*! Your father was a proud *black man*. Jews make a distinction! Enjoy your BMW and your expensive lifestyle, Mr. Steel, because your days are limited. When we drop those multiple criminal indictments on you there will be plenty of time in jail to brood about how unfair the system is. Racism," Agent Wilson said firmly, "is never a justification for criminal activity. Let's get out of here, Gomez. I smell something shitty!" They quickly exited the room.

Bodyslick stood there, helplessly, with resignation. He was worried. The FBI would now be on him like white on rice. He thought: *This is the way America handles arrogant, ambitious niggers. Niggers with a thirst for power were doomed to be locked up in the stinking dungeons of Miss Liberty.* He wondered how long could he wage his personal war against a system that was capable of sending men to Mars?

Detectives Olerhy and Tank walked back in the room.

"All right, you can go, Bodyslick. There is nothing else to say," Olerhy said.

Bodyslick lit a seagarette and slowly walked to the door leaving a trail of smoke behind.

"Body snatcher," Tank snarled, "don't try to leave town cause we will be watching you!"

"Fuck you!" Bodyslick shouted, as he angrily slammed the door.

Chapter 27

Dr. Donald Jones glanced out the Learjet's window as it climbed to almost 11,000 feet. Stars darted the milky black sky. He only hoped everything went as planned in getting the donor heart; for his reputation was at stake. He had twenty-four hours exactly to get the heart and make it back to Baltimore to put it inside Vanderbilt. He glanced down at the cryonic cooler he would use to bring back the heart in. It was really a portable liquid nitrogen refrigerator. It was amazing how something so simple could transport something so magical and complex.

There were no other passengers on the Learjet. Only him and the pilot. The trip was paid for by Louis K. Vanderbilt. He also had a carte blanche check from Louis Vanderbilt, for whatever it would cost to get his nephew David Vanderbilt a new heart.

Dr. Jones remembered when he was an intern in Chicago, how the poor who needed organ transplants were doomed to die because of their poverty, but the rich would live. In some cases the rich would get two or three chances at donor organs while the poor would get none. Being a black doctor made him especially sensitive to the treatment of the *havenots*; and yet he was required, because of his token privileged status, to accept the punishment of the poor as a price for their own impoverishment.

All his life he had wanted to be a doctor. Since grammar school he had dreamed of wearing that white mock jacket and people addressing him as Dr. Jones. But he never dreamed that he would be exposed to some of the most vile, insensitive, and brutal people one would ever meet in the medical profession. And their behavior was based on the almighty dollar.

He had learned early that the Hippocratic Oath was really a sham, because medical science, especially at the big prestigious hospitals, was not concerned about ethics. Nor was it concerned about saving lives, curing disease, or even prolonging life. His experiences with his peers had taught him that they only acknowledged one oath and that was the love of money.

He thought about Dr. Jacob. He was one of the top five heart transplant surgeons in the world, and yet greed was his motivating driving force for excellence. He really didn't give a shit if David K. Vanderbilt lived or died. But he did care about the millions of dollars that the Vanderbilts pumped into the hospital transplant program annually. He was more concerned about the continued testing of his immunosuppressive drug Trilexis on heart recipients, than the patients. The reason was because if his new drug worked, he could easily get the private venture capital he would need to market it globally. *Greed.*

Dr. Jones thought about how the federal government, with its legal mandates against procuring organs for profit, had spawned an underground hell, full of shocking horrors: where poor healthy people from Third World countries were being slaughtered like pigs and their vital organs sold to organ brokers in Europe. He remembered what a Colombian med school student named Santos Sanchez, who was studying in the U.S. under a student-exchange program, had told him about the human organ farms in his home country. Santos would grimace with nausea as he talked about it. He had told him that he was a leader of a militia that was sent to close down one of the illegal organ farms operated by a mobster who called himself General Rafara. A man who was quickly gaining a reputation as one of the most ruthless criminals in

Colombian history. A man who was head of the Cordova organ cartel. Before he fled Colombia for the U.S. he was supplying 70 percent of the world's donor organs.

Santos said that once they had rammed their way into the large facility, what he saw had to be worse than the gas chambers that the Jews died in during World War II. He said the stench of human decay was so heavy in the air that they became nauseated when they walked into the place.

Blood that was ankle-deep had congealed into a sticky, gluey, pudgy substance that gripped the soles of their shoes as if they were in quicksand. Large green liquid nitrogen tanks held dead bodies that whirled around inside, as if in a gigantic human cleansing machine. There were smaller tanks with the same liquid in it which had "Hearts," "Lungs," "Livers," or "Kidneys" stenciled on them. He said you could barely see the organs because of the thick liquid. Santos told him that the facility had been abandoned because the body snatchers had paid informers inside the secret police to notify them of any clandestine plans against them.

These human organ farms were akin to the assembly line methods used in butchering hogs and cattle for domestic consumption. Inside of the facility, almost immediately past the bloody entrance, was a series of cellular enclosures. Each cell interconnected with another by a series of plastic tubes on electric tracks, that looked like cylindrical beds and were used to transport the cadavers to each cell for the extraction of a specific body organ. Santos said that is when he saw the most abominable thing in his entire life. As they searched through the cells, looking for body snatchers, he was walking past another large tank when he felt a lurid glare beaming from the murky liquid. He sensed death floating in the smelly air, in the cells, even clinging to his skin. He wondered what kind of mad terror would compel human beings to do such a ghastly deed. He turned around and crept back to the tank. A dead silence echoed broken only by the footsteps of his comrades rummaging in search of the body snatchers. An eerie feeling blanketed him. As he neared the tank he hesitated. From a distance he could see the blurred glitter of small round white balls floating within the tank. Glistening. The white balls seemed to be staring at him. He slowly walked toward them, and as he neared the tank he wiped his eyes. Again and again. He then touched the icy cold glass of the tank. He pinched himself hoping he was having a nightmare. He put his face so close to the tank that his nose brushed against it. Suddenly, *eyes* floated toward him. Eyes without the flicker of life. Hundreds of dead human eyes were staring at him. They were floating aimlessly in the preservation solution, and all of them seemed to be piercing through him. Blue, grey, brown, black, all of them remarkably translucent. One blue eye kept bumping against the tank's window over and over again as if offering itself for pity. There was something odious about the globular blue eye staring at him with a soulless glimmer.

After that, Santos said he moaned and cried like a child. He asked with bitterness, "How could men do such a grotesque thing out of greed?"

Santos had told Dr. Jones that in some of the banana republics there were even worse cases of human organ farms.

Dr. Jones was thirsty. Nervous. He needed a drink to calm his anxiety, his uncertainty. He pressed a button on the outside of his seat and in a matter of seconds the *clitter clatter* of metallic bi-ped feet ushered down the narrow aisle. He knew it was one of the old model T robot attendants.

"I would like a beer," Dr. Jones said, as he turned around in his seat and gazed down at the four-foot-tall, tubular, washing-machine-shaped robot. He now understood why they called them model T. Tiny green metallic orbs blinked at him. Long antennas on top of a pumpkin head twitched bewilderingly. He could hear the *whir* and *whizz* of the robot's mechanical brain.

"I am only programmed to respond to my name. Andy is my name."

Dr. Jones licked his dry lips. Beads of sweat formed on his forehead. His hand clenched the arm of his chair with amazement. The robot's eyes stared at him glassily. He glanced out the window at a dark sky. Here and there stars seemed to burst with light.

"Andy, I would like a draft beer," Dr. Jones said, as he gazed at the robot noticing how old and primitive it was compared to the neurobots used in the OR at Baltimore General. He smiled at its cartoon like human gestures.

"Andy is my name. Andy is my . . . my . . . name . . . Andy . . ."

A voice came from the intercom system. "This is the pilot, Dr. Jones . . . In order to get Andy the robot attendant to work properly, you must, and excuse my language, get out of your seat and kick the raggedy *sonofabitch* in the head as hard as you can . . . over and out."

He stood up and positioned himself about three feet from Andy. Then he remembered a karate move he learned in high school, whereby he leaped and kicked his right foot into an opponent's body. He would use that against the robot's head.

"Andy is my name. Andy is . . ."

Bammmmmmmmmm!

"That was a damn good kick, Dr. Jones . . . I heard it up here. In approximately one minute the hunk of metal shit will be serving you . . ." the pilot joked.

Dr. Jones sat back down in his seat. He stared at Andy. Stared while listening. There was no sound. The robot stood absolutely still. Andy's lime green eyes were now vacant. Empty. Its antennas no longer twitched randomly. Then all at once Andy scooted next to his seat. Dr. Jones gazed at its face. Blank. Vague. Like looking at a child's toy. Suddenly the eyes lit up. He waited then he heard a *whirring* inside the robot and then a static-like sound.

Then, with a metallical stutter: "But, Massa Jones, whise usah kickin' un poe me? Jes' tells ole Anday what kinah beah usah wont me tah git ya, sah?"

"What did you say?" Dr. Jones asked incredulously.

"Mah name, sah. Yah mus' say mah name."

"Andy, what did you say?" He heard faint laughter from the pilot's intercom. Dr. Jones wondered was this some type of racist joke.

"Mah name, sah. Yah mus' say mah name."

"Andy, no . . . not that. What you said before *that*."

"Eyeeee says, sah, what kinah beah usah wont me tah git ya, sah?"

The intercom clicked on. "Doc, this is the pilot again, please don't become offended with Andy, because that particular early model was programmed to use all sorts of racist humor. Black, Japanese, hillbilly, Mexican, Italian . . . you name 'em, those old designers were at least democratic . . . they offended everyone. So don't take it personally. In fact, if it's really bothering you just tell it to knock it off!"

"Andy, a draft beer!" Dr. Jones said authoritatively, relieved that the insults weren't just hurled at blacks.

"Massah Jones, usah mus' make a choice, sah."

"Listen Andy," Dr. Jones said angrily, "will you stop talking that antebellum slave crap and speak English?"

Andy didn't answer. His arm slowly extended to Dr. Jones. Lime green eyes flickered brightly. "Sorry if I offended you." Andy held out its three fingered tubular hand.

Dr. Jones shook it. He stared at Andy with disbelief. *Damn, I need a drink*, he thought.

"Just a little early eighteenth century ethnic humor, sir. Have you decided on your beer choice?"

"Andy . . . I'd like a cold draft beer."

"Foreign or domestic, sir?"

"Andy, domestic."

"Glass or cup, sir?"

"Andy, a glass!"

"Ice or straight, sir?"

"Andy, straight!"

"Pitcher or single bottle, sir?"

"Andy, a goddamn bottle, dammit!" Dr. Jones said with anger.

"Type, sir?"

"Andy, it doesn't fuckin' matter."

"Sorry not programmed to decipher fuckin'."

The intercom clicked on again. Sounding irritated, the pilot said, "Doc . . . I'm shutting down the damn robot . . . it ain't worth it. I don't know why this company won't get rid of them. Doc, the bar is directly to the left of the john. You'd do better serving yourself."

"Thanks," Dr. Jones said, as he stood up and walked to the end of the aisle, turned left, punched the button for bar and a door opened exposing ice and a host of alcoholic beverages. He glanced back down the aisle at Andy as it moved back into its enclosure. He opened his beer and took a deep swallow then walked back to his seat. He liked the metallic taste of canned draft beer.

As he gulped down the remainder of the beer, he thought about how vastly different his life had been compared to his childhood friend, Malcolm Steel. They had called him plain old Malcolm in high school. He didn't use the moniker Bodyslick till he got in the organ business. Even in high school, Malcolm was rebellious. Where Jones was studious, Bodyslick was streetwise. Where he focused on making it in the system, Bodyslick's energy was directed toward making it out of the system. Sure he had the credentials, the respect, the adulation that came with being a token black heart surgeon intern, but it always spawned a sensation of guilt. Despite the fact that he could use his talents to help the needy. He always carried a feeling of *selling out*. He always felt like an educated *nigger*.

When he was in med school, he naively thought that by becoming a surgeon he could make a difference. That he could work inside the system and ultimately change it. How awfully wrong he was. Instead of changing it he had become as greedy, altruistic, and malicious as the very monster he had once hoped to change. How could he make moral judgments of

Bodyslick for choosing crime as a means of survival, when he had discovered that there was as much corruption in the sacred halls of science and technology as in any big city ghetto? He sometimes wondered if the hypocrisy of the system would one day drive him insane.

Bodyslick, Dr. Jones thought, at least had the guts to wage his own personal war with the status quo rather than acquiesce like he had done . . . for a sheepskin that was dripping with innocent patients' blood. Bodyslick, in a way, was a powerful link with his past, with his roots, with his ghetto childhood. Sure he was somebody. He was Dr. Donald H. Jones. He had the mulatto wife. The Mercedes Benz. The apartment in the uppercrusted white neighborhood. He had all the material trinkets that he had ever dreamed of, but the price was his silence, his obedience, his severance of old ties. No more watermelon. No more chitterlings. No more barbecue. No more Cadillacs. No more old James Brown cuts. *We don't need those old primal screams in our neighborhood; it would awaken too many ancient memories.*

Bodyslick was a means of giving something back to the ghetto. When he wrote that check for Whitey's donor heart, and the limit was a quarter of a million, that would be his own personal triumph over the system.

Suddenly the steady drone of the plane engine changed. Dr. Jones craned his neck looking out the window at the bright orange sunrise. Chicago's panoramic skyline loomed into view. The reflections of the solar rays on Lake Michigan and Chicago's magnificent urbanscape were astonishing: Sears Tower, Trump International Hotel and Tower, Millenium Park, Soldiers Field, the Harold Washington Library, and Hyde Park where Bodyslick lived.

"We are now approaching O'Hare, Dr. Jones. Prepare for landing."

He was home again. He quickly punched in Bodyslick's secret code and whispered softly, "check it out" to activate the vocal transmissions.

His special wristwatch beeped.

"Hello, Dr. Jones speaking."

"Check it out. This is Malcolm aka Bodyslick, Steel . . . homeboy."

"You got my message then, huh!"

"Yeah, but listen to me closely, Doc, tell Mr. Vanderbilt that two hundred and fifty thousand dollars must be delivered to a Mr. Jacque St. Lambrique, who is one of the Chief Financial Officers of Geneva's Union Bank, with instructions to deposit it in my Swiss bank account. And it must be confirmed by a receipt of deposit within twenty-four hours of this phone call or the deal is off . . . you got that, Doc?"

"I'll make arrangements on that right now before I land. Where shall I . . . ?"

"Don't worry about that . . . just take care of the business and contact me with my secret code. Welcome home, Dr. Jones."

Chapter 28

His menacing wolf-gray eyes were now sky blue. His shiny bald head was now covered with a brown Spanish-textured wig. He had reshaped his broad nose into a long hooked beak with organic paste. His once thick lips had been shrunken with a tissue reducing lotion. His once sienna brown complexion was now pale and white.

Bodyslick squinted with astonishment as he gazed in the mirror at his strange new image. An image that was hybrid: part Spanish, part European, part African, part clown. He smiled at his wild new age clothes: purple glittering sequined shirt, long saggy striped balloon pants, red firehouse suspenders, black knee-high leather boots with color changing straps.

In the 1990s he would have been considered a circus clown or a nut case. In 2031 he would be viewed in the streets as a NARF (new age radical freak), an underground group of cosmetically altered bohemians who based their weird lifestyle on an esoteric philosophy called Voodnarf, which is a set of beliefs and practices derived from traditional, voodoo, American and Rastafarian elements combined with the 1960s hippie movement. Voodnarf was developed by the futurist writer James Beglac in 2015. He believed that Voodnarf would fill a void caused by social alienation stemming from high tech science.

Voodnarf initiation ceremonies symbolize death and rebirth

by the drinking of human blood and the smoking of Martian-zeeg. The central belief of the sect is that the worshipping of the supernatural can alter reality.

Bodyslick touched his skin. It was chalk white and had totally bleached away his old pigment. The melanin based skin lotion had really worked its magic. His disguise was now impeccable. It would be virtually impossible to find out who he really was.

The room he had rented was in a flop house on North Wabash in Chicago, called the Tass Hotel. He could have easily afforded an expensive hotel room, because he had brought twenty thousand dollars in cash with him, but that would have made his new image more obvious. Besides, he felt more comfortable with the underground culture.

The seedy hotel room reeked of sexual human musk and cheap perfume. A broken shooter that some junkie had used was in an ashtray. There was a large king sized bed, a small table, a lamp, and a sink. He walked to his open window and gazed out at a weekend crowd of frenzied fun-seekers. The near North Side of Chicago was known for its eccentrics: bisexuals, asexuals, prostitutes, NARFS, anarchist revolutionaries, galactic drug dealers, and gangs.

The neon-lit street scene slowly metamorphosed into a surreal world of strange perverse images, and yet it was backdropped and interwoven with a stark urban reality. The night freaks were out to play. He glanced at his wristwatch phone. He wondered when Doc Jones would call.

He ducked his head as a fly buzzed around him. *Bzz . . . bzzz . . .* The fly zoomed toward him like a kamikaze pilot picking a location before it plunged to its death.

"Gotcha! Float like a butterfly, sting like a bee!" He'd once read that Muhammad Ali used to catch flies to maintain his quickness. Bodyslick opened his hand and looked at the crushed nanofly: two steel-blue, transparent, hinged, silicon wings; twin, electric-green, pinpointed, camera eyes; with a tiny, cone-shaped audio and video transmitter nestled between them. A tiny globule of liquid seeped from its shell. It was wet and smelled like ethanol mixed with water. Bodyslick wondered if it was fuel! He winked into the camera.

Suddenly he swerved from the window and reached for his .45 on a nearby table, as someone knocked on the door. He walked toward it apprehensively. All kinds of dark thoughts bounced inside his skull. Had Toejoe and the mob found him? Had someone in the hotel seen him before he had disguised himself? Maybe Detectives Olerhy and Tank had found incriminating evidence near Antonio's body? He cleared his desert-dry throat and spoke in a muffled tone.

"Who is it?" There was no answer. He slowly braced himself against the door so when and if he opened it he would not be a sitting duck. "Who the fuck is it?"

"My name is Liza, and I want to bum a seagarette if you smoke."

The voice was young, innocent, demure, and virginal.

"I don't smoke . . . sorry."

"Well could you loan me a dollar so I can buy some?" Again her voice had a melodic ring. It was as though she were singing her words. He wondered how she looked. He had learned a long time ago that a beautiful voice didn't mean a gorgeous face. He unlocked the door and stuck his gun inside a holster inside his boot. She was a NARF. But an astonishingly beautiful one. He was so stunned by her presence that he was speechless.

"I didn't mean to impose on you," she said, as she darted out her long surgically shaped forked serpent tongue. Her lime green cat-eye contacts glowed in the room. Accenting her pristine pink complexion was long rust-red hair and juicy, large, gelatin-pumped lavender lips, which complimented a Grecian nose that looked as if it was sculpted by Lysippos. Her eyelids had tiny crystal implants in them which glimmered when light shone on them. A tiny gold earring was hung around the septum of her nose. Her pearl-white teeth sparkled with small, silver, star-like shapes implanted in them. She had an hourglass

figure. She wore a morph suit that changed color with light
and temperature. It was as if it had been melted on her. Bodyslick could hear his heart pounding with excitement.

"Is something wrong?" Liza asked compassionately, as she
stood in the doorway with her arms crossed defiantly.

He hadn't made love to a woman since Malanna had been
killed. The nightmares of her carved up body had abated his
sexual drive. He had vowed he would kill her murderer before
he touched another woman. That would be his pilgrimage to
her. His way of saying I loved you. But that was before he had
gazed into the deep, sensuous eyes of Liza.

"Come on in and sit down while I get some money for your
seagarettes," he said eagerly. He walked to the window and
threw out the nanofly. Below he saw a black BMW quickly
drive away burning rubber. He knew they were the source of
the nanofly on the wall.

"What's wrong?" she asked, as she sat down on his bed.

"Nothing . . . just a little paranoid." He quickly opened the
closet and got a fifty dollar bill out of his wallet. He walked back
to her and stood over her. She looked at him. She looked at the
fifty. He gently feathered her mouth with it. She smiled. She
new intuitively what he wanted. Bodyslick's dick throbbed in
his pants. It was so hard it hurt. It protruded out of his pants
conspicuously.

Liza quickly grabbed the crisp fifty dollar bill as if he would
change his mind.

"I'll go with you. I'm hungry and I could use a drink.
What's your name again?"

"Call me Liza. My full name is Lizaveta Krelinsky."

"Lizaveta?"

"My mother is Russian. She named me after a character in
one of Pushkin's books."

"Was the book *Queen of Spades*?"

"How did you know that? Yes, that was the title," she said,
impressed with his scholarship. "Did you go to college?"

"No. While serving time in prison I read thousands of

books. Pushkin was a black Russian, a brilliant mulatto. Russians love him. I still have a passion for books. Just don't have time to read."

"What were you in the pen for?"

"I'm not a psycho killer. We will discuss that later. Now let's get out of here."

When she stood up, Bodyslick stared at her curvaceous ass rippling in the morph suit as she floated toward the door.

"You like looking at my fat derrier, huh?"

"Yeah, there is a lot of junk in your trunk," he said as he grabbed one of her cheeks tightly.

"And it's real and not fake," she said sensuously.

He smiled and grabbed her hand as they walked to the elevator.

As they walked out of the hotel into the brisk night air, he momentarily gazed up at the twinkling stars, wishing Malanna were with him instead of Liza. They started to walk north on Wabash toward Chicago Avenue, the main artery of near North Side action. His sixth sense told Bodyslick they were being followed, and he craned his neck to look around the street. Then he saw what he had suspected all along, a red Mercedes with three white men in it was slowly following them.

"Is anything wrong?" Liza asked with concern.

"No . . . just lookin' at the sights," he said as he watched the car slowly pull to the curb. He knew intuitively that he also was being followed on foot. He patted his .45 that was tucked inside his belt. Then he peered at Liza again. He wondered if she was planted in the hotel to spy on him. Maybe she was just setting him up to get murdered or she was there to get information from him? After all, he didn't know a damn thing about her. How square of him to let a pretty face and gorgeous body make him forget that quite a few people in Chicago wanted to kill him. He must watch her every move now. Watch her as if his life depended on it.

The police called the area Somellow Town because the bulk

of the galactic drug's main dealers used the strip as their personal playground and all the accoutrements of fast drug money were saturated in the area: high class call girls, any kind of drug imaginable, expensive electro-cars, robotica sex houses, and all types of galactic food shops. Somellow Town was known throughout the nation as a counter-culture haven for rebels, artists, musicians, and street entertainers. The city of Chicago, after years of intra-council squabbling, had resolved the street entertainers' problems by demographics. Stretching from the Catholic Cathedral of the Holy Name at 700 North Wabash Avenue through State Street, Superior and Chicago Avenues, school buildings, parish houses, and churches had all been converted into creative spaces. The area continued to the north on the east side of Wabash Avenue, expanding to Rush Street and then Michigan Avenue was the periphery of Somellow Town. Miles and miles of prime Chicago real estate had been created purely for artists to display their wares to the public for a price and without the threat of policemen or irate store owners nagging them about scaring off business. This was their space, and it was open twenty-four hours a day. It was a Chicago development that was hauling in multimillions of new tax dollars for the city. It had surpassed New Orleans' Mardi Gras as a national attraction because it was open year round.

"Look, that's the famous artist El Charlo!" Liza said excitedly. "Why he only comes here once a year. They say his artwork is magical."

The Chicago sky had become a velvety black. The wailing cry of a distant siren kindled a collective sigh of grief. The hypnotic notes of a distant saxophone made their souls want to soar to a place of peace and tranquillity. They walked over to a small humpbacked man who wore an ankle-length, black, hooded monk's cassock. He looked as if he was of Spanish descent.

He sat on a wooden crate, and to the side of him was a portable easel. He held a wooden palette in his left tiny hand

and a bunch of glowing brushes in the other. The paint on the palette had a faint, incandescent glow. Phosphorescent.

A dim street light popped on and cast an eerie shadow from his hood across his olive face. A sharp, beak-like nose protruded from tiny, round, gold-rimmed glasses. Piercing, slanted eyes showed vaguely through them. He had a mouth that was twisted as if he was born in pain. Stained, rotten teeth gleamed from diseased gums. His right eye twitched nervously. The scent of whiskey reeked from his mildewed clothes.

They watched.

And watched.

And were dazzled by his brushstrokes as he moved his arm with the flourishes of a maestro. El Charlo seemed as if he was trying to capture her very soul, the very life force, of the shy young woman sitting there patiently. A crowd started to gather. El Charlo slashed his paint on the canvas as if he was in some sort of mad cabalistic trance. With each stroke, the portrait seemed to reflect living flesh; a flesh magically mixed into the very molecules of paint. The portrait seemed more and more alive. And the young woman seemed more pale. More weak. Was he literally capturing her soul?

Bodyslick and Liza stood there petrified. Frozen with disbelief as the picture actually became the woman. Became a living thing. And the woman was turning a ghastly deathly white. The same color as the canvas he painted on.

"*No mas!*" El Charlo moaned from the pits of his bowels. "I can go no further. Any further is dangerous. One should never look into God's eye. This portrait you must treat with great care," he said as he stood up taking the canvas off the easel. "Senorita, it is a tiny fragment of your soul. If you should damage it, you will feel the pain; that is the price you pay for owning an original El Charlo portrait!"

He turned around and faced the amazed crowd. Agony and pain were snarled on his face. His eyes flickered like pulsing candles. He handed the young woman her portrait. She looked healthy again.

"It's absolutely gorgeous! How did you do it? What technique did you use?" she asked ecstatically.

"The great philosopher C.S. Lewis once said, 'Unless you live near a railway, you will not see trains go past your windows.' Find the window to your soul, senorita."

"But what do you—"

"*No mas* . . . please just pay me what you think the portrait is worth and leave. I am very tired. It is a curse to have this gift. It is a burden. Now all of you please go. Go! Go! Leave my wretched soul in peace! Leave me now to wallow in my own sorrow! Leave . . . you fuckin' parasites! You fuckin' *bloodsuckers!* You will never understand the creativity, discipline, and sacrifice of true genius because you're too comfortable in your dull, xenophobic, middle-class, automated lifestyles. We are all *doomed*! So drive back to your sanitized homes in the suburbs, in your air-conditioned, combustible-metal coffins, and leave me alone!"

"I don't even know your name," Liza said, grabbing his hand as they turned the corner into Chicago Avenue. She walked into a Yerba Pot Shop to buy a pack of seagarettes.

"Pete . . . Pete Wilson," Bodyslick lied quickly as they walked out of the shop looking at the thousands of people that were buying, gawking, and being entertained by a host of attractions.

"That's a real square name. I'll just call you Peter . . . git it . . . ?" The sultry warmth of her smile surprised him as she lit a seagarette and blew smoke at him.

"Yeah, I'll be your *Peter*, all right," he said, as he glanced at her succulent lips. "How did you become a NARF?"

"Look, let's go into that restaurant across the street . . . they have great food. You said you were hungry and thirsty, and I'll tell you all about me!"

He held her hand tightly as he bulldozed their way through the noisy crowd. As they neared the restaurant, a blind black man was playing a saxophone. The people were clapping and jumping up and down as if they were under some sort of spell.

Bodyslick and Liza gazed at the man. He was jet black. A tiny silver voodoo icon tattoo, barely visible, gleamed on the middle of his forehead. He wore dark shades.

He was dressed in shabby clothes. He was obviously indigent and homeless. A black top hat with a red chicken feather in it almost swallowed his small head. Long dreadlocks hung down to his shoulders. His opened saxophone case was full of money from the mesmerized crowd. He appeared to be in his late forties.

"That's Black Zac . . . he's world-renowned. People say the notes he plays on that sax have miraculous powers. People from across the world come here to listen to him play."

"Well," Bodyslick said, as he gazed again at the man's obvious poverty, "why does he seem so poor then? Why does he seem to live such a wretched life?"

"He could be a rich man, Peter. But people that know him say, out of fear of losing his power because of fortune and wealth, he never charges anything. He feels this gift would diminish if he accepted money and wealth in exchange for what he is doing. Look, see that man in the wheelchair that lady is pushing through the crowd? That's not unusual. And this is not some con game. Black Zac might make him well again."

Bodyslick watched as a wealthy white lady in an expensive dress and jewelry stood next to the pale young man in the wheelchair. The man looked as if he had muscular dystrophy. The woman got down on her knees and grasped her hands together as if she was praying, and pleaded to Black Zac as if he were a god.

"Please help my only son. Money is not a problem. Michael is a good boy. He has an incurable neuromuscular disease . . . please help him."

Bodyslick and Liza watched Black Zac as he sat almost frozen on his three-legged wooden stool. He slowly put his soprano sax to his thick lips, and then he said to the woman in a soft melodic voice, "Tell Michael to listen to the music and dream that he is healthy again."

She whispered in her son's ear. It was obvious he was paralyzed from the neck down. Black Zac started to play, and the crowd became quiet. It was as though something miraculous was going to happen and everyone collectively could sense it. Bodyslick listened to the sound. It reminded him of reggae music. From the moment air had expulsed from Black Zac's lungs into the instrument there was a popping, snapping sensation inside his head. Liza shook her head also. Then everyone in the crowd started shaking their heads, as if an insect had crawled into their brains. But it wasn't a painful feeling. It was karmic. It was soulful. It was like the sounds were coming from some distant place in the universe.

Bodyslick squeezed Liza's hand tighter and tighter as a warm glowing sensation blanketed his body. The organic rhythm washed over the crowd like healing baptismal water. He looked at her, and she nodded, signaling that everyone was feeling the same holistic sensation. Black Zac was playing the sax with such blind fury that his hands were a blur. Then suddenly everyone in the crowd moaned with anticipation as the crippled man in the wheelchair started to glow like a firefly in the summer night. His whole body was shimmering as if it was on fire. Bodyslick was amazed. Shocked! Numb with disbelief. The music dwindled. The staccato notes silenced. Black Zac snatched the saxophone from his lips. The man stirred in his wheelchair. His mother started to scream with joy and anticipation. Michael closed his eyes and attempted to catapult his body out of the wheelchair. He did it once but fell back into the chair. The crowd shouted at him.

"You can do it, Michael!"

"Come on, Mike!"

"Believe, Michael . . . believe!"

He stood up while grabbing his mother for support and walked stiffly toward Black Zac. He was healed. It was a miracle. He fell to his knees in front of the poor black man and prayed.

"May God bless you . . . may . . . God bless you. If you ever need my help just contact me!"

Black Zac nodded. The crowd shouted and filled up his sax case with money. Bodyslick tossed a twenty dollar bill into the case, and then Liza and he walked half a block around the corner to the All Souls Restaurant.

After sitting down and ordering, Bodyslick quickly glanced at his watch. He wondered what was holding up Doc. Suddenly gunshots burst through the window of the restaurant. He leaped on top of Liza, while grabbing his gun out of his leg holster and pushing her down to the floor. People in the restaurant were screaming with fear. They heard more gunshots. A mournful voice hollered from the street that Black Zac had been killed.

Bodyslick and Liza frantically ran out the restaurant, and she stopped abruptly to pick up one of the shotgun casings that was on the ground.

"Why did you pick that up?" Bodyslick asked.

"I'll explain later," she said, as they ran around the corner to see if they could help.

It was too late. His broken sunglasses tilted diagonally askew from his right eye to the corner of his upper lip. His jet black face was covered with blood. Shotgun caliber shell casings lay strewn across Black Zac's body. His beloved saxophone lay splattered with blood beside him. The money that was inside his sax's case was scattered around his limp body. He had been shot from close range with a sawed off shotgun.

The sound of an ambulance crackled through the night air. But it was too late. The man with the healing sound was dead. Liza asked a tall Asian man in a long black Buddhist robe about the murder.

"Three men in red ski masks leaped out of a red Mercedes Benz and started running toward Black Zac with shotguns in their hands, screaming 'Ton Ton.' Then they started firing their shotguns at him. It's something I will never forget."

A few moments later the Crime Scene Unit arrived and started gathering physical evidence. Liza pressed through the crowd while gripping Bodyslick's hand. She was crying and asking people about Black Zac's death.

She started beating on a detective's chest while screaming. "Why would they kill him? He helped people. He was a healing spirit. He was so damn good!"

The tall elegantly dressed detective straightened out his suit as Bodyslick grabbed Liza.

"All I can tell you people is that one of the North Side's most vicious drug gangs had something to do with Black Zac's death, and that group calls themselves the Ton Ton Disciples. For those of you who are puzzled by their name Ton Ton, their leader calls himself General Rafara. He is one of the most feared gang lords in Chicago's history. Capone and Jeff Fort were nice guys compared to this animal . . . Anyway, he modeled his organization, as he calls it, after the Haitian dictator, Jean Claude Duvaliers' Tonton Macoutes, a ruthless, murderous secret police that he used in Haiti to terrorize any opposition to his leadership."

"But why would they want to kill a poor man like Zac? A harmless soul who only loved music?" someone asked.

"My theory," the detective said confidently, "is that this was not something randomly done. This was planned. I honestly believe he was killed because he wouldn't go commercial with his alleged healing powers. He refused, and now he is dead. His death, and the way he was killed, is meant to strike cold fear into everyone who works in this area. These thugs are trying to muscle in on the money being made here by any means necessary. They already control the bulk of the somellow being sold . . . now they're trying to move in deeper with extortion."

Bodyslick and Liza started to walk back to the hotel. The once-large crowd began to dwindle, as if in homage to Black Zac's death.

"Let's not go back yet, Peter," Liza said, as she wiped tears from her eyes. "I want to visit Mama Luigi. She can help find Black Zac's assassins." They walked quietly back down Wabash Avenue.

Bodyslick wondered what was taking Dr. Jones so long to contact him. He knew his secret code. He liked Liza, but he was in no position to find the blind man's killers. Besides, he had only wanted to fuck her. Maybe it was foolish of him to invite her in his room after all. He stopped and went into a phone booth. He didn't want Liza to hear the click of his wrist phone dial. He punched the secret code in his specially made watch that was similar to the Chronor3 worn by CIA, FBI, and DOD agents. The only difference was that it had a unique holo-transmitter that enabled it to receive 3-D messages at a holo-cafe or outlet. The watch also contained a tiny microchip GPS receiver adaptor, and the message could be received vocally, by video, or by a secure text message which would appear on the watch's LCD. Dr. Jones had a matching watch. Only when a message was super-urgent would one of the parties say "check it out." Then the special code would activate the scramblers in the watches so that anyone without the special watch and its code would only hear a garbled transmission. The watch had a tiny, red, square light. When it blinked, it meant the other party was under duress.

Nothing. Doc hadn't contacted him yet. He slammed the door of the booth and wondered what the hell was going on. Liza slowed her frantic pace as they started walking up the dingy flight of stairs of an old, gray, brick, two-story Victorian house. She paused for a moment as they reached the second floor. She turned to look at him. A dangling blue light bulb hung from the ceiling casting eerie shadows on her face as the light swung to and fro. Her lime-green eyes were glowing like a cat's at night. Some deep rhythmic chant came from inside the apartment.

"Peter, this won't take long . . . just be quiet because Mama Luigi is very strange. Believe me, I'm worth waiting for." She stuck her long lizard tongue out at him. Liza knocked on the door, and it swung partially open. The door had strange chalk-white snake symbols etched in it. He wondered if Mama Luigi was involved in some sort of cult. The odorous smell of boiling

New Orleans gumbo and garlic flowed through the hallway. Liza tapped on the door again, and it flung wide open revealing Mama Luigi bent over a table with her back to them, sniffing a blue powder with a tiny silver spoon in one hand while pressing one nostril closed with her other hand. Bodyslick smiled because he used to sell the blue powder she was using. It was pure somellow, the most potent because only the blue was one hundred percent pure. He knew junkies that were fearful of its purity; yet he gazed at a middle aged mulatto woman seemingly immune to its dangers. She felt their presence and tucked the small mirror she used to cut the drug away. She wore long Rastafarian dreadlocks just like Black Zac. There were silver gray streaks in her hair, which made her demeanor appear sinister. She was banana peel yellow. She was stout. Muscular. She had light gray eyes with flecks of floating brown sclerae in them. Her nose was flat and she had thick lips. Tiny freckles covered her wide nose and cheeks. She had on a long dark gray décolleté dress with snake symbols on it and brown rubber beach sandals. Her arms were covered in cheap jewelry.

"Liza, why do you creep up on me like dat? Why don't you call first, eh?"

"Black Zac!" Liza said while stuttering and holding back tears.

"Git yersef tahgether, girl, and tell Mama Luigi yer problem."

Mama Luigi glanced in a nearby mirror to see if her nose was clean. She could feel the rush of the psychoactive drug coursing through her blood stream as it released hormones that would enable her to tap into the spiritual world.

"Black Zac was killed like a . . . a . . . dog!"

"Poe chile. Lemme hold ya."

She hugged Liza and screamed out in an octave range that rattled his soul. It was like the painful gut-wrenching cry you hear at funerals. It was the way Mama Luigi had cried in the crammed Louisiana Superdome when Hurricane Katrina unleashed unimaginable death and destruction. She could still re-

member the stench of bloated septic-soaked bodies and the sight of empty silk-lined caskets floating down Bourbon Street.

She watched Bodyslick suspiciously. "And who do yar dink yar NARF is jest standin' dar doin' nuthan'? Go git dat bottle of rum off de table and poe her ah drink!"

Bodyslick slowly walked to the table and picked up the rum. He glanced into another room. There were four people in there, chanting and drumming on congas, sitting around hundreds of burning votive candles. The smell of incense floated out of the room.

"Will yah bring de rum boy an stop nosin' yerself in mah house!"

He handed Liza the glass of rum. She gulped it down. Then Mama Luigi guided her and Bodyslick into a dark candlelit, empty room adjacent to her kitchen. Various colored bowls rested on the wooden floor.

"Sit . . . yah por girl, and tell me 'bout Black Zac. Why would dey kill such ah mon?"

"The police," Bodyslick said, as they all sat down on pillows in lotus positions in the small candlelit room.

On the wooden floor were scrawled two chalk-white serpent symbols. Written underneath one was: Baron Samedi. Under the other: Ras.

"They said three men in ski masks who were Ton Ton Disciples murdered him because he wouldn't go along with their extortion ring."

"Ton Ton Disciples ya say huh, boy? Well, dey made ah bod mistake, mon. Black Zac waz ah Voodnarf like us. We believe de world tis filled wid demons, ghouls, and vengeful spirits of de departed. One of de most dreaded and evil spirits tis Baron Samedi, who tis de ruler of the dead. Black Zac wore ah black suit and bowler hat like Samedi. Dose young fools have made ah bad mistake, mon . . . really bod."

Mama Luigi lit a huge Martianzeeg, which looked like a cigar, off a candle and passed it to Liza. "Inhale deeply, girl. The ganja will make ya fill battah."

Liza coughed violently as the pungent odor engulfed the small room. Bodyslick refused the offer and sipped on a glass of rum.

"Liza, did ya bring anything ah can use from de murder scene?"

"Yes, Mama Luigi."

Liza reached into her pocket and gave her the copper casing she had picked up outside the restaurant. Mama Luigi grabbed a male black doll out of a nearby box and covered the head with a piece of red scarf, then placed the shell casing on top of the doll on the floor directly in the center of the whitechalk serpent symbols. She started to chant, while throwing pinches of red powder mixed with cat offal from a bowl, and dry bones from an aborted fetus, a chicken's foot, a carrion bird's red feather, and a wild pig's bloody tongue mixed with ten drops of her own old dried menstruated blood onto the doll.

Suddenly, a blast of cold air whirled in the room. Bodyslick and Liza shivered while they held hands tightly. There was no window in the room. The door was closed. Mama Luigi then dipped her hands in a nearby bowl and they came out dripping with a rabid bulldog's blood. She screamed out with fear and rage, as if she was beckoning some demonic god that only her voice could awaken. She clawed at the doll with a pit bull's tooth and hummed a voodoo chant:

> "*Papa Legba, ouvri barreve poru moins. (Father Legba, open destiny's door for me.) Revenge Baron Samedi . . . Revenge Baron Lentrenc . . . We need revenge fah Black Zac . . . Revenge Ras . . . Revenge ruler of the graveyard . . . I, Mama Luigi, request revenge . . . in the name of Rasta Mon. In the name of the King of Kings, the Lord of Lords . . . in de name of Papa Legba . . .*"

Mama Luigi started floating up toward the ceiling. Foggy green halos, nimbuses, and auras started glowing around her body. Bodyslick and Liza were frozen with disbelief.

Chapter 29

Bodyslick closed the door to his room. As he turned around, Liza grabbed him tightly by the waist. He felt he was under some merciful spell as he gazed into her deep brown eyes. He kissed her passionately. His whole being heaved with animal lust. Then he thought about the Mercedes that was following him. He quickly released her and walked over to the phone.

"What's wrong, Peter?" Liza moaned sensuously.

"Just hold on," Bodyslick snapped as he waited for the desk attendant to pick up the phone.

"Can I help you?" the Korean attendant said with a thick accent.

"Yeah, this is Room 901. I would like to get another room facing Wabash Avenue adjacent to a fire escape. I have this phobia about fires!"

"Just one moment, and I'll check to see if one is available."

"Liza, take those pillows," he pointed at the bed, "and make 'em look like a body."

"Why?" she asked with bewilderment.

"Just do it dammit!" he barked.

"Sir, you are in luck. We have one room 902 which is right next door with the Wabash view and the fire escape. Do you want it?"

"Yes!" Bodyslick said impatiently.

"Well, just come downstairs and get the key."

"That looks fine, Liza," he said, as he resculptured the pillows with his hand to give them a more human-like shape then tossed a blanket over them and walked toward the door.

"Liza, go to room 902 and wait for me there. I've got to run downstairs and get the keys." He muffled her mouth with his hands and whispered, "No questions, just do what I say, okay?"

She nodded her head.

Bodyslick took the exit stairs and ran down to the lobby. As he walked toward the desk he noticed two nattily dressed white men sitting in the waiting area reading magazines. They had on black fedoras, black pinstriped suits and expensive Brutino Italian shoes. They looked like mob boys. He now realized he was a marked man.

He snatched the key from the attendant and tossed him his old key. He watched the two men as they pretended to read. Rather than take the elevator back up to the ninth floor he decided to take the stairs. He knew that once the doors opened and closed in an elevator you were a sitting duck.

Liza was sitting in a lotus position next to the door, as he gasped for air while putting the key in the lock. Once inside the tiny room, which was identical to the other except for the view, Bodyslick bent down on his knees and doggedly started checking under the bed. Then, as he gazed up at the ceiling of the closet, he noticed a door. Did it lead to the roof? He grabbed an old shade rod and poked at it. It was concrete tight. No need to worry about assassins sliding down from it.

Bodyslick waited patiently as Liza slept silently. He had bored a hole through his wall so he could watch who went into room 901; then he heard the jangle of a master key. Three white men burst in the door with Tec-9 semiautomatics with perforated silencers on them. They aimed at the bed in the dark room, thinking he was asleep. Then there was the red burst of flame and the *rat-tat-tat* as the bullets pulverized the bed.

Bodyslick clicked off the light in the room and crawled on

his knees toward the window. He climbed out and stepped onto the fire escape ladder and gazed down at the street. The black Mercedes was still there and the motor was running. A cool breeze from Lake Michigan swept past, leaving globules of moisture on his face. He looked over to room 901 to see if he could reach the ledge and straddle himself to it and open the window. He could. He leaped over, grabbing the ledge while holding the fire escape's wrought iron bars with one hand and trying to pry open the window with the other. It slowly opened. He gazed inside the room. The smell of cordite fumes engulfed the air. The walls were perforated with bullet holes. Smoke still whirled from the bed. He glanced down as he heard the loud slam of a car door. He saw the three men running out the hotel to the Mercedes.

He swung back over to the fire escape ladder and crawled back into the room. Liza was balled up into a fetus position sleeping as quiet as a graveyard. He quickly started to pack.

Chapter 30

In another part of the city General Rafara, leader of the Ton Ton Disciples, was happily driving his new red Mercedes Benz north on Lake Shore Drive toward home. He was elated because the extortion money was really starting to roll in from Somellow Town, to the point where it was actually rivaling his drug profits. He peered at the large diamond-encrusted, ice cube size gold ring on his huge bronze finger. He was making a killing in Chicago since he had fled his home in Cordova, Colombia. He smiled as he thought of being Colombia's Public Enemy No. 1 because of his war against the government over his body organ business. For ten years he had waged a paramilitary war against the state.

Suddenly, his thoughts vanished as his rear tire started to bump, causing his car to sway on the highway. His control system voice echoed: "Your left rear tire has malfunctioned, please replace." He exited at the North Avenue Beach. It was two in the morning. The beach was deserted. The waves from Lake Michigan seemed ominous as they hit the rocks on the shore line. Dark gray clouds that looked like claws engulfed a full moon. He parked the car, leaving his emergency lights blinking, and locked it because one hundred thousand dollars in drug money was in a suitcase in his back seat. As he walked to his trunk to get a flashlight, jack and spare tire, he patted his inside coat pocket for his .25-caliber semiautomatic Beretta that was loaded with a nine round chrome clip. He again glanced around the parking area. He was totally alone. He inhaled the scents of Lake Michigan. He lit a seagarette and gazed at the vastness of the lake. The smell of rotting fish and the pungent odor of beach refuse stung his nostrils. He threw the seagarette on the ground and squashed it.

It was downright weird for the beach to be so desolate on such a warm night. When he put his key into the trunk lock he swerved around nervously. He heard a distant sound. A familiar sound. It was a saxophone. He became nervous. Edgy. Probably some dude practicing his riffs near the lake. Quickly he opened the trunk and grabbed his flashlight. He beamed the light on the flat tire. Again the saxophone. Only this time the horn blasted out terse, reggae, staccato-like notes. General Rafara started to break out into a cold sweat. A creepy sensation flushed his body. It sounded uncannily like the music of Black Zac. He shook his head, grabbed the jack and spare, and put the lit flashlight on the ground. The moment he started loosening the tire lugs he panicked, as he heard the movement and panting of animals. He glanced over his shoulder and stood up while pulling his Beretta out of his coat pocket. A pack of dogs were coming toward him. He picked up the lug wrench. Trembling, he could hear his heart pounding in his chest. He knelt down, while dropping the wrench, and picked up the flashlight. It was three of them. A bolt of naked fear tore through his mask of machismo. They were only thirty feet away. It was too late to get into the car for safety. He flashed the light on them. Luminous red demonic eyes gazed at him. The dogs were short and stocky with patches of black spots on their brown coats. They were huge American pit bulls. At one time his street soldiers had used them to stash drugs in their collars.

"What the hell is going on?" he mumbled, as the dogs' shadows merged with the Lake Michigan shoreline. It was the absurdity of the situation that made him question his sanity. Why would the three dogs be romping along the Gold Coast beach, alone? Was there some rational explanation lurking behind the events that now existed because of his flat tire? The shuffle of the dogs' trotting in the thick sand made a shiver run down his back. The dogs' eyes glistened as they neared him, triggering a sense of impending doom; a feeling of how fleeting and perishable a life can be.

He thought about the Macumba cult in his home continent, South America. He remembered from his childhood, the tales in his village, of the zombies and demons rising from the dead to kill the living. General Rafara inhaled deeply trying to calm his thumping heart.

The music started playing again. The dogs continued to run toward him, their white fangs gleaming rabidly in the moonlight. They growled in ferocious primal tones. He aimed the cold barrel of his automatic at the leader's head. Hair bristled on the dogs' backs. He could tell it would only be microseconds before they launched their attack. His sweaty finger started to slowly squeeze the trigger. He wondered if this was some sort of mad nightmare! Or was this a cosmic payback for Black Zac's death? He was on the brink of hysteria. The saxophone again crackled through the night air. The pit bulls started to attack, and while growling shrieks of fiendish rage, he fired. Fired. Fired. All three of them catapulted backwards from the impact of the bullets. He only had six chances now. The three dogs were not bleeding. Their eyes were like red hot coals. General Rafara nervously wondered what he was dealing with. Were these flesh and blood dogs or something else? He swung the flashlight, as the dogs spread out in a fork formation. He realized they were now going to move in from different positions. He quickly checked his inside coat pocket for another metal clip. *No mas.* Again, the music. Then like ravening wolves all three of the dogs leaped on him at the same time. He fired the whole clip as he fell to the ground. Their razor sharp fangs ripped out his jugular vein and his carotid arteries. The moon had turned blood red. The saxophone music had stopped. General Rafara was dead. Hours later the Crime Scene Unit found a large red feather on his body.

Chapter 31

GANG LEADER AND ASSASSINS KILLED BY RABID DOGS

THE MAULED BODY OF GENERAL RAFARA, LEADER OF THE INFAMOUS NORTH SIDE GANG THE TON TON DISCIPLES WAS FOUND YESTERDAY MORNING IN THE PARKING AREA OF NORTH AVENUE BEACH. HIS DEATH WAS A RESULT OF A VICIOUS ATTACK BY A PACK OF RABID DOGS, THE COOK COUNTY MEDICAL EXAMINER STATED. CISCO MAGNETO, 27, OF THE 3800 BLOCK OF NORTH CLARK, AND HOSEA SANDIAGO, 22, OF THE 5700 BLOCK OF NORTH SHERIDAN, WERE ALSO FOUND DEAD EARLY YESTERDAY FROM SIMILAR DOG ATTACKS.

GOLD COAST DETECTIVES SAID THE THREE COLOMBIANS WERE INVOLVED IN THE RECENT MURDER OF BLACK ZAC, THE SAXOPHONE PLAYER, BECAUSE THE MURDER WEAPONS AND SKI MASKS WERE FOUND IN MAGNETO'S APARTMENT.

RAFARA'S BODY WAS DISCOVERED BY THE POLICE. IT WAS SPRAWLED IN A PUDDLE OF CHICKEN BLOOD, NEAR HIS RED MERCEDES BENZ. AUTHORITIES BELIEVE THAT HIS MURDER WAS PART OF SOME OCCULT RITUAL RITE. HIS .25-CALIBER BERETTA WAS ALSO RETRIEVED ALONG WITH A SUITCASE CONTAINING $100,000 IN DRUG MONEY. HE WAS APPARENTLY FIXING A FLAT TIRE WHEN THE DOGS ATTACKED.

Bodyslick shook his head in disbelief as he read the news-cube. Mama Luigi had actually killed Black Zac's murderers with her Voodnarf spell. Until that night at her apartment, he had always been a skeptic about the dark powers. A bonafide cynic when it came to believing in anything supernatural. Until that night, he hadn't believed there was a powerful spiritual realm that could affect reality with a magical cabalistic ritual.

He remembered in his youth how his mother was so fearful of spooks, haunts, and ghosts that she would scare the shit out of him and his brother and sister with her phobia of the un-known. Bodyslick smiled, as he thought about the time that they went to their grandmother's funeral. It was an experience that would be fixed in his memory forever. He was only about eleven years old at the time, but the terror, fear, and bone shak-ing tension stemming from his mother's irrational behavior was something he would never forget.

The incident happened after the funeral. Bodyslick, his mother and brother and sister were taken home by their Uncle Will. He remembered that gloomy brown Victorian three-flat, on the West Side of Chicago with absolute clarity. The house re-minded him of the type used in old horror movies. After they got out of the car, his mother had led them up to their second floor apartment; each step echoed a creaking forbidding moan as the stairs gave under their feet. Their mother unlocked the door of the dark apartment. It was always dark, as if sunlight refused to illuminate its deathly gloom.

Bodyslick and his brother and sister tentatively walked into their bedrooms, fearing that something dark, something un-holy, would devour them. The primeval fear of that "some-thing" seemed to boil their blood. After they changed clothes they went into the living room to look at the Bullwinkle show on television.

They could hear the windows rattling from the wind in the hallway when, suddenly, a blood-curdling scream came from their mother's room. Bodyslick, the oldest of the children, took charge and ran into her room. The other children were too petrified to move. He was astonished when he walked in her bedroom. The crackle of thunder and lightning ripped through the night sky. He could hear the pounding of the rain beating on the windows, as lightning zigzagged across the curtains. His mother was gone. He ran into the kitchen. She wasn't there. The porch door was wide open and banging loudly from the blasts of the thunderstorm's raging wind. He slowly stepped out onto the rain-drenched porch looking for his mother. He could feel his heart pounding in his chest as he wondered where she was. He hooded his eyes with his hand to shield them from the torrential rain. He strained his eyes. He looked, looked and looked; then he saw her. She was standing directly below the building in her soaking wet blue robe. Standing there as if she had seen the most abominable thing in her entire life. She was trembling. Shivering. He ran down the stairs to get his fear-stricken mother. He gently took her by the hand and walked her back up the two flights of slippery stairs. She was soaked. Shoeless. Drenched. Once they had closed the kitchen door, Bodyslick told his sister to get their mother a towel and blanket. He sat her down in a kitchen chair. He scooted his chair directly in front of her and rubbed her cold wet hands attempting to warm her. His brother made her a cup of tea.

"Mama, what's wrong?" Bodyslick asked compassionately, as a large fly buzzed fiendishly around her cup and she cried uncontrollably. The spoon in the tea cup shook violently as her trembling small hand held it near her mouth.

"I saw her," his mother said, as she unblinkingly stared him in the eyes. "Your grandma was in my room, Malcolm. I swear she was in mah room . . . just standing . . . standing . . . and looking at me."

It was difficult for Bodyslick's eleven-year-old mind to fathom the meaning of her words. Didn't she realize that they had only hours ago seen Grandma dead in her coffin? Was his mother delirious? Had she lost her mind? Besides, how could a ghost or something non-physical be a threat to anyone? His young brother, Kenny, and sister, Peaches, stood terrified around their mother, as she continued to talk hysterically. Peaches patted her face with a dry towel. Then suddenly the kitchen door flung open. All hell broke loose. His brother and sister ran into their rooms and slammed the doors and quickly, fearfully crawled under their beds. Bodyslick swiftly grabbed his mother as she leaped out of the chair. He held her tightly around the waist, as she kicked and screamed with overwhelming terror. He held her as tightly as his eleven-year-old body could muster up. Then he reassuringly whispered in her ear.

"Ma, it's only the wind. The door was unlocked, and a gust of wind blew it open. It's only the wind, Ma . . . now calm down." The porch door banged ominously. The spine-chilling roar of thunder and lightning shook the very foundation of the building. A dog howled piteously from across the alley. A neighbor's cat screeched with horror at the rumbling noise.

"Mama, it's only the wind," he said again, as he stroked her neck trying to comfort her. "Your mind is playing tricks on you, Ma. There's nothing to fear." Bodyslick sat his mother back down and went to lock the screen door.

His mind flickered back to reality as he thought about the newscube story surrounding the death of Black Zac's killers. He was no longer a skeptic. Mama Luigi had shown that there were indeed forces in the universe of which we humans have absolutely no grasp.

He tossed the newscube onto a nearby table and smiled. Liza had actually been depressed over the death of Black Zac's assassins, that after having sex she had gotten drunk and fell asleep shouting, "Black Zac's Revenge!"

The early morning light caused shadows to dance and interlace on the room's ceiling. Bodyslick peered at the shadows. He often wondered why the reflections from the light beaming through the curtains were three dimensional. They were natural holograms. Was there a scientific explanation for the 3-D shadows? He gently turned toward Liza. He kissed her on the cheek. He marveled at her naked body as she slept quietly.

Peacefully. There was a sexy smile on her pink face. A smile that seemed satisfied with the outcome of last night's bloody murder.

How many Lizas were roaming through America's decadent cities? Searching for some elusive occult god to receive them from their alienation, their depressions, and their sense of estrangement in a technological society. She had told him that before she became a NARF she was working part-time as a waitress in Davenport, Iowa, to help pay for her college tuition. Her family had lost their farm and life savings after the red rain had destroyed their crops and cattle in 2020. The acid rain made a once-fertile state a barren wasteland. The farmers called it blood rain because of the way it had scorched the earth and made once rich, fertile soul flaky and crumbly as clay.

Before the deluge Liza Krelinsky was an all-American white girl. She had middle class values, blonde hair, blue eyes, and she was very materialistic. She had swallowed the American dream hype entirely, only to vomit it up after discovering that greed, corruption, and corporate profits were used as a cover-up for the real source of the red rain.

"The samples taken from the red rain on your farm were alien to life on earth!" Professor William Pizoc, environmental physicist at Iowa State University, said matter of factly to Liza and her father.

"Darn, alien critters, huh?"

"Not exactly UFO types, Mr. Krelinsky," the professor said with a wry grin.

"Maybe more like a microbe?"

"You have a smart daughter, sir. You see, the water samples contained extra terrestrial bacteria that lacked DNA. Yet it could reproduce in water superheated to 1,200 degrees Farenheit."

"Can't some forms of life on earth survive in heat like that?"

"Only to about 250 degrees, Liza."

As Professor Pizoc talked a howling wind suddenly swept over the barren cornfields creating eddies of reddish dust in a twisting wrath.

"What's interesting is that even without DNA, we have pictures of these microbes reproducing mutant scavenger bacteria that ate your crops and killed your livestock!"

"There ain't no cure for these darm critters, huh, professor?"

Rage and fear flushed across Mr. Krelinsky's face as he squeezed Liza's shoulder with reassurance while waiting for the professor's answer. He momentarily sighed as crows *caw caw caawd* and plotted the sun, which had once radiated the most alluvial soil in the world.

"I believe carbon dioxide, the burning of earth's land for cattle and food, industrial pollution, the parasitic demands of human development, and most importantly, the alien microbes, what I call the mutant soup, are causing the blood rain showers that are being reported throughout the world."

The sky was a deep blue with streaks of orange and vermillion slashed through it making the once fertile cornfields look skeletal.

"Yeah, that's doing my father a lot of freakin' good," Liza pointed her finger accusingly at his chest. "now that his entire life's work is gone. Because rich industrialists, the government, and scientists like you don't give a shit about the working class! Why, when I was in the first grade they were predicting the effects of global warming!" she moaned tearfully.

"Liza," Dr. Pizoc whispered passionately while rubbing his hand on her shoulder, "carbon dioxide is only one influence; there are others, sun cycles, a reduction in cosmic rays. Why 150 million years ago dinosaurs had higher carbon dioxide than us!"

Sunlight glittered on her blonde hair and ignited her blue eyes as she rattled her throat as if cleansing it of phlegm and then spat in Dr. Pizoc's face.

Liza told Bodyslick that after that incident, she came to Chicago and became a NARF as a means of escaping her sense of despair. Her sense of aloneness. Her sense of loss.

As Bodyslick gazed at her he only hoped she would one day find real meaning, real substance in her young life. He leaped out of bed to take a shower. His dick was still rock hard and throbbing from the terrific sex he'd had with Liza early that morning. As he walked into the bathroom his wrist phone started to beep. The tiny square red light blinked. Something was wrong. His dick went limp. He quickly closed the bathroom door and punched in his secret code number then whispered into the watch's micro-transmitters "check it out." Nervously he waited, his naked body shaking with anticipation.

Doc Jones had finally contacted him. He put his wrist phone to his ear, as the heavy breathing of a man's voice echoed through the phone: "Two hundred and fifty thousand dollars have been delivered to Mr. Lambrique at Geneva's Union Bank and deposited in your Swiss account, and I have a receipt of deposit. Sorry it took so long to get back to you, Bodyslick, but I am now at the O'Hare Hyatt Hotel, Suite 5012. I have access to a helicopter, limousine, rental car, or taxi. Whatever is needed to get that heart is at my disposal. So, wherever you want me to rendezvous with you, I can get there quickly. I now have only fifteen hours to get the heart and return to Baltimore. I'm ready when you are . . ."

Bodyslick quietly packed his belongings, took one last look at Liza, and walked out the door. Bodyslick sensed something was wrong.

Chapter 32

Beads of sweat rolled down Dr. Donald Jones' forehead as the cold steel muzzle of a .357-caliber Magnum jammed into his temple. He only hoped that Bodyslick would detect through his strained voice that something was wrong. That something was deathly wrong. They had captured him the minute he had touched the ground at O'Hare Airport. He was then put into a limousine and driven to a hotel and forced to contact Bodyslick at gunpoint. He had told the hoodlums everything. If he hadn't, he would had been dead hours ago. They had blindfolded him in the limo. He was existing in a blind world of terror. The voices that he heard in the room were both black and Italian. His entire life unfolded before him like a movie. He wondered if he would ever see his wife and daughter again. He trembled in the chair uncontrollably. Drops of urine seeped down into his pants leg. His heart pounded with unquenching terror. He listened with horror at the many voices that crisscrossed the room.

"Once he arrives, Toejoe . . ."

Jones could tell the voice was Italian.

". . . you, Pumpkin, and Butch will be in the room 5013 which is right across the hall. We will hit him from every conceivable direction. It's important we take the dude out decisively because Vinnie might go nuts if we botch this job," Gino

Sartucci said, as his comrade Nicky Sigichi nodded with agreement.

Gino ran his hand through his thick black Sicilian hair. He had his doubts about Dr. Jones' sincerity. Even at gunpoint, it seemed that he was holding back information from them. But it wouldn't do them any good to torture him, Gino thought, because whatever secrets he had wouldn't stop them from annihilating Bodyslick. Gino walked away from the doctor toward the bar to get a drink. He then walked back over to a leather sofa, directly in front of the doctor, and sat down. He sipped his drink, and then spoke to him.

"So you and Bodyslick are childhood friends, huh?"

"Yeah, we grew up together," Jones said nervously while blindly turning his head to find the direction of the voice.

"Are you surprised that we knew that you were coming to Chicago to get a heart for Vanderbilt?"

"I was shocked!"

"Well, Doc, we got connections everywhere in the world. Our connections can supply us any information we want about anything . . . including your family, Doc."

"My family?" Dr. Jones asked in utter fear.

"Doc, at this very moment a car is parked in front of your house on Grove Street. Inside the car are two of the most ruthless assassins in our outfit. These animals will kill babies, women, and priests for a price."

"Look, please don't hurt my wife and child. I've told you everything I know. I swear I don't know anything else!"

Gino sipped his drink and smiled as the doctor started to shake nervously. He had planted the seed in his mind that his wife and child could be murdered. If he was holding back any secrets, the death threat would quickly unveil it.

"When Bodyslick arrives here, if you give him any indication that something is wrong . . . your wife and child will be killed instantly . . . you got that, Dr. Jones?"

"Yes, I understand . . . just don't hurt them . . ."

"Now listen up, Doc," Gino said authoritatively. "When

Bodyslick arrives and the desk clerk phones us before he lets him come up, I want you to sound real anxious about the heart. Tell him that time is running out and you must hurry up and fly back to Baltimore with it, you following me, Doc?"

"Yes, I understand!" Jones said obediently.

"And another thing, Doc, about that heart for Vanderbilt . . . what kind of blood type does he have?"

"He has AB blood type Rh-positive, the rarest type."

"Dr. Jones," Gino said facctiously, "you been looking for a donor with his blood type in all the wrong places."

"I don't understand your logic. We have a nationwide computer donor bank at the hospital. Like I said his blood type is rare."

"Dr. Jones, did you know that Bodyslick has AB blood type?"

"You're lying," said Dr. Jones with disbelief.

"Don't call me a liar, doctor. I've killed men for less serious things. Now, all you had to do was a little investigation and you would have found out that Malcolm 'Bodyslick' Steel has AB blood type."

"So what?" Jones asked, knowing where Gino's conversation was headed, but hoping he could dampen the brutal realization of what he was on the brink of hearing.

"So that quarter of a mil that you deposited in his Swiss account will be ours, because you're going to take Bodyslick's *heart* back to Baltimore with you!"

"There is no need for that," Jones said confidently," Bodyslick already has a fresh AB cadaver donor heart for me. A perfect specimen. Believe me, there is no dire need for Bodyslick's heart!"

"Doc," Gino said, as he rose up off the sofa and walked over to him then stooped down, "you will take his heart back with you. When we capture him, we have already made arrangements with a private hospital for you to use their facilities to cut his heart out. It's something you can't refuse, Doc. Of course, if you don't care about seeing your family again you don't . . ."

"Just don't harm my family. I'll cooperate, dammit. Just don't fuck with them!"

Gino glanced at his watch. It had been three hours since Jones had made contact with Bodyslick. He realized it would be only a matter of minutes before he arrived. He picked up the phone and asked the operator for room 5012.

"Toejoe?" Gino said anxiously.

"Yeah, Gino what's up?"

"Bodyslick should be arriving anytime now. Are your guys ready over there?"

"We're ready."

"Good, I've got Nicky downstairs in the lobby. The minute he walks in I'll ring ya. And leave on your video cameras for the hallway!"

"Remember, Toejoe, we don't want to kill him if possible. Because the punk's *heart* is worth a quarter of a mil . . . so if we can capture him all the better. Vinnie has made it clear that his heart is of utmost importance!"

"I understand what you're saying man. I personally think Bodyslick is too dangerous to be fucking around with . . . but if that's what Vinnie wants!"

"Well, that's what he wants, and I'll buzz you when he arrives!"

Chapter 33

As Bodyslick gazed at his speedometer, he was moving at eighty-five mph. With increased acceleration it sounded like the whine of a jet taking off. He glanced at the fuel gauge. Ten miles more, and he would need to fill up at a hydro-station. He exited I-94 at River Road and made a quick right listening to the *hiss* of the fuel cell's compressor. He marveled at the silence of the powerful BMW's hydrogen engine: a 120 kilowatt fuel cell under his seat which translates into three seconds to accelerate to 60 mph.

Suddenly a genig boy ran in front of the car chasing a two-headed pink Chihuahua. Bodyslick quickly released the steering wheel and pressed the emergency button. In microseconds, the database triggered the brakes' vacuum pump sensor monitoring system and the video steering guide system mapped braking distance of the object, compared that against velocity, thrust, and momentum relative to analogues stored in its brain bank and instantly the car stopped three feet from the boy, as the regenerative brakes whistled, capturing wasted friction energy.

Bodyslick angrily lowered his window and shouted, "Will you get your stupid genig ass outtah the street before ya get killed?" The dwarfish, huge helium headed, blue-eyed genig snatched up the two-headed poodle and walked up to his windows. His droopy eyelids twitched. His pinkish blue color had

a slight glow. Saliva drooled from his Cro-Magnon mouth. His tiny simian hazel eyes blinked moronically. His canine sharp teeth gleamed as he shouted.

"You think you're better than me, shithead! You think you can call me racist's names, you fuckin' moolie! Get your ass outta the car, and we can see who's the real man right here!" he said as he slammed his hairy fist on Bodyslick's hood. His dog barked viciously. Bodyslick grabbed his 9 mm laser pistol next to his thigh. He pointed it between the genig's eyes. So quick it caught him by surprise. Bodyslick had to hold back a laugh as the genig looked at the barrel cross-eyed with absolute terror. His face was even more deformed as it grimaced with fear. He looked like a frightened Quasimodo.

"Bitch," Bodyslick said as he poked the cold barrel of the gun deeper into his forehead. "Bitch, step back from my car, or I'll blow your fuckin' brains out on this street!"

A stench like piss and shit stung his nostrils. He raised up his windows. The genig turned around holding his poodle in his arms and ran across the street. A brown spot plotted the back of his pants as a trail of pee dripped from his pants leg.

Bodyslick swerved around him and drove three miles and parked almost half a mile from the O'Hare Hyatt Hotel. He sat in his black BMW as he gazed with binoculars at the hotel. The roar of airplanes vibrated the area. He quickly glanced at his watch. It was 5:45 p.m. It would soon be dark and the chances of Dr. Jones getting that heart back to Baltimore were becoming very dim. He peered into the rearview mirror because he could actually feel the roots of his hair tingling as it metamorphosed into its old texture. Faint brown translucent blotches had started appearing through his white skin. The skin changing lotion was starting to fade. The organic paste that he had reshaped his nose with was weakening and his broad nostrils had started to flair. The tissue-reducing-lotion he had used on his lips was starting to dry causing his once fleshy lips to expand. It would only be maybe four hours before he became his real self again. His NARF disguise was disappearing before his very eyes.

He reached inside his boot holster and grabbed his .45-caliber Colt and checked for ammo. He had stuck a small laser pistol inside the belt of his pants. He liked the laser because, when it fired out its white hot pellets of hot hydrogen, it did not have the kick, the recoil of the old pistols. It was great for a silent kill.

He must act fast now. It would be his own personal war against Toejoe and the mob. He would wait till dark before he made his rescue attempt of Dr. Jones at the hotel. He realized he must treat the doctor's kidnapping as a hostage situation.

Suddenly he heard a noise. He quickly grabbed his .45 out of his leg holster again. It was now pitch black outside. Someone was tapping on his window. His finger slowly tightened around the trigger of his pistol. Then he heard a voice. A muffled voice. A woman's voice.

"Peter, it's me, Liza. Open the door."

"Liza?" he said with both bewilderment and surprise. He pressed the window button and lowered it about three inches.

"Peter?"

He was confused. The woman sounded like Liza. But she certainly wasn't the woman he had been with at the Tass Hotel. The woman outside his car was blue-eyed, blonde, and white, not pink. He lowered the window all the way down.

"Okay, so you say you're Liza, right?"

"Yes, it's me, Peter. It's just that my NARF identity has changed."

"Stick out your tongue!" Bodyslick said, baffled. He realized she might have shed her NARF image, but she couldn't alter that long lizard tongue.

"See!" she said, as she flicked her eight-inch serpent tongue at him through the window then slowly licked the glass. He momentarily flinched at the abnormality of it.

He unlocked the door and Liza jumped in the car. He was nervous. Fidgety. He was now gazing into the eyes of a white girl. She was no longer the lost freak he had met earlier. She was still dressed unorthodox. She still had the gold ring around the septum of her nose. Her teeth still had the silver implants. If he could just get past her whiteness.

"Peter?"

"That's not my real name!"

"Good. Because I hated calling you that. What is your real name?"

"Malcolm Steel, but people in the streets call me Bodyslick!"

"I can understand after last night."

He smiled. "Liza, to make a long story short I'm a bad guy. A criminal. I sell human body parts for big bucks. I became a NARF because I was hiding. I was just biding time until I was contacted by a very important person. How did you find me anyway?"

"I woke up the minute you walked out the door. You didn't notice my metamorphosis because I had the bedsheet up to my neck and I was lying on my stomach. I forgot to rebathe in the melanhue. But this time, mostly because I have fallen in love with you, I wanted to be my real self."

"Liza, don't love me. I live in a very fast violent world."

"Bodyslick, I followed you out here in a taxi and I'm not leaving without you."

He gazed at her blue eyes. She smiled. The tension and magnetism between them blinded their differences. He no longer saw her white skin. Instead she was a woman who loved him.

"Bodyslick, you are changing. I can see the difference already in your lips, hair texture and skin color. But that's not important to me. I love you. The you that doesn't weigh anything. The spiritual you. The human you. I only hope your feelings for me transcend my lily white skin."

Bodyslick nervously tapped his finger on the steering wheel. He thought about how his entire life had been spent waging his own personal vendetta against the status quo. The capitalist class. The elite people in power who had made poor people live a horrible insane nightmare in America. Was Liza, a lost white girl from Davenport, Iowa, the reason for his victimization? Should he reject her white love because of the class war being waged against his kind? His logic answered *no*.

"Bodyslick, do you love me? I mean the *real* me that has absolutely nothing to do with my skin color? Because I know, dammit, that's what's fucking with you!" She started to cry and grabbed the door handle.

"Don't leave, Liza." He grabbed her and pulled her toward him. He kissed her passionately. He felt that even his beloved Malanna would approve of Liza's purity of heart. "Liza, I don't know if I *love* you. But I do know I will protect you. I'll even die for you. You can bank on me being honest and loyal. And what I do feel for you transcends petty societal laws. All I ask, Liza, is not so much you love me but that you respect me. Stand by me. Baby, those things are far more important to me than love. We must be a team. We must be strong. By being with me, you are asking for public scorn and ridicule. Liza, we must stand like granite as one!"

Bodyslick hugged her tightly. He kissed her again and again on the cheek. She smiled. She smiled like a woman who was madly in love. She held his hand tightly.

"I don't care about society. I don't give a damn what people think. That's the reason I became a NARF, because I hated the hypocrisy, the lies and the corruption. I love you, Bodyslick."

Bodyslick glanced at his watch. It was getting late. Liza would be an advantage in rescuing Dr. Jones.

Chapter 34

A long white Cadilectro stretch limousine pulled up in front of the hotel. Bodyslick adjusted his binoculars lenses to get a closer view. Liza was asleep and curled up next to him. He watched as the chauffeur quickly got out of the limo and opened the door. It was Snow. His view was blurred because of the darkness. He pressed the infrared red button for night illumination. They now became crystal clear. Four men, all dressed in dark blue Italian designer suits and light blue silk shirts open at the neck exposing ropes of gold, got out of the car. He watched them as they scanned the hotel entrance. Nervously. Apprehensively. As if someone was stalking them. As if they were in some predatorial jungle whereby a broken tree limb, the crunching of grass, even the howl of the wind would kindle their fear of the unknown. The way they were dressed only validated what Bodyslick sensed all along. They were Mafioso. One of the henchmen then signaled to a man inside to get out.

He strained his eyes, as a short stout nattily dressed man with a receding hairline rose out of the car. He wore the same type of expensive designer suit. His demeanor. His regal gestures. His charisma telecast. Leader. The man looked strikingly familiar to Bodyslick. He sharpened the focus on the lenses. Yes, it was him. The animal who had sent Antonio to kill him. The beast who had ordered the butchering of his beloved Malanna. The maniac who had Bubba's heart carved out. The

scum who had a quarter of a million dollar contract on his life.
It was Vinnie "Lucifer" Luziano.

Bodyslick suppressed his fury. His hatred. His violence.
Rage that he couldn't kill him here and now consumed him.
He could feel the blood pulsating in his head. He was so overwhelmed by hate that his heart thumped as if it were going to
leap out of his chest. He elbowed Liza in the ribs. She quickly
woke up.

"Liza, press that orange button on the door!" Bodyslick
had his BMW equipped with a state of the art electronic control system. When Liza pressed the button, it opened a small
door underneath the glove compartment revealing a shiny,
pearl-handled .38 special.

"Have you ever used a gun before, Liza?"

"Of course, on the farm back in Iowa, my father used to take
me hunting all the time," she said, as she clicked the safety of
the gun and checked it for ammo.

"Well, we don't have much time. We have to move very
quickly . . . you see that white limo over there, Liza?"

She quickly peered out the window. "Yes."

"Well, that short Italian dude with the receding hairline is
Vinnie Luziano."

"You mean the Chicago Mob boss?"

"That's him."

"What has that got to do with us?" Liza asked with fear
and astonishment.

"It's a long story, baby, and we don't have enough time.
Please, just listen to me."

"I'm listening."

"Liza, there is a good friend of mine in that hotel, who the
mob is holding as a hostage, and his name is Dr. Donald
Jones."

"But why . . . ?"

"Shush, lemme finish. Dr. Jones has come to Chicago because he needs a very important favor from me. To make a
long story short, I need your help to get him out of that hotel."

"But why are they holding him hostage? And why were you hiding from them?"

"I need you to help me now, Liza. We're running out of time. I'll explain all that later. I need you to help me get him out of that hotel, dammit!"

"But, Bodyslick, I've never done anything like this before."

"All you have got to do is listen to me. Just listen and follow my instruction. I love ya, and believe me we will come out of this on top. Just listen to me and do what I tell ya."

"I'll try."

"You must, Liza. There's no time for trying. There's no room for failure. A mistake can mean death. If you're the tough woman I believe you to be . . . you won't lemme down."

"Okay, just tell me what to do."

"All right, first of all, we've got to move fast before Vinnie gets inside the hotel. Liza, I want you to put that .38 special in your purse. And don't be afraid to use it. You might have to kill, Liza."

"Kill?"

"Liza, it's either them or us."

"I understand."

Bodyslick and Liza peered out the car window at Vinnie Luziano, as he joked with the chauffeur and then handed him a fifty dollar bill. He smiled. The chauffeur was Snow. His bodyguards surrounded them while he talked.

"Liza, we're going to slowly walk toward Vinnie and his boys, and when I spank your butt, I want you to run over to one of his bodyguards and fabricate an argument. Say anything you want to, just make it sound sincere."

"Why though? These guys are murderers. These guys are hoodlums. They would kill their own mother for a price."

"No questions, Liza. Are you with me or not?"

"Yes."

"What you will do is merely a ploy to get us into the hotel. Okay, they're starting to walk toward the hotel. We must act quickly now. Do you understand, Liza?"

"Yes."

"Kiss me, Liza. Are you with me?"

"Yes."

They leapt out of the car and started to walk toward the men. Snow quickly lowered his window and nervously pointed at his watch indicating he would contact Bodyslick later as he drove the limousine away.

Chapter 35

Bodyslick gritted his teeth with raw anger as they approached them. He could feel the crinkling sensation of his physical disguise changing. The four hoodlums circled Vinnie Luziano as he stopped and started to talk to them. Bodyslick grabbed Liza's hand. She was shaking with fear. Trembling.

He whispered to her. "Liza, don't be afraid. Remember there's no room for mistakes."

He then gently tapped her butt signaling for her to walk toward them and go into her act.

She quickly trotted toward the biggest of the hoodlums. She screamed and pointed at him. "You bastard! You didn't pay me my money. I want my money now! Who do you think you are, using me and walking out on your part of the deal?"

Vinnie and the other goons stood there, surprised by the woman's guts. Vinnie looked at Reggio, the goon Liza was screaming at, with bafflement.

Liza continued to holler at him. "Now if you don't give me my fuckin' money, there's going to be a lot of trouble!"

"Reggio," Vinnie said, irritated, "will you give the *bagascia* her money? We don't need this type of action."

"And who are you calling a damn *bitch*? I'm a lady, and I want to be treated like one. Now, scumbucket, give me my money!"

"Who are you?" Reggio asked, as he walked toward her

while cracking his knuckles. "I don't know you. What kind of con are you up to?"

Liza nervously glanced at Bodyslick wondering when he would make his move. Snow winked at Bodyslick as he sped off in the limo.

"This ain't no con, and I want my . . . my . . ." She started beating him on his chest. He grabbed her by the waist and picked her up.

"Who are you? What are ya trying to prove? If you don't cut this shit out, you gonna get hurt real bad." He put her back down.

"Come on, Reggio," Vinnie said impatiently. "We got business to take care of. Give the dame a C-note so she'll let you alone!"

At that moment, while the goons' backs were facing Liza, Bodyslick pulled his .45 out of his leg holster and quickly walked up behind Vinnie and grabbed him around the neck while stabbing the barrel of the .45 into his temple.

"All right, if you go for your guns, Vinnie's brains will be helping dandelions grow. Liza, search them!"

"Liza methodically searched each one of them. Her hands trembled uncontrollably as she tossed .45s, .38s, laser pistols, switch blades, and razors onto the grass.

Vinnie's eyes widened in panic as he gazed at Bodyslick's hands. Hands that were white with patches of black skin.

"Look, you want money? I got money. But you're a dead man if you don't let me go. You don't know who you're fucking with!" Vinnie said in disgust.

"I don't want your money. I want Doctor Jones. And you're going to help me get him!"

"I don't know any Dr. Jones. Who are you?" Vinnie caught a glimpse of his NARF clothes out of the corner of his eye.

"Shut up! Now tell your goons to circle us and walk toward the hotel entrance as if nothing is going on. Go on . . . tell 'em!"

Beads of sweat started to form on Vinnie's forehead, as the icy cold muzzle of the .45 pressed harder against his temple.

"Tell 'em or I'll blow your fucking brains out!" Bodyslick shouted.

"All right . . . all right . . . Reggio, you guys walk around us toward the hotel entrance or this clown nigga's going to kill me!"

Bodyslick swiftly moved the .45 from Vinnie's head and stuck the barrel deep into his lower back.

"Okay, let's start walking toward the hotel." Liza fearfully walked in back of Bodyslick and Vinnie as his four henchmen led the way.

As they entered the hotel, Reggio approached the desk clerk and told him his name and that the people in Suite 5012 were expecting them. The clerk buzzed the room and waited for someone to pick up the phone. Then he nodded his head to them signaling that it was okay to go up. As Reggio pressed the elevator button, the door instantly slid open.

Bodyslick immediately took control. "Let me, the girl and Vinnie get in first . . . if any of you try anything I'll blow his fucking brains all over this elevator."

"You fucking NARF, you'll die for this!" Reggio mumbled.

"Shut up and punch fifty . . . now!"

The door slammed shut, and the elevator climbed quickly to the fiftieth floor. The door slid open.

"All right, everybody out. Now! Remember Vinnie's a dead man if you even fart too loud. Now let's keep walking."

Bodyslick's eyes were tired as they tried to grasp each move of the four men, gobs of sweat started to drip from his fore-head. Then his peripheral vision caught one of the goons as he quickly reached inside his coat pocket and turned toward them with a laser pistol. Bodyslick pushed Vinnie against the wall just as the gunman was on the verge of squeezing the trigger. The recoil of Bodyslick's .45 with a silencer on it, and the rib-boning orange nozzle smoke, tore a hole through the man's gold rope chain and silk shirt. Vinnie and the other hoodlums dropped to the floor. Liza stood there, frozen with disbelief, as the blood gushed from the man's chest like a water fountain while he lay sprawled on the floor.

Bodyslick grabbed Vinnie off the floor by his suitcoat and said, "Anybody else want to try me? Don't be shy, 'cause the sight of blood gets me high!"

The voice sounded familiar to Vinnie. "Bodyslick!" he screamed. "You ain't no fucking *NARF* you . . . !"

"You're a dead man if you don't close that trap of yours! Now, we're near Suite 5012. When we get there . . . just act normal."

They slowly walked down the thickly carpeted hallway. Bodyslick tried to suppress the gnawing fear that crept over him as they reached the door.

"Listen," Bodyslick said in a quiet voice. "If you mess up, Vinnie's a dead man!"

Reggio tapped on the door. Gino glanced out the peephole. He smiled. He picked up the phone and asked for room 5013.

"Toejoe, they're here in the hallway. I can see 'em through the peephole," Gino said, excited. "Bodyslick is dressed up like a NARF and he's got a .45 jammed in Vinnie's back . . . and he's got a white dame wid him."

"Toejoe, make your move . . . *now!*" Gino said anxiously.

Chapter 36

As Reggio waited for the door to open, a middle-aged, grey haired white lady came out of her suite with a tiny dog. She glanced at them with a puzzled look on her face. Her tiny rodent looking Chihuahua's fangs glimmered as it nervously barked until it started to choke. At that moment the elevator door opened and several young seemingly high teenagers alighted from it. They became quiet and looked at them suspiciously.

Suddenly a young girl screamed out, "Look! There's a dead man on the floor down there!"

All of them started screaming and hollering with fear as they stampeded back to the elevator. The middle-aged lady's dog broke loose from her and headed straight toward Bodyslick's neon bootstraps and started biting and pulling on them. Bodyslick tried to kick the dog loose, but it continued to bite his neon straps while growling menacingly. The old lady panicked and left her door ajar with the keys in the lock, and nervously walked toward the dog.

"Fefe, come to Mama, be a good little baby."

Suddenly, Toejoe leaped out the adjacent suite, grabbed the old lady around the neck and cocked his .357 python, as he stuck the large pipe barrel at the base of her skull. Pumpkin and Butch ran down the hallway with their Uzi submachine guns pointed at the terrified teenagers.

"Shut the fuck up now! And all of you get away from the elevator!" Butch shouted.

"They gonna kill us! Oh Lawd, Jesus . . . they gonna killll!" a black girl screamed. Pumpkin slapped the girl so hard her face, for a split second, seemed like a loose mask. She stopped screaming, and she looked up at the ceiling with her hands clasped as if praying silently.

"Bitch, don't make me kill ya. Naw shut the fuck up 'cause de Lawd Jesus can't help yo silly ass. Now all of you step back away from the elevator." The doors slid open.

"You! Get in there, and shut it off!"

"Me!" a tall freckle-faced white boy said fearfully.

"Yeah, you punk!" Butch said in a murderous snarl.

"All right, Toejoe," Pumpkin shouted, "everything's straight down here!"

"Bodyslick, let Vinnie go and drop your weapon or I'll blow this old lady away," Toejoe said, as he shook the gun barrel at the lady's head. "And you too, bitch!" Toejoe shouted at Liza.

The old lady whispered pleadingly to Bodyslick. "Please, son, don't let him kill me. I'm an old widow. There is just me and Fefe!"

"Shut up, you old cunt!" Toejoe said, as he pulled back the trigger. "I swear umma blow her away, man, now let him go, and you and the dame drop your weapons!"

"I want Dr. Jones," Bodyslick said unshakingly, "give me the doctor and we can settle this!"

"Fefe!" the old lady screamed.

The tiny Chihuahua darted toward Toejoe and started biting his ankle. He yelled in pain as the dog's fangs gnawed, tearing flesh. The pain from Fefe's bites caused him to release his chokehold on the old lady. She quickly picked up her dog, as Bodyslick fired and shot Toejoe in the chest. A dark carmine blot started to spread and quickly branched out like a cancer.

A muffled *whop* echoed off the walls of the hallway as Toejoe began to fall against his suite's open door. He braced himself and aimed his gun at the old lady. Bodyslick fired again.

Toejoe fell down on both knees still aiming. Then he shot the old woman in the back. She fell down near her door. Her body started to twitch and quiver as if she were having a seizure. A bucket of carmine blood gushed from a gaping hole in her lower back. Pumpkin and Butch aimed their Uzis, but they stood there dumbfounded because the only way they could kill Bodyslick would be to wipe out Vinnie and his goons who shielded him and Liza.

"Gino, open the door, dammit!" Vinnie called in a nervous raspy voice. "Before this animal kills me!"

Liza glanced at the old woman as she lay on her stomach, in a puddle of her own blood. Toejoe had shot her in the spine. She was dying. Her dog mournfully licked her bloody face. Her bulbous eyes stared passionately at her dog. Her mouth was open as if praying. Then her eyes closed and her head tilted. She was dead. Liza strained her eyes as a small indefinable shadowy substance *whooshed* from her body and vaporized. The dog barked frantically at the shadow as if he knew it was his master. Liza wondered if it was the woman's soul? She thought about how the old woman's death would affect the human condition. She also thought that she could have been her.

When Gino appeared at the door, Bodyslick shouted, "Throw your weapons on the floor and lock your hands behind your head. Any surprises, and Vinnie is a dead man!" Gino instantly tossed his pistol on the floor. The three goons filed in the room first; then Vinnie, Bodyslick, and Liza nervously followed.

Butch and Pumpkin had locked the teenagers in their suite after they had tied them up and cut off the telephone cord. Both of them were on their knees gazing at the bloody lifeless body of Toejoe. They angrily stood up and started *banging* on the other door.

"You're a dead man, Bodyslick!" Gino shouted. "Toejoe will get his revenge! You ain't gonna leave this hotel alive! You in a goddamn war that you gonna lose!"

Doctor Jones smiled with relief as Bodyslick walked into the room and snatched off his blindfold. He rose up out of his seat and playfully punched him in the shoulder and said, "You haven't changed a bit. You're always where the action is . . ." He pointed toward a bedroom down the hallway.

"Come out of there," Bodyslick yelled, "but throw your weapon out the door first! If you try anything your boss is dead!"

A small, pearl-handled laser pistol thumped on the gold carpeted floor. Then a tall lean elegantly dressed Nicky Sigichi walked out of the bedroom.

"Doc, pick up the gun, and use it if you have to while I check out this place!"

"There is no one else here," Jones said confidently.

"I still want to check the place out! Liza, use that gun without hesitation to back up Doc!"

Bodyslick quickly walked through the suite, searching and checking under the beds, closets and cabinets; everywhere that could be used as a potential hiding place for a bomb or an assassin. He glanced at his watch. If it flickered red there were explosives hidden somewhere. There was no change. He walked back into the living room.

"I want all of you to take off your clothes. Everything except your undershorts. And throw them in the middle of the room!" He pointed with his gun at the space he wanted the clothes tossed. He noticed that his hand was completely black.

"Liza, watch them while I go take a leak!" He clicked on the lights in the bathroom and was shocked as he peered into the mirror. He was his old self again. If it weren't for his NARF clothes, it would be a complete transformation. He put his .45 and his laser pistol on top of a nearby shelf and started taking off his clothes. He stripped out of the costume until he was wearing nothing but his underwear. He then grabbed his .45 and put his laser pistol back in his ankle holster then hurriedly walked back into the living room.

They were almost naked. Bodyslick winked at Liza and Dr.

Jones as he picked up a suit, shirt, socks, and shoes from the pile of expensive clothes on the floor. He held his gun in one hand while switching to the other as he put on the clothes, trying to maintain his balance.

"You're a dead man, Bodyslick, nobody can do us like this and live. There is nowhere on this planet that you can hide!" Vinnie said venomously.

"Vinnie," Bodyslick said, smiling, "it's too bad you won't be around to see me dead. Now I want you and all your goons to lie on the goddamned floor, belly down, and lock your hands behind your heads!"

"You'll die for humiliating me like this! You're a dead man!" Vinnie sneered, as he knelt down head first on the floor.

"Liza, I want you to take all their belts out of their pants, and then Doc and I will tie them up—that is except for Vinnie. I've got a special request from Malanna's and Bubba's relatives for Mr. Luziano."

Dr. Jones glanced at his watch and said, "Bodyslick, if I'm not back in Baltimore within five hours . . . forget the deal."

"Don't worry," Bodyslick said confidently. "You'll make it back in time. Have I ever let you down?"

"No, you haven't."

"Just be cool, Doc, and leave everything to me!" Liza gave them the belts. "Doc, you'll make it. Now let's tie these punks up."

"What's your plan?" Jones asked, as he pushed his knee deep into Gino's back.

"Wait a minute, lemme finish this knot," Bodyslick said, as he pulled the belt tightly. "All right, Liza, watch Vinnie while I talk with the Doc in the back room!" Liza held the pistol with two hands the way her father had taught her back in Davenport, Iowa.

As they walked down the hallway they shook hands renewing an old childhood friendship. When they entered the room Bodyslick gestured to Dr. Jones to come to the balcony. "Doc, are you scared of heights?"

"No, not really!" He peered at the glass enclosed balcony.

"Before you say that," Bodyslick said, as he walked toward the sliding window door and then opened it, "come and check out this view from fifty floors up."

"Goddamn, man!" Dr. Jones said fearfully. "The people down there look like specks of dirt . . . you don't mean we have got to . . ."

"That's just what I mean, Doc, we have to climb sixty floors up to the roof."

"But why the damn roof?" he asked, as he glanced at the vastness of Chicago's horizon and quickly stepped back, feeling momentarily dizzy from the height.

"Because you are going to use that *carte blanche* check to rent us a helicopter to take us to my organ storage facility in Robbins, Illinois . . . to get the heart you came here for. O'Hare has a helicopter transport service—you call them up and tell them to get over here as fast as they can and that price is no problem. Tell them that we'll be waiting for them to land on the helicopter pad on top of this hotel. Tell them to give us at least ten minutes extra for any unforeseen event. After you do that, get all of your personal stuff, 'cause we have got to climb out of this balcony to the roof."

"You mean sixty floors up?" Dr. Jones said in astonishment.

"That's what we must do. Now I'm going up front to check on Liza." Bodyslick grabbed a pillow off the bed and ran back into the living room.

"Liza, you go in the back with Dr. Jones." She scampered out of the room. Bodyslick walked over to Vinnie Luziano and peered at his livid face with hatred. With rage. With murder. He stood over him with the pillow shaking with anger in one hand and his .45 cocked in the other.

"Vinnie," Bodyslick said solemnly, "put the pillow on top of your head!" He dropped it on the floor near him.

"If you going to kill me, nigger, kill me like a man. I want to die standing up!" Vinnie sneered.

"All right stand up then, you rotten wop muthafucka!"

Vinnie slowly rose up from the floor then he suddenly lunged toward Bodyslick grabbing his legs. As Vinnie tried to wrestle him down, Bodyslick quickly pointed the barrel at the top of his head and pulled the trigger. He fired. Cocked. Fired. Cocked. He liked single action on people he hated. Vinnie's neck jerked back from the impact of the small bullet hole as it cracked through his cranial vault and exited through a gaping hole underneath his jaw. A geyser of scarlet blood streamed from his head.

Bodyslick turned around toward the hallway then slowly walked away, as he listened to Butch and Pumpkin bamming on the door.

"Open this door, punk! 'Cause you backed up against the wall!" Bodyslick realized it wouldn't be long before the police came. He ran into the back bedroom. Jones had just hung up the phone . . . and Liza was nervously looking at the view on the balcony.

"They will be landing on the roof in approximately thirty minutes, and everything I need is in here." He held up his suitcase. "Inside is a collapsible cooler that I will use to transport the heart."

Pumpkin and Butch started firing at the doorknob.

Chapter 37

"Liza, lock the door! Doc, you help me push this bed against the door," Bodyslick said. They dragged the heavy bed to the door and then stood it upright to slow down the henchmen.

"Let's go out to the balcony," Bodyslick said impatiently, as he gazed at O'Hare's busy runway, which looked like a gigantic polygonal spider spewing a neon web as far as the eye could see. He looked down and nervously bit on his thick lower lip. They were fifty floors up from sidewalks, and there was nothing between them but air. The people below looked like tiny dots. The cars looked like strings of colored zigzagging lights. He squinted as the orange sunset shone luminously on Lake Michigan.

"We've got five floors to climb up before we get to the roof, and we have now . . ."—he glanced at his watch—"twenty-four minutes to do that." Liza closed her eyes and prayed. Guns she could deal with, but height terrified her. "This wrought-iron parapet here . . ."

"Parapet?" Liza asked curiously.

"This railing, Liza," Bodyslick condescended, "is our salvation. As we look up . . ."—he pointed toward the next balcony directly above them—"as you can see, luckily underneath that balcony there are enough cantilevers, girders, and rafters to grab to support our weight as we climb each floor toward the top. The biggest hurdle and most difficult will be to maintain your balance on this, I'd say, foot-wide decorative lip molding on the railing here." Bodyslick pointed to the black sill lip of the railing. "Liza, bring me that small chair out the bedroom!" She rushed into the bedroom and came out with the folded chair, opened it, and put it next to the railing.

"Now, we don't have much time, in a matter of minutes the goons are going to break down that bedroom door and we've only got . . . twenty minutes to get to the roof. So watch me, I'm going first. Then, Liza and then you, Doc."

Suddenly, they heard submachine guns being fired at the bedroom door and the screeching of the bed as it gave under the weight of Vinnie's boys.

Bodyslick kissed Liza and hugged her then shook Dr. Jones' hand.

He leaped onto the small chair then carefully stepped on the foot-wide lip of the parapet. A strong gust of wind made him sway to and fro. He momentarily felt like he was walking on a tightrope. He was facing Liza and Jones, as he stood on his tip-toes and grabbed a girder from the above balcony, and then walked with his hands toward a projecting beam to pull him-self up. He swung in a wide arc over the railing and onto the floor of the balcony. They saw nothing but Bodyslick's dangling feet as his body fell and thumped loudly on the floor above.

"All right, Liza baby. You can do it. Just don't look down!" Bodyslick said encouragingly.

Liza inhaled deeply. Her heart felt as though it was going to burst out of her chest. She gazed at a sun that was turning into a blood-red ball enveloped by pristine flaming clouds. She closed her eyes. She prayed. She was trembling with fear. The bedroom door began to open more. She could hear the angry voices of the goons, as they continued to bulldoze the bed from the door and fire their guns.

"Liza, hurry!" Bodyslick yelled nervously, as he peered at his watch. "We're running out of time. Come on now, baby, you can do it!"

She leaped onto the chair. Her back was against the view. Jones pulled out his laser pistol from his waist, and started firing at the bullet-ridden bedroom door.

"Go on, Liza. Go now and we can make it!"

She stepped onto the foot-wide railing lip and peered up at the crisscrossing girders and cantilevers. She felt as if she were teetering on the edge of the metal slab.

"Liza," Bodyslick shouted, "you remember when you were a kid and you played on monkey bars?"

"Yeah, I remember," she said, as gusts of wind whirled through her shaking body.

"Baby, it's the same thing. All you got to do is balance yourself and leap directly up and grab one of those steel beams and imagine you're on monkey bars. Then walk with your hands over till you reach the girders and then grab the railing. I'll help swing you up here. Now let's go, Liza!"

Jones continued firing at the slowly opening door. Suddenly Butch was firing at him and the glass window crashed to the floor. He shouted fanatically at Liza, "Move, dammit! Go!"

She jumped up and grabbed the girder then started walking with her hands toward the projecting steel beams. Two small orange eyes with vertical slits stared at her from behind one of the beams. She panicked as a large bird with a black hooded face, grey underbody and black wings specked with silvery white feathers hissed at her. She blinked her eyes while praying that it wasn't the treacherous urban bird of prey that she'd seen so many times in the city, swooping down on pigeons for food. She prayed that it wasn't a peregrine falcon. It was. She screamed, as the bird ferociously started tearing into her fingers while she tried to hold onto the beam. The bird's yellow hooked beak was as sharp as a razor blade. She tried to release one hand to hit it, but that only provoked it to use its talons, sinking them deep into her hands, ripping flesh and veins. She closed her eyes as the wind sprayed her own blood into her face.

"Bodyslick, I can't make it! Help meeeee!" She felt the steel beam start to slip from her bloody wet hands. She heard Bodyslick ask, "Liza! What's wrong?"

She could feel the whooosh of the wind as it clawed at her falling body. The now dark sky became a whirling kaleidoscope of lights, stars, and specks of moving neon colors below. Her clothes flapped loudly as if she had wings, as she descended down and down. She could hear the helicopter zoom past her. Liza screamed from the pit of her soul. She was falling upside down. She heard Bodyslick's voice as he moanfully shouted, "Liza, I love you!"

As she continued to accelerate, her whole life seemed to be unfolding before her like a moving picture. Her weight seemed to be doubling each second. She felt faint. She clasped her hands and prayed. She hit the street with such overwhelming impact that she died instantly.

Jones looked down at her crushed body with contempt, as he swung over the iron parapet and bumped into Bodyslick, who was on his knees, moaning. He knelt down beside him and hugged him reassuredly.

"Man, I know what you're going through, but neither you nor I will do Liza any good dead. Look! The helicopter is landing on the roof. Come on, man, we've got to go!"

Bodyslick stood up and gazed down at the blot of blood that was once his beloved Liza. He wiped tears from his eyes.

"Just one more floor, Brotha, and we're out of here," Jones said with exhaustion and relief.

"You insensitive sonofabitch! Is that heart all you care about?" Bodyslick shouted.

"Be realistic, Bodyslick," Jones said emphatically, "she was just a white trashy slut anyway."

"What did you say, man?" Bodyslick yelled, not believing what he was hearing.

"She was just a slut, white trash. The world is better off without her. Now come on, man. You've got a quarter of a mil waiting for you in your Swiss account."

Bodyslick swerved around and kicked Jones to the ground

then jumped on top of him with his knees anchoring his arms to the floor. He pulled out his laser pistol from his belt and stuck it so deep into Jones' mouth his knuckles and the pistol handle scraped against his wet lips.

"I loved Liza, punk. Now, I want you to apologize to her!" Bodyslick twisted the doctor's head so he could see the grotesque view below. "Okay, umma, blow the top of your weasy, tommin' Bourgeois negro fuckin' head off!"

"I dit tent meeen nit, moaan!" Jones mumbled, the laser pistol stuck deep in his mouth.

"Yes you did, muthafucka! Now say you sorry . . . 'cause if you don't, you gonna be one dead tommin' ass nigger!"

Bodyslick raised one knee off of his arm, grabbed him by the collar, and pulled him further over the balcony's edge. Jones broke out into a cold sweat as he peered down at the twinkling red lights of an ambulance below.

"I'm sorry dammit! Now will you let me up." Dr. Jones moaned.

"Say her name. You didn't say her name!" Bodyslick demanded.

"I'm sorry, Liza . . . is that good enough?"

"Now, say it with feeling. Like you really mean it," Bodyslick said angrily, as he jammed the shaking barrel deeper down his mouth.

"I'm sorry, Liza. I'm really sorry!" Jones moaned with humiliation.

Bodyslick momentarily forgot he was holding him down, as he watched the ambulance attendants pick up Liza's crushed remains. Even the loud noise of the helicopter landing on the roof above didn't shift his attention. He watched as they slammed the ambulance door and drove away. To them she was probably nothing more than another statistic of urban suicide. To him Liza represented a new breed of American woman. A woman who had ignited his love by being a rebel; a rebel who would rather live on the fringes of society than acquiesce for material gratification. A rebel who had once told him that without a *real* social and economic revolution there will never be full equity for minorities.

Bodyslick often felt that what Liza had experienced as a youth in Davenport, Iowa, during the red rain that destroyed her family's means of survival, was one of the seeds that had helped shape and molded her radicalism. A radicalism that compelled her to leave her rural farm life and search the fetid concrete jungle of the urban cities for an answer: a utopian answer that one could swallow like wine and get high and euphoric from its false claims that it could abolish man's inhumanity to man. Disillusionment was the key word in understanding the millions of zombies, like Liza, in the urban cities, searching for some magical elixir that could eliminate the rot in their lives.

Liza could never fully reconcile how quickly her father's years of labor had been wiped out by the red rain. She felt her father was merely a tiny pawn that had been shit upon by industrial technology and global corporations; that shit was merely a metaphor for acid rain, a dangerous ozone layer, and the new orbiting waste dumps. Liza had often told him that she felt as if she were being strangled by a money-hungry, capitalistic monster.

"Will you let me up now? Dammit, the goons will be on the balcony in a matter of minutes," Jones moaned. Bodyslick peered angrily at him. He wondered what kind of doctor he could be if he made judgments based on material appearance and embraced a philosophy that sought dignity, humanity, and status through the acquisition of money and power at any price. He wondered how many black Dr. Joneses were out there in the world, masquerading as responsible citizens with their degrees, their credentials, and their status quo jobs serving as mere props that hid the wretched evil that lurked deep within their rotten hearts. The evil that consumed their very being with self-hatred, contempt, and malice toward the less fortunate members of their race.

"Look, man, the helicopter is here . . . will you let me up so we can get outta here!"

Bodyslick angrily released the doctor's collar and stood up. Grabbing the railing, he leaped onto a rafter and started walking with his hands toward a projecting beam. Then he swung into a wide arc and landed on the rooftop. The wind from the helicopter's whirling blades momentarily made him lose his footing, as he walked on the slightly concave rooftop toward it. He could hear the *rat tat tat* of machine gun fire below.

He quickly activated vocal transmission on his watch. "Check it out . . . Geronimo, Snow, and Shondell, this is urgent. I'm in route by helicopter to the organ storage facility. Bring weapons and contact Choi Tse Tong and the Hip Hop Sung Gang for fire power . . . ASAP."

Outside the helicopter window, the dark clouds heaved and rumbled. A storm was brewing. *I hope they get that message*, he thought, *because my life depends on it.*

Chapter 38

Gina Luziano rubbed her temples as a volt of piercing pain shot through her head. She braced herself on a nearby door as she walked down the long cavernous hallway toward her office to count the money receipts. As she opened her door, again the explosive pain. It was as if someone was releasing tiny atom bombs inside her head. She clicked on the light in her tiny pink office then glanced at a recent picture that Vinnie and she had taken at a Chicago Cubs game. She squeezed by her entertainment center that was encased in gleaming pink and white marble. Everything in Gina's office was pink. Her vidphone. Her computer system. Her holo-television. Her answering machine. Gina quickly sat down in her pink swivel chair while tossing the money box and receipts on top of her small desk. She slumped in her swivel chair and shook her head as if whatever was causing the pain would somehow slip out. She sensed intuitively that something was wrong with her brother, Vinnie.

She quickly opened her desk drawer, looking for some packets of aspirin. Then she loudly slammed it shut after not finding any. Suddenly the phone rang. She was nervous, fearful, and overwhelmed with a sense of grief. Her hand trembled as she reached for the phone. "Hello, Wise Guy Lounge, this is Gina. Can I help you?"

"Gina, this is Gino. We had some problems," he said solemnly.

"Is Vinnie okay?" There was silence. A pause. Apprehension. "Is Vinnie okay? Dammit, don't you fuckin' play with me, Gino!"

"Gina," Gino said nervously, as he cleared his throat, "Vinnie is dead." The phone dropped and all Gino could hear, as the phone swung in side arcs, hitting the side of her desk, were agonizing screams, wails, and moans of grief. Almost five minutes passed before she picked up the phone.

"Gino, how fast can you get back here?" she asked, as she tried to sound authoritative and strong. The way Vinnie told her to be if something happened to him.

"As it stands now, Gina, Nicky and me and four soldiers are here. The nigger made us take off all our clothes and tied us up, and then, after he murdered Vinnie, he and this white dame and a black doctor climbed to the roof of this hotel."

"What hotel, Gino?" she asked, as she bit her lower lip trying to hold back tears.

"The Hyatt at O'Hare. At this very moment . . ." Gino craned his neck over the taut telephone cord. "I can hear a helicopter landing on the roof. Dammit, Gina . . . the cops just busted down the living room door. Get our bond ready, Gina!"

"All right, all of you get your hands up, and spread your legs . . ."

As Gina heard the police, she slammed down the phone and cried.

Her huge bodyguard, Angelo Beresio, tapped on the door. "It's me, Gina, Angelo! Is something wrong?" He swung open the door and saw her weeping like a baby in her chair. "Gina, what's wrong? Don't cry. We can handle it." Snow walked in behind him.

"Vinnie was killed by . . . by . . . Bodyslick!" she sobbed.

Angelo gently caressed her shoulder. "Gina, now calm down and tell me everything you know."

"That weasly punk ass Gino called me from the Hyatt O'Hare before the cops came and busted him . . . when I get through with him he's going to wish he had died with my brother . . . the rotten coward."

"Don't worry, Gina," Angelo said consolingly. "He's a dead man already!"

"Good!" Gina snapped viciously, "because all I care about right now is killing that nigger that murdered Vinnie like like . . ." She started to bawl.

"Easy, Gina," Angelo said.

"Like a no-life . . . like he was a penny-ante bum. All I care about right now, Angelo, is that my brother is dead . . . and the way he was killed. I don't give a fuck *why* he's dead. It's just the way he died. Now I want you to call New York and tell Tony Saccardo I need ten of his most vicious assassins on the next plane to Chicago!"

"Gina, Vinnie was kind to me," Snow said, sounding like a skilled actor. "He took a chance on me, and I want to help in any way I can!"

"Joey, you're such a sweet kid. Vinnie really liked you," she said, starting to cry again.

Angelo smiled. His simian eyes twinkled. His large nostrils flared. He clenched his fist with the anticipation of killing Bodyslick.

"Did Gino say how this Bodyslick got away?"

"He said they escaped by helicopter. It was Bodyslick, a white girl, and the doctor."

"You mean it landed on top of the roof of the Hyatt?" Angelo asked impatiently.

"Yes . . . yes . . . yes . . . dammit! Just do something." She started to cry again. Every ten seconds, the outside neon sign flickered eerie red shadows on Gina's face, as her sky blue shadow melted with her tears, giving her a demonic demeanor.

"What's wrong wid Gina?" Uncle Carillo asked, as he walked into the small office along with four young newly recruited henchmen.

"Vinnie was killed tonight," Gina squealed, as she rose out of her chair and hugged Uncle Carillo for moral support.

"Did dem niggas kill Vinnie?" he asked. His whole body seemed to tremble with disbelief and grief. "I told him towa let de dope alone!"

"We know who killed him," Angelo said confidently, "believe me, within the next twenty-four hours, he will be subjected to unimaginable horror!"

"Someone calla Tony in New York . . ." Uncle Carillo said mournfully.

"Joey, you and Franky take Gina upstairs so she can lie down and get some rest," Angelo commanded.

"Franky, Mother Nature's callin', I'll meet you outside," Snow said, as he walked into the bathroom. He whispered into his wrist phone, "Check it out." He then punched in Bodyslick's number and read the text message scrolling across his screen. *"Geronimo, Snow, and Shondell, this is urgent . . ."*

Meanwhile, Angelo dialed Tony Saccardo's New York number then listened intensely as the phone rang and rang and rang.

"Hello, this is Benny. Who is this?"

"This is Angelo Beresio with the Luziano outfit in Chicago."

"Hey, what's up, Angelo? How's everything in Chi-town?"

"Bad, man . . . Vinnie Luziano was murdered tonight by a black dude called Bodyslick!"

"But, Angelo, you're one of Vinnie's top capos and one of his top aides. How could you let this happen?"

"Benny, I haven't got time for all the fuckin' grimy details. I got to talk to Tony Saccardo. This Bodyslick is the craziest nigger we've ever run into."

"You mean one *moolie* has got all you mean *dagos* scared?" Benny asked derisively.

"Listen, Benny," Angelo said angrily, "this ain't no fuckin' joke. I told you Vinnie Luziano is dead. He was gunned down. We don't want the Chicago outfit involved in this hit. It would bring too much heat down on us. Benny, we need outside help."

"Okay, I'll call Tony right now, Angelo, he's in Florida taking care of some business. I'll get right back with you. How many soldiers you think you need to take out this crazy moolie?"

"Tell Tony we need ten of his most skilled assassins."

"Ten," Benny said skeptically.

"Yeah, ten!" Angelo repeated.

"Okay, Angelo," Benny laughed, "but this Bodyslick must be one bad ass dude!"

"If Tony gives the okay on this, Benny, what's the fastest they can get here?"

"If Tony okays the use of the family's Learjet . . . Jesus, they could be at Midway in less than two hours."

"Great, now by the time you call back I should have all the logistics on the whereabouts of Vinnie's killers. By the time the New York assassins arrive . . . but right now I've got to go, Benny. There's a lot to do here. You know, tryin' to keep things organized."

"Angelo, you and Uncle Carillo got to stick by Gina!"

"I'll be right with her when she picks up his body, and I'll help her with the funeral arrangements."

"Good, Angelo, you always was dependable!"

"Thanks, Benny, I know I can also depend on you to tell Tony about Vinnie's death."

Benny snarled, "Don't worry about nothin', Angelo. I think I'll make this trip myself. Me and Vinnie go way, way back, and for him to get taken out like this is a slap in the face to any wise guy! This, Angelo, is an insult to all five New York family Mafiosi."

"Listen up, Benny, this is important!" Angelo said in a low serious tone.

"Go on, I'm listening."

"Benny, I tried to talk Vinnie out of getting into the body organ business because this nigger Bodyslick has it sold up here in Chicago, and rumor has it he has some heavyweight people on the city payroll helping him cut through a bunch of red tape . . . like that weasly Jewish coroner, Weiner. I told Vinnie that we didn't need that type of business. Why, we been making a killing just selling that galactic drug somellow. But you know Vinnie, he was greedy, and he didn't mind dealing with blacks or anybody else that could help him make more money!"

"Somellow ain't that big here in the Apple yet, but I heard the Puerto Ricans and Jamaicans are going crazy over the stuff. They say this shit makes cocaine and heroin seem like Kool-Aid. They say this shit can make you actually levitate. Fly, and float like a bee. You ever try the shit, Angelo?"

"Hell no, man! I wouldn't snort that shit with your nose, let alone shoot it up! Some of that stuff they sayin' might be true, but what I do know is that money is floatin' from their hands to mine!" Angelo laughed.

"Angelo, if it's true that these junkies are floating, then dealers gonna have to get ankle weights to keep them in sight. Ha ... Ha! I didn't mean to trip out on ya ... but to get serious ..."

"Go on, Benny, get serious about what? I'm running out of time!"

"What's an uncut kilo of somellow selling for in Chicago right now?"

"Vinnie got it wholesale, so we would sell it at a discount rate ... you know, depending on volume and how much you buy, but, on the average in the street, it sells for one hundred thousand dollars a kilo. We talkin' one hundred percent pure somellow. Uncut. Straight from a Martian mining colony."

"How's it moving?" Benny asked, curious.

"Right now it's slow ... I'd say about four kilos a week."

"Holy fuck, Angelo! Why that's good money," Benny yelled excitedly.

"And that's when it's slow," Angelo replied arrogantly.

"Four hundred thousand dollars a week ... is slow, huh?" Benny asked.

"And we're talkin' *uncut*."

"So's you can double that by steppin' on it?"

"You got it, Benny boy!"

"Tony is against the shit and so is the commission, which

consists of ten families. They view Vinnie Luziano in Chicago
and Franky 'Ears' Calossi of Cleveland as renegades. Angelo,
as you know they are totally against selling body organs and
somellow, but that won't interfere with getting the help you'll
need for Vinnie's death!"

"I've got to go, Benny . . . but if you come to Chicago with
the hit squad, I can personally show you how to get around
that . . . I'll talk to you later . . . got to go now . . ."

"All right, Angelo, I'll get right back. Give me a couple of
hours or so. Okay, *Paisan*?"

"Just take care of business, Benny."

The two young rookie soldiers stood quietly in the room as
Angelo slammed down the phone. He stood up and cracked
his knuckles as he walked over to them.

"Me and Luigi have an appointment with that weasly Dr.
Weiner. Joey, you and Franky are going to kill Gino and Nicky
Sigichi. Both are locked up at 26th and California. They are
fuckin' cowards. If Vinnie is dead and they are alive, they
fuckin' got to be killed. Besides, if they talk to the feds we are
doomed. I don't give a fuck how you do it. Dress up like
chinks . . . just don't come back here without proof that they
are dead! You got that?"

"We got you, boss!"

"And then we'll all meet up at Bodyslick's warehouse out
south in Robbins."

Franky and Joey nodded their heads and quickly walked
out of the room.

Chapter 39

Angelo Beresio and Luigi Moloto, one of his new soldiers, sat on their cans, quietly smoking seagarettes while waiting for the coroner of the City of Chicago to leave the County Morgue at 2121 West Harrison Street. Angelo glanced at his wrist watch. He smiled. In less than three hours the payback for Vinnie Luziano's death would soon be known to the world.

"There he is!" Luigi said anxiously. They watched as Dr. Weiner nervously walked along the crowded sidewalk toward his shiny new Lincoln. They watched him as he uneasily put his key into the door lock. Angelo gritted his teeth and his left eyebrow started to twitch, the way it always did when death was near. Luigi laughed loudly as he pointed at Dr. Weiner.

"Angelo, you ever see them shows about wild antelope and how they react to everything before they just drink a little water? I mean these fuckin' antelope are so wired up that every five seconds they lookin' around for the lions, wild dogs, and beasts of the jungle. Now look at Weiner, don't he kinda remind you of one of those neurotic antelopes? Look at him. How could he be so neurotic?"

Angelo snarled, "He does kinda remind you of one of those sissy ass deers all right. Showtime, Luigi!"

Dr. Weiner tossed his briefcase on the passenger seat, switched on the ignition, put the car in reverse, and started to swerve out into the brightly lit night streets. Then suddenly, Angelo put the pedal to the metal of his car and ripped it into the Lincoln's rear end. Dr. Weiner quickly leaped out of his car and slammed the door. He held his tiny fist in the air with anger as he walked to the rear of his car and peered at his broken tail-lights. He waved his fist at Angelo as he strolled toward them. Angelo and Luigi sat calmly in the car. Angelo lowered the automatic window as the bird-like, bespeckled, livid face of Dr. Weiner peered in, yelling at him.

"I hope you got fucking insurance. What's the matter with you? You drunk or something? Look at the damage you've done!"

"I'm sorry, old timer," Angelo said arrogantly.

"You think a couple C-notes will straighten things out, pops?" Luigi asked, as he waved them at him.

"Absolutely not! As soon as I see a cop we will resolve this matter!" Dr. Weiner said, craning his neck and looking for a patrol car.

"No need for that, Doc!" Angelo barked.

"What do you mean by that?" Dr. Weiner crouched down and gazed at Angelo through the window.

"I mean get your weasley, conniving, Jew ass in the fucking car, Dr. Weiner. Luigi, get out and help the good doctor into the car."

Dr. Weiner's knees rattled as he stared at the 21-inch barrel of a Remington Model 870P shotgun brushing against his large nose. Luigi opened the passenger door and pushed Dr. Weiner into the seat then slammed the door and sat back down in the rear seat.

"What do you want from me?" Weiner asked, as he squirmed fearfully in his seat.

"Dr. Weiner," Angelo said gravely, "you shouldn't have done business with Bodyslick!"

"What are you . . . ?"

Luigi quickly looped a leather belt around Dr. Weiner's neck from the backseat and handed the buckled end to Angelo.

Both of them started to pull in opposite directions. Five hundred pounds of combined brute strength extinguished the life out of Dr. Weiner.

"Luigi, open the door and dump him out. We got to get moving," Angelo said as he muscled the electro-powered Chevy into the street. He picked up his vidphone.

"Listen up! This is Angelo. Me and Luigi are headed out to Robbins, Illinois. We're going to Bodyslick's LL&T facility to kill him. Your GPS system will guide you there. Just be there . . ." —he gazed at his watch—"by eleven o'clock!"

Louey Rufino and Sammy Gallo were in the parking lot directly across the street from the neon blinking Hip Hop Pot Shop on 35th and Martin Luther King Drive on the South Side of Chicago. Winos and junkies peeped into their car wondering if they were NARC agents. It was unusual to see two white men just sitting in a car in that neighborhood.

Louey and Sammy smiled at the voluptuous black women as they swayed down the street. Sammy wiggled his tongue at one and she gave him an angry glance.

"Louey, will ya look at the ass on that girl. My dick gets hard and my mouth gets watery just looking at her."

"You ever fuck a black dame before, Sammy?"

"No!"

"They not like white women. Unless you're really long-winded, they will wear you out!"

"You mean they *fuck* that long?"

Louey lit up a cigar and started to thump it repeatedly in the ashtray. "They fuck like animals, Sammy. They got *gourmet* pussy if you're man enough to eat it."

"Will you look at that frantic crowd, Louey!" Sammy said, as they looked at the customers going in and out of Bodyslick's Real Steel Chicken joint. Louey grabbed his binoculars and sharpened the focus, as he stared at Pumpkin and Butch who were at a payphone just one block down from the chicken joint.

Butch dialed Louey from the payphone. "How's it going, Butch?"

"I bought me a five piece extra spicy wing dinner and left the bomb in a corner of the place in a brown paper bag."

"Was it crowded in there then? Because the place is like flies on shit right now."

"Hell, yeah! Won't nobody notice it! They too busy waitin' fah that bird."

"You time it for closing, right?"

"Yeah, they close at two in the morning." Butch looked at his watch. "We got four hours before liftoff."

"We don't want any unnecessary bloodshed, you know . . . women and children," Louey said with concern.

"When we blow it up . . . believe me it will be empty. I been casing the place for a week. In fact, I'm trying to fuck one of the girls who works in there, and it would be a sin against Gawd Almighty to destroy all that pussy."

Louey and Sammy laughed.

Butch continued. "The detonation requires two radio signals . . . yours and mine. At exactly two o'clock we press the red button on the black boxes simultaneously. That's why it's important that our watches are synchronized. What time you got, Louey?"

"Ten o'clock!"

"Good, that's what I got, alright, at two o'clock *capoooow*! No more Real Steel Chicken!"

"There's a text message coming through from Angelo. We all got to put the pedal to the metal. He wants us in Robbins in thirty minutes. Let's get outta here!"

Chapter 40

"Where do you live?"
"5515 . . ."
"5515 what?"
"5515 . . . sah."
"Naw, look, if you wanna get out of here I've got to verify your address. You're only in here for vagrancy. Now, 5515 what?"
"I said 5515 . . . sah."
"Will you quit your goddamn mumbling and tell me where you live?"
"Dats mah address, sah."
"5515 could be a vacant lot, a street corner, a goddamn bench. Now, asshole, your ID card states something else. Is it phony? Are you really Willie Orethorn Simpson? Do you know how to spell your fuckin' name?"
"My name is O.J. Simpson, sah."
Laughter boomeranged off the metal cells. Even Nicky Sigichi smiled.
"It doesn't say O.J. on your ID, fool!"
"Dat's whut dey call me in the streets, sir!"
"Now look, fool, is your name Willie Orethorn Simpson?"
"It depends, sah, on whose askin' me."
"You just sit in here awhile longer and think about who you are, okay!"

"Yessah."

"Get Doc Franklin in here, Reggie. Something's not right with this guy!" Detective O'Brien said.

"Will do, boss. I'll call him now. But we need to quarantine him. He's stinking up the whole building." Officer Reggie Miller pinched his nose as he walked out of the interrogation room.

Detective O'Brien looked at his mildewed shirt and pants that were caked with dirt. A sour body odor of feces and urine clung to him. He smelled like he had fallen into a sewer. His long, unkempt, filthy dreadlocks hung down to his shoulders. Lice and gnats seemed to be doing Olympian somersaults in them. His waxen coffee brown face was a grotesque caricature of Stepin Fetchit. As if someone had made a death mask of him and glued it on his face.

Dr. Franklin walked into the room dressed in surgical greens, with his holoviscope on the top of his head like a Viking helmet. He shook his head, momentarily stung by the vile stench of the man.

"We have got to get him out of here and clean him up before he contaminates the entire building. I'll just do a basic exam now."

He opened his leather medi-box and pulled out a pair of latex gloves and a mask. He was a short, squat, bald, middle-aged man of German descent. All police precincts were required to have an M.D. on the premises.

"What is the problem, Detective O'Brien, besides his wretched odor?" Dr. Franklin asked through his mask while walking up to the man and looking at his waxen complexion.

"The guy is cold as a corpse, Doc. He doesn't even blink his eyes. Every ten minutes he has a seizure like someone is trying to put a firecracker up his ass!"

"I think he's a somellow junkie. That galactic drug produces the same symptoms," Officer Miller said as he scooted away from his desk.

"O.J., will you stand up please?" Dr. Franklin asked softly.

"Yessuh."

"Now open your eyes—wide?"

"Yessuh."

Dr. Franklin scanned the holoviscope beam into his eyes. He shook his head in disbelief then strapped the holoviscope back on his head and grabbed the man's hand.

"Jesus Christ! You are ice cold. Open your mouth."

"Yessuh."

"Just what I thought. You can sit back down, O.J."

"Well, what do you think, Doc?" Detective O'Brien asked.

"Come out of the room for a minute!" Dr. Franklin whispered. They all walked into an adjacent room. "O.J. is a cyborbot!"

"You shittin' me, Doc!"

"I knew something was weird about him. But a fuckin' bot?" Reggie said.

"He's the most advanced I've seen. Of course I haven't seen many since med school. But he is advanced because he doesn't know he is not human. Let's go back into the room."

"O.J.," Dr. Franklin commanded, "stand up and take off your shirt!"

"Yessuh . . . but is something wrong, Doc?"

"No. But we just want to make sure."

He quickly snatched off his filthy shirt.

"Now watch this!" Dr. Franklin whispered to Detective O'Brien and Reggie. "O.J., open your mouth! Good . . . now let me grab your tongue!"

"Jesus fuckin' Christ!" Reggie said with astonishment.

"It's fuckin' twelve inches long!" Detective O'Brien said, laughing in disbelief. "Doc, why would they give it a tongue that long?"

"Before I answer that let's get some more data about him." Dr. Franklin walked around to his back. He pointed to a tattoo-like stamp on his right shoulder blade that read:

> *Model:* Z134-DZ
> *Date:* 2021
> *Comp: Hwang Tao Robotics, Inc.*
> *Patent:* 2020-13-2A
> *LOC: Made in China*

Dr. Franklin then pointed to a twelve by twelve gray piece of plastic film that bisected his spine. He pressed a tiny button on top of the square and two beams of reflected blue laser light interfered on the film creating a holo-screen. 3-D encoded data beamed from this film:

> *This cyborbot is the property of Hwang Tao Robotics, Inc.*
> *Patent and proprietary information is subject to all global sci-tech copyright laws. This cyborbot cannot be re-sold without title transfer from original owner.*

Dr. Franklin pressed the button and held it down as the three of them glanced at the holo-screen.

"Let's see here," Dr. Franklin said as the information scrolled down and he lifted his finger at interesting data. "He was originally owned, in 2021, by the Baroom & Bayly Circus for their Freakbot show. In 2026, he was sold to a used 'bot' dealership called Heavenly Toys. They customized and re-programmed him in 2027 and sold him to the Robotica Erotica House Franchise. By 2030, he was outdated and they didn't want to de-charge him, so they let him out in the streets! Open your mouth, O.J."

> *Yessuh . . . Docta', but doncha do me like you do po shine . . .*
> *gave him so much medicin' till he went stone blind.*

"Amusing, O.J., where did you learn poetry?"

I once was a clown for the Baroom and Bayly Circus.
Now I live on a park bench without
fans
Or
purpose.

"Excellent, but I need you to open your mouth, O.J."

"Yessuh."

Dr. Franklin pulled out his long tongue and wiped his finger on the inside of his mouth then pointed it toward the ceiling light.

"This gel-like substance is both a liquid and a solid. When pressure deforms the gel, the voltage ignites electrodes imbedded in the plastic tongue along with thousands of nano-sensors which enable it to sense the texture of satin, concrete, or even a woman's vagina."

"Did you say pussy?" Detective O'Brien and Officer Miller both said while laughing at the same time.

"No. I said vagina . . . but remember your earlier question, O'Brien, about why they would make a twelve inch tongue. Well, most men don't realize that millions of women go to Robotica Houses to have sex with these cybobots yearly. It's a billion dollar underground business. So companies like Heavenly Toys retro-fit them for different sex acts . . . in O.J.'s case it was oral, his tongue. But they only operate for seven to ten years, and then they start to de-charge. That's why I think O.J. is having the seizures."

"Doc, he kept saying his address was 55th and King Drive in Washington Park!"

"Unfortunately, that's what happens to these old bots. They are let loose like stray dogs until they de-charge!" Dr. Franklin reached into his green trouser pocket and took out a Swiss Army knife. He slid out the screwdriver and punched it repeatedly into the holo-screen. A noxious green vapor seeped from the hole. The holo-screen dimmed.

O.J. started shaking uncontrollably and fell to the floor.

Jaws sagging. Teeth rasping. Positron brain fizzling. Fists clenched defiantly.

"That should do it," Dr. Franklin said almost mournfully. "He is de-charged. Dead!"

The three of them stood over him as if viewing the body of a dead friend at a funeral home, staring at his dark waxen face as if he were human. Dr. Franklin gazed at him feeling like a monster that wanted to plead for forgiveness.

O.J.'s liquid brown eyes fluttered then he sighed with a peaceful sound as if drifting into a deep, fathomless electric abyss.

The slam of the jail door closing bounced off the walls. Nicky Sigichi nervously paced his cell. He wondered if Gina would send him a lawyer. His whole being shook with terror, just the thought of freedom meant he was a marked man by the Triad. He nervously grabbed the cell bars as he heard the footsteps of a jail attendant walking toward the exit.

"Turnkey?" he hollered. The attendant quickly glanced back toward his cell. "It's me . . . Sigichi! Any word on my lawyer?"

"No!" he snarled.

"Look, will ya lemme know when you hear somethin' 'bout my bail being posted?"

He was a short stocky Irish cop with red hair and a freckled face. There was a small scar over his left eyebrow. It looked like a razor wound. Nicky glanced at his badge. His last name was Malahy.

"Well," he said, glancing at his watch, "my shift is over in ten minutes, but they'll let you know on the next shift."

Nicky walked back to his steel cot and noticed a newscube crystal on it. He picked it up then clicked it on to read the headlines:

UNIVERSITY PROFESSOR MURDERED IN
HYDE PARK

A LONE GUNMAN AMBUSHED AND KILLED UNIVERSITY
OF CHICAGO PROFESSOR JONATHAN GRAHAM WHILE HE
WAS WALKING HOME AFTER A LECTURE. LAST WEEK,
GRAHAM ANNOUNCED AT THE LECTURE THAT HE HAD
SUCCESSFULLY TRANSPLANTED A DONOR BODY TO A
HUMAN HEAD. THE STATE ATTORNEY'S OFFICE BELIEVES
ORGAN TRAFFICKERS HAD SOMETHING TO DO WITH HIS
MURDER . . .

Nicky lay back down on the steel cot and closed his eyes. He dreamed . . .

He *dreamed* he was walking down the squeaking, dark hallway of an old abandoned house. A house where he had once raped and sodomized an eight-year-old girl, named Susan Carlson, and left her to bleed to death. The hallway was pitch black. He touched the walls trying to find his way. He could hear old curtains flapping in a nearby room. Suddenly, he turned around. He heard footsteps. Tiny footsteps. Or was it just his weight on the old wooden floor? Or maybe rats? He froze in his steps as the *screech* of a door hinge made his heart valves pound deliriously. He gazed down the hallway, as a foggy red light shone through the crack of a door. It slowly opened. He could see whirling dust particles in the luminous crimson light. He flinched, as some magnetic force started to pull him toward the opened door. He tried to resist, but his feet were no longer implanted on the floor. He felt tiny fingers on his back nudging him forward. He started to float a good foot off the floor. The door swung open. He entered the room; it was dark red, and hundreds of candles flickered. The smell of roses and incense wafted past his nose. He hovered at the door entrance. He blinked his eyes as he gazed at an open small white casket at the front of the room. It was a child's casket. He could see the profile of a girl's face. Susan? Was he in a funeral home, he wondered? There were twelve little girls sitting in metal chairs in front of the casket. They all turned around and looked at him. They bared their lips revealing glistening fangs. They all *hissed* at him like angry felines. Their faces were chalk white. Dead faces. Blonde, black, or brunette hair looped down on their shoulders. They were all dressed as if going to church. They stood up as he floated down the aisle toward the casket. They were holding gleaming knives, razors, and ice picks in their small hands. Were they the little girls who died in that arson job he did last year?

Nicky's body was immobile. He could feel the small fingers poking in his back as he slowly floated toward the casket. He screamed as he felt the *swish* of a razor slit the flesh on his arm. Children's laughter echoed from a distance. The girls started to slash at him with the weapons.

"Jesus!" he hollered, as a knife dug deep into his back. "Please, do not do that!" he yelled piteously, as he felt a cold small hand grab his penis. He peered down and saw Tong's niece's fanged smile. He closed his eyes and bit down on his tongue as she scraped the razor across his dick. His body continued to float toward the casket. The girls walked back to their seats. Blood blotched their pretty dresses. He grimaced with pain as he levitated in front of Susan's dehydrated body. Nicky gazed with ghastly horror at her shrunken cheeks. Her milky white skin. Her hands were neatly folded in her lap. He floated closer. Closer. And even closer toward her. A cool breeze swept through the room and snuffed the candles' flames. The room was coal black. Then the candles rekindled their fire. His eyes were riveted on Susan's dead face. The other girls were gone. Susan's mouth moved? He gasped with naked horror. Susan's eyes opened. Dead eyes. Soulless eyes. Prostrate, she slowly rose out of the casket. Her alabaster face snarled, making blots of purple and lavender flush her skin. She *hissed,* baring sharp bone-white fangs. Her fingernails became long and vulture-like. Her eyes became a fiery red, as if they reflected the scorching heat of hell. He was frozen. He could feel her hot breath as her mouth neared his neck . . .

Hours later he awoke with fear, as someone shook him. He groggily opened his eyes. He glanced at an olive, hard knuck-

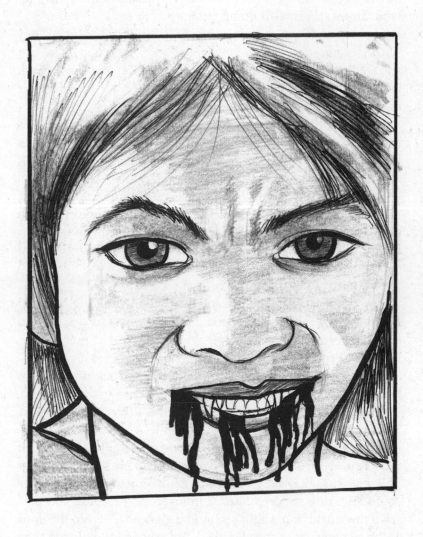

led hand as it roughly pulled on his shoulder. Nicky squinted in the darkness. He smiled as he pushed his upper body up with his forearms, as if doing pushups.

He looked down, thinking, *I knew I could trust Gina to pay for my bond.*

"Damn, I'm glad to . . ." He glanced up at the loose black pants of the man who was shaking him. Someone else was there. "Did Gina come, too?"

He heard the quiet laughter of two men. He froze. He was too scared to turn over. He gazed up with terror as his eyes locked with Chinese eyes. Ninja eyes. Deadly eyes. Black hooded masks covered their noses and mouths. He blinked with disbelief. He painfully bit down on his lower lip to make sure this wasn't another dream. It wasn't. He gritted his teeth as he looked at the glistening serrated blade of the ninja, as he held it over his head like a human guillotine. Again he heard their laughter.

"Hey, can I say somethin' off the record to you?"

The two ninjas smiled at each other while looking down at Nicky Sigichi. The blade reflected the cell's bars, it was cocked over his head.

"Sure," the ninja with the sword said. "It is a last request?"

"Well, I just want you goddamn motherfuckin' gooks to kiss my Italian ass!"

Nicky bared his teeth as he heard the *swish* of the hurling blade as it sliced through cold air while speeding toward his neck. Nicky's head *plopped* down on the floor. A geyser of blood gushed from his neck. His headless body's arms and legs twitched spasmodically for a moment. For a nanosecond he could still move his eyes. For a millisecond he could still perceive the world. For a split second he glanced up from the floor at the two ninjas, as they laughed and reached down, and then grabbed Nicky's head by his hair and tossed it into a garbage bag. And then there was only silent darkness.

Chapter 41

"Ma, this is Malcolm."

"I can barely hear you, boy. What kinda noise is dat in the background? Where are you at, son?"

He couldn't tell her he was in a helicopter headed for his organ storage facility in Robbins. He couldn't tell her that the Mafia had him on their hit list. He spoke louder into the cell phone, as the helicopter's blades chopped through the wind.

"You heard about your Uncle Will, huh?"

"I was over his house recently. Aunt Eltha is tryin' to nurse him back to health."

There was silence. He glanced out the window at twinkling stars as the helicopter roared through the air.

"Your Uncle Will died this morning, Malcolm."

"No, Ma . . . I just talked to him. No, Ma . . . No . . ." Bodyslick said as pain and sorrow gripped his heart.

"He had his faults, but he was a good man. He loved you like a son. Even on his deathbed he whispered to me that he had talked to you about goin' straight. About . . ." She started to cry.

"Don't cry, Ma. Believe me, I'm goin' to change my life. I swear, Ma," he said, as he bit down on his lower lip trying to hold back tears.

His mother cleared her throat and continued. "May Gawd have mercy on you, boy."

He remembered the same scorching words his mother had said while sitting on the couch and holding his small five-year-old hand. Listening. Watching people on television leaping from two burning towers as satanic fire and smoke billowed upward.

"Ma, why the planes flyin' into the buildings, huh?"

"Didn't Malanna's death teach you anything? What about Bubba? How many people have to die before you realize that worshipping a false idol will sooner or later get you killed."

"I listened to Uncle Will. I'm also listening to you. Once I tidy up a few business deals, I'm out. Finished, Ma. I'm goin' to be at Uncle Will's funeral. I just called to check on you."

"Malcolm, listen to me."

"I'm listenin', Ma."

"I had a dream and you was running with fear. Son, please be careful."

"I will, Ma. In Yamba's name I promise I will."

"Yamba?" she asked, confused. "Who in God's name is Yamba, son?"

He smiled inwardly. "Yamba is an African word for God, Ma. I just say Yamba instead of God."

"Okay, Malcolm, you've always been a complex and mystic child. If you want to call *God Yamba* it's fine with me. Just pray, Malcolm. Pray to Yamba to give you enough strength to stop makin' money from the dead."

"Ma, remember I love you and if *anything* should happen to me you are the trustee for my estate, in my will."

"May God be with you, Malcolm."

"Bye, Ma."

"I love you, Malcolm. Pray to Yamba to change your ways."

Suddenly the red light on his watch flickered. He glanced at the message as it beamed across the screen: *Check it out. We got your message. Geronimo, Shondell, and I are en route. We also got the message to the Hip Hop Sung Gang . . . Snow . . . Yamba!*

Chapter 42

In the distance, Dr. Jones could hear the helicopter's whirling rotors fade away as they neared Bodyslick's underground dungeon of cadaver organs. He had programmed the helicopter's Robot Request System to wait one hour before returning to O'Hare Airport. He had already booked flight 224 to Baltimore at two in the morning, which means he had only one hour and forty-five minutes to get the heart and make his flight time.

As they lumbered through the tall dense weed stalks and trees, Jones quickly understood why Bodyslick had chosen Robbins, Illinois, as the site of his storage facility; for miles and miles there was nothing but huge trees and tall shrubbery. It was pitch black. Everything seemed hidden in the impenetrable frame of the night. It was difficult to even see your hand in front of you. The yellow glares of light that beamed from nearby frame houses were the only visible signs of civilization. Huge weeping willows and cottonwood trees towered over them as Jones stumbled while following Bodyslick through the perilous darkness. Bats darted past a full moon, their tiny red eyes ablaze with a neon light that seemed to glow with the very flames of hell. Dogs howled piteously from a nearby field; it was a sound that was agonizing, mournful. He peered up at the moon as black clouds seemed to claw at it. Then the dogs began to howl again as if the moonlight had some ghastly effect on them. Owls hooted as if warning of impending doom. Crickets cried loudly. Ominously. His whole body seemed to shudder with cold fear.

As they zigzagged through the dense foliage they passed a house. Jones was shocked. Flabbergasted that in 2031 there were still black people living in such squalid, impoverished conditions. He stared with disbelief as a faint light from inside the house held his sight. It was like walking through a time warp. The house was more like a shanty. It reminded him of the makeshift houses that black sharecroppers lived in during the antebellum South. As they scampered past it, he shook his head with amazement that his life was so radically different than the blacks that lived in that shanty.

Suddenly a sleek black Cadihydro pulled into the graveled driveway of the shanty, and a young black man stepped out of the car. He had on a red baseball cap cocked defiantly to one side. Pipe-thick ropes of gold gleamed from around his neck. A red and white Bulls leather jacket draped his lanky body. Bright red turbo gym shoes accented his baggy black pants. He leaped up some groaning stairs and knocked on the door. Some words were exchanged. Jones heard a woman's voice. The deadbolt released. A light from the living room popped on and made a silhouette of him and the woman as she gave him some money and he placed tiny aluminum foil packages in her hand. Somellow? Martianzeeg? Chunocoke? The door *slammed* shut; the young dope dealer strutted to his car then sped away leaving clouds of whirling dust behind.

"Come on, Dr. Jones," Bodyslick whispered, "we're almost there! We'll enter through my secret underground passageway."

After they had walked about a half a mile, Bodyslick pointed with his flashlight at a sign that seemed hidden in shadows, cast from trees, in some unknown place:

LL&T
NO TRESPASSING
ELECTRONIC FORCE FIELD
ENTER AT YOUR OWN RISK

"This is the underground section of my organ storage facility, Dr. Jones, where I keep my *high* quality organs!" Bodyslick
said with quiet elation, as they stood in front of a tall man-
made hill surrounded by a high fence. "I can't wait for you to
see this." Bodyslick's voice had taken on a religious fervor to
it, as if God would let them see some inaccessible temple in
which were hidden the secrets to immortality.

Doctor Jones was amazed how Bodyslick had built part of
his facility underground. He couldn't help but notice how it
blended in so well with the surroundings that it was virtually
impossible to find. He stood there in awe as Bodyslick walked
toward a small box built outside the entry gate of the fence.
He signaled Jones to follow. Bodyslick then pressed a button
on his special wristwatch, and a small door from the metal
box flopped open. He hurriedly gazed at a keypad set inside
the box and punched in the defuser code: 1968. Jones wondered if that was the same year that Martin Luther King Jr.
was assassinated? A small green light blinked on signaling the
force field and the retinal scan system was deactivated. The
eight foot high gate screeched open, and the entry door within
the ten-foot hill trundled up like a garage door.

"Let's go, and hurry," Bodyslick said, as he ducked a spider-
web while sprinting into his underground grotto of organs.
"Doc, this facility cost me a cool three mil, but it's paid for itself four times over," he said. As they stepped into the vestibule, he reached for a duplicate keypad and punched in 1968
to reactivate the security system.

"This represents the state of the art in organ storage technology. The place is totally automated, and don't worry about
anybody bustin' in on us because that electronic force field

covers a mile radius and is so sensitive it can differentiate a mosquito from a fly. It's one gigantic electric trap out there that triggers minefield detonation and electrocution for any human that's stupid enough to stumble into it."

Another door slid open, and Jones followed Bodyslick inside. A long cavernous hallway was lit by a series of small square signs over doors: LIVERS, PANCREAS, LUNGS, KIDNEYS, EYES, SKELETAL PARTS. He began to shiver from a dry refrigerated cold that seemed to engulf the morgue-like place. The facility was quiet and one could *feel* a blanket of deathly gloom. It was silent except for the random bursts of electric energy from the automated storage computer system. About three meters down the hallway a sign flickered over a door: HEARTS. A light shone from underneath the door. Immediately adjacent to the room was another sign that read: DISSECTION LAB.

"All right, Dr. Jones, this is what you've been waiting for," Bodyslick said, as he pressed a button on the wall near the door. It slid open. They were about to step into the room when the alarm system voice started to wail: *"Intruders are attempting to penetrate electronic force field! You are being attacked!"*

"Shit!" Bodyslick shouted. "Come on, Doc, let's get that heart and get the fuck outta here!"

Bodyslick led him into a state-of-the-art heart storage facility. Jones was stunned because even at Baltimore Memorial Hospital, they didn't have an advanced self-contained organ storage system like this. There were hundreds of interlinked cylinders containing beating floating human hearts. Each cylinder had handwritten labels denoting ethnicity and blood types. They were connected to multicolored electrical cords on long tables. The walls constantly blinked from a barrage of electrical sensors, gauges, dials, and television monitors. Security cameras were mounted on the ceiling.

"Bodyslick, I've got to give you credit, because this is a superb facility," Jones said, while pointing and listening to the rhythmic beat of the floating hearts. "Are the organs in liquid nitrogen?"

"Yes, they are," Bodyslick said, "and because the nitrogen needs constant replenishment, each organ container is closely monitored by its own miniature computer."

"How ingenious . . . but how can you guarantee that these are healthy organs? After all, machines break down. Entrophy and Murphy's Law are unavoidable constants of science. How do I know that the heart I'm buying is totally healthy?"

Bodyslick smiled mischievously and cleared his throat as if eager to share his secret.

"Doc, the minute the organ is extracted from the cadaver by the surgi-robot, it is packed in dry ice and transported here in an electro igloo-container." He pointed to a robot that stood quietly next to a nearby shelf. "Afterward, the organ is submerged in oxygenated plasma, various anticoagulants, and then liquid nitrogen is added at a temperature well below zero to fight off infection from the organs. Now I'm not a scientist, Doc, but maybe in the future, if we get out of this alive, I'll arrange for you to meet the great Japanese genius, Dr. Shurito, who developed the system."

Jones nodded.

"Now, Doc, time is against us. We must hurry." He glanced at the video camera. "We only have thirty-five minutes to get you back to O'Hare with the heart. The helicopter should be landing now. Over there in the closet are thermal insulated surgical smocks and gloves you can put on to protect you from the dripping nitrogen once the robot retrieves the heart."

"Which robot?"

"I'll activate it, Doc." Bodyslick walked over to the robot, and let it make a retinal scan of his eyes.

"Master, can I help you?" the robot droned, as it nodded its head like an obedient slave.

"Clarence, this is Dr. Jones . . ." Clarence quickly did a body scan of Jones for his databank. "Follow his instructions carefully, you understand?"

"Yes, master!"

"He's state of the art compared to that metal robot crap that served us on the jet ride here," Jones commented.

"Ready for your instructions, Dr. Jones," the robot said.

"We need an AB blood type. Preferably Caucasian. Age range eight to twelve. I want to see it scanned for viral infection and structural defects."

The robot walked to a large nitrogen vat full of hearts. He opened the lid and stuck his hand in it then grabbed one gently.

"This one is a perfect specimen, Dr. Jones."

Chapter 43

Angelo Beresio squinted through the night vision scope of his 7.62 mm chambered AK-47 which had a fixed wooden butt that measured 34.21 inches and weighed 11.31 pounds. He smiled, as he patted the thirty round box magazine. He lay crouched in the tall weeds at the base of a tree, as he swept the barrel of his weapon over the wavy impenetrable electric force field. The Mafia assassins that flanked him were growing impatient. Angelo lowered his weapon and nervously whispered to Benny Torrilo who was crouched next to him.

"We've got the entire place surrounded with four assault teams. All of them are positioned and ready. I've instructed all of them to use their Skorpion 61 submachine guns with attached silencers sparingly since they only have one 20-round magazine each and we also don't want to rouse the local cops out here."

Benny looked at Angelo with confusion. "That's fuckin' great except for that electric field . . . unless we figure out some way to cut off the electrical power we ain't goin' nowhere!"

Angelo looked surprised. "Any suggestions?"

"Yeah, you see those power lines over his facility? I'm going to get six of my best marksmen to knock 'em out." Benny put down his sterling L2A3 submachine gun with silencer attached, picked up his nightscope and scanned across the power lines over Bodyslick's facility.

"Yeah, Angelo, a stream of laser fire from some trees will

knock out his power source." Benny then crawled away from Angelo toward three of his men who were positioned near trees that were closer to the facility. He whispered in their ears and then crawled back to Angelo.

Bodyslick smiled as he locked the door to the storage room and he and Dr. Jones sprinted toward an underground escape tunnel that would emerge near the helicopter. Then, suddenly, all of the lights shut off.

"Down here!" Bodyslick shouted, as Jones held the cryonic igloo cooler tightly and gazed down a dark deep cavernous stairway that was black as night.

"Listen up," he said, "we don't have much time so just do what I tell ya, all right?"

"Let's do it!"

"Once your foot touches that first step this door will seal up from the other side and become undetectable. I had the escape route built just for a situation like this. No need to worry, Doc, once your eyes make the adjustments to the darkness below there are only three flights of stairs and a small short tunnel that will take us to the helicopter pad. Freedom is only minutes away. Are you ready?"

"Let's go!" Jones said, as he felt a trickle of pee sliding down his leg. After he made that first step on the ladder the door slammed shut. He held the igloo container tighter and nervously stared down the dark stairway. He squinted as the once faint images became solid and sharp. Bodyslick's boot almost struck him in the face, as he grabbed the two handles of the metal stairway and started to climb down directly behind him.

Poooot!

"Excuse me, Doc!"

"Why you want to fart on me?"

"Umm, sorry?"

"Sorry? I believe you did that on purpose."

"I said I was sorry, Doc!" Bodyslick said with bafflement, as

Jones locked his grip on the stairway bars and gazed angrily up at him.

"Didn't your mammy teach you any manners?" he raged.

"Don't talk 'bout mah mama, Doc!"

"And don't you be fartin' in my face, man!"

"It was ah mistake, Doc! Now we're running out of time. Lemme down so we can git outta heah!"

"Yeah, well consider this a mistake too, muthafucka!" Jones shouted as he set the igloo cooler on the ground.

Jones grabbed Bodyslick in a full nelson, as his feet touched the ground. He used his weight as he turned to the side to angle Bodyslick's back across his knees with all the strength he could muster.

"What the fuck you think you doing, Doc? You wanna miss your damn plane over bullshit?" Bodyslick grabbed his arms, gulping air as Jones choked him.

"This is the payback for humiliating me over that bitch Liza!"

He could feel the panic in Bodyslick, as his veins became writhing worms on the side of his temples. He could hear the grating of his spinal cord as he tried to crush him. Suddenly Bodyslick seesawed his legs and clamped Jones' head, scissoring him while applying pressure with his locked feet to his neck. Jones' head felt as if it were going to burst. He fell underneath him. Dizzy. Exhausted. Bodyslick sat on top of him, breathing hard.

"Okay, Doc, we're even now, okay?"

"Just respect me, man! I know you have comtempt for me because I played by the system's rules. But you have no more right to judge my life than I have to judge yours. Since childhood you've been challenging my manhood because I was a nerd. Because I preferred science over slam dunking. To you I was the sissy, the prissy . . . well, I'm just as much a man as you."

"You mean over all these years you've carried that grudge?" Bodyslick asked, astonished.

"Yes," Jones said bitterly.

"Well, I'm sorry, Doc, I didn't know you had such toilet tissue feelings."

"Let me up and then say that to me, punk!"

"All right, Doc, time is against us." Bodyslick stood up while dusting off his clothes. "Can we shake on it, Doc?"

Jones extended his hand and they stood there eye to eye, reaffirming their childhood friendship. Then, suddenly, they heard the loud *thumps* of trotting boots above. The assassins had penetrated the fortress. Bodyslick started sprinting down a dark tunnel.

"See that red light?"

"Yes, I see it!" Jones replied anxiously as he grabbed the igloo cooler.

"That's where our journey ends. Come on, Doc, run . . . 'cause time is running out!"

Jones ran with all the adrenaline his stiff, middle-class, out-of-shape body could produce. The farthest he had run in recent memory was from the elevator to the emergency room and that was only thirty seconds away. He gulped air in exhaustion as they neared the exit door. As Bodyslick pressed a tiny orange button on the side of the wall, the door slid open revealing the gleaming helicopter only a minute away. They stepped out the door. Bodyslick glanced around quickly. He took the laser pistol out of his leather jacket and cocked it. It was quiet. Even the crickets were silent. Dr. Jones' heart pounded in his chest as if it was going to burst out. He took the .38 Smith & Wesson out of his smock jacket. He had forgotten he had it.

"Let's go, Doc, there's no turning back!"

Jones leaped into the helicopter and instantly pressed the ignition button which activated the auto-pilot system. The rotors started to whip up. He glanced at his watch. He had less than an hour to get to flight 224 to Baltimore. He glanced to the door looking for Bodyslick, as a bullet whanged off the metal door. The hydrogen fueled TCH-7077 Peregrine Hawk helicopter started to lift. It quickly pulled away from Bodyslick's dark underground grotto. Jones sighed with relief, as he released his grip on the cryonic igloo container that held Vanderbilt's heart.

Chapter 44

Bodyslick looked up at the helicopter as it sped northwest toward O'Hare Airport. He grimaced in pain from a bullet wound in his right leg, as he tried to conceal himself in the tall bush, shrubs, and weeds. He could feel the shattered bone in his leg. He quickly tore off a shirt sleeve and tied it around the bullet wound that was spurting a geyser of blood. He then picked up his laser pistol. Suddenly, he heard a cacophony of voices. As they neared, he listened. Was that a woman's voice? He panicked. He checked the automatic button on his laser pistol to off. He wanted single action. He ran a hydro-shell into the chamber. The *swish* of weeds and the *crunch* of grass became closer. He crawled toward a tree and rested his back on it for stability. He brought the cocked laser pistol up and steadied it on top of his bent knee. He could see them clearly now. There were ten of them. A white woman, dressed in a black leather jumpsuit and dark glasses, led them. His trouser leg was drenched with blood. It felt as if it had been doused in water. Blood poured down into his shoe. He gritted his teeth from the excruciating pain.

He wondered where was God when you really needed Him? He felt all alone in the universe. He psyched himself into a warrior mood by reciting a street rap he had learned while in prison:

"I was weaned off the tit of a wild boar,
and I cut my teeth on a Colt .45.
I can be mean without even trying.
I'm a bad muthafucka, and I don't mind dyiiing!"

He wondered where Snow, Geronimo, Shondell, and the Tong's Triad ninja soldiers were. He wondered if Choi and the Hip Hop Sung Gang had even gotten his message.

"That's him over there by the tree, Gina!"

His thoughts vaporized as they plodded through the weeds. He strained his eyes, as he aimed the gun at the woman's chest. The assassins stopped six meters from the tree. They aimed their Skorpion 61 submachine guns with silencers at him.

The woman in black screamed at him with delirium. With rage. With diabolical hatred. "You killed my brother, Vinnie Luziano! Now you must die!"

"And they better dig another grave for you, bitch!" Bodyslick blasted a 0.9 millisecond blue laser pulse into her chest, vaporizing her heart, as a barrage of machine gun fire hammered his body into the tree. He could smell the stench of his scorching flesh as the bullets sizzled through his being.

His mind raced back through his life as his vision became foggy. He attempted to gaze up into the milky black sky. His vision became dimmer and dimmer as the electricity seeped from his dying brain. His eyes closed. He heard the assassins' voices:

"Don't worry, Gina, it's just a bad wound."

"Is the nigger dead, Angelo?" the woman in black asked mournfully.

"Yeah, Gina, he is one dead punk!"

"Good!" She smiled. She slowly closed her eyes. She was dead.

"Angelo, look!" Benny shouted, as he pointed toward the storage facility with his machine gun.

"Jeezus Christ, they're everywhere!"

Snow, Geronimo and Shondell, along with hundreds of Hip Hop Sung ninjas surrounded them.

"Shit!" Angelo shouted. "If we gotta die let's die like men . . . fire!"

Benny turned to Angelo and grinned as a bullet slashed through his heart. Angelo threw down his weapon and started to run.

Snow glared at his fearful, fat wobbling body, as his finger hugged the trigger of his Galil sniping rifle. He waited. Then he slowly pulled the trigger as Angelo's body merged with the intersected lines of his telescopic sight.

Bammmm!

Angelo screamed and fell to the ground as blood gushed from his spine.

"That's for Bodyslick, goddamn it!" Snow whispered.

Epilogue

Bodyslick heard women's voices. Familiar feline voices. Then he saw a burst of light. A white light. A shimmering pristine light. The faint shape of two women walking toward him crystallized out of the light. He sighed with relief as he felt his soul snapping free from the gravity of his physical body. He soared toward the women's magnetic voices bathing over him like warm baptismal water.

One was Liza's voice: "Bodyslick, it's me," she said, as she darted her long serpentine tongue at him.

"I will always love you," Malanna whispered like a bird's song.

"But both of you are *dead*!"

"Dead is only a man-made definition used to describe a metamorphical process that is infinitely more complex than is perceived by humans."

"Am I also dead?" Bodyslick said in disbelief.

"Yes, and we are here to help you make the transition from the physical to the spiritual realm."

His soul trembled with euphoria as they took his hand, and a volcanic sense of peace and contentment erupted through him.

"Bodyslick, do you hear me?" Snow hollered, trying to drown out the exchange of gunfire as he felt his wrist for a weak pulse. "Shondell, spray his bullet wounds with the re-animative cryonic spray that will stop his blood loss and hold off decomposition till we can get him to Dr. Sanbury in Chicago!"

Shondell pulled out the aerosol can from his jacket, stooped down and sprayed the foam on Bodyslick's bleeding bullet wounds. The wounds slowly sealed. Snow, Shondell, and Geronimo ducked down, dodging gunfire as they gently lifted his limp body and quickly trotted toward Snow's hydrovan.